ARMAGEDDON

OSGUARDS: GUARDIANS OF THE UNIVERSE

By

Malcolm D. Petteway

Homecoming
Revelations
Armageddon
Revenge

OSGUARDS: ARMAGEDDON

BOOK THREE

OF

OSGUARDS: GUARDIANS OF THE UNIVERSE

MALCOLM DYLAN PETTEWAY

Rage Books LLC
www.ragebooks.net

Osguards: Armageddon

Second Edition Published by Rage Books LLC February 2010

Edited by:
Karen M. Petteway
James Barnes

ISBN: 0984364528
EAN-13: 9780984364527

Printed in the United States
Rage Books LLC
www.ragebooks.net

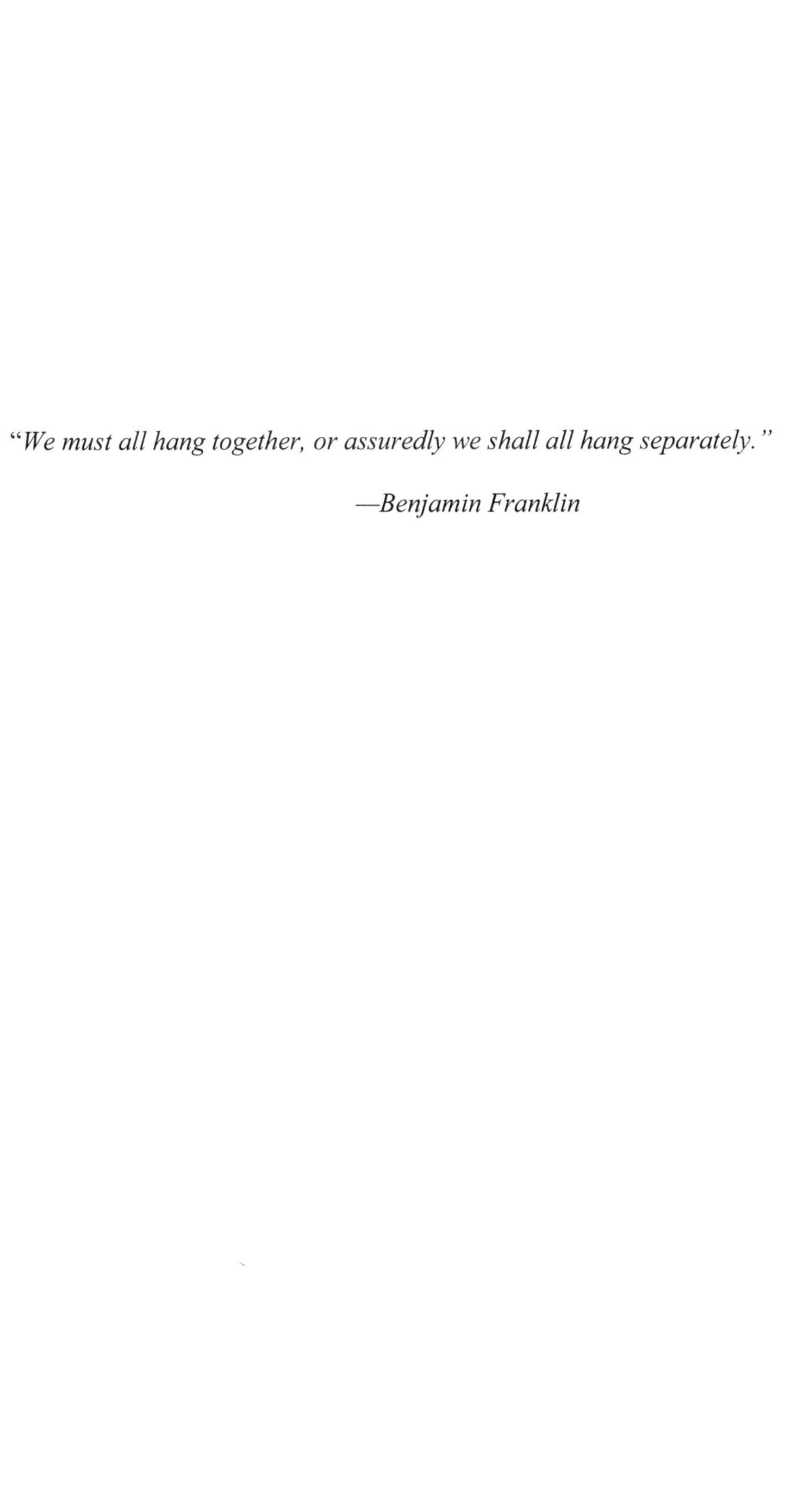

"We must all hang together, or assuredly we shall all hang separately."

—Benjamin Franklin

Prologue—Thirty Days Later

It was dark, warm and soothing, but also scary and lonely at the same time. The black liquid kept her nude body warm, matching her body heat to the nth degree. It caressed, washed and lifted her into a weightless state as it wafted over her like a gentle breeze. She floated in a prone position, arms and legs extended and unable to move. A blindfold covered her eyes and a mask supplied the proper mixture of air to her lungs. It was called a sensory deprivation tank. However, it was more like a coffin, molded to her body size and structure ... a liquid coffin letting nothing in and nothing out.

Her heart was the only thing she could feel as it pounded hard in her chest. At least she imagined she could feel it. She was alone in her thoughts, without the outside environment to interject. No sight, no sound, no feeling, no smell and no taste, just the sense of her own existence that was fighting to keep a grasp on reality.

Even the feeling of expectations was lost to her. Life and death were benign concepts in the tank. All she had were memories, or were they dreams of an existence long gone? No...she had memories...she had regrets. She remembered killing Kie Ritchen. She also regretted doing it in front of Osguard 55, who was stalking in the shadows. If only she had kept her mouth shut. If she had just not engaged in frivolous bravado with Kie, before and after she had assassinated him. Now she had nothing to do, but think, remember and regret.

Time had no meaning in the tank. It already felt like an eternity. Without use of her five senses, time had become distorted. What she calculated as an entire cycle could have been a day, a week or even an hour. Her grip on sanity was all she had, and she was losing that.

She took in a deep breath so she could feel the air rush into her lungs. That along with her heartbeat was the thing her mind could focus on. She imagined she could feel her toes, fingers, and arms, but she couldn't. She imagined she could hear the liquid in the tank sway back and forth, but it wasn't. She imagined she could smell a metallic presence in the air she breathed, but there was none. She imagined she could see patterns of light through her blindfold, but she was in complete darkness. She licked her lips, imagining the taste of food on them, but she was fed intravenously. Therefore, her semblance of reality, of sanity, of her own being, was her breathing and her heartbeat.

She counted her heartbeats, and then she counted her breaths. Something had to keep her mind occupied, or insanity would rush in and envelop her consciousness. She didn't know how many times she had executed this mundane chore, but it was keeping her mind active. It was reminding her she was alive…she was somebody.

Then a sharp pain shot through her right arm. At first she was shocked, then relieved. She could still feel pain. She tried to laugh, but could not, or she couldn't hear herself laugh. Either way, the pleasure of laughter escaped her at the moment, but the feeling of pain was exquisite and well welcomed.

She heard the sound of the liquid rushing around her. Several seconds later she felt her body descend in the tank. Finally, she felt the bottom of the tank. Her back was on the bottom. At first it was irritating, almost painful, but like the pinch of the intravenous needle being removed, it was a welcomed discomfort.

Someone ripped the blindfold off. The light was so bright it hurt. She shut her eyes and covered them with her arms. Then the air mask was pulled off. She screamed with delight, or pain? At the moment she did not know which. All she knew was she could scream, so she did.

"Quiet Rina," the voice ordered.

Rina stopped her yelling. She didn't know why she was being pulled out of the tank or who was pulling her out, but she wasn't going to ruin the opportunity by screaming now.

"Who are you? What is going on?" Rina asked.

"Rina of Jaywick, daughter of Rena, granddaughter of Dina, your appeal has been accepted by the Daughters of Fire. You are to appear in the Hall of Fire for your sentencing."

Rina squinted in the direction of the voice. Her eyes were still unable to focus, but she deciphered the person talking was a guard from the Daughters of Fire. The figure wore a white cloak and hood and carried a firestaff, the weapon of choice for the Daughters of Fire.

Then two other guards, she did not see, grabbed her and forced her to her feet. Her feet fought for balance on the slippery floor of her tank. Then they picked her up and planted her on the dry deck. The black liquid dripping from her nude body littered the deck and speckled onto the guards' white cloaks.

"Clean her up," commanded the lead guard.

"Kiza," the two guards replied in unison. Then they whisked her down the deck and into the cleaning area. They threw her into a shower room. Rina's head banged against the wall as she slid into the room, lost her balance and crashed to the floor. It was hard for her to regain her balance after the long period in the deprivation tank. Rina thought it was worse than suspended animation. At least in suspended animation you were unconscious throughout, but in the deprivation tank, you were conscious, floating in mind and spirit, devoid of a body. It was freedom and prison at the same time. Now she had to get accustomed to gravity and walking again—both appearing to be difficult tasks at the time.

The sonic wave, mixed with water and air pelted her like a hailstorm. Any other time she would have welcomed the shower, especially after a long and grueling day. However, it was another source of pain, tearing at her skin. She screamed, not like she did before, not out of shock or surprise, but out of pure torture. The sonic wave pushed, pulled and ripped the black liquid from her skin. She remained on her hands and knees unable to move or stand, just screaming as if someone were cutting her with a knife.

"Why is she screaming like that?" one guard asked the other.

"It's the after effects of the tank. They have no balance, they can't walk, gravity is too much for them and their skin is super sensitive to any pressure, even a sonic shower."

"Kiza!" the first guard replied.

Inside the shower, Rina of Jaywick, daughter of Rena, granddaughter of Dina, fell unconscious, unable to cope with the pain the sonic shower was delivering. Upon seeing this, the guards turned the shower off, dried her and dragged her into the changing room. They clothed her with her traditional black robe of a soldier then slapped her into consciousness.

"You awake now?"

"Kiza," Rina whispered, massaging the sting from her cheek.

"It's time."

Then the guards picked her up by her arms. Rina stumbled to her feet, trying to regain her balance. Gravity was still a hard phenomenon for her to conquer. However, she felt she was making progress. The door disappeared in front of them, they walked through and the door reappeared behind them. The guards pushed and pulled her down the circular corridor. They took several turns and negotiated several stairwells until they came upon a giant doorway. The door vanished opening to a dark arena.

"You want help?"

"No," Rina asserted. "I can do it myself."

The guards let her go and Rina stood for the first time since her release from the tank, on her own power. She plodded through the doorway. The door reappeared behind her, locking her into the arena. She looked up and on the first tier of seats, fifteen feet up, sat the Daughters of Fire, the five leaders of the Tuit Consortium. In the other tiers of the circular arena were magistrates and other dignitaries of the Consortium. Rina estimated all five hundred Fireholders were in the Hall of Fire staring at her.

"Rina of Jaywick, daughter of Rena, granddaughter of Dina," called the First Daughter. "You are charged with gross negligence and gross incompetence during a mission. Because of your actions, our enemies of dimension level four now know of our existence and are suspect to our plans. What do you say for yourself?"

"My First Daughter," Rina bellowed, summoning strength she did not know she had. "I have no excuse for my arrogance. Although, I was unaware of the enemy's presence in the room as I spoke, I shouldn't have spoken. I failed you, and I failed the Consortium. All I have to offer is my life as a warrior to the Daughters of Fire to do as they wish."

"Fine," the First Daughter replied. "We have discussed your mistake and feel internment in the deprivation tank was…well, it is too harsh for your actions."

Rina recognized the First Daughter spoke of it as a mistake and not a crime. Joy filled her heart, for she thought she was about to be pardoned for her actions.

"However," the First Daughter continued. "Your actions did cause irrevocable damage to our cause, and a full pardon is out of the question."

Rina's heart dropped. She was now confused. Her confusion turned to fright. The one thing left was a prison sentence on an uncharted, uninhabitant planet. She tried to think of this as something she could do. It was better than the tank.

"Therefore, I give you a choice," The First Daughter continued, "A Hall of Fire challenge or life in prison."

Before she knew it, Rina said, "I will take the challenge."

"Very well. Spoken like a true warrior. Begin the challenge!"

The door on the opposite side of the arena vanished and in its place stood a warrior guard. She wore a breastplate, a metal bikini bottom and knee high metal boots. On her left hand she wore an elbow length glove with a blade attached to the fist, littered with different size spikes. In her right hand she carried a machete type blade.

The sight of her forced Rina into a combat mode. Her adrenaline pumped and fueled her body with rare power. She navigated to her left. She stumbled and fell on her knees. At first she thought she was still too weak from the tank, but then she realized it was the robe. It bonded her and hampered her warrior movements. She jumped up and pulled the robe off, exposing her nude body to the arena. A loud gasp rushed from the crowd. At the moment, she didn't care. She was fighting for her life, and a little bit of embarrassment was a small price to pay for her life.

The warrior sprang at Rina in a full sprint. Rina hopped to one side and slung the robe wrapping it around the warrior's head and neck. Rina then twisted the robe as the warrior stopped, turned and swung the blade. Rina ducked while still hanging on to the robe. The blade whooshed over her head. She reached up with her left hand, grabbed the warrior's wrist, and twisted it. The warrior's arm bent, sending a sharp pain to her elbow. She dropped the blade. Rina let go of her wrist and continued to weave the robe around the warrior's neck. The warrior struggled, wildly swinging her gloved left hand and blade. Rina ducked, swung around and coiled her body in several directions to avoid the spikes from the glove and the attached blade, and then she delivered a blow to the warrior's head while never letting go of the robe wrapped around the warrior's neck.

When the robe was as tight as it could be, Rina let go and dove, tucked, rolled and picked up the blade. She sprang to her knees facing her opponent who was busy trying to get the robe from around her neck. Blood soaked the robe from where she cut herself with the spiked glove while reaching for it. That mistake told the warrior she had one hand to try to free herself with—the right hand. Rina studied her opponent for a second, and then she looked around the arena at the audience. She saw the look of fear in their eyes and smelled the fright in the air. It burned in her soul like fire. It fueled the rage in her heart.

She then turned back to her opponent who stood five feet from her, screaming in anger and tearing at the black robe around her head. She stood and rushed the warrior and swung the blade. The blade sliced through the robe, and cut clean through to the other side, separating the warrior's head from her body. The head plopped on the black shiny floor with a heavy thud. Blood spewed from the warrior's throat like a volcano. The warrior's body went limp and crashed to the floor next to the head.

Rina remained motionless, still holding the blade in the air where it came to rest, staring at the carnage in front of her. Blood spotted her face and body. She licked her lips and tasted the blood on her tongue. After several seconds, she turned to the Daughters of Fire and threw down the blade. Her dark hair was mangled and her perspiration glistened in the light, making the blood on her look like rivers coursing over her naked body.

"The challenge is complete!" exclaimed the First Daughter. "You are absolved of any wrong doing."

Rina glared at the First Daughter. Her body was racked with pain and her mind dazed with exhilaration. She felt vindicated, but also sick that she had to kill one of her sister warriors. She glanced over at the body once more, wishing it peace in the afterlife.

"Rina of Jaywick, daughter of Rena, granddaughter of Dina," called the First Daughter. "You have met the challenge after spending an entire cycle in the deprivation tank. Only the strongest of the Consortium have done this. Your courage and strength tells me you are the right person to take over the invasion of the fourth dimensional level. Come take your place among the Daughters of Fire. You have earned the right to be called a Daughter of Fire. You are now the Sixth Daughter of Fire."

Chapter 1—Return to the Siryman Galaxy

Jarod Stone, Osguard 11, sat on the edge of his bed, staring off into the dark room. His port window displayed the majestic beauty of Millmum Capitol Station, the heart and hub of the Universal Science, Security and Trade Association of Planets (USSTAP). Millmum Capitol Station was an amalgamation of seventy self-contained black-coated stations, peeking out of the shadows of space through thousand of distant stars. They littered the space line like drifting snowflakes. They were diamond shaped and of different sizes, placed asymmetrically surrounding the biggest station. The bigger stations including the main one in the middle had large docking rings around them. The main station dwarfed the others and was eight miles wide at the base and two hundred decks long from point to point. The nearby sun of the Chaktun solar system framed the beauty of the station, which had a mosaic arrangement of window ports of different sizes and shapes decorating the black energy absorbent skin, called slitanium. Some ports were oval, some square, some rectangular and some shapes only Picasso could have invented.

Around the main station were other galaxy protectors, like his ship, the *G.P. Gentry*, two miles long, one and a half miles wide and twelve decks high. The galaxy protector had concave engines that ran the length of the ship on the port and starboard sides, each engine melded into a sharp edge point at the bow and aft of the ship. The engines attached to the ship with a doubled triangular spar at mid section. The main ship, reminiscent of a submarine, flared in the stern where it contained a launch and receiving pad for its fighters, called defenders and its multifaceted space transports called startrams.

God gives you no more than you can bear, Jarod reminded himself, staring out at the beauty of God's backyard. However, right now he felt overwhelmed. What was so surprising was that he was overwhelmed over such a simple matter. To anyone else it would be a simple matter, but to Jarod it was a matter of serious magnitude. Nothing was more daunting, or more soul chilling than what was on his mind now…dealing with his father. With a deep breath, Jarod rose to check his messages, trying to shake his father, Wilson Stone from his mind.

He moved to the outer room and shuffled to his desk, still fighting the onslaught of sleep. He plopped behind his giant oak desk with a smoky glass top, and stretched his arms above his head. The bear yawn that followed, punctuated his need for more rest. But time was short and he needed to be awake.

"Lights!" he ordered.

The Artificial Intelligence, also known as the ARIT, flicked the room lights to on, screeching illumination throughout and assaulting his tired eyes.

"Half illumination," he requested with extreme agitation.

The ARIT complied with his wishes, as Jarod rubbed his eyes, trying to chase the blinding spots away. After several seconds, and after his eyes had adjusted to the new illumination, Jarod tapped his desk monitor to display his messages. One message displayed on his screen:

TO: ALL OSGUARDS

FROM: MICHAEL D. GENESIS, OSGUARD, MILLMUM GALAXY

REFERENCE: THREAT ASSESSMENT

UNIVERSAL DATE: 09.07.48255

When our ancestors, Nausona and Laurona Osguard, left Chaktun to escape the Kulusk invasion over one hundred and twenty five universal years ago, lived as slaves in America, unwittingly left their children on Earth as they returned to the stars and founded the Universal Science, Security and Trade Association of Planets, they never imagined the mantle of leadership they would leave upon their descendants. When Ortho found us, some seventeen universal years ago, and indoctrinated us as the leaders of the association, we never imagined the wonderful things we would do, or the monstrous dangers we would face.

In the beginning and after our accession to leadership, we have seen and participated in many space confrontations and peacekeeping missions against the Mosleck Pirates, Grudgea Federation and the Toniea Republic. During those times, many opponents attribute an unwarranted amount of deaths to us in our quest for peace. But the galaxy protector became a godsend deterrent to space pirates and planetary governments bent on revenge or domination. In the last seven universal years, this association has brought peace to sixty Galaxies and over fifty thousand signatory planets in the Virgo Star Cluster. For one, I am proud of our accomplishments. And I'm proud to have served with my family in bringing peace to the universe.

However recently, our mortal enemy has challenged our efforts. In the last three universal months, we have staved off a Kulusk plot to annihilate Earth through nuclear confrontation between Russia and the United States, an attempted assassination on me that almost killed my father, an all out coordinated attack throughout the known universe, and a biological attack that incapacitated all but one Osguard—Osguard 55, Juanita Genesis-Clark. Luckily Juanita was able to retrieve the antidote and facilitate a regime changeover on Kulusk favorable to the association.

However, in her endeavors she learned the unsettling news that the Kulusk aggression was orchestrated by another source...the Tuits from the Centauris Star Cluster. There is not much known about the Tuits, we only achieved a small glimpse at them when they bore an attack on Millmum Capitol Station. As you know, they retreated without firing a shot; once they found out the Terinolice virus no longer incapacitated us.

As you depart Millmum Capitol Station for your own galaxies, I want to express to you my fear that we have somehow awakened another enemy against the association. Please be careful and be on guard for anything suspicious, no matter how insignificant it may appear. Unlike the early days, when we had each other for back up, in these days of peace we are all alone...aliens in our Galaxy of Responsibility. I urge caution and a heavy reliance on your Intelligence Corps

Take Care and Godspeed
Michael D. Genesis,
Osguard 01, Millmum Galaxy

***

Jarod emerged from his quarters, in his black overall uniform, wearing the four golden thunderbolts of an Osguard on the collar of his environmentally controlled jacket. His dark, almost mahogany auburn hair, freckled with a touch of gray, and hazel eyes, characteristics of all Osguards, seem to glow with his magnificent smile. His swagger was confident as his lanky basketball frame marched toward the coaster.

He rode the coaster to the top deck and stepped out. He surveyed the corridor and then turned right, walking past several cabin entrances that housed the offices of his senior staff. At the end of the corridor were two steps that went up and a set of five steps that went down on either side of them. The sign *'Command Bridge'* overhung the steps that went up and the sign overhanging the downstairs steps, said, '*Control Bridge.'* Jarod stepped up toward the command bridge

"Osguard on the bridge," boomed the sentry at the doorway.

The bridge was an oval design decorated with brown and black polished metal and glass railings, stations, and fixtures. It sat up over the control bridge like a balcony. His command chair with its multifaceted buttons, sat in the middle. The smaller Centurion of Operations and Centurion of Engineering chairs with an equal amount of buttons flanked his command chair. In front of the three chairs sat the ship's pilot and navigator. They had a miniature screen that sat between them, displaying an array of information and a star map. Around the outer walls in clockwise rhythm from the navigator station sat the security; communications; offensive; defensive; life-support; and science stations.

"How is she shaking out?" Osguard 11, Jarod Stone, asked.

"She is good as new, Osguard," The Centurion of Operations Regina Dawson responded, spinning her seat around to face him. Her shoulder length light brown hair was full and framed her face perfectly, highlighting her green eyes. Her chin was handsomely stern, all business. When she smiled, her female softness electrified the area. And she was smiling. "The *Gentry* handled the test run perfectly. I'd say all the repairs are complete."

"How about the engines?" Jarod queried, stepping down to his seat.

The Centurion of Engineering onboard the *USSTAP Galaxy Protector Gentry*, Kelly Sterling, stood with a wide grin. "All engines…thrusters, hypersonic, hyperlight, Mass Object Projection and Intragalactic Gate Portal, are functioning at one hundred percent." Her nature was almost unbearably perky. She wore her brunette hair that fell below her shoulders, curled and puffed, like a movie star. Her zest made the words she spoke seem like they were happy as well. Jarod imagined she never had a bad day in her life. If she did, he doubted she knew it.

"Great!" Jarod replied, sitting in his command chair, catching the infectious smiles from his senior officers. "When can we go home?"

"As soon as we get clearance from Millmum Capitol Station," Regina chimed in.

"Well what are we waiting for? We have been here an entire month and as good as it is to spend time with my mother, I think it is time for me…I mean us, to get back to our own galaxy." Jarod turned toward the sixty feet high by eighty feet wide view port screen located in front of the command and control bridges. "We are one of the last ships still here and I can't wait to get back to Siryman Capitol Station."

"I'm sure the station admiral took perfectly good care of the station for you," a female voice came from behind him.

Jarod swung his chair around and chuckled, "Well, I was wondering when the Security Centurion would join us," he teased.

"Wouldn't miss it for the world," Gail French laughed.

Gail was not as attractive as Regina or Kelly, but she had an unmistakable sexuality about her that men took note of. She also was all business. She had to be, to be in charge of security for the flagship of the Siryman Galaxy. Her demeanor was always on trial, her decisions were always scrutinized and her actions were always challenged—at least so she thought. Unbeknownst to her, Jarod had nothing but the utmost respect for her and nothing but confidence in her ability.

"Yeah right!" Jarod laughed. Then he swung his chair around front and let loose a heavy sigh. He gazed at the screen again, almost mesmerized by what he was seeing. In the fifteen years Jarod had spent in space he could never get over the beauty it projected, or the peace it seemed to bring to his soul. Every opportunity he could take, he would study the stars—not like a scientist, but like a lover…admiring, longing and wanting. It was in his blood…in his spirit. The coldness…the vastness, gave him no fear. He was in love; and he imagined the stars were in love with him.

His senior staff recognized the look. They knew their Osguard was in deep thought, conversing with his spirit, with his soul mate, with his love…the stars. It was a ritual, it seemed, that Jarod engaged in before every trip into the Galactic Gate Portal. He sank into the ritual, unaware and without doubt, but the crew knew, and they were patient.

After several minutes in solitude, Jarod took a deep breath and blew it out hard, "Request clearance for departure."

"Tiah," said the communications officer, Lieutenant Jeremy Ryan, from his right. Then he selected a channel, spoke and nodded at the voice coming over his speaker.

"*USSTAP Galaxy Protector Gentry*, this is Millmum Departure Control…Siryman Capitol Station has been set in GGP number three…you are cleared departure through GGP number three. Have a good flight."

"Acknowledged," smiled Jarod. "Pilot…take us into GGP number three."

"Tiah!"

The pilot maneuvered the two-mile long, one and a half-mile wide, twelve deck ship up and over Millmum Capitol to the GGP field. The gate was two quarter-mile thick, three mile-long ARIT rods, bent at a one hundred and twenty-degree angle and separated from port to starboard by five miles of space. When the ship came within ten kilomarks, the rods illuminated a majestic white light that reached across the five-mile void of space to wash the area with inner space.

"Gate activated," announced the navigator.

"Continue," ordered Regina.

The ship maneuvered into the white light at half subsonic speed. To the outside observer, it appeared the light was swallowing the ship like an Anaconda snake devouring its supper. Inside the gate, the white light of inner space penetrated the ship's hull, making everything and everyone glow with angelic radiance. However, the ship's crew contained veterans of inner space travel, and the light gave them a familiar comfort.

"Thirty seconds until normal space," announced the navigator.

Jarod kept his eyes on the screen, admiring the beauty of the light. He always thought of inner space as the light people saw as they approached death. He felt that traversing the light was the closest man could get to God. He swore inner-space was the corridor to heaven, and he always felt at peace while he was in it. He also felt guilty, like he was sneaking around God's house without his permission—like he was a kid sneaking into his parents' bedroom without them knowing. This feeling began to overshadow his blissfulness, as it always did, just as they were entering normal space.

The Siryman Galaxy, M87 to the scientist of Earth, located at the core of the Virgo Supercluster, fifty-seven million light years from the Millmum Galaxy, welcomed the crew with audacious darkness. The crew blinked several times to adjust to the drastic change in light. The ship crept through an exit GGP and the white light vanished.

"All stop!" Regina ordered.

After several seconds, their eyes adjusted to normal light.

"Adjust axis!" bellowed Regina.

The Siryman Galaxy was a southpaw galaxy, where up was down and down was up due to the standard of space travel. Therefore, the *Gentry* had to roll on its axis to match the standard. The pilot adjusted his control panel and the ship rolled to the right. As it rolled, the artificial gravity adjusted, allowing the crew to remain upright with little disturbance to their equilibrium. However, as Jarod knew, the trick was to close your eyes until the procedure was complete. That way the eyes would not send false messages to the body, causing a loss of balance. On Earth, pilots called it the leans.

"Axis adjustment complete," the pilot announced.

"Fine, take us home," Jarod commanded.

The ship maneuvered from the GGP field toward Siryman Capitol Station. The Station was similar in design to Millmum, but a little smaller. This station did not have to house the parliament. It just housed the Siryman Galaxy Congress. However, it was littered with smaller precinct stations like its big sister.

"Siryman Capitol Station…this is the *Galaxy Protector Gentry*…request arrival and docking procedures."

"*Galaxy Protector Gentry*, this is Siryman Control…slow to thrusters…you are cleared approach corridor alpha to docking station one. Welcome home Osguard."

The ship slowed and maneuvered on the approach path, like a float on a parade route. Lights from the smaller stations blinked on and off like

Christmas trees, welcoming their Osguard and the Flagship of the Siryman Galaxy. The ship floated to the docking ring around Capitol Station. The pilot guided the ship with mature finesse. The docking clamp kissed the dock like a mother kissing her child.

"Good job Captain," Jarod complimented the pilot.

"Thank you sire."

"Start debarking and lockdown procedures, Centurion."

"Tiah," Regina responded with glee

Jarod stood, straightened his uniform and left the bridge.

***

Dock one reception area splashed with brown, red, and crimson colors. Similar to the corridors of the galaxy protector, Dock one and the rest of Siryman Capitol Station's corridors boasted of a thin burnt brown color carpet blanketing the floors and ran waist level onto the walls. Similar to its sister stations, the walls contained murals, a continuous painting from end to end.

The station's sire, Admiral Amierwat B'Kailine made his way through the station's corridors toward Dock one to meet the Osguard. When he heard of the Osguard's arrival he had mixed emotions of dread and pride. More or less, dread seemed to occupy his emotions more than pride. For the last two universal months, B'Kailine had responsibility for the entire galaxy, during a time of extreme stresses…the *'First Universal War.'*

He had protected the Siryman Galaxy from the Kulusk financed attackers. He had devised and initiated strategy and policies that he felt were as good as anything Jarod could have come up with. But still the glory went to the Osguard for his part in the final demise of the Kulusk Empire and no glory, no accolade, not so much as a thank you came his way for protecting over one hundred and ninety thousand light years of space.

B'Kailine stopped at the end of the corridor, the entryway onto Dock one, to admire his favorite mural. On the wall was a picture of his direct ancestor, Blothil B'Kailine in the midst of the Battle of Scevilla, the last battle before the expansion of the D'Ardin Empire into the far-reaching corners of the galaxy, some three hundred universal years ago. The frieze captured Blothil standing on top of a hill, overlooking the battlefield, pointing in the distance with one hand and holding the traditional borax blade in the other. The smoldering ashes framed his large physique and a devilish grin pursed his lips. This is the battle that put the B'Kailine name in the history books as military leaders of the empire. He was staring at his inspiration, the legacy he was expected to live up to. However, with the D'Ardin Empire living within the confines of USSTAP, and him living under the shadow of the Osguard, living up to his family's legacy was getting damned near impossible.

He huffed as he gathered his thoughts, and moved on to Dock one. He waited in the reception area to greet Osguard 11, the savior of the Siryman Galaxy. Several minutes later Jarod emerged from the *G.P Gentry* and onto dock one reception area.

"Sounds like you had a little bit of excitement back in Millmum Galaxy," B'Kailine laughed.

"So did you, according to your reports," Jarod countered.

"Yes, but it wasn't anything we couldn't handle. Several skirmishes occurred in the outside sectors. The Eierre system in the eighteenth sector suffered heavy damage; the Kulusk sympathizers made Eierre their prime objective."

"I guess they wanted to secure the dialairtic crystal from the Eierre satellite mining operations," Jarod commented as he started to walk to the exit corridor.

B'Kailine understood the dialairtic crystal was the only energy source used by USSTAP and the capture of the dialairtic mines would have severely hampered USSTAP. The Eierre mines were the fourth largest supplier of dialairtic crystal. It was a natural target and he realized it could be a target again. He made a mental note to fortify the security for the mines as soon as possible.

"I suppose," B'Kailine shrugged. "Anyway, I sent the *G.P. S'Coril* and the *G.P. P'Togi* to investigate. The *P'Togi* was in the fifteenth sector; she used the sector GGP and stepped into the eighteenth sector in time to help the *S'Coril* to stop the invasion."

"Yeah, I read the report. Great job, man. It looks like you handled everything right. I knew there was a reason I picked you as my Capitol Station Sire."

"Thanks Osguard."

"Now admiral, if you will excuse me. I have to go over my notes before I address the Siryman Congress this evening." Jarod shook the admiral's hand and moved through the doorway out of sight.

B'Kailine stared in awe at the doorway, wondering why Jarod didn't want a full debrief of how the battle affected the galaxy. B'Kailine was a prideful man; a man of many characteristics, which he thought Jarod didn't appreciate. He thought his actions during the most challenging day in USSTAP's history would spark more than pleasant gratitude. He thought the incident would spark hardy conversation, strategy planning or even a retrospective analysis of the situation. None of which he had ever had with Jarod. Apparently, none of which he will ever have with him.

B'Kailine took a deep breath and shook his head. '*Why should he work so hard to gain the Osguard's approval?*' Until ten universal years ago, the Siryman Galaxy had never heard of the Osguards or USSTAP. They were aliens to this galaxy. For some reason the D'Ardin Empire and the four other governments signed on to USSTAP and practically gave the galaxy to them. He always resented that. He was the military leader, the Kushcan, of the D'Ardin Empire. Deep inside, he knew the D'Ardin Empire should be where USSTAP was, and he, as the Kushcan, should be where Jarod was—the economic benefits of the alliance notwithstanding.

His king, the Kinsile, wanted the alliance and wanted him to run the Capitol Station. He knew Jarod didn't pick him. It was the Kinsile who picked him, as his price for joining USSTAP. He knew USSTAP capitulated and accepted him as the Capitol Station Sire, and he has been trying to prove his mantle for the past ten years.

B'Kailine headed for the main observation deck, still shaking his head. He counted his blessings that the other four governments in the galaxy did not push the same proposal. Or did they? Is that what Jarod meant, '*he picked him*?' No, the other governments would have revolted. He knew the D'Ardin Empire would have revolted if he were not chosen. USSTAP gave each government the same amount of ships, and technology; but, the D'Ardin Empire acquired Capitol Station, and the others received ownership of the most powerful ship in the inventory—the galaxy protector. He always suspected it was a compromise.

Now that the governments didn't need to spend money for defense, they concentrated their assets on economic and societal growth. And that was just what the D'Ardin Empire did. Even though B'Kailine resented the arrangement, he understood it. Monetary cost for defense, exploration and trade were the responsibility of USSTAP, leaving more governmental assets for economic and societal growth. His people had prospered, as he was sure the other governments had as well. The galaxy had enjoyed internal peace for the past nine years, since the inception of USSTAP. Regardless of whether he liked it or not, USSTAP's inconceivable ideology of balance of power and a shared alliance was working. If it ever did break, it would not be because of him.

Yes, he resented USSTAP, but he also respected them. That is why he worked so hard to catch Jarod's eye. He wanted Jarod, and USSTAP, to respect him as a warrior. He wanted acceptance as an equal, and he was not sure he was getting it.

B'Kailine popped onto the observation deck and moved to the command chair. The observation deck was at the tip of the diamond, with a continuous view-port providing a three hundred and sixty-degree view of space. It was majestic and breathtaking. Around him was the command and control staff, occupying three tiers of decks. His plank ran behind the chief controller, Commander Toevph, from the Yo Republic. A short fifteen years ago, the D'Ardin Empire and the Yo Republic were at war. B'Kailine could no longer remember what started the conflict. All he knew was Commander

Toevph was a top-notch Sixana Warrior, a superb ally and his best friend—another benefit from the USSTAP alliance.

"Sire, Toevph addressed B'Kailine.

He nodded in her direction. Her sapphire eyes and caramel skin radiated in the light of the observation deck. However now, for some reason her eyes had a different sparkle in them, which B'Kailine noticed.

"Yes, what is it commander?"

"I just received a communiqué from the Osguard…He wants you to meet him in his quarters. He says he wants to bounce some things off you before he addresses the congress tonight." Toevph smiled

B'Kailine's obsession with Jarod was evident. Jarod had never invited B'Kailine to his quarters before, for work or pleasure. This was a first and it was a sign, Jarod respected B'Kailine's opinion and valued his thoughts.

A smile broke across B'Kailine's pale green face. His golden eyes sparkled with the same gleam as Toevph's. This is what he was hoping for, and the day was finally here. Jarod wanted to run something by him.

He laughed, "About damn time!"

Chapter 2—First Shot

The mixture of gases and ice in sector eighteen of the Siryman Galaxy made this part of the galaxy the most beautiful. They formed streaks of white, orange, blue and red light, making space appear as if it were on fire. The darkness of space dare not show its face in the eighteenth sector. The bright colors acted as a solar star, chasing the dark like a dawn light. The rainbow of colors mystified and captivated all who saw it. The streaks would spiral for miles in certain areas and thin out in others. The luminance of the area never dissipated. The light washed out the stars, which made navigation in the area quite challenging. Star charts were useless in this sector. Sensors were the primary navigation aid.

In the heart of the sector lay USSTAP's space station eighteen. People from around the galaxy traveled to *SS 18* just to see the beauty of the Siryman Lights. This made it the most popular spot in the galaxy and the most traveled, giving the security corps a headache. Nothing proved the difficulty in defending *SS 18* more than the recent attack on the Eierre system by the Kulusks' allies. The Eierre system contained five Earth sized planets at equal distance from the sun sharing the same orbit, although located at different spots.

The D'uins, a fringe and extremist subset of the D'Ardin Empire, led the attack in the sector. The D'uins used the blinding Siryman Lights to hide their advance on the star system. However, the Eierre defense system detected them in time to send out an alarm to USSTAP. The alarm reached *SS 18* within five minutes. The station was already on alert due to the message sent out by Osguard 11, just hours before. Commodore Duiq, the sire of SS 18 immediately responded. He requested the quadrant's galaxy protector, the *G.P. S'Coril* be dispatched. Her sister ship from the third quadrant, the *G.P. P'Togi*, soon followed her.

On the red horizon of the Siryman Lights, five D'uins battleships sailed to the main planet, Eierre Prime. Their sensors were on frontal search, aiding their targeting scanners in finding Eierre Prime through the blinding light. The D'uins miscalculated they had four hours to crush the system before the nearest ship could reach them; which was true for the galaxy cruisers. They did not realize USSTAP was expecting a fight and they had galaxy protectors with the ability to get to the Eierre Star System in minutes, due to secretive Intergalactic Port Engines, IPEs.

The *G.P. S'Coril* sailed through the white light of inner space, undetected and undaunted, under the camouflage of the Siryman Lights. She parked fifty above the galactic plane and seventy-five kilomarks off the lead D'uins port bow. She hailed the D'uins and requested they cease their attack. In response, the lead ship trained her aft pagenays unto the *S'Coril.*

The *S'Coril* did not hesitate. She fired full weapons onto the lead D'uins ship. The D'uins' chromerion field took the blunt from the pagenay beams and coronet guns, but the Asher torpedoes sailed undisturbed through the field and destroyed the ship's sensor and scanner array. Then a firefight ensued. The *S'Coril* attempted to hit primary functions on the ships, but the D'uins were relentless. Five minutes into the battle, the *G.P. P'Togi* arrived.

She parked fifty below the galactic plane and fifty kilomarks off the starboard bow. The *P'Togi* gave no warning. She opened full spread with all weapons and struck at strategic points. The sire of the *P'Togi* was aware of the battle occurring in Millmum Galaxy and had no sympathy for the enemy. The *P'Togi* destroyed the lead ship's starboard engine, setting it ablaze. She also took out the two starboard flanking ships' engines. Yet, the damage did not deter the D'uins. They limped forward at one-quarter hypersonic speed toward the Eierre Solar System. The two USSTAP ships continued firing all weapons. The rear ships were the first to go.

The weapons barrage crushed the rear flanking port ship and the rear flanking starboard ship. They both collapsed as if under a great weight of outside pressure, like a beer can under a car wheel. Then the ensuing implosion pumped, pushed and shook sending a compressed wave of metal, wire, blood and guts through space. The other three ships rocked from the invisible force, turning them sideways and about. Several more pagenay beams pushed the ships toward each other and momentum did the rest. Without friction to slow the ships, they hit at half hypersonic speed. The two flanking ships sandwiched the lead ship. The ship on the port stern hit the lead ship, nudging it into the oncoming starboard stern flanking ship. Then an eerie blue light, like runaway electricity, framed the impending massacre.

One of the D'uins dialairtic energy converters had ruptured and was about to blow. The two USSTAP ships retreated at hyperlight speed, as the D'uins ships imploded then exploded like a supernova, spewing dialairtic radiation like black rain for one hundred thousand kilomarks. Fortunately, Eierre Prime's atmosphere protected it from the radiation. However, the radiation, which was dangerous to human life and interrupted hypersonic, hyperlight and MOP engine efficiency, had a life of forty-eight years, if not cleaned up.

That is why the USSTAP Science Vessel, the *Y'Tamin* was in the area. The *Y'Tamin* was equipped with dialairtic sensors and sweepers to safely collect and neutralize the radiation surrounding the solar system. Science Vessels like the *Y'Tamin* were routinely dispatched to the aftermath of a battle for radiation cleanup, as they were dispatched to the area around Millmum Capitol Station after the Kulusk encounter.

The sire of the *Y'Tamin*, Centurion Vezec from the Yo Republic, was a burly man, with a husky voice that vibrated off the bulkheads when he spoke. His light sapphire eyes seemed to smile as he spoke. His white hair gave him a grandfather appearance. His demeanor was similar to a Santa Claus—an extravert with friendly overtones.

He sat in his command chair, watching the readings flow across his smoky glass screen, displaying his patent smile. Everything was going as scheduled. He thought he would have time to travel to the Yo Solar System and give his crew a much-needed shore leave.

"Sire," his science officer called, breaking his concentration.

"Yes Captain…what?" he responded

"I'm getting high energy surges off our port stern…five hundred kilomarks—four…no…eight…no ten surges. They look like gate portal openings, but different."

"On screen…maximum view," Vezec ordered.

The captain complied. The main viewer filled with the images the captain described. Ten red ovals dotted the blue, orange and white tapestry of the Siryman Lights. Then shadows began to emerge from the red dots. Cone shaped white ships, as large—if not larger than galaxy protectors, were lumbering out of the red holes.

"Identify!" Vezec commanded.

"Working!" yelled the captain. After several initial attempts, the captain found a match in his database. It was a new entry, just recently added. His eyes swelled with fright. "Elim!" he cursed in his native language.

"What? What is it?" Vezec queried.

"Sire, ninety-four point fifty-eight percent match…they are Tuit ships."

"Tuit? Who the hell are the Tuits?" Then Vezec's eyes rolled up. "You mean the Tuits…the same Tuits on the last warning message?"

"I'm afraid so, sire."

Vezec turned back to the screen. He counted the ships out loud. Then he huffed, "Hail them!"

The communications officer to his right acknowledged the order and began working his magic at his console. "No response," the young lieutenant said. "All channels, all languages…no response," he repeated in exasperation.

Even though it took a split second, several images ran through Vezec's mind. He was a science officer. The *Y'Tamin* was a science vessel with a crew of two hundred, equipped with one pagenay generator for self-defense. It was not equipped for combat. It was never intended to be in combat. His ship was always intended to be in friendly territory or at least surrounded by other combat ships. However, now he was alone, facing ten galaxy protector size ships. His mind saw the impending destruction of his ship. For the first time in years, his patent smile erased from his face. He knew he did not have the resources to engage the Tuits.

Although, he was a science officer and always part of the science corps, his command instincts kicked in. He had to save his ship and he had to warn USSTAP. Orders rang from his lips like a well-rehearsed script. "Chromerion field up. Alert 1! MOP Engines engage on my mark…course three–four–five decimal seven–eight, mark one–two–zero. Pagenays on line! Comm…send warning, all languages, all frequencies…ten Tuit ships stepped into Siryman Galaxy…give last plotted position. Warn the Eierre Solar System defense to go to Alert 1. Get the nearest galaxy protectors and galaxy cruisers here now!"

The flurry of activity and head nods assured Vezec his orders were being carried out, but he still had an uneasy feeling in the pit of his stomach. He wanted to stay and see what the Tuits wanted. He stood and moved closer to the screen as if it would give him insight. All he knew was he didn't want to be the one to fire first.

"Comm…continue the hail…all languages and frequencies," he reiterated.

"Tiah!"

"Sire, the ships are two hundred and fifty kilomarks and closing," the pilot announced.

"I see that captain…I see that." Then Vezec looked toward his comm officer. "Any answer to our hail?"

The comm officer shook his head.

"Elim" he cursed. "How about a USSTAP response?"

"Not yet sire."

"Sire, they are one hundred kilomarks and closing!" the pilot said with a raised voice.

"Thank you," Vezec said in a softer tone to calm his bridge crew.

"Sire, they are charging weapons!" the navigator announced.

"Pilot…Lock on pagenay to the lead ship," Vezec ordered, wondering where he was getting his courage.

"Weapons discharge sire, it is melenai charge wrapped in ionic plasma," the navigator announced.

It took Vezec a microsecond to realize his predicament. He knew the melenai charge was the shockdel weapon used by the Kulusks, and the chromerion field was useless against it. If he went to stealth to energize the slitanium hull, the ionic plasma would rip him to shreds. He had to retreat or at least maneuver. He had to keep them busy until the big boys got there.

"Engage MOP engines now!"

The bright yellow ball of energy, from the melenai ionic plasma gun ripped through the vaporous image of what was once the position of the *Y'Tamin*. The ship was no longer there. In the blink of an eye, the *Y'Tamin* moved and now was thirty kilomarks above the Tuits starboard bow.

"Target lead ship's weapons. Fire pagenay…two second intervals!" Vezec screamed.

Blue beams shot from the *Y'Tamin* bow, slicing through space. The protective shield surrounding the cone shaped Tuit ship soaked the beam up, like a sponge and dissipated the energy.

The Tuit ship reacquired the *Y'Tamin* and charged their weapons once more.

"Engage MOP engines, on these coordinates," Vezec ordered as he rushed to input the coordinates on his command board. He knew he was violating operating policy. MOP engines needed a fifteen-minute recharge between use, and short distances overloaded the dialairtic converter, but he had no choice. He was buying time and he could not face the Tuits in a conventional fight. His one hope was that he could use the Siryman Lights as camouflage in his insane attempt to conduct a battle.

A screech vibrated in the ship's hull as the strain on the engines increased.

"Sire, the engines cannot take another jump," the pilot warned.

"They are going to have to," Vezec commented.

Once again the *Y'Tamin* moved, violating the laws of physics. The melenai ionic plasma beam missed its target once more. This time the ship appeared fifty kilomarks behind the Tuits.

"Target the last ship's engines and fire…three-second bursts," Vezec ordered. This was the first time he saw the engines. The hull from the cone shape denied a view of the engines from the front. Vezec knew he was collecting valuable data, but he didn't know if he could get the data to USSTAP. He was sure he would not survive, but he was doing his part. He was slowing the Tuits down, delaying their attack on Eierre and buying the combat ships some time. "Comm…send images of the battle to the nearest USSTAP space station. I want them to have this for analysis."

Once more, the pagenay blast dissipated on the Tuit protective shield. Vezec knew he was targeting a different ship and his weapon's effect would be limited at best. He had to keep hitting the same ship, at the same point. He had to weaken the shield; however, he did not have the proper instruments onboard to tell him if his weapon's fire could weaken the shield. He punched his armrest in frustration.

"Engage hyperlight engines to these coordinates," he ordered, punching in new coordinates. He wanted to give the MOP engines a rest, but he was taxing the dialairtic converter, which was still dangerous. Most battles were fought under hypersonic speed, where the dialairtic converter was not strained to the max, but he had to keep moving.

The *Y'Tamin* dotted the space fifty kilomarks above the lead ships port bow and fired a pagenay blast at its weapons array. Again, the Tuits reaction was slow. The melenai ionic plasma blast ripped through another ghost. Then the *Y'Tamin* appeared twenty-five kilomarks off the starboard and fired. This time it appeared thirteen kilomarks below the starboard and fired. It then appeared seventeen kilomarks above the starboard and fired. At one time the *Y'Tamin* displayed in five areas simultaneously, seemingly firing its pagenay. The energy from one pagenay barely reached the weapons array, before another one rocked the Tuit ship. Soon the Tuit lead ship's defensive shield was down and the *Y'Tamin* was doing damage to the weapons array.

"One more hit!" Vezec screamed. He knew he could knock the lead ship out of space with one more hit. He pushed the pilot his new coordinates and prayed for victory. However, this time when the pilot pushed the engine engage sensor a blue static enveloped his console, indicating a rupture in the converter. The ship moved once more in a blink of an eye, displaying in two locations—where it once was and twenty kilomarks below the lead ship's port bow.

When it appeared below the Tuit's port bow, the blue static now gripped the entire ship, shooting arcs of light like electricity. The *Y'Tamin* was doomed. The pressure of the converter's implosion, crumbled the hull. Then the subsequent explosion blossomed into a fiery red, blue and orange ball, shooting shredded metal, dialairtic gas, dialairtic radiation and dead bodies out like a broken piñata.

***

Rina of Jaywick, the Sixth Daughter of Fire, daughter of Rena, granddaughter of Dina watched the drama unfold in front of her. She commanded the lead Tuit ship and had ordered the shockdel plasma cannon to open fire on the small vessel, which was in her path. At first she was amused at the small ship's sad attempt to confront her, but then her amusement turned to irritation, and then to anger as the ship appeared to be untouchable. Somehow it self-destructed. Rina did not know how, or why, but she made a point of finding out. The lesson learned may prove invaluable later. Although for now, she had a mission to do, and very little time to do it.

Two Tuit ships sailed toward each of the five planets in the Eierre System, unhampered by the dialairtic radiation. The USSTAP Eierre System Defense Grid board on Eierre Prime lit up. One hundred and twenty-five robot defense ships, twenty-five from each planet, raced on an intercept course. These small unmanned defender size ships, which one galactic month earlier valiantly fought off the D'uins attack, pierced the pastel sky of the Siryman lights, shooting blue pagenay flames of fire in an undaunted effort to delay the inevitable. The Tuit ships dwarfed the unmanned defenders like an elephant to a Chihuahua. And like elephants, the Tuit ships moved slowly, powerfully and gracefully through the mix, ignoring the defenders and their pagenay spray of fire. The invisible protective shield surrounding the Tuit ships absorbed the pagenay blasts and harmlessly released the energy into space.

Seconds later the Tuit ships released an onslaught of weapons fire, slicing yellow balls from their melenai ionic plasma guns. Each defender caught by a plasma ball disintegrated into glowing metal embers of confetti. The first barrage destroyed twenty ships; the second barrage destroyed thirty more. Then after a thirty-second lull, the last barrage destroyed the remaining defenders. The Tuits dismantled Eierre System's entire defense capability in fifty-four seconds flat.

Each ship then maneuvered so their bow faced their respective planet. Then from the four points of their cone bottoms, beams shot forward. Two were red and two were blue. The beams converged into one spiraling color twisted beam two kilomarks off their bow. The mixed beams shot toward the planets, drilling deep fissures into the grounds.

From space, red veins seemed to crack each planet. The veins swelled and multiplied. Soon each planet glowed red as the atmosphere heated. On the planets there was no life left. Molten lava or the unbearable heat had killed all in its quake. Then the planets bulged, becoming bigger and bigger—looking like balloons about to burst.

Then the Tuit beams stopped. The ships reversed course and left their orbits, but as they left, a single melenai ionic plasma ball discharged from the rear gun. This was the last pressure the planets could take. The last remnants of cohesion collapsed as the planets popped with red, yellow and orange explosions. Millions of meteor chunks, of what had been the five planets making up the Eierre planetary system, spewed into space like vomit, spraying dust, ash, and rivers of molten rock in a disorderly array for hundreds of thousands of miles.

Rina smiled, watching the destruction with glee. She tasted victory and it tasted good to her. The conquest had begun, and she was the lead warrior. Then, the Tuits disappeared into the red ovals of ultra space, leaving in their wake the newly formed Eierre Cloud, where once thrived five Earth size planets, housing approximately one billon people on each. The total destruction—five and a half billion lives and the entire Eierre race wiped out in four minutes.

Chapter 3—Return To Earth

Parker Genesis stood in the backyard of what formerly was his house. It seemed like yesterday, when that chaotic day occurred. The day Earth almost met its destruction. He remembered Michelle running toward the front door screaming for Elizabeth and him. He remembered stepping out on the porch, and then everything else happened so fast—Michelle dragging them into the light—stepping onto a space ship—and then finding out about his heritage. All of it was so unbelievable; especially the assassination attempt on his son, which left him without his legs.

He reached down to massage his MARIT thighs as he remembered feeling the pain from the Kulusk weapon pierce his body. He felt the pressure of his hands massage the MARIT thighs. He cracked a smile as he stood back up. At first he thought the MARIT legs would be an abomination. Now, he had to remind himself they weren't real. They felt real, looked real and moved like real legs. In the morning they would cramp up and in the evening his feet were tired. Even when his wife tickled the back of his leg, he would laugh and jolt away. They weren't his God-given legs, but they were real.

He shook his head, and looked back at the empty space. The Kulusks blew his house up in their ill-fated attempt to kill him. His prize possessions were gone—his medals from the war, his books, his photos and other memorabilia he collected over his sixty-seven years of life—were all gone. It was like his life never existed. There were no signs of him or his accomplishments. All he had were memories, and they were fading in his old age.

He missed their parents' wedding pictures, which were in the downstairs foyer, flanked by his and his children's wedding pictures. On the opposite wall he'd hung pictures of himself and his siblings as children, as well as his wife and her sister when they were teenagers. He had a picture of all his children and grandchildren in a multi-picture frame on the same wall. He was so proud of his family. Family meant everything to Parker. Now he didn't have that.

He kicked at the dirt in frustration, "Damn those Kulusks…Why the hell did they have to do this…Why me?"

"Because you are an Osguard," came Michael's voice from behind him.

Parker spun around, half embarrassed Michael heard him, and half angry because Michael witnessed his frustration. He forgot he was not alone. He had walked away from Michael, Michelle and Elizabeth to what was once the backyard of his house to steal this time of solitude. He never intended it to be shared. He just wanted to be alone with his thoughts.

Michael moved closer to Parker. "Dad," he continued. "You may not be an Osguard like us…I mean, you aren't running USSTAP, or commanding a galaxy protector. But you are a direct descendant of Sharyla, daughter of Nausona, making you an Osguard. Plus, you were a threat to the Kulusks—the operative word being '*WERE*.' Now the Kulusks are our friends and you have nothing to worry about."

"Yeah right!" Parker shrugged. "That doesn't help me. I lost everything, my house, my car…everything—"

"Dad," Michael interrupted. "You lost nothing that can't be replaced," he said, looking at his father's legs. "You have your health, your family, and you know more about your family than you ever did." He looked skyward. "You can trace your genealogy to the stars and back. You have more history today than you had a month ago." He looked back at him, allowing his hazel eyes to help him make his point. "You can build new memories, try new things, and travel to places throughout the universe. This is an opportunity of a lifetime. It is your birthright—your heritage. Not this piece of land or what it once stood for. Remember, you only moved into this house five years ago. And guess what? In thirty more days our Engineering Corps will have built the house again—like new."

Parker just stared into Michael's eyes, chewing on his words. "I suppose," he said, "but I lost a lot of memories here."

"No Dad…you lost a lot of stuff here. You still have your memories."

"Michael, much of that stuff was irreplaceable—family treasures that meant a lot to me."

Michael grabbed his father's arm and pulled him closer. "Dad, I almost lost a treasure that was irreplaceable. I almost lost you. And no amount of stuff is worth my ability to reach out and hug you whenever I want. No picture, no tape, no record, nor a certificate could ever match that treasure. So as long as I have you, Mom, Patricia, Shawn, Michelle and the kids, I am the richest man in the universe. And I would hope you would feel the same about us."

Parker looked skyward and huffed. "I did get to visit another planet."

"Not just another planet…your homeland. You got to see the very house Nausona and Laurona were raised in. The same house countless generations of Osguards were raised in. How many African Americans have a heritage that deep? Not many, I tell you. Well you have it. You have it all. And you have the entire universe at your disposal. Damn it dad. You are an Osguard. I guess it is time you started acting like one."

Parker huffed again, never taking his eyes from the sky. "I guess you're right, son. I guess you're right." Then he looked at the empty lot where his house once stood, shook his head and turned around. He hugged his son by the shoulders and they walked toward the ladies.

"You know, you're pretty smart to be my son!"

"Thanks, Daddy—I think!"

***

She was amazed. A few weeks ago the area looked like a combat zone, or at least what she thought a combat zone would look like. Burnt-out houses spackled the twilight sky; rubble and debris littered the landscape. On the road, abandoned cars with doors ajar told the story of a rushed evacuation and impending doom. The pictures were illicit and vile. Her home was destroyed and her life turned to shreds.

However today, there were no signs of the fight in Osguard Gardens. The roads were clear, the burned out houses were gone and the landscape was clean of all debris. Residents had already moved into several houses that staved the attack. Lights danced from their windows as if the world was right again. However, for Elizabeth Genesis, there was no such luck. Her house was not only scathed in the attack, it was demolished by a Kulusk Torko bomb.

She realized if she or her husband were home during the attack, they would have died. She thanked God almost every day for allowing them to live to see another day. Even though she almost lost Parker on Millmum Capitol Station, she recognized God was with them. However, things were moving so quickly, her mind could not comprehend it all. She was in her late sixties, and never expected such a life altering change to occur for her.

She looked skyward at the setting sun. The day had been a beautiful one. The temperature was cool for an August day, around eighty-five degrees. The clouds were light and the breeze was gentle. The sun had done its job and now was retreating from the full moon that approached. Elizabeth saw the stars make their appearance in the orange sky. Before, she never took much notice of the stars. She always thought them beautiful. She always thought of them as God's blanket on the world, but now she had another appreciation for them.

The stars were her children's home. The stars were her children's life. Now when she looked in the sky, she knew she was looking at her children. Patricia and Shawn had left for their respective galaxies of responsibility. Michael called it their GOR. So they were out there somewhere—somewhere in her sight, but she could not see—somewhere in the sky, doing who knows what, for who knows whom. They were her children and she vowed to love them, no matter where they were. And she did.

"Momma," the virtuous voice echoed from behind her.

Elizabeth turned around and nodded to Michelle. Then she turned skywards once more.

"Momma, what are you looking at?" asked Michelle.

"My children…I suppose."

Michelle turned to the sky as well. She wanted to tell her mother-in-law that she could not see her children by looking at the sky. Shawn was in the Minor Man Galaxy, known to Earth as Triangulum or M-33. This galaxy was the third galaxy in the local group of galaxies, along with the Millmum Galaxy alias the Milky Way Galaxy, and the Mermian Galaxy better known as the Andromeda (M-31) Galaxy. Patricia was in the Miter Line Galaxy on the outer realm of the Local Group, over seven million light years away in the Maffei Star Group. Even if she could see these galaxies, the light containing the image of Shawn would not reach Earth for at least another three million years. In Patricia's case, it would take another seven millions years to reach Earth. In fact, she thought, if there was a strong enough time-light ARIT, the images it would receive would show the formation of life—the cultivation of civilization—and a thousand other things in those galaxies, which would answer many scientific questions. The possibilities were endless. She smiled toward the sky as if she had just received an epiphany. She wanted to share her thoughts.

Nevertheless, she decided to forgo the astronomy lesson and just enjoy the view with her mother-in-law. "It's going to be a beautiful night," she commented, pushing the thought out of her mind.

"Perhaps!"

"Well, I hope the weather is just as nice, tomorrow in Connecticut."

"Why?"

Alliyah…you remember…your niece's wedding," Michelle responded in surprise.

"Oh my God!" shrieked Elizabeth. "I forgot all about Alliyah's wedding. That's tomorrow?"

"Ah…mm! Your sister is expecting you tomorrow morning."

"Well I guess I better call and tell her I can't make it," huffed Elizabeth.

"Why on Earth not?"

"Because I have too much to do here," she said waving her arms.

"This is your sister's only daughter. She wants you there. Besides, you can't do anything here for a couple of weeks. Plus, I am the maid of honor. It wouldn't look right if Michael and I showed up and you and Papa weren't there."

Elizabeth lowered her head and turned to the side in a reflective manner. "I suppose you're right," she sighed.

"You know I'm right!" smiled Michelle. "Besides, it will do you good to be around your folks for a while. You've been around Papa's folks all this time." Then Michelle looked back at the heavens. "You just can't talk about what happened here. It's best you tell them the house flooded or something like that, if you have to say anything at all about not being home for the last month."

"Okay, point taken!" Elizabeth looked back at the heavens again. "Point taken," she repeated. "Who'd believe me anyway?"

***

Washington D.C. was enjoying the same cool breeze as Osguard Gardens. The president of the United States, Frederick Walter Peters, was enjoying a brandy and watching the beauty of the sunset from his oval office. The last month was particularly harrowing, but the past week had eased the pain somewhat. It appeared Congress was supporting his amendment on the strategic arms reduction treaty. Therefore, he could proceed with his plan. The House Majority Leader, Republican Representative Joyce T. Eldridge from Texas became his spokesperson for the amendment, leaving Senator John W. Bass, the Senate Majority Leader, from the State of Washington, licking his wounds.

Then there was the report sitting on his desk. He picked it up and flipped through the pages, for the hundredth time. Peters cracked a wide grin. For he knew, in his hands he had the names and affiliations of all the Osguards. *I got you,* he thought.

Peters had created a special task force to capture all the data on Juanita Genesis-Clark. Then he had them cross-reference her with Unlimited Associations. A simple audit of their tax records cross-referenced with family relations produced the sixty partners of Unlimited Associations. The bad news was none of the partners listed an address in the United States as their primary residence. Yet that didn't matter either, because he had Osguard Gardens. However, the report also named over two hundred and fifty thousand people as employees of Unlimited Associations worldwide—twenty-seven thousand from the United States. Peters realized, even if half of them were really USSTAP it still was a big chunk. Furthermore, for the organization to have been so covert, for so long with so many people was astounding.

USSTAP was not just an alien organization it was an organization with roots on Earth and especially the United States. There were Americans, other than the sixty Osguards, in the organization. Also, there were people from almost every nation and religion in the world. They were Africans, Asians and Europeans. They were Jews, Buddhists, Muslims, Catholics, Protestants and more. The name Unlimited Associations was very apropos.

The report stated UA had offices in every major city in the world, throughout Europe, Asia, the Middle East, Africa, Australia, South America and North America including the United States—Boston, Richmond, Atlanta, Dallas, Los Angeles, Seattle Washington and Chicago—seventy-five cities in all. Peters thought it a very successful operation if nothing else. He didn't know if he should be embarrassed or angry at the operation. USSTAP, under the guise of Unlimited Associations, managed to not only operate, but also thrive under his nose.

Now he was pondering his next step. What should he do? Technically, USSTAP was a foreign power in his land. They had no consent of the U.S. government to operate. On the other hand, they also had set up shop like a big business and had officially conducted themselves in that manner. Peters was confused. *On the surface, had USSTAP broken any U.S. laws?* He knew exposing them would be disastrous, especially after pushing Congress to ratify a false Strategic Arms amendment. Why couldn't he let it go, like Presidents Truman and Kennedy did? Peters didn't know what he wanted. All he knew was he wanted something. He wanted access to USSTAP's technology. No, he wanted USSTAP technology.

Peters poured another glass of brandy. He stood and walked to his oval office window, staring outside at the orange glow that followed the setting sun. He closed his eyes, as if to make a wish, and then sipped on the brandy and opened his eyes. He had made his decision. He was ready. He had to act.

Peters turned and picked up the phone. He pushed an automatic dial button and waited. The phone rang several times. He thought no one would answer the phone.

"Yeah!" a tired voice answered.

"It's me," Peters whispered. "Did you get the file?"

"Yes, I did sir," FBI Special Agent Anthony Musoto snapped.

"Well if it was up to me, I would have cut you out after the Shreveport screw up. But—"

"I understand sir," a humbled Musoto whimpered.

"Good…then I have a job for you…And Musoto, you better not screw this one up, or I'll have your badge. I hope I make myself clear!"

"Perfectly clear, Mr. President…perfectly clear."

Chapter 4—Meetings

B'Kailine stood outside Jarod's door, trying to hold his nervousness in. He had passed the door a million times, but never dared knock on it. All of his meetings with Osguard 11 had been on the observation deck or in his office. And those meetings were spontaneous and short. Now, the Osguard wished to confer with him over how to proceed next. Sweat beaded his forehead and rolled down his spine. He never felt this way before, nervous and anxious at the same time. He was nervous because he didn't want to come off as a complete idiot, and anxious, because he wanted to make a great impression. He wanted to accent the fact the Osguard had never conferred with him prior and that it was not just an insult but also a breech in protocol.

B'Kailine took a deep breath, straightened his jacket and then pushed the door chime. A few seconds of silence followed. He pushed it once more. Still there was no answer. He shrugged his shoulders. Now he thought the entire episode a practical joke.

"Enter!" rang Jarod's voice from inside. The door slid open and B'Kailine walked in. "I'll be right there," Jarod announced from the bathroom. "Please make yourself at home. The bar is to your right. Pour yourself a drink. I'll only be a moment."

B'Kailine looked around. The room was very spacious. Two couches and two easy chairs surrounded a coffee table in the middle of the room. His comm board, containing video and audio, was to his left. To his right was the bar as Jarod promised.

"Nice quarters you have here, sire," B'Kailine shouted. "Very comfortable," he added, walking behind the bar and smiling to himself because he had thrown the opening salvo. He wanted Jarod to recognize this was the first time he had seen the inside of his quarters.

Behind the bar he saw a bottle of D'Ardin Bourbon. It was more than half empty. In fact the other bottles were practically full, but the bourbon was almost gone. He grabbed a couple of glasses, assuming this was Jarod's favorite drink, and poured the bourbon.

Jarod appeared out of the restroom, drying his hair. "I had to take a quick shower. It is a ritual with me. Every time I return to the station, I just don't feel quite right until I take a shower. Call it silly…I guess…It's just one of my crazy idiosyncrasies." Jarod threw the towel down on the sofa and joined B'Kailine at the bar.

"I took the liberty, sire, of pouring you a glass of bourbon."

"Yeah…great. You know D'Ardin Bourbon is one of my favorite drinks."

"I can tell."

"How?"

"It's the only bottle half empty. The others are hardly touched."

"That's what I like about you, admiral. You have a discerning eye."

"Oh sire," he replied in awe. "I never imagined there was anything you liked about me."

Jarod picked up his glass, sat at the stool, and sipped from it. "Touché!" he replied.

"What?"

"It's from a language on Earth. It means good shot."

"Oh!" he replied. *So far so good*, he thought to himself.

"Look B'Kailine…I know I have not been…well let's say, I have not included you in galaxy business like I should've. But you've not included me in station business either. So we're even." Jarod took another sip of his bourdon, laid it down and moved to the communication center. B'Kailine followed.

"Yes sire, this is true," B'Kailine admitted.

"Well, I want to put that behind us and start afresh." Jarod turned back to B'Kailine. I need you more now than ever, admiral. As you know, we have a new threat which requires us to work better together—the Tuits."

"I know sire."

Jarod clicked some buttons on the comm center and a document flipped on the screen. "This is what I haven't told you. My assessment of the Tuits and the danger I think they pose to this galaxy and the rest of USSTAP. I would like you to read it and give me your opinion. I plan to present this to the Congress this evening and I want to know if I am hitting the mark."

"Of course sire, but…"

"But why now and why you?"

"Exactly!"

"Look admiral, I always admired you and your ability. But I have my own demons to control. Where I come from…well where I come from your lifestyle is not normal. In fact, the politically correct term is Alternate Lifestyle back on Earth. And I am…was a little uncomfortable talking to you."

"My lifestyle?"

"Look…you come from a system where women live on one planet and men on another. You have partners of the same sex."

"I'nmo?"

"Yes, I'nmo. Isn't an I'nmo your sex partner?"

"Yes, they could be for some. But most of the time, they are just partners in rearing offspring."

"Offspring?" shouted Jarod. "Offspring is another thing. This arrangement you have with the women of D'Ardin, surrogate mothers we call them on Earth. Well, I am…I mean I was uncomfortable with that as well." Jarod returned to the bar and then downed the rest of his bourbon and poured another glass. "Test tube babies, surrogate mothers, incubator babies, what's next—cloning."

B'Kailine sighed in disbelief, but he expected this was the problem and he was prepared. He emptied his glass. "Before the Restoration," he began, "two thousand years ago, we were as you—married to opposite sexes and having children. Then one day we turned around and our society had deteriorated. Fathers weren't around, marriage became a joke and children were hurt. Violence became a way of life and no one gave a damn about anything. The religious leaders blamed it on our disrespect of morality, our preoccupation with sex." He returned to the bar and poured another glass of bourbon.

"A small group of female I'nmos came to power and restored our society, by splitting the sexes," he continued. "The females stayed on D'Ardin Prime and the males moved to D'Ardin Two. Once separated, sex and violence left our minds and life was pleasant again. Children no longer suffered. Children were now born under contract using what you call test tube babies and surrogate mothers; and raised to full term in incubators. Then two partners who contracted the birth shared in the rearing of that child. Women partners contracted for female children and men partners contracted for male children."

"It sounds so sterile," Jarod pronounced.

"I admit, over the years sex has entered our society again, but only a small portion of our society actually practice it."

"Yeah, but they practice it with each other, not with the opposite sex."

"Maybe, maybe not. Travel is permitted between planets. Nonetheless, those who practice it do not do it with the consent of our laws. The law calls for celibacy."

"You mean they can be punished, whether homosexual or heterosexual?"

"Technically yes – in practice, no. Our government prides itself in granting its people freedom—Similar to the USSTAP constitution. As long as their actions are not infringing on others and they are consenting adults, our government looks the other way. As long as it is discrete."

"That sounds ominously familiar," Jarod snapped. "Isn't that what the Restoration was supposed to kill? If you treat everything like that, you will have anarchy again."

"Well, let's look at your history. Alcohol was once banned and now you drink it freely. Gambling was once banned, and now you have lotteries in nearly every state and casinos throughout your country. Prostitution is banned, except for the State of Nevada, and it hasn't hurt them. Some of your states are even granting same sex marriages. And there is a move to legalize recreational drugs. All these are cases of consenting adults making decisions on how to spend their time and life. These are victimless crimes. Our government believes that if there are no individual rights being denied by their actions then they will look the other way."

"You know a lot about American History."

"I made it a point to study it in case we ever had this conversation."

"Touché again! But you can use those arguments to justify anything from being a pedophile to having sex with animals," Jarod pushed as he poured another bourbon. B'Kailine finished his glass and offered it for a refill.

"True, but a child is not a consenting adult and neither is an animal."

"You mentioned drugs. Don't you know the United States has a big drug problem?"

"No, I guess I didn't," B'Kailine admitted, "but let me tell you how we handled our drug problem during the Restoration. Those who wanted to do drugs had to do it under the observation of a hospital. Those found doing drugs at home or in the streets, were taken to the hospital where a doctor could watch them. Once identified as a drug user, it was placed on their identification card. Then we gave employers the option to deny work to those identified as drug users. If anybody committed a crime under the influence of drugs, they were shipped to D'Ardin 4, our outer planet. There it was very cold…inhumanely cold. But they got all the free drugs they wanted, so I guess they didn't notice. Well anyway, after the first hundred years, of spending their lives in hospitals, not getting work or spending their lives on D'Ardin 4, the people lost their taste for drugs. We killed the demand, so the supply dried up."

"How about alcohol?"

"Same difference," B'Kailine shrugged, "Except you didn't have to go to a hospital to drink. If you were at home or at a bar, the ARIT would not allow you to go pass a certain blood alcohol limit. You were cut off when you were near the limit. So the Restoration cured alcohol abuse in about fifty years."

B'Kailine sat at the bar once more and looked at his Osguard. "So why the talk now?"

"Let's say, I had a life altering experience at home."

"You mean the war?"

"No, not that." Jarod sipped on his bourbon as he tried to muster the courage to speak. "You know my father left my mother when I was fifteen. Well we, my sister Rachel, Osguard one-five of the Miopsolan Galaxy, and my brother Tim, Osguard two-four of Breilon Galaxy, finally saw our father for the first time in twenty-five years." Jarod looked down at his feet. "He's dying and he wanted to see us one last time before he died."

"Well can't USSTAP save him?"

"Yes, I'm sure we can. The question was did I want to save him. I mean he left without saying good-bye and we hadn't heard a word from him since. To us, he was dead a long time ago."

"You didn't try to find him after you became an Osguard?"

"No! Besides, we always knew where he was. We just never went to see him."

"Why?

"Because he left my mother for another man. My father is gay and he is dying of AIDS."

"Oh, that explains it. You think by talking to me, it will absolve you of your prejudices," B'Kailine smirked. "Well Osguard, it won't work."

"I'm not looking for absolution. I'm looking for answers."

"Good, because I can't give you absolution…I'm celibate."

"What?" Osguard 11 was shocked. "You're celibate? But I thought you had an I'nmo."

"I do. We reared three sons together. But we are both celibate—not practicing homosexuals like you assumed."

Jarod lowered his head in shame. "I'm sorry B'Kailine. I didn't know and I should've. All this time I had a preconception of the D'Ardin people that was in error."

"I figured that," B'Kailine shot back, "but as long as you were fair in your decisions regarding the D'Ardin Empire, we had no problems. And as long as I had free reign in running the station, we were fine."

Jarod looked into B'Kailine's eyes and read his sincerity. He felt a weight; he did not know existed, lift off his chest. "I've made a rash decision about your society and about you, without knowing all the facts. This is the most heinous sin for any Osguard. I guess I had let my own family demons affect my judgment."

"Okay, no problem. But what about your father." B'Kailine wanted to change the subject. He got his point across and didn't want to belabor it any longer. Deep down inside he knew Jarod was a stand up guy. He just needed to know why he was on the outskirts of his circle. "He's still your father and you are still an Osguard."

"I am, but he's not. I am an Osguard through my mother."

"He's still your father," B'Kailine pleaded.

"I know that," Jarod conceded. "We all knew that, but it was hard."

"What was hard?"

"With the blessing of the other Osguards, we sent my father to a USSTAP hospital. The doctor says it may be too late, but he has a fifty-five percent chance of beating this thing. The question is when he beats it; he will forever be part of USSTAP—him and his lover.

"Again, I ask. So?"

"Look B'Kailine," Jarod began, shifting his weight while searching for the strength to continue. "I'm not comfortable about my father being a homosexual. It isn't something I can subscribe to. It is a matter of my religious upbringing." Then Jarod cocked his head to one side in confusion. "But I believe my religious upbringing might have been a little hypocritical."

"How so?"

"When I was growing up in the church, it was no secret that the organist and the pianist were both gay men who lived together. And it was no secret that the choir director and one of the associate ministers were gay and lived together as well. All were highly regarded and respected members of my church. In fact, the church, especially the pastor, refrained from preaching on the subject, which now causes me to wonder, where I obtained this *'high and mighty attitude'* on gays from." He took a sip of his drink, shrugged and let out a cleansing sigh. "Most likely peer pressure, I guess. Either way, I'm convinced, homosexuality is a perversion that I don't want to associate with or be exposed to."

"I believe it is much too late for that," B'Kailine surmised. "Your father is in a USSTAP hospital fighting the AIDS virus. You're already exposed to it."

"Yeah, I know," Jarod acquiesced, averting his eyes from B'Kailine. "That means I will have to move him and his lover to Osguard Gardens, once he is well," he growled. "They will always be there as a reminder to my mother of the most painful day in her life."

"What does she say about all this?"

"Nothing! She acts like she doesn't care," Jarod said looking up at B'Kailine. "What shall I do?"

"Sire, let's cross that bridge when we get to it." B'Kailine relished in throwing Jarod's catchphrase back at him. "For now you have to deal with his illness."

The comm center beeped, startling the two men.

"Osguard here," Jarod forced.

"Sire, report from the *Y'Tamin*. The Eierre System is under attack," Toevph's voice rang out.

"What?" B'Kailine yelled.

"Yes sire, it's the Tuits."

Chapter 5—The Conspiracy Begins

New Haven Connecticut was enjoying a perfect Saturday afternoon. The temperature was a pleasant seventy-five degrees with no clouds to hamper the beauty of the sunshine reigning over the city. The First Olive Baptist Church, in the north of New Haven just off of Whalley Avenue, displayed a mighty fine majestic aura during this mild summer day. The tan brick structure was a newly constructed church to house a hundred-year-old congregation. The church sat a thousand people in its sanctuary and another two hundred and fifty in the balcony. The oak pews were decorated with red plush cushions to match the red carpet. The altar was large enough to hold three full choirs and the pulpit. The orchestra pit on the right side of the altar housed the organ, piano, drums and other instruments of praise. The church was outfitted with a state of the art sound system, even downstairs in the fellowship hall. The church had become the demanded festival area for many religious events, including weddings. Today, Jamel Roget, a twenty-five-year-old graduate student of New Haven University, and Alliyah Whitmore, Elizabeth Genesis' niece, were getting married.

Jamel met Alliyah three years ago on campus. He had bumped into her. He was deciphering his class schedule and wasn't paying attention to where he was walking. Fortunately, neither was she. He knocked her down onto her butt. Her books flew up in the air and papers scattered all around them. He was so embarrassed. He profusely apologized and picked up all the papers and books, leaving her sitting in the grass dumbfounded. When he realized his mistake, he dropped the books and papers on the ground and offered his hand to help her up. This was the first time he captured a glimpse of his victim. He thought her the most beautiful woman in the world. Her caramel skin was so soft and perfect. Her high cheekbones highlighted her deep brown eyes, and she had softly tinted her dark shoulder length hair with brown streaks. He fell instantly in love with her. He also fell instantly dumb. He couldn't speak. He couldn't utter a sound, other than the occasional grunt so common to men when they are awestruck…and Jamel was awestruck.

It took him several days to ask her out. He was afraid she would turn him down. Fortunately, he met someone who encouraged him to follow his heart and ask Alliyah out. It was later that he discovered that someone was her cousin, Shawn Genesis.

Shawn had returned to New Haven for a visit and met with his cousin, Alliyah. She could not stop talking about the encounter. She feigned being galled at Jamel's rudeness, but Shawn recognized the interest in her voice. She was intrigued with Jamel. During her outrage, she described him as rugged, handsome, strong and somewhat sensitive. These were words of endearment, and Shawn knew it. So he sought the young man out and befriended him. He too talked endlessly about the encounter with Alliyah. Shawn played cupid and put them together. Now Shawn, who'd just returned from his GOR just before the start of the wedding was the *'Best Man.'*

"You may kiss the bride."

Standing as the best man, Shawn gazed at the couple, sporting a big smile. He saw Jamel place such a passionate kiss on his baby cousin that he blushed. He also felt warmer. He knew Jamel was a good man. He wasn't like any of the thugs on the streets. He had a plan, he wanted a future and he was going after it. He was pleased with his cousin's choice.

One hour later the wedding party and two hundred plus guests were in the banquet area in the church's basement. Shawn stood to make his opening toast.

"In every life, there is night sprinkled with thousands of stars. Each star is so beautiful and so bright. So bright, you think you can touch them. And when you look up in the sky, it makes you feel happy that the stars are there. Besides beauty, the stars in the night sky have little for you. However, soon the night is chased away by the one and only perfect star—the sun. The sun rises, shining the brightest light, washing the sight of any other star from your view. The sun destroys the darkness, so you can see more clearly. It provides everything one needs to sustain life, energy, warmth and passion. Well Jamel, you have found your sun in Alliyah. She has washed the sight of any other star from your view. Her devotion has chased the darkness so you can see your dreams more clearly. Her passion fuels you like no other source of energy. And her love will keep your soul warm for eternity. May you always cherish her as the Earth cherishes the sun!"

Shawn raised his glass of champagne in a salute, followed by all the guests. Michael thought it peculiar Shawn directed his comments toward Jamel and not to the both of them. He concluded that was Shawn's official warning to treat Alliyah right, which Shawn confirmed with a little snicker as he drank his champagne.

Two hours later, Michael and Michelle had danced and eaten their way to a stupor. Shawn and Patricia, along with their families had left. Shawn and Patricia had to rendezvous with their ships so they could get back to their respective galaxies of responsibility or as it was abbreviated—GOR. Michael was ready to go as well, and so were his parents. He bid his farewell and congratulations once more to the lucky couple and exited the church to get the car, while Michelle and his parents waited in the church vestibule.

The parking lot was a block away. It was really an abandoned lot, where several houses once stood. Michael walked the narrow sidewalk toward the parking lot, passing several three-story, three-family New England Victorian style houses. The houses were early twentieth century, some were even late nineteenth century, but all were one hundred or more years old. Most were showing their age, rotted wood, broken banisters, chaffed paint, overgrown shrubbery, and other signs of age and dereliction. Michael thought it a shame. If the houses were in other areas of the country, they would be proclaimed a historical sight. However, for the New England area, one hundred-year old houses were commonplace, and for something to be considered historical it had to be dated as colonial. Nonetheless, to him the houses were of significant historical importance. They just needed repairing, but that was too costly. Now they were just low-income houses for the elderly or those on welfare.

Michael marveled at how much history was wasting away in front of him. It made him a little emotional, He didn't know whether it was the champagne he had drunk, or the culmination of stress and fear boring into his shield of self-confidence, but a tear filled his eye and escaped onto his cheek.

Michael then crossed the street to the parking lot, still mystified at the wasted history. When he was growing up, he never thought of the houses as history. He thought of the houses, especially the three-family house he grew up in, as cold and old but still home. Only when he became an adult did he realize the importance of his house and others like it. However, no one else did, especially the bureaucratic idiots at City Hall. That is when he gave up and joined the movement to start Osguard Gardens in southern Virginia for the family.

A noise caused Michael to stop. To the side of the parking lot he saw a homeless man, dirtied by street grime and inebriated by cheap wine rummaging through the garbage cans, looking for food or something of value to hock. He turned and walked toward the man with a spirit washed in sympathy. He checked his pockets and produced a twenty-dollar bill.

The man looked at him with distrust in his eyes, but with a hopeful smile.

"Go on take it," Michael urged, stopping and offering him the money.

The man looked around as if to see if this was a joke. While smacking his lips, he reached out and then snatched the money from Michael's hand. Then with the grace of a sprinter, he ran down the street, looking back like he expected Michael to change his mind and chase him down for the money. When Michael waved at him, he just turned around and continued running, never looking back again.

After the man was out of sight, Michael looked skyward. The stars were unusually bright tonight. *Maybe that is where Shawn got the idea for his toast*. Many times the stars have been an inspiration for him as well. It kind of went with the territory of being an Osguard. However, the stars weren't soothing enough tonight to calm the growing beast inside of him. Anger began to fill his aura as he seethed in agony over what he had just witnessed. Here he was, the leader of the most important organization known to man and the Chairman of the Osguard Senate, and in the past twenty years he has been unable to help his own people…like this homeless man. It was the beginning of the twenty-first century, a new century of promised hope. But poverty, drugs and violence rose to wretched proportions, killing what hope the new century promised it would bring. Additionally, Michael just sat back and watched as war; famine and disease pushed its vile rule across the world. He did nothing in the name of USSTAP.

Michael searched the heavens once more; trying to capture the peace the stars had always brought him before. The secrecy of USSTAP was an albatross hung around his neck, choking the compassion from him one universal year after another. Once he was full of spit and fire to change the world. But as Ortho promised, the business of the universe and the politics of the greedy stole his attention. Twenty years ago, Michael let Ortho talk him out of spreading USSTAP's wealth and knowledge for the benefit of mankind on Earth. Ortho convinced him that the chaos that would follow would outweigh any good he could possibly bring to Earth. And he brought it, hook, line and sinker. Now Michael gazed at the stars, wondering, *how would the homeless man feel if he knew I had the power to ease his suffering?*

The spiraling black hole of depression that chased him before the Kulusk aggression three months ago, and disappeared under the excitement of battle, now tapped him on the shoulder. With it were its cousins, despair and frustration. Michael shook his head, took a deep breath and blew it out hard. He straightened his tie and walked to his car holding a mental conversation with his newfound feelings.

"Osguard?" the voice came from behind him as he reached his car.

Michael spun around. In the shadows was a man, a white man; which was odd for this neighborhood on a Saturday night. He reached for the pagenay in his coat pocket. He now had an odd feeling in the pit of his stomach.

"I'm Special Agent Anthony Musoto."

"Prove it," Michael demanded.

Musoto offered his identification as he stepped toward him. Michael inspected the identification and nodded in recognition.

"Okay, you're Musoto. What do you want?" Michael asked, turning his back to Musoto to unlock his car.

"President Peters sent me."

"Yeah, so what," Michael huffed.

"Sir, the president wishes to speak with you."

"About what?" Michael bellowed, turning back toward Musoto and showing his agitation. "Quick, you tell me so I can run right off and help him, and leave the galaxy's business on the back burner."

Musoto casted a heavy sigh. "I don't know why, Osguard. All I know is the president wants to speak to you. So I've come here to invite you."

Michael shook his head, "How the hell did you find me anyway?"

"Easy! You and the other Osguards filed tax forms as board members of 'Unlimited Associations Incorporated' with you as the Chairman. A quick look at birth and death certificates and the FBI has your entire family. Your cousin's wedding announcement sent a flag. And voila, here I am."

Michael shook his head in disbelief. "I should have known Peters just couldn't let it die."

"What did you expect?"

Michael gently but with authority grabbed Musoto's arm, while pushing his own irritation with the situation inwards, "I expected him to be secure in the knowledge we are here and leave us be." Michael lowered his hand, his hazel eyes burned with ire as he looked into Musoto's eyes. "I also expect the president to do his job and be this nation's leader and protect it from self destruction and…or self annihilation…without my help, or my technology," he added, finding someone else to lay his personal guilt trip on.

"Well…" Musoto huffed. "He obviously isn't satisfied with that. So I say again, the president of the United States wishes to talk to you."

"No."

"No? What do you mean no? This is the most powerful man in the free world. You can't just say no to him."

Michael scratched his head, displaying a perplexed look. "Excuse me! Is that supposed to frighten me or impress me? Let me tell you something. I am the most powerful man in this galaxy. I am one of the most powerful men in the known universe, and I am supposed to cow down? Well it's not going to happen." Shame penetrated the tone in his voice as his anger trailed off.

***

While Michael was blurting out his outrage toward Musoto, unbeknownst to him a red light from a sniper's rifle spotted on his chest. The light illuminated from atop a service garage adjacent to the parking lot.

The sniper was clad in a black jumpsuit and ski mask, wearing nothing shiny, no buckles, no buttons, and no studs. Only the cuts around the eyes and mouth revealed the sniper as white. The sniper had been watching the exchange between the two men. Michael didn't stand still during his tirade. His voice was audible even at the sniper's distance. Luckily no one else was around, so the sniper thought. Michael was very emotional, no doubt a little inebriated as well. However, Michael's irritation soon began to lessen and his movement slowed until he was standing still, while he blasted

Musoto. The sniper flicked the guiding red beam and swung it up to his heart.

***

Musoto took a deep breath in a vain effort to deflect Michael's harsh words. He looked away in disappointment, trying to think of a diplomatic way to ease the tension. He didn't know why Michael said those things. Perhaps it was because he was trying to place the president on the same level as the Osguard. Peters and Michael weren't on the same level. Michael was right, and that is what he wanted to say. '*The Osguard was right.*'

He turned back to Michael after letting a moment of silence cap his last words. He saw and recognized the red dot on Michael's chest. Without hesitation he yelled, "Gun!" Then he pushed Michael to the ground. At that precise moment the shot cracked in the air and shattered Michael's driver side window.

Two more shots rang out in quick succession, hitting the car with two distinct pings. Musoto and Michael crawled behind the car. They knelt behind the trunk as Michael reached under his shirt for his communications collar. The one inch black form fitting elastic collar with silver stripes wrapped around the lower part of his neck was his two-way communication lifeline to USSTAP. He pushed the emergency beacon. Musoto pulled his revolver and Michael pulled his particle generator array weapon—pagenay. The silver remote control-looking device fit in his hand and had three buttons. The blue button fired the blue beam that quickly and neatly burned its target with high unbearable heat. The red button corresponded to a red beam of energy, which overloaded the human axons and dendrites in the nerve cells with heat, rendering its victim unconscious. Lastly, the yellow button corresponded with a yellow beam briefly disconnected its victim's axons and dendrites causing momentary sensory deprivation and momentarily disorienting its victims. They looked at each other for a split second before both of them turned, draped the hood and returned fire in the direction of the shots.

Musoto's 9mm clattered three quick times as Michael's pagenay threw a red light, piercing the darkness like a beacon for two two-second blasts. Then they ducked behind the car again.

"What the hell Musoto?" Michael whispered. "I tell you no, and your partner tries to put one in me. That ain't smart buddy. That ain't smart at all."

Musoto looked at him in surprise. "This ain't me."

"Yeah right! Who else knows I'm here? Who else would take a shot at me? Everyone else who wants me dead would use a more sophisticated weapon than a gun."

On the edge of the parking lot, seven white gate portal openings flashed as security personnel emerged from them.

Michael hit his CC, "Osguard security, shots fired from the garage roof at your nine o'clock."

The men jumped for cover and marched from car to car to the garage. Two security personnel adjusted their Personal Gate Portals (PGPs), the portal device that controlled gate portal openings, and stepped to the roof. Thirty seconds later, the CC receiver implanted in Michael's ear cracked, "Roof is secure…no one here."

"Scan the area!" Michael commanded. "Scan the area," he repeated.

In the distance sirens blared, announcing the arrival of New Haven's finest. They both stood and Michael turned to Musoto, "Your play."

"Get your men out of here. Let me handle the cops."

"Do you want me here?" Michael asked as he saw people peeking out their windows.

Soon there will be a crowd of curiosity seekers, wanting to know who was shooting at whom, and if anyone was dead. The busy bodies will swarm on the spot at the same time as the cops. To come any earlier would be too dangerous. And one thing the blacks of New Haven did was, make sure they were safe before they became the hood investigators.

"No, I guess not."

Michael tapped his CC, "Dr. Michelle Genesis…This is Osguard zero–one." He waited for the protocol to finish and for Michelle to find a quiet place to answer.

"Dr. Genesis."

"Michelle, grab my parents and the kids, step to the ship…Alert two. Break…break. Osguard Security, step back…repeat…step back…Alert two."

Then Michael pulled and activated his PGP. He looked back at Musoto, "This shit isn't over. Tell the president he doesn't want to fight me. But this little stunt—"

"I promise you, Peters had nothing to do with this."

"Bullshit!"

"I can prove it…give me a chance."

"Okay, Mr. Musoto, prove it."

"How can I reach you?"

"You don't. I will reach you when I want to see you. That's how it works…and don't you forget it." Michael turned and disappeared into the white light of inner space as the invisible door slammed shut, leaving Musoto alone to explain to the police what had happened. No, not explain, but fabricate a story the police would buy.

Musoto shook his head as the first police car pulled up. He holstered his weapon and pulled his badge. "Special Agent Anthony Musoto…FBI," he announced.

***

The small red brick two bedroom house in a southern suburb of Richmond Virginia was soaked in darkness. The nearest streetlight was a half block away and the lights in the house were turned off. It was approaching midnight in the suburb and the streets were quiet. The only sounds in the air were the crickets serenading the moon, which were silenced by an owl's occasional *'hoot'* from the oak tree in the front yard.

Inside the living room the red light from ultra space washed the room from a portal opening. A person dressed in black, wearing a ski mask and carrying a high-powered rifle slung over the right shoulder stepped from the light. An invisible door slid down, bringing with it normal light and depth to the room. The person pulled off the ski mask and allowed her long brunette hair to fall upon her shoulders. She rushed into the bedroom, dropping the rifle onto the bed, and then she hurried into the bathroom.

She crowded the sink, staring into the mirror. Her yellow pupils were wide with fright and disappointment. Mona Richards' mission was to kill the First Osguard and have USSTAP believe it was the U.S. government behind it, but she failed to kill him. She missed and she knew her superiors did not bear failure easily. Up until now, she had executed her assignments without a hiccup. Regrettably now, when it counted the most, she failed. Michael was still alive. She knew it would be only a matter of hours before Eldridge would find out, and then it would be a matter of minutes before the Daughters of Fire would find out. She had to do something and she had to do it now.

She thought about running, but where would she run? Her PGP would just take her within the confines of the planet. And with her unique DNA it would be a matter of days before Eldridge would find her. Basically, running would make things worse.

She thought about lying and stating she thought she made a clean kill. However, that would imply incompetence, and incompetence was just one step away from failure. Yet for some, it was the same and she did not know how the Daughters of Fire would take it. Either way, she saw herself in the sensory deprivation tank for life. Or what was left of her life. *No, pleading ignorance would not help.*

There was only one thing to do. She had to come clean. She had to say she missed her assignment and take her medicine. She knew her life was not worth anything now. All she had left was her honor, and she was convinced she would maintain her honor, no matter how painful it was. Truth, even in failure, was the Tuit way, the honorable way, and the single way to go.

She shook her head in disbelief as she pulled her PGP from her belt. "No time like the present!" she whispered. Then she activated the device and stepped into the red light. The door closed behind her and then a door opened in front of her. She stepped into the darkened black room. She blinked several times to help her eyes adjust after being in the red light of ultra space.

"Well?" the voice came from behind her.

"I failed," she whispered.

"How? What happened?" asked the Republican Representative from Texas, the House Majority Leader and the commander of Tuit insurgency on Earth, Joyce Thelma Eldridge.

"I missed," she whispered as she spun around to face the voice. "Musoto recognized the red laser dot just as I fired and shoved the Osguard to the ground. I tried again, but they moved behind the car. I was going to go down and finish the job, but the Osguard called for security and they were there so fast, all I could do was get out of there."

"Oh…" was all Eldridge could manage. She turned on the bedroom light and hopped out of bed. She walked toward Mona, slipping on her robe.

"He was so furious with Musoto; he just didn't stay still enough for me to get a good shot at first and when he was finally still…well, Musoto got in the way."

"Are you making excuses?"

"No, commander…I failed. There's no excuse."

"You say the Osguard was agitated at Musoto?"

"Yes, commander," she added, hoping she had stumbled on to a way out of the problem. "He was very agitated, especially after I shot at him. I stayed long enough to hear him shout at Musoto. The Osguard thought the attack was ordered by Peters."

"What else?" Eldridge was leaning in, showing more interest.

"Nothing, commander. I left soon afterward for fear of being captured."

"So perhaps you didn't fail. It appears it may have worked out better this way. Instead of having USSTAP catching Musoto holding the First Osguard's dead body and coming to the conclusion Musoto was involved. We have the victim himself blaming Musoto. It couldn't have worked out better even if I had planned it."

"Do you think?"

"Yes, but we will have to wait and see. For now, I will consider your mission as a partial success…but only a partial success. I will give you another chance to finish the mission…but not right now. Let us see how much further we can take this before we kill him." Eldridge's yellow pupils sparkled with satisfaction as a new scheme hatched in her mind.

Mona knew Eldridge wanted to pit USSTAP and the people of Earth against one another. She knew if Eldridge could dissolve the psychological tie the Osguards had with Earth, the more vulnerable they would be.

"Go back home…pump Musoto for details when he shows up and report back to me," Eldridge commanded.

"Kiza!" Mona responded with relief. She had reported her failure honorably and she was not faulted for the failure. In fact, the failure worked to their advantage. She smiled because she did not lie or run. Either one of those choices would have been fatal. She did the right thing and she knew it.

She pulled her PGP and activated it for her home. She looked back at her commander, still displaying the smile of confidence. Eldridge smiled back and waved her to go on. Mona stepped into the red light and disappeared behind the invisible door, leaving her commander content. She could not have hoped for a better ending to the night.

Chapter 6—The Aftermath

Chunks of rock, meteors, dust and ice floated on invisible highways, of what once were planetary orbits, around the Eierre Star. The supernatant chunks varied in size, shape and depth, and some looked like mountains tumbling on an imaginary string. The small ones were building size. As if some spiritual hand had swept upon the masses, the chunks assumed an organized position and space from each other. Some pieces traveled faster than others, and several bumps and collisions occurred. For the most part, the mangled and twisted sea of rocks moved in an orderly fashion. In the distance, the supernal moons that once perched in the heavens over the Eierre planets were flying away from the debris, no longer held in place by gravity, but freed to explore the cold dark emptiness of space. What was not seen, but morbidly present were the billions of Eierre lives. The newly formed Eierre Cloud was the graveyard for an entire race of people.

On board the Universal Science, Security and Trade Alliance of Planets *Galaxy Protector Gentry*, the picture played out on the large view port screen for the inhabitants of both the command bridge and the control bridge to witness. Jarod sat in his leather chair in the center of the command bridge with his mouth agape. The fact he was witnessing a floating memorial to an entire race cooled his soul. He massaged the side of his head as if to rub the image from his brain. He had never witnessed such ruin. He did not know of any weapon capable of such devastation. He didn't even know of anybody capable of such destruction.

Siryman Galaxy USSTAP Intelligence estimated the entire episode, including the destruction of the *Y'Tamin* took approximately ten minutes. Jarod's mind could not grasp the enormity of the destruction is such a short time. With each passing chunk of the Eierre Cloud, his eyes widened with disbelief. *It wasn't real*, he wanted to shout. But it was and he knew it. He just didn't want to accept it.

"Osguard," Regina called.

He turned to her, with his eyes still showing the shock of the situation. "The ship's sensors are picking up residuals from an unidentified energy. The science lab thinks it was the weapon used to…"

Jarod nodded, but his eyes told the rest of the story. His hazel eyes changed from shock to anger. The science lab had to identify the energy and do it quickly.

Regina turned to her control arm. "I'll push them for answers," she added.

"They attacked here because it was our fourth largest producer of the dialairtic crystal," he whispered. "Within sixty universal hours, they destroyed the Sirus system in Millmum Galaxy, the Sirap system in Memlan Galaxy, the Nidra system in Axer Galaxy, and the Darreck system in Telo Galaxy. Systematically, they destroyed all our major mining systems for dialairtic crystals…each attack lasting no more than ten minutes. They came out of nowhere, hit us and disappeared like ghosts." He looked skyward and sighed heavily, "Who the hell are these people?"

Strategically, it was simple. His attackers knew USSTAP and practically the entire known universe depended on dialairtic crystal to fuel everything from coffee makers to Capitol Stations. It was the only energy source they had. Until now, there was an abundance of it throughout the association. Now, only small pockets scattered throughout USSTAP's sphere of influence contained the crystal. Small independent contractors, who supplied small areas, owned those mines. Even if USSTAP took over the mines, there weren't enough crystals to outweigh the damage done. USSTAP's supply of crystals could last anywhere from two years to twenty years, depending on the fracture rate of the supply.

In theory, the crystal contained an endless supply of energy. Unfortunately, the strain put on the crystal in obtaining the energy often fractured the crystal and made it useless. The *Gentry* had fractured three crystals in six universal years, and that was under normal space duty. He could not imagine the fracture rate under sustained combat operations, which he suspected was coming.

He never imagined USSTAP's energy dependency on one fuel would be so critical. He knew as long as the fuel came from different sources, it should not have been a crippling matter. At least that much he learned by watching the U.S. give away its sovereignty by creating a dependency on Middle Eastern Oil. No, USSTAP didn't fall into that trap—No, USSTAP had five areas in which to obtain their energy. Thus if one area became a problem, the other four would increase production. Hell, USSTAP could have gained all their energy requirements from one mining system if it came down to that. No, USSTAP could never fall into a trap where energy became an issue. Sadly, no one figured on all five solar systems being out of commission, or worse…destroyed.

Yet, what was really upsetting and what he did not dare say aloud was the destruction of life in those systems. From all the reports flowing in, he realized an estimated thirty-five billion people and five races were wiped out—annihilated—within sixty universal hours. And just last month, he was worried about the destruction of one planet…Earth! How trivial that appeared now, in comparison to the destruction he was witnessing. It hurt…it hurt badly. The sadness of the moment clouded his mind and controlled his thoughts. As an Osguard, he could not show his grief, and in the past, it was a simple thing to hide his grief. But now…but now…his grief was hiding him. It was hiding who he was and what he was. It was as if his mind was in neutral and his emotions were in charge.

"According to Centurion Vezec, he believed them to be the Tuits," Regina commented, shaking him from his thoughts. "His was the only ship to come into contact with the attackers, and the data he pushed out to us confirms his suspicions. His images, of the attacking ships and that of the Tuits that showed up at Millmum Capitol Station, are a ninety-three point seventy-eight percent match."

"What's the difference?"

"Vezec got some rear images. The ARIT is unable to match the rear images."

"Without the rear images?"

"The ARIT calculates a perfect match."

"Push our analysis to all stations and galaxies," Jarod ordered, looking back at the devastation consuming his screen.

"Tiah!"

***

Her yellow pupils were brazened and smug with pride. She stood triumphantly in the midst of the Hall of Fire. Only days before, she was a prisoner fighting for her life in the arena—shamed by a mistake and deprived of her will to live. What a difference in an impulse…the impulse to live. Although her will to live was vanishing, a spark of vitality ignited it again, and she fought like there was no tomorrow. For if she had lost, there would not have been a tomorrow.

She smirked at the spot where her opponent had breathed her last breath. It was a befitting justice she thought. Now she commanded the attention of the people. Rina of Jaywick, daughter of Rena, granddaughter of Dina was a Daughter of Fire. Not just any Daughter of Fire, but the Daughter of Fire in charge of the newest invasion. She was a warrior who had delivered what she promised.

With the inside information she received, she had led a complement of ten attack ships in the destruction of five solar systems under USSTAP's sphere of influence. The new rhetonic cannons had worked as advertised.

The planets exploded with the fury of a supernova. The image played in her mind over and over again. With each replay, her smile broadened more. This is what she wanted to do all along. Using the Kulusks as an intermediary was never her intent. However, the Daughters of Fire wanted a surrogate agent to drive the opening punch into USSTAP, but all the Kulusks were able to do was bungle the plan from the beginning. Kie Ritchen's hidden agenda to destroy the Osguards first only awakened a sleeping giant.

Luckily, now the Daughters were doing it her way. She had earned the right and the privilege to conduct the battle in her fashion. It was her plan…no one else's…all hers. And it took days of pleading and pestering to get the other Daughters of Fire to buy into it. *But so far, so good!*

Striking the five solar systems did two things for the Tuits. First, it killed the economic backbone of USSTAP and many of the governments associated with it. In many strategic reviews, one thing became abundantly clear. The dialairtic crystal was the lifeblood of their economy. The lost of the crystal would send the alliance into a recession. The alliance's economic currencies would devaluate and fall into disarray. Second, the strikes would destabilize the alliance's military cooperation. Once the governments of the alliance realized USSTAP couldn't provide the security they promised, they would pull out from the alliance to form their own defense. Consequently, their struggling economies and their dependence on the crystal would prevent them from shaping a formidable defense.

It was a strategic error for USSTAP to introduce the crystal as the only energy source to its members. The fact that it burned cleaned, and was cheap made all the members drop their own energy sources for it and jump at the chance to join USSTAP. Economically it made the members stronger but strategically it made them weaker. Now that they were dependent on the crystal, they were just as vulnerable as USSTAP. Fortunately, USSTAP thought spreading out the mining facilities throughout five different galaxies was a stringent protection plan. They never expected all the facilities to be hit.

However, if Kie Ritchen had stuck to the plan, the Kulusks and their allies could have completed the task with one fell swoop. Unfortunately, the Daughters of Fire wanted control of the facilities, and not destruction—which meant automatic failure for the Kulusks and their allies. Even if Kie did not deviate from the plan, they did not have the manpower or the strategic leadership to accomplish the objective. Luckily, the Daughters of Fire only gave them technology to develop the shockdel gun and not the phase shockdel gun or the rhetonic cannon. When she found out that Kie intended to attack the Tuits as well after he supposedly dispatched the Osguards, she knew she had to eliminate him. Of course, she was to eliminate him anyway. It just happened sooner than planned.

"Rina of Jaywick," the First Daughter called. "You have implemented the first part of your battle plan. Do you have anything to report?"

Rina looked up at the pit where the Daughters of Fire sat. They were dressed in the golden robes of command, hoods covering their heads with only their glowing yellow eyes piercing the shadow of the hood. Then the First Daughter lowered her hood, allowing her blonde hair to fall freely over her shoulders and her chest. She was about forty years old. Age lines that came from command faintly circled her eyes, but did not diminish her beauty, which all the Tuits prided themselves on. As with Rina and the other Tuits, her skin was a pasty pale, because the sun on Tuit did not provide the rays sufficient enough to tan or color the skin.

"Their economic basis is destroyed. Soon the alliance will be in economic upheaval and chaos will follow. The alliance members will splinter and split from the alliance, trying to thwart the threat on their own. That's when we move in." Rina smiled at the simplicity of the plan. "For now all we have to do is stay on the offensive."

"Are you sure?"

"Certain!"

"How long?" The First Daughter sighed, squinting with impatience.

Rina knew her tenure with the Daughters of Fire was contingent on results—results she did not have at the moment. "Six cycles at most," she guessed aloud.

"How about their current supply of crystals? How long do you suspect they will last? The energy source of the crystal is almost indefinite. They could continue as is until they find another source for the crystal or another energy source. USSTAP is not about to give in just because you struck them. In fact, I suspect they will increase their resolve."

"I do too," Rina agreed, "but we will keep hitting them and destroy their resolve."

"No!" the First Daughter said. "I want live lolwes to replenish our needs. Killing every planet you come up against is not in our purview. We need these people alive."

"I know First Daughter," Rina responded, "but we do not need them all alive, only half. So I separate the lolwes we need, and kill the rest."

"Sorry to say, every time you destroy a solar system, you change the tapestry of space and ultimately of ultra space," the First Daughter warned. "Eventually our coordinate system will be worthless, for our scientists can't tell what changes occur. I'm sorry, but we have to limit your plan until we know the effect on our own system."

Rina looked up in surprise, "What do you mean?"

"Our scientists warn us, every time you use the rhetonic cannons and destroy a solar system, you throw off the coordinate system in ultra space—

gravitational forces alter and space changes. As for now, it is an insignificant change, but as you destroy more, the change raises exponentially. We cannot afford that. Our scientist cannot determine how the system will change anymore."

"Then that kills my plan!" Rina screamed.

"No, it alters it. I am sure you can adapt and still make your strategy work. However, the scientists do agree that the change will not be significant, if you slow your pace to one use per three cycles. That way, they can adapt to the changes in our coordinate system and maybe be able to forecast it. Can you adapt your plan to that?"

Rina looked to the side to hide her disgust. Then she turned back to the pit. "It will elongate the outcome. Can the consortium wait?"

"No, your timetable remains the same…six cycles."

Rina looked down to the floor. She knew the First Daughter wanted her to resume the original plan and this was either a ruse to do so, or a convenient happenstance. Either way, Rina had to incorporate the original plan back into hers. Then she turned to the side and nodded. She finally realized that the original plan could work. It would call for some adaptation, but it could work, especially under her leadership. However, she needed an edge.

"Give me one more use of the cannons in one cycle and another use in four cycles and then I promise the outcome in six cycles."

The First Daughter turned to the other Daughters and they conferred in whispers for several seconds. Whispers waffled throughout the arena as the other dignitaries in the hall engaged in their own conversation about the subject. Rina watched the commotion with childlike awe. She wondered if she had pushed the Daughters too far on the subject, but it was the only way she could ensure victory.

The First Daughter turned back to her and raised her arms as if to welcome her. "You are the Sixth Daughter of Fire," she said. "We have entrusted you with this task and we must trust you have the consortium's best interest at heart. So you proceed as you see fit. However, if the scientists return with concrete evidence we are losing our continuity of ultra space, we will hold you accountable. Is that clear?"

Rina nodded, "Kiza!"

"Fine, Rina of Jaywick. Come take your seat with the Daughters of Fire."

***

It was the first time Anthony Musoto was invited to the White House. Even though he had been working directly for the president of the United States for the past couple of months, he had never met Peters in person, only spoken to him on the phone. The thought seemed odd. Here he was working the most sensitive project for Peters and he had never met him. Well today was different. He didn't know whether it was different for the worse or the better. Nonetheless, he was here.

Two Secret Service men stood outside the Oval Office entrance, each dressed in a traditional black suit with a white wire protruding out of one ear, which disappeared underneath their jacket collar.

To their left, the president's aide was working on something on the computer. He seemed young, almost college age. Musoto thought him some intern working on his political science or international affairs credits. Yet, it seemed odd that someone so young and obviously so inexperience had daily contact with the president. *Some people were just born lucky,* he guessed.

Mrs. Charles, the president's receptionist, sat across from him. She occupied a large mahogany desk with mounds of paperwork straddling the corner. Around her sat the trappings of a modern day secretary, a phone with computer key buttons, and a computer with a twenty-two inch flat screen monitor. A combination color printer, color fax machine and color copier sat to her side. A digital camera, a microphone and a PDA mount were connected to the computer. She wore a headset with a microphone that was also connected to the computer via the telephone. She also seemed intensely busy with something.

Neither she, the aide, or the secret service men looked at him. They all were in their own little world, or at least that is what they wanted him to believe. He knew all were acutely aware of his presence. Even though they did not look at him, he knew they were keeping him under surveillance in other ways, by listening or using their peripheral vision. They wouldn't be in this position if they weren't keeping an eye on him.

Security was amazing getting into the White House. Musoto had to present several forms of identification at the gate, where he had to leave his service revolver. Then he was escorted to the entranceway where he passed through four metal detectors, went through two wand inspections and even was frisked from head to toe by one security guard. Then a secret service agent escorted him to the foyer outside the Oval Office.

Musoto made up his mind. He had to get a pass or identification or something that gave him unfettered access to the president. *Going through this kind of security each and every time he wanted to see the president or when the president wanted to see him,* he corrected, was too time consuming. He needed to mention it. He wanted to feel like the first string, not a third class citizen. After all, how many people knew of his mission?

"Mr. Musoto," Mrs. Charles called. "The president will see you now."

"Thank you," he said, standing and moving toward the door.

The agent on the left swiftly opened the door for him. Musoto nodded in appreciation and walked in. Peters sat with his head bowed into paperwork behind the famous resolute desk. The same trappings that surrounded his secretary were present in the room. On the desk sat a computer with a large flat screen monitor. Behind him sat a phone with more buttons than the computer keys. And to one corner sat the same bulky four foot high color copier, color fax and color printer. Musoto wondered why the president needed the administrative machinery in his office, when his secretary and aide right outside the door had the same equipment. However, the image only intrigued him for a split second.

"Sit," Peters ordered without raising his head. The gruffness of his voice told Musoto, this wasn't going to be pleasant.

Musoto walked toward the seat in front of the president, passing the two couches and coffee table that appeared to be for informal visits. He knew this was definitely formal. Peters continued editing a paper in front of him, grunting at some points and smiling at others. Musoto sat quiet for several minutes, watching Peters, trying to get some insight into his character—wondering what kind of man Peters really was.

Soon thereafter, Peters put down the paper, placed it in a folder and slipped it into his desk drawer. Then he looked at Musoto for the first time, with his head slightly cocked to one side.

"You're not like I pictured you," Peters huffed. "In fact you aren't at all like I pictured you."

"Oh!" Musoto managed.

"Yeah! I thought you a worn down, gruff, kind of broken spirit of a man," Peters responded. "But look at you. You're impeccably dressed, nice haircut and I can see you work out."

"Thank you, Mr. President."

"Then why all the screw ups, Musoto?"

"Sir?"

"You heard me! Why all the screw ups?"

"Look, Mr. President. I don't know what you are talking about."

"First Shreveport and now New Haven. Someone took a shot at the First Osguard. Why?"

Musoto bristled at Peters' comment. Ever since he returned from Shreveport Louisiana, he wanted an opportunity to explain what happened. However, he didn't know what quite happened. Nonetheless he was suspicious of the similarities between the two incidents. He was more leery of the fact he was involved in both. He sighed and stared Peters in the eye, "I don't know. But all I can say, is my presence at both situations stopped it from becoming more severe."

"How's that?"

"In Shreveport I saved the mother and in Connecticut, I saved the Osguard."

Peters cocked his head to the other side, "Hmm!"

"I don't know what's going on," Musoto added, "but things aren't right. And until they are, I don't think you are ever going to meet the First Osguard. He's gone…vanished…disappeared from the face of the Earth…and so are the residents of Osguard Gardens."

"What about your contact?"

"Stelana is gone too. She left her position at UAI."

"How about the others at UAI?"

"I checked all the offices throughout the country. The only people left in those offices don't know anything. They are the front people. I would like the CIA to check the overseas offices?"

Peters thought a moment and slowly shook his head. "If they are gone from here, I know they left all their overseas offices as well. No…I still want to keep this low profile…just you. I don't want to spook this Osguard anymore than he already is."

"Okay sir, but I don't think he's spooked. I think something is up. Something is wrong. Why else would they empty Osguard Gardens again? I mean until yesterday, the residents were coming back. And now today, it's a ghost town again."

"How do you know?"

"I checked."

"You can still get in?"

"No, I watched with binoculars from outside the gate."

Peters looked upset at first, when he heard what Musoto was up to. Then he turned his anger inward. "Someone tried to kill the First Osguard and he blames us. We have a leak somewhere. Have you told anyone about this?"

"No sir."

"Then it is on my side," Peters announced. "Someone in my inner circle has betrayed me."

"Are you sure? Couldn't the Russians have done this?"

"Perhaps…but I doubt it. They didn't have the information we had to track the Osguard down. I haven't shared anything about Shreveport, or the UAI with them. All they know is that USSTAP exists and that they saved us from nuclear annihilation."

"Couldn't they have found out?"

"Perhaps!" Peters stood from behind the desk and walked over to Musoto. Musoto stood. "I want you to change your mission a little. I need you to check on these people." Peters handed him a folder. "I am authorizing you full access to the Secret Service and the CIA files. If one of these people betrayed me, I need to know and I need to know before we attempt another contact with the Osguard." Musoto opened the folder and scanned the names. His eyes widened with shock. "I know," Peters calmly said. "Some of those names are the most trusted people in my administration. Also, they are the only people that know what is going on. One of them is trying to frame me and I need to find out whom."

Musoto closed the folder and stared into Peters' eyes. He saw a strong man fighting for his life, fright gripping at him. Musoto was his only lifeline. He was the only one who could do this without tipping his hand. No wonder Peters was complimentary toward him; a far cry from the character bashing Peters had done so far. Peters was searching for someone he could trust and he picked him.

"I have full access to the Secret Service and the CIA files? And I have immediate unfettered access to you…right?"

Peters grabbed Musoto by the shoulders and stared him directly in the eye. "It's all set up. Here are your contacts in the Secret Service and the CIA." Peters handed him an envelope, keeping one hand firmly on his shoulder. "You contact them and only go by the codename Millmum. When you use that codename, you have the full authority of my office. They will get you anything they can…without breaking the law of course. As for access to me, well we still need to be covert about it. The secure communications is our best means. In your office I am having a secure phone, e-mail and fax set up. Mrs. Charles will assign a secretary with the necessary clearance to assist you." Peters let go of his shoulder. "Musoto, I need you, and for God sake don't screw this up."

Musoto looked at Peters and nodded, "I'll find out who it is sir." Then Musoto glanced at the folder once more. "What if it is no one in here?"

"Then we search somewhere else. Someone took a shot at the First Osguard."

"What if it is someone else from some other…"

"We exhaust all earthly possibilities before we jump to that conclusion. Your job is to make sure we do. Got it?"

"Yes sir! I got it."

Chapter 7—Confession

"I'm pregnant!"

Upon hearing those words, Michael's mind went blank. The fork and knife he was using to cut into his eight-ounce steak crashed into his plate. They clanged like a church bell, resonating throughout the kitchen area.

Questions raced in his mind. Michael's first impression was to ask '*How?*' However, he knew how. He knew how ever since he was eight years old. His next impression was to ask '*When?*' Then he realized he and Michelle had been as intimate as newlyweds after the Terinolice virus scare until the Tuit attacks. Those weeks were the most blissful days of his life.

During that time, he thought the universe had finally found order, and peace would forever reign. His happiness had found a newfound release in Michelle. They spent hours exploring, once again, their love and lust for each other. So the question, '*When?*' was answered instantly as evident by the twinkle in his eye. '*Why?*' came next. Yet, he knew only God had that answer. '*But aren't you too old?*' crossed his mind. Thankfully, common sense smothered the words before they formed in his mouth.

Michelle witnessed the transformation of questions on his face. His face was quizzical for a split second—then comical—and finally it glowed with pride. It seemed to take forever for the glow of pride to push through the fog of confusion. But once it did, she flashed her most sexy smile at him.

Michael reached and gulped down his drink as if the information was a pill and he just swallowed it, needing water to wash it down.

"Are you sure?" he asked, putting the glass down on the dinner table.

"Yup! The doctor confirmed it yesterday."

"You're pregnant?"

"That's what I said," Michelle huffed.

"We are going to have a baby?"

"Yup!"

Michael reached over and hugged Michelle, squeezing her tight. The connection of love flowed through his arms into her soul. Then he pushed back and looked into her eyes. Tears started to form in them.

"What's wrong?" he asked.

"I just thought you might be upset…you know about the timing."

"Yeah, the timing sucks," he admitted. "But we can't do anything about it now." Then he let her go, "Unless…"

"Unless what?" she whispered.

"Unless you want to use the baby bank?"

"What? Why on Earth for?" she screeched. "The baby bank is not my style. This baby will grow inside of me…not in some ARIT incubator." She tilted her head and Michael knew he was in for a scolding now. "Besides, isn't the baby bank for unwanted children, those embryos up for adoption, or products of rape and incest—the equivalent of advanced abortion?"

Michael lowered his head for a moment and then looked at her. "At first—yes, but lately, women have been using the bank as an alternative to pregnancy. It saves them from the trauma of gaining weight, giving birth and losing time on the job." He poured another glass of water and sipped it. He could feel Michelle's eyes burning through his skull. Immediately, he regretted ever mentioning the bank. He was now on the defensive and he needed to plead his case. "I think it appalling also, but it is legal and another way to discourage abortion. The bank has countered every argument for abortion. The embryo is removed from the women's body and allowed to gestate in an ARIT. The baby remains alive and the woman maintains her right to do what she wants with her body. Shit! Now men can have their children even if the woman doesn't. I know a lot of women who had abortions over the father's objections. I mean if the woman wants the child and the man doesn't, he's tied down by child support. However, if it is the other way around, the woman gets rid of the baby. In either case the baby suffers. I think the baby bank is a fair compromise."

Michael realized he was on his soapbox and didn't need to lecture his wife about this. They had always agreed and the look she was giving him now confirmed he needed to get back to the subject of them. "I only suggested it to you, because of the war."

"The war?"

"Honey, as you stated the timing sucks. We're at war. You and I will be in harm's way and I need you to be at one hundred percent. And you being pregnant won't allow you to perform at one hundred percent. Plus, the stress of war may be harmful to the baby. Allowing the baby to gestate in a quiet, peaceful and safe environment may be warranted in this case."

"No!"

The word thundered in his eardrums. He looked into her eyes and saw her unwavering motherly instincts. He knew the conversation was done and he needed to change the subject.

"No, it is." He hugged her again; capping the fact he was not going to push the subject again. "We're having a baby," he whispered.

***

Centurion Regina Dawson stood outside Jarod's ready room, licking her lips in nervous anticipation. She knew the time had come for her to come clean. She had kept the secret all her life and now the secret had an opportunity to affect the outcome of the war. That is what USSTAP was calling it—a war—more precisely a Universal War.

USSTAP now considered the Kulusk battle as the opening shots of the war and not the end-all they had initially proclaimed it to be. Now they understood the Tuits were the true enemy, only using the Kulusks and their allies as a staging partner in the assault. Consequently, since the Kulusks and their allies failed, the Tuits needed to be more forward in their strategy. Meaning, the Tuits needed to take over the fight, and they had done so with a vengeance.

For the past three universal weeks, the Tuits had attacked sixteen systems in four galaxies. Luckily, they did not destroy the planets as they did earlier in their attacks. But they still wreaked enough havoc, death and destruction to set the civilization of those planets back into the Stone Age. It was frustrating. The hit and run tactics the Tuits used seemed indefensible.

USSTAP cruisers had to use Intergalactic and Intragalactic Gate Portals to step huge distances of space. It was like looking for an elevator in a fire. The galaxy protectors IPEs could not step more than one thousand light years at a time, and then the engines had to recharge for six hours before another step could be attempted. Each galaxy only had five galaxy protectors to guard hundreds of thousands of light years of space. She thought it phenomenal that USSTAP had maintained such a tight control over the known universe thus far.

Conversely, that control was weakening. The association was on the verge of splintering. Members were talking about recalling their people and their support in an effort to strengthen their home defenses. Confidence in the association was waning and the Osguards were doing all they could to hold it together. Now she held in her hand a piece of the puzzle that may allow the Osguards to maintain the association.

She massaged the corynx crystal that contained the HVP between her fingers. The blue texture felt smooth to her fingers and the oval shape seemed to fit perfectly in the palm of her hand. Although, what it contained was more explosive than a coronet blast. She blinked several times as if to clear her vision, but in actuality she was stalling. She did not want to do this, but she knew there was no other way. She sighed and studied the crystal like a picture, now holding it closer to her face.

"Well, I best get this over with before I change my mind," she whispered.

She pushed the door chime.

"Enter!" rang Jarod's voice.

The door split at the USSTAP emblem in the middle and slid into the walls. Jarod was working at his desk, poring over the latest reports. The despair was evident in his eyes, which tugged at Regina's heart. Jarod was usually outgoing and fun. His character was so jovial; he could bring laughter to a funeral.

"Sire, do you have some time to spare?"

Jarod looked up. He wasn't wearing his climate-control jacket, used to regulate the body temperature. The jacket was specifically designed to keep the body at a specific temperature, dependent on the specific race's physiology. Nevertheless, this was his office, and the temperature was a perfect twenty-two chimes. He had rolled the sleeves of his black crewneck shirt up to the elbow and he had zipped his sleeveless jumpsuit down to the stomach. Regina could tell he was harried with worry.

However, his distinguishing jovial gleam slowly resonated in his eyes. She knew he always had a fondness for her. In fact he had a soft spot for Kelly and Gail as well. Any one of them could always lighten his spirit. It was love, but not romantic, strictly platonic. They were family in spirit if not by blood. She felt it and she knew he felt it as well. She did not know why he felt this way; she just knew that he did. Right about now, especially after poring over the latest reports, she knew he needed to see a friendly face. But she was afraid the information she was bringing would change all that.

"Yes Regina, I always have time for you. What can I do for you," he said motioning for her to take a seat.

Regina removed her jacket, laid it on the back of the couch as she passed by, sat at the side of the desk and politely crossed her legs. She usually felt as comfortable in the Osguard's office as she did her own. However today, her comfort level was awry. She flashed her electrifying smile as normal, which automatically made Jarod smile.

"What?" he asked again.

Regina shook her head, letting her brown hair softly wave around her shoulders. She took a deep breath and placed the HVP crystal on the desk.

"What is this?" asked Jarod.

"What does it look like?" she coyly responded.

"It looks like an HVP?"

"Tiah!"

"Regina, I don't have time for an HVP right now," Jarod said, stretching his arms above his head.

"Sire, this is no ordinary HVP," Regina interjected. "I got this from my mother…I think you need to see this."

"Your mother?" Jarod asked with surprise. "What is your mother doing with an HVP?"

"Please sire, calm down. It's legit."

"Okay…explain!"

Regina reached into her cargo pocket and pulled out a gold coin with an emblem on it. She placed it on the desk. Jarod reached for the coin. His eyes no longer gleamed. Curiosity filled them. He picked the coin up and studied it for several seconds.

"This is from the House of Chting—Ortho's family!" he exclaimed.

"Tiah!"

"How did you get it?"

"My mother."

"Again…explain!" he ordered placing the coin back on the desk.

"My mother is Ortho's daughter. I am Ortho's granddaughter. That is why he recruited me."

"But how? You're from Texas…you're from Earth…aren't you?"

"Yes and yes," she meekly responded. "However, my mother is from Chaktun. After my grandmother died, she was sent to Earth to be with my grandfather during one of his many sojourns to find the missing Osguard children. My grandfather did not want to confuse her, so he raised her as if she was from Earth. She went to school, ate, danced, partied and even fell in love as an Earthling. She met my father in college. Against my grandfather's wishes, she married and moved to Dallas. They stopped talking to each other. My mother forsook all that was Chaktun and became a Texan. She raised me as an Earthling. I didn't know until my father was killed in a car accident. Then I met my grandfather. He and my mother made up and he gave her this…for safe keeping, or until it was needed."

Jarod's shock resonated throughout the room. He was visibly taken aback and couldn't respond. Betrayal and awe washed across his face. After several painful seconds of riding this emotional roller coaster, he just beckoned her to continue with his eyes.

"It is an HVP of Nausona and Laurona…" she swallowed hard, still looking into Jarod's eyes. She felt his disappointment in her reach across the edge of the desk and slap her. She wanted to beg for his forgiveness for keeping her identity a secret from him, but she simply smiled, hoping to deflect the disappointment.

Jarod shook his head, fighting her disarming smile. "Go ahead," he pushed.

Regina sighed and looked up at the bulkhead as if searching for God to help. She really wanted to apologize, but her smile slowly disappeared. The atmosphere turned business-like and any family warmth Regina thought existed, soon faded.

Jarod perked his lips to one side, flipped the coin in his hand and then twirled it on the desk like Ortho used to do. The coin spun on its edge in place, catching the light from the bulkhead and sprinkling it like a disco ball throughout the room. It was hypnotic and soothing. The light eased the tension and pain that weighed in the room.

"Jarod," she finally said. "Ortho made me promise not to tell anyone… even you or the other Osguards."

"We can discuss that later," Jarod responded, obviously hurt from the revelation. "I want to know about this HVP."

The smile returned to her face as she stopped the coin from spinning. Then she pocketed the coin. Her smile then disappeared, and the business look, which made her the excellent leader she was, took over.

Jarod swallowed, reached out, and placed his hand on top of hers. "Go ahead," he urged.

She nodded, "The HVP is about when Nausona and Laurona met the Tuits."

"What?" Jarod shrieked.

His outburst startled Regina. She jumped back a little, but her hand never left Jarod's. "That's all my mother said in her note. I didn't know about this until an hour ago, when I received this from my mother. She suggested we watch this together."

She bent over the desk and slid the crystal over into the HVP receptacle. Four feet in front of the desk a forty-two-inch clear glass screen dropped down to eye level. Colors swirled and streamed, lighting the screen. Then Ortho appeared in the screen.

***

Ortho appeared much younger than Jarod remembered. He sat behind the Osguard's desk at Millmum Capitol Station. Jarod recognized it immediately. However confusion still reigned in his mind.

"Hello," he began. "I am Ortho Chting, Vice Osguard for the Millmum Galaxy and acting First Osguard. I assumed my position upon the death of Laurona Osguard two years ago."

Jarod mentally calculated the HVP was made around 1941, prior to his portion of the Pandora's Box HVP Michael sent to the presidents of the United States and Russia.

"My duty is to find and indoctrinate the descendants of Laurona and Nausona Osguard. However, the association is growing rapidly, and governing the association is stealing time away from that mission. To date, we have twenty galaxies as members of the association—a far cry from the five galaxies, in which Laurona and Nausona saw become members during their lifetime. But there is also another realm out there…a realm that I just learned about. It is called ultra space. I came across a personal HVP of Laurona's after her sister's death three months later. It was in her private effects. I thought it personal so I did not view it. But upon my thirty-ninth birthday, I received a strange time-delayed communiqué, requesting I view this particular HVP. Laurona made the communiqué on her deathbed with instructions for me to hear it then. I viewed the HVP as Laurona instructed and found it recounted an encounter the two Osguard princesses had with a race of people called the Tuits, and the death of my father."

The tape skipped as if it were stopped during recording and then started again after a split second delay. Jarod suspected the mention of Ortho's father may have caused an emotional moment and he needed some time to regain his composure.

"The events you are about to witness concerning the Osguard Princesses occurred Earth year 1901. I feel these events may be of some importance in the future so I decided to pass them on, but this HVP will stay within the Chting line until deemed necessary to make it public. If you are not of the Chting House and are viewing this, I must consider things dire."

Chapter 8—Start of an Untold Story

She closed the lid to the wooden box and cradled it in her arms like a newborn. Her mind was adrift in a faraway land, remembering a time so long ago. Nonetheless, no matter how much time had passed, the memories seemed fresh, as if they were of yesterday. The pain…the suffering, all bore in her mind, but not like the sorrow of leaving a child behind. That emotion prevailed over all the others. It was the rock to her memory. It was the stable to her being. Nausona could never forget. Nor could she ever forgive herself. She felt she was to blame for leaving her child on Earth—her beloved Sharyla, never to be seen by her again.

Time had been somewhat pleasant to Nausona. In Earth years, she would be fifty-three years old, but in Galactic years, she was barely forty-five. She still stood strong, with a formidable, svelte physique. Her daily routine still consisted of a two hour Sixana workout, where she was still able to defeat the youngest member of the class in two out of three challenges. She took pride in her physical well-being and mental sharpness, the tools of command she always preached.

Her skin still maintained the majestic golden glow of her youth, however highlighted with tiny age wrinkles around her eyes, giving her the badge of maturity needed in her position. Her auburn hair was darker and salted with gray streaks on the side, enhancing her beauty and strength. Presently, her hazel eyes reflected the sorrow in her heart that awakened with the contents of the wooden box.

After a few seconds of living in the past, she placed the box back onto the shelf. She had watched the HVP several hundred times in her life. The HVP detailing hers and her sister's visit to Earth over forty years ago always brought tears of remorse. She didn't know why she tortured herself with it, but she did. It was a quiet ritual for her to watch the entire HVP once a week. Every week, she took four hours from her day and watched it as if it were a religious duty to do so.

The intercom beeped, bringing her back into reality. She moved toward her desk and pushed the reception button.

"Yes!" she responded.

"Approaching Millmum Capitol Station," the voice rang from the speaker. It was Alar, her Centurion of Operations.

"Understood…request standard docking and hail my sister."

"Tiah!" The intercom went blank.

***

Outside, the *USSTAP Star Cruiser Nary*, Nausona's ship, sailed through the thin blanket of stars like a black dove. The front of the craft was shaped like an arrowhead, slicing through the thick darkness of space. The arrowhead narrowed into a shaft, which widened again, revealing long barreled rods. Then the rest of the ship, behind the weapons grew in all directions in perfect symmetry. The USSTAP star cruiser was the predecessor to the galaxy cruiser and the grandfather to the galaxy protector.

USSTAP outfitted her as well as the other fifty-five ships in the fleet with gravogenic engines, giving them speeds up to and exceeding thirty light years per hour—MOP thirty.

The docking ring glowed when the *Nary* approached. And then with the softness of a mother's touch, the *Nary* hooked onto docking station one. Nausona was now on the bridge and her sorrow was gone. The gallantry of the newly completed Millmum station had chased her remorse away, replacing it with awe. On the other side sat the galactic gate portal field, where the three-mile-long, one hundred and twenty-degree-curved ARIT rods, glowed with the same majestic light as the docking rings, awaited its first ever transport of a USSTAP cruiser to another galaxy.

Nausona sat in the command chair on the bridge entranced in her own thoughts. She stared off into space, through the front screen as she remembered when she and Laurona made contact with the neighboring galaxies in the local group, the Memlan and Minor Man Galaxies. It was almost twenty galactic years ago when the voices crackled through galactic gate portal technology. Through two decades of intense negotiations they brokered an agreement for planets in each galaxy to join the association. Now was the time to physically meet the recipients of the treaty. She smiled at the thought of her and her sister traveling for the first time, through the Galactic Gate Portal to another galaxy. An advance team had traveled to Memlan and Minor Man Galaxies several years earlier to set up a set of return Galactic Gate Portals. Also, the advance team set up space stations in those areas to mirror Millmum and she could not wait to see them. Her smile widened, as she knew her and her sister's dreams were within a stone's throw—a truly united universe. And she was to become the emissary to the Minor Man Galaxy.

"Permission to debark?" Nausona chimed into the interlink

"Permission granted," Laurona's playful voice responded. "Welcome back dear sister," she added.

"Thanks." The interlink went dead as Nausona gave her patented smile to her bridge crew. "Proceed with debarking," she ordered.

"Tiah!" Alar responded from behind her. He barked orders to the bridge crew and a flurry of expected activity swarmed around her.

Thirty minutes later she and Laurona were on the docking platform tightly hugging each other. It had only been three months since she last saw her sister, but it felt like an eternity.

"How are you," Laurona whispered to her sister.

"Tired!"

"Understood, it has been a long outing," Laurona said while staring into her sister's eyes. "I can tell you had a rough time this time."

"No, it wasn't rough. But for some reason it seemed longer than usual…just when I thought I was getting use to these types of tours."

"Well, when you take over as emissary for the Minor Man Galaxy, you will be doing more of these type of tours…I dare say longer than three months," Laurona teased with envy and pride.

Nausona heard in Laurona's voice the wish to trade places, but they had decided because of her situation, she was the one that needed to lead a new galaxy. "Yeah, that's right," she gleefully responded like a schoolgirl. "I'll have my hands full, won't I?"

The glimmer of happiness resonating in her voice told them both that it was the right decision. The challenge of organizing an entire galaxy, foreign in language and culture would keep her busy and most of all happy. Nothing seemed to pep Nausona up more than visiting and learning about other cultures.

"Don't rub it in. We could have a revote in the congress and see if they still want you to go," Laurona playfully warned.

"You wouldn't do that…would you?" Nausona bristled. "Because if you do, you will see how much of a witch I can become."

"Damn girl, you still have a little bit of Earth in you…don't you?"

Nausona stepped back and cocked her head to the side, "Apparently so, and so do you." The tiredness in her eyes vanished, swallowed by sisterly playfulness. Soon the gleam spread into a smile and they both began giggling like teenagers. The small crowd on the docking platform seemed to stop doing whatever they were doing at that moment to capture a rare but positive scene displayed by their leaders. The Emissaries looked around and noticed the small crowd staring at them and quickly straightened up. They then traipsed through the docking bay door and vanished from sight. However their laughter resonated back through the door like an echoing ghost. The people in the docking bay resumed their activity, inwardly cherishing what they just saw, but outwardly acting as if nothing happened.

***

The sisters walked to the end of the corridor and stepped into a coaster. The coaster glided through magnetic ican coils of air in a vacuum tube, with a ride so smooth; one hardly noticed they were moving. Ican coils were made out of a delicate metal alloy, first invented by the Viks several decades earlier. The coil was lightweight and exuded an energy like an electromagnet, but exponentially more powerful. The energy caused the cylinder shaped coaster to magically float through the air. Fifty-five seconds later it stopped, and the door hummed opened to the operation deck located at the tip of the Capitol Station diamond. One flight of stairs, and they were on the command plank of the operation deck.

Laurona sat at the command seat. Nausona began to slowly walk the circular plank, taking in the view of the stars that made up the heavens surrounding them. She stopped and took a deep breath, staring into space in the direction of Earth, some eight hundred light years away.

"I wonder what they are doing now?" she whispered.

Laurona swiveled around in her chair and studied her sister for a moment. Then she stood, walked over to her and grabbed her hand. "Sister, I have not forgotten our vow. We will find them and bring them home."

"Do you really believe that Laurona?" she responded. "It's been so long and so many things could have happened to them. They could be dead by now. You know how the white people of Earth treated our people."

The words *'our people'* flowed from her lips as if she were talking about Chaktuns. After their escape from Earth, both she and Laurona thought of the black inhabitants of the planet as their people. She was not quite sure how they were related, or even if the people were truly of Chaktun blood, but they just felt in their heart that it was so.

"I know we sent countless exploration teams to search. And I read Mitiah and Wtong's reports. But it's been thirty-two galactic years and not a single lead. Don't you think it is about time we go to that planet and search for our children?" Nausona continued in a demanding tone.

"Nausona, I know you are hurting now…more than ever," Laurona calmly stated. "But too much is at stake here. We have two galaxies wanting to join our alliance. We fought for thirty-two galactic years to unite our own galaxy and now we have the opportunity to unite two more. This is the chance of a lifetime…our dream come true."

"Once maybe, but no more…My dream is to see my daughter, to hold her once more in my arms and to let her know a day hasn't gone by without me thinking of her. How about you? You are going to stand there and tell me you don't miss your daughter as well. You don't miss Kashara?"

Laurona lowered her head in shame. "I do miss Kashara. I miss her so much that it hurts, but like you, I've buried myself in work, in the completion of our dream…a united galaxy, which now has evolved into a united universe. It's a grand project; one I know won't be completed in our lifetime. Nevertheless, I want to lay the foundation."

Nausona looked over her shoulder and viewed the crew at work, pushing buttons, controlling traffic and other details she had long forgotten about. They were working on automatic. She smiled, because she realized their dream was coming to fruition and had taken on a life of its own.

She turned back to her sister and stared into her eyes once more. She saw something else this time, something she never saw before, or chose to ignore before, but right now it was very prevalent. It was controlling her soul, her mind, her spirit and her will. It was like the specter of death; always looming over the body, but never acknowledged until it was too late. It was frightening and it was also reassuring. Nausona saw desperation in her sister's eyes—that spur that either drove people to do great things, or forced them to do foolish things. The emotion was strong in her sister and for the first time, she knew it was strong in her.

"Listen Laurona," Nausona blurted, "I lost my husband and you still have yours. Maybe you don't know how it feels. But Sharyla is all I have to tell this universe I was somebody, other than a great diplomat. She is my seed, my only seed. And even though your husband still lives, you are like me—barren—left that way from our fight with the Pathgo brothers so long ago. Kashara is your one and only seed as well."

"Don't you think I know that?" Laurona exclaimed, trying to catch her temper in a strained whisper. "Don't you think I know that," she repeated. "A day doesn't go by in which I am not reminded I can't have any more children. I hurt every time I see a child and know I have been robbed of the joy of motherhood. The Pathgo family has done more to bring pain to me than any Kulusk has ever done. The Pathgos were lucky. They only died once, but I die little by little every day wishing I had children. Now it's too late, our children are grown with families of their own. And hopefully, they have had a better life than we could've provided for them here. As backwards as Earth was or still is, our children had a fighting chance to stay alive there instead of here running from the Kulusk threat."

"Bullshit Laurona. The Kulusks have not been a credible threat for over ten galactic years. We could have gone with Mitiah Chting and Sergeant Wtong and retrieved our daughters then. But no…the great Laurona had to push her will onto the known galaxy, and now you are about to push your will upon the known universe, instead of searching for your family like we promised years ago."

"Look…I was not alone in pushing my will. You were right beside me. Damn…you were in front of me on many occasions. Who volunteered to negotiate the Vik treaty, or the Shani treaty or the Ory treat? That was you. I didn't have to twist your arm. You wanted to go. Then after you met Loclam, your world was suddenly fine. Sharyla was a distant memory."

"Do you really believe that?" Nausona said with distain. "Do you really believe my love for my husband, Loclam, overshadowed my love for Sharyla?" She shook her head. "My husband is dead. Nitram is still alive. Is that it? I'm only acting this way because I lost Loclam. Tell me, does Nitram do that for you? Does Nitram make you forget about Kashara? Or do you stay awake at night wondering, wanting and wishing about her, like I did and like I still do about Sharyla?"

Laurona lowered her head in embarrassment. "I just told you, I miss my daughter just as much as you miss Sharyla. My marriage to Nitram doesn't curtail the pain. Don't you think I want to stop the universe and go after my child? But it's too late now. Sharyla is grown, or worse…dead. Dwelling on it only complicates things more than they already are." She looked up with swollen eyes, piercing at Nausona like flying daggers.

"You're right, baby sister. I am sorry. But it is too late. We can't capture what we lost. It is gone forever. I'm afraid Kashara and Sharyla are just a memory for us now."

"Perhaps…perhaps not," Nausona wondered aloud. "No matter if they are dead or not, they are still our children. And if they have families…children of their own, we can indoctrinate them into the fold? We will need someone to carry on our vision. You…yourself said it was too large a vision to be completed in our lifetime. Who else could we trust with this vision, but our own blood? Besides, don't you want to know if you're a grandmother?"

"I always thought that Mitiah's descendants would carry the dream. Alar's wife is pregnant now. Mitiah will be a grandfather soon." Laurona softly said. "His family has become our family. I mean he did save our lives. And how about Sergeant Wtong—Jus watch his soul—His son Ecned is my Centurion just like Alar is yours. Shit I thought we were grooming them to take our place."

"I know that! I'm not suggesting we stop or forget them. But I would like our descendants to be part of our dream."

"Okay!" Laurona relented after several seconds of reflection. "I will go to Earth after you are settled in Minor Man Galaxy, and I will search for our children."

"We can delay the trip and we both can go," Nausona gleefully said.

"No, little sister. You must go. The Minor Man Galaxy needs you right now. Any delay will be considered a drastic breach in protocol. No…I will go. Ecned can take the reigns as acting emissary here. I will keep you informed…I promise."

"Okay…when?"

"When you feel you no longer need me here to back you up—when you are comfortably set in Minor Man Galaxy. But it will have to be quick. Ecned is slated to take over Memlan Galaxy in eighteen galactic months as the emissary."

"Tiah, I will do as you suggest," Nausona conceded. "But sister, please do not let anything else stop you from this. You need to attack this as you attacked the Kulusks, as you attacked this project. You must find our children."

"Don't worry, you have my word."

Chapter 9—The Accident

"What's that?" asked Nausona as she stepped onto the observation deck. A black hole, like a tear in the fabric of space, bordered by red, blue and white flashes appeared on their starboard side. It was a zeshion storm approaching the station at hypersonic speed.

The zeshion storm was one of those unexplained freaks of nature. Space was empty, devoid of anything, except radiation. The entire spectrum of space was a chasm for radiation surges from stars, black holes and other phenomenon. Chaktun scientists believed that the radiation in space was life in its truest form, and that the zeshion radiation contained the beginning spark of the big bang theory, or at least the left over residue of the beginning of the universe.

A zeshion storm was truly one of those phenomena of energy that inhabited the galaxy and intrigued scientist. For one thing, no one could predict a zeshion storm. It would appear as if transported by the hand of God. Then it would disappear just as mysteriously. The storms would last from five galactic minutes to thirty galactic days, devouring everything in its path like a hungry shark. The only saving grace was that it was a very rare phenomenon. Scientist counted only two hundred occurrences in known space since Chaktun began space travel. For some unknown reason, the storm never occurred within a solar system, but usually light years away from a solar system. Unfortunately, the newly constructed Millmum station was fifty light years away from the Chaktun solar system and not excluded by nature in experiencing a zeshion storm.

"Chromerion fields up…all stations all ships," Laurona shouted from her command chair. "Prepare for evacuation of all ships and all personnel."

"Do you think that's necessary," Nausona asked.

"I'm not sure, dear sister. But I'm not going to take any chances."

"Tiah!"

"Ten minutes until the first wave hits," yelled the captain from the science station on her left.

"Nausona, you must get the *Nary* out of here," Laurona commanded.

"How about you?"

"I'll be right behind you in the *Tharen*. I just have to make sure all is secure and ready for automatic retrieval once this thing passes."

"Then I'll wait for you. I have an interest to protect in ensuring you get off the station…remember your promise."

"Fine, I don't have the energy to argue with you. Go and make sure all ships are ready." Then she turned to her crew. "Find your evacuation assignments and go. My sister and I can handle this." The five operators on the observation deck crew looked at her in disbelief, eyes wide, mouths opened and necks cocked to one side. "Go…I said go…go now…that's an order!"

The crew ambled down the flight of stairs, with their heads craned back, halfway expecting and fully hoping the emissary to rescind the order. Laurona and Nausona just eyed the crewmembers as if to say goodbye. The moment was serene and almost ghostly, but the crew finally disappeared into the coasters.

Nausona moved to the main controller station and began barking orders for ship evacuation. She contacted Alar and told him not to wait on her, she would ride on the *Star Cruiser Tharen* with her sister if need be. Then she contacted Ecned and told him he was in charge of the *Tharen* until they came aboard…and if they weren't there in nine minutes, they were to leave immediately.

Men and women raced through the brown tunnels of the station and the satellite stations searching for their evacuation ships and pods, awaiting the command to launch. All were frightened, but their Sixana training hugged and covered their fright, and took charge of their emotions.

The sisters had insisted that Sixana warrior training be a requisite for any member to join USSTAP. They understood the training had allowed them to survive as mere teenagers on a strange planet, through slavery, beatings and a rape. They knew any other person would have broken in spirit, mind and body, but their stay on Earth only made them stronger. They credited their Sixana training in keeping them sane, strong and free willed.

At the moment, the recipients of the Sixana training were thanking the sisters in their silent prayers for forcing the training onto them. It gave them clarity of mind, strength of purpose and inner peace—all of which they were calling on right now. For it was easy to face an enemy. You could see the enemy, and you knew how to battle the enemy. However, the zeshion radiation was unfamiliar, it was a mystery and the unknown was a character breaker. The unknown caused panic, caused trepidation and caused people to make mistakes. Not knowing what would happen or what could happen just grated on a normal person's ability. Yet, to the Sixana warrior, it was how the universe unfolded—one surprise at a time. And a Sixana warrior was always ready for a surprise, thus eliminating the advantage that usually accompanied it.

The storm approached at a steady pace setting upon the Gate Portal Field. A blue charge reached out and struck the left rod of the first Gate Portal—the one designated for intergalactic travel. The rod illuminated, activating its sister rod and the white glow of inner space pushed opened between them. Nausona and Laurona looked on in astonishment. Nausona raced to the controls to deactivate the rods, but the helm was unresponsive. She pushed the manual override, but a blue spark enveloped the panel, throwing her back and out of her seat.

Laurona rushed to her and helped her to her feet. Nausona was groggy, but conscious. The blue spark continued to surround the panel like a shield, moving throughout the control area. Laurona reached out to the controls, but the blue spark burned her fingers like a pagenay. She pulled back her arm in utter pain, a screamed formed in her throat, but she muffled it with her pride—not giving it a release. However, her eyes watered and tears crept down her cheeks. She wiped her face, took a deep breath and reached for her sister's hand. Soon the entire observation deck was covered with the blue energy and they stood in the middle surrounded with no way to escape.

Outside, the zeshion storm began to cover the gate portal field. Suddenly, the white energy from inner space shinning from the number one gate portal mixed in with the zeshion storm. The flow of the light turned from white, to blue then to red. Then the red energy sucked the storm inside the gate portal like a vacuum cleaner, stretching the dark cloud into its jaws.

Then a blinding explosion of bright red radiation tore through the space from between the rods, causing the sisters to cover their eyes and fall to the floor. The energy of the explosion traveled through the vacuum of space instantly reaching the main station and its satellites. The chromerion fields surrounding the stations and the ships turned a ghostly white as the fields fought to absorb and neutralize the energy. Every part of the station began to shake as if a quake had hit. Pieces of the station cracked, shook and fell onto the floor. Chairs unbolted and toppled over, floors cracked and bulkheads ruptured. Control panels overheated, connections melted and lights flickered on and off throughout the area. For an instant, Laurona and Nausona thought the end was here. They felt as if Armageddon had arrived, brought by Jus as the Book of Lonson foretold.

Laurona wondered if she had crossed the line. Was this her punishment for crossing over the great void to another galaxy? Had she violated Jus' word? Slowly the fear she was hiding in her heart, turned into acceptance. "Jus' word is law and the law is Jus' word!" she whispered.

"Tiah!" her sister agreed.

Soon after she spoke the words, the blue light engulfing them faded away. The Chromerion field became invisible again, as the last of the energy dissipated harmlessly into space. The shaking vibration ceased, and all seemed to quiet.

Laurona rose, shaking the dust and debris off her uniform and surveyed the station. It looked like a fleet of Kulusk ships had attacked the station, but the station withstood the accident. A broad smile emerged on her face as if her life had been validated with the station's survival.

Nausona, still bent on one knee, shouted to the ARIT, "Damage report!"

The feminine voice, a synthesize recreation of her mother's voice, thundered through the overhead speaker, "Structural damage to docking ring, section 4–A, 5–A and 7–A.... Life Support down to fifty-three percent...Weapons off line...dialairtic crystal fracture...implosion in five minutes..."

"Stop!" Nausona ordered. "Eject dialairtic crystal…authorization Nausona Osguard…two…five…zero."

"Crystal ejected," the ARIT replied.

"Casualties?" Laurona asked.

"None."

"The ships?"

"Specify," the ARIT commanded.

"Casualties…any casualties on the ships in dock?"

"None…all ships are ejecting their dialairtic crystals."

Nausona hopped to her feet and rush to the window. She saw the thirteen ships docked to the station drop balls of dialairtic crystals from their emergency ejector ports. She knew the resulting explosion from the crystals would be almost as dangerous as the energy surge they just experienced. *Armageddon wasn't over,* she thought. *It was just warming up.* "How long to the first explosion?" she asked the ARIT.

"Four galactic minutes."

Then we have three GMs to get the weapons on line," she commented as she rushed to the weapons array control panel. She ripped the lower cover off the panel and dove her hands into a deluge of wires and lights. "Laurona, get me some power…quick!"

Laurona rushed over to the chromerion field generator panel. "ARIT open interlink to all ships in dock," she commanded.

"Opened."

"If anyone has weapons capability, this would be a nice time to take out those crystals. If not…everyone should evacuate their ships and pods back into the stations. Take cover deep in the stations…now!" Then she paused. "Engineering," she shouted.

"Engineering!" the voice replied. The engineering officer, Colonel Ti Oria from the Patt solar system, had never left her post. She knew that her skill would be needed if the zeshion storm had done damage. No matter what automatic features the station had, she realized it needed a human touch, and she was the only human that would ever touch engineering.

"How long before you can get another crystal in place?"

"Already done, sire."

"How'd you get back to your post so fast?" Laurona wondered aloud. Then she realized Oria never left her post. Part of her wanted to scold her for disobeying an order and another part wanted to praise her for not leaving. "Never mind…we'll talk later. Just get me emergency power to the pagenays. We have some shooting to do."

"Tiah," Oria responded with glee.

"How's it coming, Nausona," she asked.

"I think I can bypass the bad junctions to get it working. But for how long or how many shots we can get out of it, is anyone's guess right now."

"Fine," Laurona added. "I know you can do it. I'll try to get us some cover in case...well you know." Then she looked at her timepiece. "Two GMs left," she announced.

"Almost there," Nausona pursed. "Just a few more seconds."

"Baby sister, I just want you to know, the entire USSTAP is counting on you. I mean...no pressure...no pressure at all."

"Thanks...and stop calling me baby sister. You're only the oldest by two GMs. Just because you came out of the birth canal first doesn't mean a thing."

"Testy...testy...testy. What's wrong, old age getting to you?"

Nausona fought the smile, but lost. She knew her sister was trying to put her at ease, and for some reason, sibling jousting seemed to do the trick. She imagined her sister standing above her grinning from ear to ear at her last statement. "Well in that case, I'm glad to be the baby...making you the older one, thus the more testy of the two of us."

"Right!"

"Got it!" Nausona said, buttoning up the cover to the weapons array panel. She fingered the targeting scanners and selected the closest dialairtic crystals. Sweat beaded on her forehead, for the crystals were still too close. Even at that range the explosion caused by the pagenay blast might send explosive energy waves toward the station. "How is the chromerion field?"

"I got it up to sixty percent!"

"Well that's going to have to do," she commented. "Pagenay...pagenay...pagenay," she announced, fingering the firing solution.

Five thin blue razor sharp beams of energy sliced through space and connected to their two hundred and fifty pound, spherical yellowish crystal targets. The crystals exploded like fireworks, shredding blue, yellow and green light particles in a blossom array. The chromerion field smoked gray for a split second as it absorbed, neutralized and dissipated the radiation out to space.

"Five down...nine more to go," Nausona announced. Then she fingered the targeting scanners once more, and sighted her next five targets. "Pagenay...pagenay...pagenay," she hollered again. Then she thumbed the firing solution and again, five thin blue razor sharp beams of energy pierced the darkness of space, hitting five crystals, which were further out than the last set. The resulting explosion did not make the Chromerion field turn white, while it was digesting the energy, indicating the field was well within its limits for energy absorption.

"Good shooting," Laurona praised. "Chromerion field holding at fifty-five percent."

"Good, only four more to go," said Nausona. "Pagenay...pagenay...pagenay." She fingered the targeting solution and captured the last four crystals, and then she pressed the firing button, but nothing happened. She pressed it again. This time the button sparked and flashed, causing Nausona to draw back her hand in pain. The board then sparked again, and fire soon popped out from under the panel. Laurona grabbed the fire extinguisher from the rear bulkhead and doused the fire.

"Thirty seconds to dialairtic explosion," announce the ARIT.

Through her targeting scanner, Nausona could see the blue spikes of fracture dance on the crystals like spider webs. She knew that fifty-five percent on the Chromerion field was not enough to stop the chain reaction of energy from the resulting fracture explosion. Again, Armageddon seemed to be near. Death was working overtime to get her today. At first she accepted it, then she fought it, but now she didn't know what to do, pray for a quick ending or pray for an escape.

Laurona looked at her sister and a tear rolled from her eye. "This is it; I guess…I love you."

"I love you too, big sister," she tearfully responded.

They held hands as they looked out the observation window. They wanted to face death together and unafraid. Then suddenly a red light came on the docking panel, indicating a ship broke dock without permission tearing the clamping locks from the deck. Laurona turned to her left and saw it was her ship, the *Star Cruiser Tharen.*

It moved at subsonic speed, maneuvering toward the crystals. At first Laurona thought Ecned was going to ram the crystals, but that would be foolhardy. The resulting explosion would increase in power, and then she thought he was maneuvering the ship to shield the station.

She punched the interlink, "*USSTAP Star Cruiser Tharen* …what the hell are you doing?"

"Saving our butts, I hope," Ecned responded without any sense of protocol.

"Centurion Ecned, if you got power, get my ship out of here."

"Sorry sire, we only have subsonic, we wouldn't be able to get away. I pushed all my power to the pagenays. If I can get around the corner, I can have a clear shot. Wish me luck, Ecned out!"

Just then, the *USSTAP Star Cruiser Tharen* shot four pagenay blasts wildly toward the crystals. The shots were widespread and thick. Luckily, at the *Tharen's* angle, nothing but open space was behind the crystals…so he thought.

The crystals exploded in the same firework fashion, but the wide spread of the pagenay engulfed them and pushed the radiation back into the Gate Portal Field.

"What the hell is that?" Laurona shouted.

Unbeknownst to Laurona and Nausona, two ships sat at the entrance to the intergalactic gate portal. They had slipped through the portal during the first explosion.

***

Dina of Jaywick's mind was still groggy. Her and her wingman were traversing ultra space to the third level when suddenly a force seemed to grab them and yank them at incredible speeds through the red plane of ultra space. Her engines buckled and her ship's integrity failed in several key positions. When it was over, she awoke to the sight of a great diamond shaped space station surrounded by smaller diamond shaped stations in the middle of a firing exercise. The blue beams seemed to cause small explosions at a point of contact.

"Analysis shop…record and decipher this. What is that? Where are we? And what are they doing?"

"Kiza!" came the reply.

"Damage report!" Dina ordered.

"Phase engines out. Weapons are gone and energy deflectors are inoperative."

"How about the *Snikle*…what's her situation?" Dina questioned, worrying about her wingman.

"Damage report coming in now, Command Daughter."

Dina slowly read the report from her chair monitor. The *Snikle* was in the same situation as her ship, the *Tesle*. "Neither one of us is in a fighting condition. So let's keep our distance and hope they don't see us."

"Command Daughter…a ship has departed the structure," announced the Daughter of Defense, Sasha of Tellwick." Her instruments caught the *Star Cruiser Tharen* maneuvering around the station. "It's coming about. I'm picking up communications between the structure and the ship. I can't make it out."

"Record and analyze," Dina ordered.

"They are charging weapons," Sasha screamed. They are firing weapons…incoming…repeat incoming."

"Fireships *Snikle* and *Tesle*, brace for impact. We are under attack. I repeat, brace for impact. We are under attack," ordered Dina.

The pagenay beam from the *Star Cruiser Tharen* had dissipated with the dialairtic crystal explosions, but it still had enough power to reach the Tuit fireships. The beam struck the *Snikle* on the port side and the *Tesle* face on. With their deflectors down, the fireships took a large beating from the pagenay hits. The ships rocked as if they'd hit a brick wall. While reaching for something to steady themselves, the daughters smashed and banged up against bulkheads, doorways and fell down stairs. Dina flipped over her command chair and down the two steps, hitting her side against the last step, cracking a rib.

"Engineering," Dina called, holding her rib and pulling herself up with her other hand. "Give me what you got. I know phase engines are down. Can you give me integral or single engine? I don't care if you have to get out and push, get this ship out of here." Then she flipped the frequency, "Isha," she called to the Command Daughter of the Fireship *Snikle*. "Do what you can, but get out of here. I am passing a rendezvous point for you. Meet us there in two days. Dina, out!"

The two fireships, maneuvered at a snail's pace. The Fireship *Tesle* dove to her starboard fifty degrees and engaged her integral engines, traveling at sublight speeds. The Fireship *Snikle* ascended to her port side, trying to limit the exposure of her damaged frame and engaged her single engine, limping at hypersonic speeds. After several minutes, the ships slipped into the darkness of space and out of view of Millmum Capitol Station.

***

"Cease fire…cease fire," Laurona screamed over interlink to Ecned. "We have unknowns in the area!"

"Tiah!" Ecned replied. "Our sensors and scanners were inoperative. We didn't see them."

"Nausona, can you identify?"

"Negative…that ship configuration is not in our databanks," she responded in disgust. "Where the hell did they come from?"

"I don't know!" Laurona screamed. Then she took a deep breath and blew it out hard, trying to capture her composure and let her Sixana training kick in once more. "Try to hail them."

"Working!" her sister said, showing her agitation at the situation.

Laurona then flipped the station's interlink button, "All warriors to station…repeat…all warriors to station." She disconnected the interlink and turned to her sister. "We better damn well figure out what just happened here and quick."

"Tiah!"

Chapter 10—The Investigation

"It's been ten galactic days and we still don't have a clue about what happened, or whose ships they were," announced Nausona to the staff. Laurona was to her left and down the right side of the table sat Centurion of Operations for the *Star Cruiser Tharen*, Ecned Wtong. Next to him sat Centurion of Operations for the *Star Cruiser Nary*, Alar Chting. On the left side of the table sat, Station Engineer, Colonel Ti Oria and Station Head of Security, Colonel Ke Lee. At the end of the table sat Station Science Officer, Colonel Vid Son.

"All we can gather from interpolating the data, is those ships were brought through the IGP when the zeshion storm activated the rods," she continued. "However we do not know what the hell it activated. The medium the ARIT registered was not inner space. It was something completely unknown to us."

"Do you think the ships were captured and pulled into our space or do you think they are an advance for an attack force?" Alar asked.

"We don't know," she answered, "but I suspect it was an accident brought about by a bizarre chain reaction due to the zeshion storm. If they were an advance team, they would have been stealthier. If they were to attack, they would have stayed and fought. All I know is that we have two unknown ships sailing in the heart of USSTAP territory." She activated the briefing HVP screen. "Because we had to re-supply our dialairtic crystals for the stations and all the ships, we were unable to get a positive track on the intruders."

The HVP rang to life with two bright red tracks leading from Millmum station toward the fourth sector.

"All the data collected from our scanners and sensors indicate the ships took this routing, or approximate routing toward the fourth sector. It looks like they stayed in the area to affect repairs to their ship. I don't believe the pagenay blast hurt them that much. I think their damage was caused because they were ripped into our galaxy." She flipped the picture to the IGP. "Vid, do you want to explain?"

"Tiah!" Vid Son responded. He stood and walked over to the HVP screen and pointed to the projection of a simulated zeshion storm. "No two scientists will ever agree what radiation is in a zeshion storm. No one has ever been as close to one as we were several days ago. My analysis suggests a rare type of radiation, never seen before by humankind. However this radiation is surrounded by trachion particles as denoted by the blue, and restion particles as denoted by the red. Also, the white particles are benion particles, suggesting tiny fissures opening our space into inner space."

Vid expected the hum in the room after his last statement. He just batted his blue eyes and scratched his baldhead waiting for someone to ask the question. He did not have to wait long. It took about eight seconds.

Colonel Ti Oria spoke up load and clear, showing her disbelief in Vid's hypothesis. "You mean there is a natural occurrence of inner space within our space?"

"Apparently so," Vid countered. "But that is not all. Somehow the trachion and restion particles have some type of effect on the fissures. Inner space cannot last more than several seconds in our space. Yet somehow, these particles have captured it and prolonged its ability to survive in our space."

"What about the black matter? Is it a threat?" asked Colonel Ke Lee.

"Spoken like a true soldier," Vid countered. He then magnified the cloud to show the dark matter within the fissures of inner space, the trachion and restion particles. "The dark matter inside is consistent with what we call zeshion radiation, but we didn't know what caused it, or its properties—until now!" He flicked a secondary screen on to show the atomic properties of the dark matter. It showed a sequence of different atoms, bonding, swapping and sharing electrons, protons and neutrons. "At a closer look you can see what the dark matter is." He flipped another switch. "First, let's take out the known elements that make up energy in our space—the gravitational particles that give us propulsion, light, heat and so on and so forth. Then we subtract the invisible particles from inner space that do the same. Now we are left with this configuration."

The screen still contained a conglomerate of atoms and particles that only a scientist could decipher.

"So, what is that?" Ke knocked.

"That, my dear Colonel, is the atomic make-up of the red light that was in the gate portal just prior to the ships appearing. I believe it is another medium of travel. I believe the zeshion cloud is a combination of normal space, inner space and this new kind of space. A clashing of dimensions if you will."

"Prove it!" demanded Ti.

"Fine, I will," Vid chuckled. "Watch the screen. Our gate portal activated on its own, correct. That is because it registered the presence of inner space and thought there was an incoming ship. When the gate portal activated, the blue particles, the trachion particles, shot from the storm to either grab the occurrence or neutralize it. Either way, it was too large an opening for the particles to handle." The screen played the scenario out as Vid narrated. "The occurrence reached out and penetrated the cloud, finding the fissures at first and then finding the atoms that made up inner space inside the dark matter. It ripped the atoms from it, leaving what we know as normal space and this other space. Well this other space, like inner space cannot keep a gate opened for long in normal space. So the atoms that made it up rushed into the gate portal and somehow altered the trajectory and opened up a portal to its own space. This all happened with one big explosion. The three spaces separated into their own particles. It's sort of like water, H_2O separating into two parts hydrogen and one part oxygen. Separate, they are two totally different entities, but united, they are the basis of life—water. People...the zeshion cloud is the basis of life as well. It is the mixture of our living medium. It is the ultimate space."

"Great scientific breakthrough my friend, but it still doesn't answer the question—who are these people and where they are from?" chimed Ke.

"Vid, as far as I can tell, you are telling us, these people are from another dimension, another universe per se?" questioned Ecned.

"No, I didn't say that. They could be people who transverse this other medium like we do inner space, or they could be from the other medium. Just because we haven't found life in inner space doesn't mean it doesn't exist. Therefore, life could exist in this other space. Shit, it could be the first or second generation of humankind. I hypothesize; one generation is each of these spaces. Remember the first generation was liquid breathers and the second were carbon oxide breathers. This much all scientists seem to agree on. Archeological evidence is irrefutable.

"Okay Vid, let's slow down, before you go chasing after the USSTAP Wolbo Award for the greatest scientific discovery of the galactic year," Laurona said, stepping in to kill the debate.

"Well sire," Vid continued without thought. "You know Wolbo discovered inner space and then developed the theory that led to gate portal travel. So it would only be appropriate for the next Wolbo Award to go to the person who discovered the next dimension of our universe. And this may very well be that dimension."

"Be that as it may," Laurona interrupted, "we still have a problem. Two ships think we attacked them without provocation." She shot a stern look at Vid to tell him his time was now up. "Technically, we just declared war on a people we don't know anything about. We need to correct the situation and fast."

"Sorry sire," Ecned offered.

"Nothing to be sorry about, Centurion," Laurona countered. "Your actions saved the station and everybody on it. Your pagenay blast shouldn't have done any damage to those ships. It is just a shame that they didn't stick around to find that out for themselves."

In fact, I personally am going to see you get the Order of Osguard for your heroic actions and quick thinking. And all those on your crew shall get the Star of Victory for their professional handling of the situation. No! Nobody blames you. Because if it wasn't for you, we wouldn't be here in the first place."

"I concur," Vid added. "The science corps calculations surmise without your actions, the station would have lost the front quarter of the diamond and the security and mining stations to the right would have been totally obliterated. You saved approximately twelve hundred people from an unbearable death. Ecned, in my book, you're a hero."

"Yeah, but I have to talk to you about your impatience," Laurona interjected. "Did you see the damage you did to the station and to my ship because you didn't declamp first? Did you forget to declamp or you thought it would take too much time to do it?"

"Every second counted sire," Ecned murmured. "And the truth is…I couldn't wait. We were down to seconds and I knew the declamping procedures would take ten seconds. As it was, I destroyed the crystals with only five seconds to spare."

"And you did all this math in your head before you took off?" Nausona added.

"A rough approximation…"

"Fine! We'll leave it at that," volleyed Laurona. Then she turned back to the first HVP. "I will be taking the *Tharen*; Nausona will take the *Nary* to these coordinates. We are going to see if we can find our friends and explain this unfortunate accident."

"Tiah! I will prepare the ship," responded Ecned.

"No mister," Laurona interjected. "After what you did to her, I don't want you touching her again."

"What?"

"That's right. You are a menace to her. You need to get your own ship to destroy. How about the *Jessup*? I figure you are going to need a ship when you become emissary to Memlan Galaxy."

"What?" he said in surprise.

"Yes, the *Star Cruiser Jessup* just arrived in port yesterday. Her crew is waiting for her new sire…you. You can join us in our trek once you shake her out. I'll give you twelve hours."

"Thank you sire," was all he could manage.

"Ti, I need you to find your replacement. You are my new Centurion of Operations. Congratulations Centurion."

***

It was the twelfth day after the accident and maybe one of the greatest discoveries for humankind. The USSTAP star cruisers, *Jessup*, *Tharen* and *Nary* departed from their docking clamps and moved at subsonic speed toward Sector four. The *Tharen* took the lead with the *Nary* on her right flank and the *Jessup* on her left flank. Once they were clear of all traffic, the ships slipped into hypersonic drive. They traveled to two thousand kilomarks away from the station, and then engaged hyperlight engines, causing them to disappear from the visible spectrum. Once in light travel, they increased speed to MOP thirty, sailing the black vastness of normal space traveling thirty light-years an hour.

Scanners provided the routing through mathematical calculations and geometric projections to ensure the ships cleared all heavenly bodies and not so heavenly bodies floating in space. Since they were traveling faster than light, the view screen offered no visual clues. So the ships projected a route of flight from departure to destination, with an icon depicting where they were on that route. Forty minutes later, they had reached their destination.

"Fleet, all stop on my mark," Laurona ordered. "Three...two...one...Mark!"

As if by magic the ships dropped into the visual range and slowed through subsonic speed to a complete stop in unison. It was picture perfect maneuver considering if one person delayed, even a fraction of a second, the ship could have traveled thousands of miles further before stopping. The fleet stop out of MOP was the most practiced piloting maneuver in USSTAP, because it was the most critical to perform. When done right, it could bear arms on an enemy before they had time to react. It employed the element of surprise, tapered with economy of force executed with precision timing.

Laurona looked through the view screen and saw the area was empty. "All scans...all sensors!" she ordered.

"Tiah!" responded her defensive officer.

"Spread to arrow formation...two thousand kilomark spread," she ordered the *Jessup* and *Nary*. Without a flaw, the ships split formation and took up position pointing outwards off the *Tharen's* flanks.

Immediately sensor and scanner readings streamed in on the defensive officer's panel. He studied them for a quick second, made his notation and sent the findings to analysis and intelligence. "Sire, some interesting data coming in over sensors and scanners."

"Initial impression?" she inquired.

"Rough estimate is two ships; approximately one point three kilomarks long...point seventy-five kilomarks wide, using gravitational wave metering propulsion had stopped at one–two–three–eight decimal two–two–nine, mark eight–nine–nine through one–two–three–eight decimal two–three–four, mark one–zero–two–one. They were here approximately fifty-eight galactic hours...probably affecting repairs. I'm detecting a discarded energy source. I can't quite make out the material, but it is some type of organic crystal similar to our dialairtic crystal. Readings suggest it's in the bolemincic family...I dare say tribolemincic. Sire, it's not a naturally occurring element in the known universe."

"So that means we have a new player in the game," Laurona wondered aloud, "a larger ship than I've ever seen before, using wave metering propulsion. Imagine if we master the wave metering technique in our propulsion, we could travel at MOP fifty or even MOP sixty. And the fuel source, I've never heard of it."

"Sire, the dialairtic crystal is still cleaner and more efficient," the Calentic pilot offered. "More important, it is more stable."

"How'd you know?" the defensive officer countered.

"We used to use the bolemincic crystal as a warhead for our torpedoes back on Calen. It was the only thing they were good for," the pilot refuted. "Tribolemincic would be more unstable, unless you had an energy converter cold enough to handle it. And I mean cold…we're talking negative seven hundred and ninety eight chimes."

"Space is colder than that," the defensive operator continued. "Just put the converter and the crystal in an unpressurized area."

"Possible, but not practical," Laurona interjected. "Exposure to space means exposure to enemy fire."

"Not necessarily," the defensive officer countered, "but I would like to see how these people did it. Obviously, they found a way to overcome the problems we see."

"Obviously," Laurona noted. "Do we have an exit track to follow?" I mean does this Godsend of an energy source leave a trail we can follow?"

"Yes sire," the defensive officer said, realizing he may have offered too much information. "Heading two–three–three decimal three–three."

"Plotted," the navigator announced.

The screen came up and the projected line pointed to Earth's Solar system. Laurona's eyes watered and her heart pumped with fear. "Are you sure?"

"Yes sire, I am sure," the navigator confirmed.

"Pass all information to the others. Have us rendezvous in five galactic minutes," Laurona ordered. Then she turned her head to the side and flicked the private interlink between her and her sister. She picked up the writing tool and scribbled, "Nausona, we are getting to go look for our children sooner than I thought." With mixed emotions and a troubled heart, she pushed send.

On the *Star Cruiser Nary*, Nausona read the message and pushed a slight smile. Just a few days ago, she thought she would be standing in judgment of Jus. Today, she was on her way to Earth to search for the new visitors to her galaxy and maybe to search for her child as well. She closed her eyes and whispered, "Jus' word is law and the law is Jus' word."

Chapter 11—Efas Escapes

"Ten minutes till we reach the Gentry Star System," the navigator announced to Laurona.

Laurona looked up into the viewer. The ARIT projected route was still on the screen. At that moment, she realized she'd never seen the planet from space. She had stepped to the planet with her sister using the outdated Kulusk Gate Portal before, and when Mitiah and Wtong rescued them, she was unconscious.

Soon anxiety filled her spirit—a sour mixture of fear, guilt and uneasiness. She did not know how to handle the feeling. She felt fear because of her distaste for the people of the planet. Her memories were bitter, and her only sweet memory was of her child, and now that was painful. She also felt guilt, for never having returned to the planet as she promised to look for her child. She had convinced herself that Kashara was better on this archaic world—free from the pain of the Kulusk tyranny; especially, if she was able to get North—North to the promise land. Once she heard the war had freed the slaves, she had hoped Kashara was living a better life. Besides, what right did she have to alter that life?

Because you are her mother, a voice rang in her head. *Because she is your child! Because she is an Osguard, destined to lead a galaxy if not a universe. Your selfishness may have eliminated any chance for Kashara to fulfill her destiny.*

The uneasiness came with the shame. She wondered if she found her child, *what would she say? What would she do? How would Kashara take it? Would Kashara hate her? Would she denounce her for life?*

Laurona lowered her head and slowly shook it in amazement. She finally realized how accurate her sister was. They should have made a more concerted effort in searching for their children. Their children should have been more important than the dream of a united galaxy, or a united universe. Those were lofty dreams and seemingly unattainable. However, Kashara was a gift, no matter if she was a product of rape. Kashara was still her daughter, and she threw her memory away like a rag doll.

Now, because of some unforeseen accident, she is being forced to face her demon…her inner self. How would she cope? That was the true question. It was about her. How could she cope? She abandoned her child—the worst thing a mother could ever do.

The emotions started to overwhelm her. Her body started to shake. It was barely noticeable, but it was happening. The great emissary, the great leader, the great diplomat, who united over a hundred races, was about to face her biggest fear—her daughter.

Ti Oria saw her sire going through some type of thought process, possibly a flashback and also noticed how it was affecting her. She moved over to Laurona and whispered to her, "Sire, why don't you go to your office. I can handle this from here. You can come back when you feel up to it."

Laurona looked over at Ti and realized she was correct. She nodded in agreement, "Transfer screen images to my office. I need to see this…but I need to see it alone."

"Tiah!"

"Ti," she whispered back.

Ti looked up and peered into Laurona's hazel eyes, wet with pain and wide with anguish.

"Thank you," Laurona managed to say. Then she stepped back into the archway. "Centurion, you have the bridge," her voice broke. Then she rushed off the bridge.

***

Nausona sat in her office, filled with anticipation. She never thought she would see this day. Her mind raced at how to proceed with the search. She knew the search would be secondary to the mission of finding the strangers, but she had no doubt they would take time out to try. There was no way she would come this far and not attempt to find Sharyla. Deep down she knew Jus was with her.

She pulled out the old reports from Wtong and Chting, from their earlier search ten galactic years ago. Their report was not promising. The landscape had changed. A lady named Caroline Pathgo was running the Pathgo Plantation. Jessica Pathgo had died—to Nausona's chagrin—and left the land to relatives. The Gentry farm was but a shell of itself; being run by somebody she had no knowledge of. Furthermore, the cave left no clues on how to follow the Underground Railroad.

Wtong and Chting stayed on Earth for two galactic years, questioning people, investigating incidences and scanning for leads. The people were hostile—as she remembered—all events were dead-ends and all leads were cold. The good news was that the South was in a period called *'Reconstruction.'* This period gave voice and integrity to the blacks. The war had allowed them to gain power, wealth and self-respect. In all, it gave them their freedom as human beings. It looked like the blacks of Earth were going to have a good life and she was happy that her daughter was able to share in that good life. She hoped her daughter and niece had made it to the North.

That is where she decided to start the search. Since the earlier search in the South proved fruitless, that could only mean one thing. Her family made it North. With the new scanner and sensor ARITs, she hoped they would be able to find a Chaktun DNA signature from orbit. Even though their children weren't pure Chaktun, her specific DNA would probably be a sufficient tag to compare to. At least she hoped and prayed it would.

The intercom buzzed, indicating an incoming message for her.

"Osguard two," she responded. Because she and her older twin sister had the same last name and because they often traveled together, it became a habit to refer to herself as the second Osguard or as Osguard zero-two. Her sister loved calling herself the First Osguard. It had a regal sound to it—like royalty, which they were both truly of. Conversely, Nausona often referred to her as Osguard one, when she spoke to her on interlink or vidcon.

"Sire," Alar voice rang out. "We are approaching Earth."

"Tiah! Transfer view screen image to my office."

Nausona turned on her desktop viewer and watched as the blue ball of ocean and land grew. *So that's how Earth looks*, she thought. She had studied the HVPs of Earth that Chting and Wtong made, but there was something majestic about seeing it firsthand. It made it more personal. She touched the screen with her fingertips. "Sharyla, I will be there soon," she whispered.

***

"All ships, Alert one…chromerion fields up…all hands, battle stations…defensive stance *'Copper one.'*" The words flowed out of Centurion Ti Oria's mouth in rapid succession as she stood from the command chair. "Repeat…all ships, Alert one…chromerion fields up…all hands, battle stations…defensive stance *'Copper one.'*"

The Alert one buzzer rang over the intercom throughout the ship, like a loud piercing bullhorn. The crews scrambled throughout the halls like ants—their mission clear—get to their battle stations as fast as possible. The bridge crew responded even quicker. Seat belts were snapped, chairs were locked and ankle restraints emerged from the floor and snapped on with a loud thud.

A chime came from Oria's earpiece. It was Laurona's special chime. She inserted the earpiece into her right ear. "Centurion Oria," she answered.

"What's going on?" Laurona's command voice thundered.

"Sire, we have a Kulusk Transport Battle Craft orbiting Earth…intentions unknown. Obviously, they ignored the space markers declaring this solar system as *'A Protectorate of USSTAP'*. I must assume their intentions are hostile until otherwise known."

"Tiah! I am on my way up." The connection went dead.

Ti shook her head allowing her closely cropped dirty blonde hair to frizzle, and then she brushed it back with her hand. She took a deep breath and stepped toward the view screen. "What the hell are you doing here," she whispered to the screen.

"Centurion, the butch is bugging out," the defensive officer announced. "Engine signature indicates it is a calogenic engine…top speed…hyperlight."

"You're kidding…right?"

"No centurion," the captain said, checking his readings again. "Top speed is full hyperlight only."

"Tiah!" she responded half laughing. "What the hell is that old ship doing out here? I thought the Kulusks upgraded their ships to gravogenic engines as well." The crew gave her nothing but blank stares. They were just as perplex as she was.

"Hail the idiot," she commanded.

"No response," the major at communications announced after several attempts.

Ti flicked the interlink, "Ecned, this one is yours. I want to get the emissaries to Earth in one piece. I figure you would want to shake out your new ship."

"Tiah and thanks," Ecned replied.

"Alar, you are with me…standard orbit!"

"Tiah!" Then the interlink clicked off.

***

"Okay crew…you heard the lady. We get to go Kulusk hunting," Ecned said with pride. "Mute Alert one buzzer. Set in a pursuit course."

Alar took his seat in the command chair, placed his seatbelt on and disengaged his ankle restraints. He never did like the restraints. They made him feel like he was in an execution chair and it restricted his flow of freedom. Besides, he thought he worked better this way.

"Send our boy a message…Pagenay at will!"

His command resonated in his offensive officer's ear for a split second before he yelled, "Pagenay…pagenay…pagenay!" It was the first time he'd ever fired the weapon at a living target. He had scored excellent in all his simulator evaluations, and he was surprised how smooth and natural his reactions were to the orders.

The blue steel of energy sprang from the ship's bow, slicing through space and connecting to the Kulusk TBC's stern starboard side quarter plate. The tiny Kulusk ship rocked and slid off its trajectory. The pilot compensated.

"He's doing the old Kulusk Coronado-three maneuver," exclaimed the pilot.

"Thanks, I'll program that into the ARIT," the young lieutenant at the offensive station responded. "It will keep the targeting scanners on him more readily."

The young lieutenant announced three more firing solutions in a row. Three blasts tore at the stern starboard quarter engine plate in an effort to destroy his propulsion and send the TBC into a spin.

"He's changing defensive maneuvers," the pilot rang out. "I don't recognize this one. But it looks like he is trying to outrun us."

"With calogenic engine drive?" Ecned laughed. "Is he serious?"

"Apparently so, sire."

"Stay with him," Ecned ordered.

The *Jessup* moved in closer to the Kulusk TBC, eating the space between them in large chunks.

"Oh! He's stopped maneuvers and he is scurrying like a shredant into the meteor cloud," the pilot reported.

Just as the pilot was becoming comfortable in the chase, the TBC launched a nova flare, which flashed a blinding light equal to one tenth of the sun, blinding and confusing the Chaktun ship's sensors, scanners and the pilot. Then the Kulusk ship pumped out several more decoys that saturated the *Jessup's* sensors and scanners, making the defensive and offensive officers lose the ship in the clutter. Next, the Kulusk TBC deployed a full load of space mines, a complement of forty-five, ten-foot wide floating spheres packing two hundred megatons of nuclear explosive power, giving the arrogant pilot of the *Jessup* something else to worry about other than following him—his own survival.

The pilot careened to port, applied reverse engines and ascended at a forty-five-degree angle. The ship slowed and climbed, depleting all kinematic energy. The crew fell backwards and to the left, held in place by their seatbelts and ankle restraints. Ecned grabbed the armrests of his chair and squeezed until his fingers grew numb. He knew he was going to meet his death. The mines were solid matter that could rip through the chromerion field and send shockwaves to the hull of the ship, tearing the skin and blasting view ports within seconds. It was an old weapon, but still highly effective. Ecned cursed under his breath for not expecting such a technique from an old Kulusk Transport Battle Craft. He was so arrogant about it being an old ship using old techniques. He forgot to call up its known weapons load. If he did, he would have known about the massive quota of mines and would have used an attack procedure other than direct pursuit.

His eyes lit up as he followed on the sensors the mines as they drifted closer to the ship. The lead mine was within fifteen marks of the ship. He knew it would only take one explosion. He needed distance and he needed it now. His only option was to jump the engines again. It was an uncommon practice, and it could cause a crystal fracture, but he needed to do something and he needed to do it now.

"Hyperlight engines full…climb…climb…climb," he yelled.

The pilot obeyed. The ship's hyperlight drive engaged from a dead stop and zoomed the ship into hyperlight speed, causing the ship to seemingly vanish and reappear on the other side of Mars. The dialairtic wave disturbed the gravitational pull around the first ten mines causing them to draw closer together. The mines collided in a hodgepodge of metal on metal. The resulting explosions, one after another, vibrated about a one hundred-mark radius, as the vacuum of space sucked in the mushroom cloud waves and doused out the resulting fire within seconds. Fortunately, the *USSTAP Star Cruiser Jessup* was safely two million one hundred and twenty-five thousand kilomarks away, with her sire licking his wounds.

"*Star Cruiser Jessup* …report!" came Laurona's voice over the interlink.

Ecned didn't want to answer. He considered this his second mistake in two weeks. He let an outdated Kulusk TBC outmaneuver him and almost kill his crew. He bit his lip, knowing his crew was watching to see what his next move would be. This incident and how he handled it would be the defining moment of his command. His mind raced for answers, but his training led him to only one—the truth.

"Ecned here," he answered, after flicking on his interlink.

"Report Ecned…What happened?" Laurona's voice seemed more motherly than commanding.

"We lost the butch. He deployed mines and we had to take evasive action," he reported.

"Tiah," she responded. "Damage report…any casualties?"

Ecned looked over to his Centurion of Operations, Paq Ario. Paq Ario was a Chaktun as well, muscular build with broad shoulders. He was dark skinned with a flared nose, close cropped brownish hair, and he usually sported a bright smile. Presently, his smile was gone and he had a stern look on his face. Ecned did not know how to read it. Did he just lose favor with his second in command or was he calculating bad news to report.

Ecned lifted his hands as if to say, *well?* Paq checked his incoming reports and the smile slowly returned. He gave Ecned a thumbs up and mouthed *'Grade A…no casualties.'*

"Grade A…no casualties," Ecned relayed to Laurona.

"Good!" Laurona huffed. "Tell that pilot of yours, that was some fancy flying. He kind of reminds me of me when I was younger. Gutsy move Ecned! I suggest you run a diagnostic and check your crystal. Make sure that little stunt of yours didn't put you in a critical situation."

"Tiah," he replied. Laurona was now preaching to him in front of his new crew. She had lessened his authority in their eyes. He was a Centurion. He knew the proper procedures. He didn't know if Laurona did that on purpose, or was it that she wasn't ready to let go of him yet. Either way, the effect was the same. His defining moment was ill executed. He would have to achieve another defining moment or he would lose the respect of his crew, which meant he would lose control of them.

"How about the butch?" he asked.

"Forget him…we have to see if he has done any damage here on Earth," Laurona said with a more commanding tone. "Rendezvous in orbit around Earth as soon as you can."

"Tiah, Ecned out." With that he broke communication and barked the command orders to start the diagnostic. Then he turned to his pilot, "Great job…thanks for getting us out of there so quickly."

"Thank you sire," sounded a sheepish reply. "I'm sorry I got us in that situation."

"Son, it wasn't your fault. I am the sire of this vessel, and I take full responsibility for what happened." Then Ecned turned to the rest of the bridge crew. "Believe it or not crew, you guys did well. I take full responsibility for not following the pursuit procedures to the letter. I should have checked on the weapons armament on that ship while we pursued it from a safe distance. We are lucky; it didn't have any fancy upgrades we didn't know about. It was a lesson learned, and I promise it will never happen again."

The six-member bridge crew nodded in agreement and smiles started framing their faces. It was like a great weight had been lifted from their shoulders. Paq gave an approving smile, easing the tension of the situation.

"Sire, we won't make the mistake again either," bellowed the defensive officer. His voice was deep and soulful with pride. You can tell he was a strong man by the tone of his voice and his mannerism.

Ecned knew this man was a person he would rather have as an ally than as an enemy.

"I will have a weapons layout of any ship we encounter—friend or foe—before we do anything from now on. That is my job…I am the DO, not you."

"Thanks Major Somi," Ecned smiled. "We will both do our jobs from now on. We will all do our jobs from now on—to the letter."

"Tiah," they responded in unison.

Chapter 12—Earth Again

The USSTAP star cruisers *Nary* and *Tharen* established a trail formation geosynchronous orbit in the same spot they calculated the Kulusk ship had been. Both Laurona and Nausona wanted to find out why the Kulusks were on Earth. Now the priority of their mission had swapped around a little. First, they had to find out the Kulusk mystery, then they had to find the strangers, then they would look for their children. A gut feeling told both sisters that two or maybe all three issues were related. At first, the sisters thought they should divide their forces and assign each ship to one of the tasks. However, the eerie feeling that it was what '*they*' wanted, whoever '*they*' were, halted them from executing the option. Something wasn't right, and neither sister could put her finger on it.

"All sensors…all scanners!" Laurona had ordered from her command chair two hours ago. The feeling of dread had long left her and the feeling of combat was upon her. She did not know the Kulusks even knew about the planet. Could they know about her family on the planet? Could they have been after her family, if they did know? *Worse of all, did they succeed?*

These questions plagued her like a migraine headache. The doubt just wouldn't go away and it made her ill. She knew if she was this sick over the turn of events, her sister was going out of her mind. She kept the private interlink between them open and her earpiece on, but Nausona had not contacted her since their initial conversation when they entered Earth's orbit.

Laurona agreed, they should start looking in the North of the United States for their children, but Nausona agreed they needed to find out where the Kulusks had been. When the initial sweeps indicated the last PGP disturbance occurred from a northern city in the United States, their heart was troubled.

"Let's go down now!" Nausona urged.

"No, we have to wait," her sister warned. "Let the ARIT try to track our bloodline in the city. Maybe, the bastards did us a favor. Maybe they did find our children, but we got here before they could act."

"Laurona, you are grasping at straws. If the Kulusks found our children, they are surely dead by now. The only way they would have left this planet is if they had completed their mission."

"Or at gunpoint. In which I think they were—at gunpoint I mean."

Nausona huffed and blew out hard. She paced the bridge behind her command chair. She was hoping against all hope that her sister was correct. "Listen Laurona, I have followed you from hell and back, but I'm too close to my daughter to let your pride or your dream get in my way. I will find my daughter."

"Yes Nausona, we will find our daughters. I promise we won't leave here until we do. Have I ever lied to you before?"

Nausona looked up at the ceiling and grunted a heavy sigh. "No you haven't lied to me yet, but you have left some promises unresolved—including this one. And I am telling you. There is an expiration date on this promise. If you aren't fully with me by the end of the day, in looking for our children, then I will take the *Nary* and do it myself. Is that understood?"

"I wouldn't have it any other way," Laurona relented. Deep down inside she wanted to find her daughter just as much as Nausona wanted to find hers. However, Nausona had had the feeling of desperation longer than Laurona. Laurona recently achieved that feeling of desperation when she saw the Kulusk ship orbiting Earth. She knew her pathetic thought process on why the children should have stayed on Earth was in error, but it took a battle with an aging enemy to see the light. "I promise, we will do this together," she whispered into the interlink.

"We better!" Nausona replied, shutting down the interlink.

Now, two hours later, all Laurona could do was let her crew do their job. She needed information that she knew the sensors and scanners would provide. Also, she needed to let her sister calm down. This was the first time she could remember Nausona openly contradicting her. It was unfortunate that the bridge crews of the *Nary* and the *Tharen* witnessed the conversation. Even though they spoke in whispers, she knew the crews sensed a rift developing between her and Nausona. She hoped she could repair the rift before it became a fracture in their relationship, or worse, in USSTAP. She wanted to hail Nausona, but she thought it not wise.

She understood the recent death of her sister's husband had put her on an emotional roller coaster. She knew she would be acting the same way if Nitram were killed in a totally preventable hunting accident. Loclam would still be alive if he took certain safety precautions. To be mistaken for the prey by some overzealous, crazed hunter, who was hunting in a prohibited area and hunting out of season, was a senseless death. One minute Loclam was camping with his troop and the next minute he was laying dead in a pool of his own blood—shot in front of fourteen disadvantage teenagers from the war torn planet—teenagers who he wanted to show how fun camping could be.

Instead they witnessed another massacre, sealing the message that life is too short, so go and get yours now—do everything fast and to the limit—throw caution to the wind—violence is a way of life, so learn it. All the messages she and her sister tried to erase from young peoples' minds. *What a waste!* Loclam was a good man, and her sister loved him dearly, just like she loved Nitram.

She thanked Jus everyday for Nitram. She was happy that Nitram was back home on Chaktun visiting with his parents. His parents were getting up in age and needed Nitram to take care of some legal issues for them. He had left four galactic weeks before the entire episode began. In her last transmission to him, she did not disclose all that had happened. She did not want to worry him about the situation, but Nitram was a smart man, and he would figure it out sooner or later. It would be better if she told him personally, but it would be even greater if she could introduce her daughter to her husband.

Yes, she thought it would be the height of her life to introduce the two people she loved and cared about the most, besides her sister, to each other. For some reason, the thought brought an overwhelming peace to her soul. It chased away the doubt, the fear and the shame that had been eating a hole in her stomach until now. A smile broke out on her face for the first time in days. Her spirit was calm, her mind alert and her body at ease. Now she was happy to be back at Earth.

"We have the coordinates of the Kulusk PGP," Ti interrupted.

"Great!" she responded. "Open a vidcon to the other ships." She waited for the split picture of her sister and Ecned to appear. "We have the coordinates. I am passing them to your gate portal rooms now. Nausona…"

"Sire…" Alar interrupted. Laurona stopped and gave Alar the floor. "Sire, sorry for interrupting, but when I placed a scan on those coordinates, I found two Chaktun life forms exhibiting Osguard DNA…your DNA…about four marks from there."

"What?" Nausona shouted.

"Yes sire…two Chaktun life forms…females. The blood type is not as tight as you proposed, but they are Chaktun…well at least more Chaktun than the other twenty-five thousand. And they have the Omega two-four-four DNA sequence, characteristic of the Osguard family line."

"Now Nausona, I know this looks promising, but remember, the blacks on this world carry a strong Chaktun DNA. Our daughters are half Chaktun and half whatever. It might not be them."

"Must you always be so pessimistic?"

"No, I am praying to Jus I am wrong, but here is what I propose. You and I go to the coordinates and search for these girls. Alar and Ti take an Exploration Team and search the coordinates of where the Kulusks were last. Ecned, when you get here, I want you to try to trace the strangers' energy trail. We lost them when we entered Earth's orbit. They're either on the surface or they backtracked on us. But whatever they did, I want you to find them." Laurona stopped and squinted her left eye in deep concentration. "I think that about does it. Does it sound like a plan?"

Nausona and Ecned nodded with smiles.

"I really didn't want to split the forces," Laurona continued. "But the details dictate that we do. Everyone be careful. Common clothes are warranted."

***

On 42nd Street in New York City, west of Harold and Time Squares, better known as Hell's Kitchen and the Tenderloin, the fire that engulfed Dr. Thomas Gentry's office had long dissipated. The smoldering wood still crackled and popped, with the red glow of destruction still alive in the embers. The firefighters had retreated and the burnt bodies, which the police assumed were Dr. Thomas Gentry and his brother Dr. Richard Gentry, had been removed. Smoke still filled the air and the few people who still remained, pointed in whispers, as if they had just witnessed the most spectacular event of their lives, not knowing they were witnessing the after effects of a great universal turning point in history. The onlookers did not realize that two princes from the planet of Kulusk, Erif and Efas Ritchen, had lived among them for several months and had introduced morphine, a cocaine derivative into their society in a bold attempt to eradicate the Chaktun gene from their DNA—only to be stopped by two drug addicts in search of the white taste of hell. The spectators were a blend of black and white, but mostly black people from the neighborhood. The police had completed their cursory interview with everyone who wanted to talk, but neither the police nor the spectators were too helpful in deciphering what had happened. Therefore, the police left, happy to report this as a tragic accident that took the lives of two faithful and dedicated doctors.

In the alleyway across the street and in the back of the grocery store, a white light flashed, as an invisible door lifted and exposed a portion of inner space to the New York City night, giving the brilliance of the full moon momentary competition. Ti Oria, dressed in an ankle length flower-print skirt, white-buttoned long sleeve blouse and a wool jacket, stepped from the light onto the rocky pavement of the alley. She turned around just in time to see her light close and disappear into infinity.

Then as if by magic, but really a synchronized orchestration of inner space, another invisible door lifted open, producing the Centurion of Operations for the *Star Cruiser Nary*, Alar Chting. He stepped through the heavenly portal and stood next to Ti. He was dressed in non-distinct black pants and a long sleeve white shirt. He also wore a gray wool jacket. Each carried a pagenay in the right front pocket—their only form of self-defense besides their Sixana fighting ability.

When the door closed, the chill of the late fall night wrapped around both of them, welcoming them to Earth's northern climate. The sensors had estimated the temperature to be approximately fifteen chimes, but it felt colder to Alar's Chaktun skin. He bristled as he saw the white evaporation of his breath flow out of his mouth. He estimated it to be around ten chimes. "It's sure cold enough out here," he complained.

Ti just looked at him for a short moment then nodded her head. She pulled out her Portable Artificial Intelligence, PARIT, to scan the area. The PARIT was black and was form fitted for the human palm. The display window was about ten centimeters wide and five centimeters long situated at the top of the device. The portion that fit into her hand had a thumbwheel to the right and a trigger button on the left. She turned the thumbwheel counter-clockwise until she saw the direction outlined in her screen. "It's that way," she noted after a moment. "How's your Earth speak?" she asked him in Chaktun.

"I believe it is called English and I think it is very fluent," he responded in English. "My father taught me after his return from this lost world," he continued in Chaktun. "How's yours?"

Ti stopped and looked at him and gave him a slight smile. "It was never my best subject," she admitted in Chaktun. "I suppose you need to do all the talking for the both of us."

"Come on! You must know some words."

"Yes, I do," she admitted. Then she broke into heavily accented English, comparative to a deep Southern accent, "Shit for brains! Damn fool!

Bastard!" Then she smiled, "And my favorite," she announced in Chaktun, "Asshole!"

Alar shook his head giggling, "I'll let you know when you can speak. If the stories my father told me are true, you'll get plenty of practice."

"Don't laugh, my friends and I spent many a nights calling each other Earth names. Hey, we thought it was funny."

"Well, I bet you wished you paid a little more attention to your English lessons?"

"Yeah, you're right. For the life of me, I never thought I would step foot on this rock as long as I lived."

"Life is funny like that," he commented.

Just then two gate portal lights flourished in the darkness, one in front and one behind the pair. Two security guards from the *Star Cruiser Nary*, one dark skin female Chaktun and one light skin tall Chaktun male, similar in tone to Alar, stepped from the rear light, and two security guards from the *Tharen*, both tall white males from Patt, stepped out from the front light. Each Centurion gave their respective team a head nod as the portals closed. All six pulled their PARITs in order to synchronize them to each other. Alar took the command node with his PARIT.

"Jewel and Thesis, you go to the far corner over here," he picked the coordinates from the PARIT. "I want you to keep your ears open, ask questions if necessary, but find out anything and everything you can about this building. "You other two, take up positions here on the other side of the street, I want you to do the same." He passed the coordinates to their PARITs. The four acknowledge their orders and left the centurions in the alley. When they were out of sight, Alar pushed passed Ti to exit the alley. "This is my mission from here on out. You sit back and learn."

Ti shrugged and put her PARIT back into her jacket pocket and followed the more experienced and highly adaptable Alar. They exited the alley across the street from the burned out building. It was a two-story structure, made of brick and wood. However, only the brick remained, giving a ghostly appearance of a bombed ruin. Two people stood in front of the structure, whispering to each other and still pointing to different spots of the demolished structure.

Alar looked up and around the neighborhood, craning his neck and turning in place in several directions. He saw two and three story brick buildings adjacent to one another, paved roads and a combustion engine automobile traversing the street. "This does not look like Earth. My father never mentioned buildings, or roads like this. Nor did he mention traveling machinery like this. It's like they jumped a century in technology in a span of a few short years."

"You sure we are on the right planet?" Ti quipped.

"Yes! My only guess is the North was more advanced than the South, where my father and godfather were. But this is not any better; it's just different. It's crowded; it stinks, and just look at the people…"

"What about the people?"

"No life, no luster…they just look like they are existing," he commented. "This reminds me of the curries I read about in our history book."

"What are the curries?" Ti asked, not knowing much of Chaktun history.

"About five hundred galactic years ago, there was a big economic gap between my people. There were the rich and the poor—no in between. The curries were where the poor, the down and out, the outcast of our society lived in squalor. I don't know much about it. I considered it ancient history. But I imagine they lived like this. I imagine they had the same look on their faces, the same lack of luster in their walk and the same wish for internal peace as these people."

"Alar, you are crazy!" Ti laughed. "I don't see that."

"Oh no? Then what do you see?"

"I see another race of humankind, in a stage of growth behind ours, but steady. I see people, living their daily lives, with troubles as well as happiness. I see a big city, a sign of considerable intelligence—not perfunctory inanity. I see a mix of colors, unlike the stories I heard from the Osguards, getting along and coexisting in the same area." Then she pointed with her chin to the burnt out building across the street. "I also see the objective. Get in front of me while I scan the area more."

She then pulled out her PARIT and pointed the head to the building. She pushed several buttons, to change the parameter of the request. Then she rolled the thumb wheel and pulled the trigger to lock in on the building. Different readings scrolled on her PARIT. One reading in particular caught her eye. She honed in on the reading. "Scanmons…Kulusk's scanmons!" she whispered. "At least residue of Kulusk's scanmons—among other things. I'm catching Kulusk's medical supplies, Kulusk's blood. I'm recording a lot of Kulusk material in that building. All damaged beyond repair, and doubtfully recognizable by the people around here as anything but burnt out chunks of debris." Then she turned the thumbwheel once more and pulled the trigger. "Wait, I am also picking up a lot of other blood patterns. However the fire has altered the DNA. I would have to get a sample to analyze in order to tell you for sure who is who, or if the Osguard children were in the fire."

"Hopefully, they weren't. I mean the reading I took from the ship has them several marks from here. We are just trying to surmise why the Kulusks were here and for how long."

The tone in his voice told her, she had stepped off into a tangent that he did not want to venture. So, she took the rest of the readings without further comment.

"I need to get closer," she pushed.

"Fine, let's cross the road, I will distract those two and you can get all the readings you want.

Chapter 13—Family Reunion

No other word but shanty could describe the structure. Nausona and her sister looked on in horror. The scene was devastating. The structure reminded them of the slave houses on the Pathgo plantation—a wood box of tinder, just waiting for the right conditions to light it into a fireball. The full moon coupled with the spots of lanterns burning from the window, gave it an unholy glow—like the devil's playroom. Not many things frighten the sisters, not since their initial visit to Earth. Even so, something about the structure pierced their heart, cut their soul and ravaged their emotions.

For Laurona, it was the fact she was so wrong. The five children, she counted, crowded around the front of the structure were shabbily and filthily dressed, with dirt splashed on their faces like camouflage. However, what tore more at her heart was that they were kids. None older than ten Earth-years, she suspected. If her child or grandchild was living in this filth, she had committed the worse sin against Jus. She did not take care of her own!

For Nausona, the sinking feeling in the pit of her stomach came from the deplorable conditions they were witnessing. To her, neither child, nor adult should live in such conditions. What she saw was worse than she ever read about concerning the curries of her planet. It was worse than the slave conditions she witnessed on Earth almost four decades earlier. At least the slaves she remembered were clean, proud, strong and a family. What she was witnessing was the worst of unsanitary conditions, humbled children with no adult care.

The small child, no older than five years old, pointed to the sisters, alerting the older ones of their presence. Suddenly five pair of suspicious eyes gazed upon them as unwelcome strangers. Nausona froze in her tracks, not sure whether to speak, or continue walking. She tugged at Laurona's arm, beckoning her to stop as well.

Laurona shot a daring glare, and mouthed *'What?'*

"Something isn't right," she whispered. "I have a gut feeling, we need to tread lightly," she suggested.

"Why?" Laurona whispered back stepping back to her sister.

"Runaways!" she said without thinking. Something in her mind just grasped at the word and pushed it through her vocal chords, before she had time to fully understand it herself. Then after a moment of silence, and a chance to digest the information, she repeated, "Runaways."

"Runaways?" Laurona questioned.

"Yes, runaways."

"What do you mean?" Laurona whispered while checking over her shoulder. As she did she noticed the children filing into the structure. They looked like they were scared. Scared of what, she did not know. At that moment, the feeling her sister was correct crowded her consciousness.

"Take a look," Nausona commanded. "No adults."

"That doesn't mean anything," Laurona demanded more to convince herself than Nausona.

"Maybe not…maybe so," she complained. "All I know is that our family could be in there and if we go in like soldiers, we may never see them."

Laurona tilted her head sideways, contemplating what her sister had said. "You may have a point. What do you suggest?"

"I don't know, but we must take it nice and slow from here." She turned away from the house and pulled out her PARIT from under her coat. She adjusted the controls, clicked the trigger and it hummed to life. "I'm reading Osguard Omega two-four-four DNA in the house from two life forms near the right rear."

"Any way out, other than the front?"

Nausona adjusted the thumbwheel and pulled the trigger once more. "A window," she read.

"I'll take the back," Laurona suggested. "You see what you can do from the front."

"Always the strategist," Nausona grumbled.

Laurona shrugged, turned and scurried toward the right rear corner.

Once her sister was out of sight, Nausona marched to the house. She barely thought it habitable, let alone a house. Nevertheless, it was home to the children she saw scamper inside. She climbed the makeshift stairs, made of old crates, and walked into the front doorway. There was no door, just a rag hanging from a rope. She pushed the rag aside and walked in.

She scanned the room. As her Sixana training kicked in she placed her other hand around her pagenay inside her pocket. She did not know if it was a trap or not. However within an instant of scanning the room, she realized she was safe. Because staring back at her were the same five children, bright eyed and scared. Four other sets of eyes had joined them from the right rear corner. They also showed the same fright and uneasiness.

A tiny voice in her mind echoed. *What should I say?* She felt helpless, more helpless than the children. "Hello," sprang from her lips. "Hello," she murmured more softly, "I am…Nausona Osguard."

"What do you want?" challenged a child she deemed the oldest and the leader from her right.

"I'm looking for…I'm looking for…" Her voice trailed off as she studied the girl closer. She had hazel eyes and auburn hair and she had an uncanny resemblance to her father's sister on Chaktun. Then her eyes skipped to the girl standing next to her. She had the same deep-set hazel eyes and the same auburn hair. *Osguards!* Her mind resolved in an instant. *The children?* She queried herself. *No! The grandchildren,* she realized.

Just then Laurona rushed through the makeshift doorway and stood next to her sister. Immediately her eyes focused on the two taller children. The recognition in her eyes told her sister she was thinking the same thing. They had found their family line.

"I'm looking for…I mean we are looking for…you!" exclaimed Nausona.

"And who the hell are you?" the taller one challenged.

"I guess we are…or at least one of us is your grandmother," Laurona announced.

"Grandmother? My grandmother is dead!" the tall girl said stepping closer to the sisters.

"Tell me something?" Nausona asked. "Have you ever heard of Sharyla or Kashara?"

The tall one moved even closer, almost studying in the poor light of the lantern. "Why?" she huffed.

"Because…they are our daughters?"

The tall one's eyes widened with recognition. "Can't be," she doubted aloud. "Those were old witch tales our grandmother told us."

"Your grandmother?" Laurona questioned.

The younger girl stepped out and moved next to the bigger girl. The other children remained cowering in the corner.

"Big Momma was a runaway slave," the smaller girl announced. "She told us stories about plantation life and about Momma being the daughter of some spiritual savior. She called my mother Sharyla and she called Betty's mother Kashara." She gulped as she stared at Nausona's hazel eyes. "But we thought that was their African names or something. I never paid much attention to the story."

"Shush!" Betty commanded. "You fool…those white men already tried to kill us. What makes you think they won't do the same?"

"Look at them Betty," she pleaded. "They are just like us. They look like our mommas. I believe them."

"Well I don't," Betty stomped.

"That's your grandchild alright," Nausona pointed out to Laurona. "She has your stubborn streak and more."

Betty looked at Laurona upon hearing the comment and squinted. "Is this really true?" she asked to no one in particular. "Are you the Great Spirit my grandmother told us about?" Then she shook her head. "No, Big Momma said you were killed fighting the plantation owner. It can't be you."

"We were left for dead, but we survived," Laurona said, eyes moistened with tears. "It took us a long time to recover and by the time…well…" Laurona was searching for the right words. She could not explain why they hadn't come looking for their mothers personally. It sounded so cold and unloving. And that was the last thing she wanted to share with them now. "They were gone," she whispered.

Nausona reached out for Shirley. Shirley initially drew back from her reach, but she saw something in Nausona's eyes. She saw the look of a worried mother longing for her touch. And deep down inside, Shirley had been longing for her mother's hug…any mother's hug, and at this point, even this lady's hug would do. They had been out on their own for over two years and she wanted to go home…even if home was momentarily in a stranger's arms.

She reached out and touched Nausona's hand. Instantly a spark ignited in her blood. She was overcome with emotion, causing her to rush into Nausona's arms and bury her head into her bosom. Tears rolled from her eyes as she felt love cradle her as soft and warm as she remembered it was with her own mother. She clinched her arms around Nausona's waist, as if to draw the energy and love of a mother from her hips.

Nausona cradled her package, rubbing her cheek against her grandchild's forehead and saying a silent prayer to Jus. Tears rolled down her cheeks as well, as the moment she had waited for all these years played out in perfect harmony. She was hugging her offspring…her descendant…her love.

Laurona looked on with quiet passion. Her heart ached for the same response from her grandchild. After a moment of quiet contemplation, she held her arms out, inviting Betty to hug her. Betty looked perplexed. However, she still wore the unwavering steel look of defiance. Laurona realized it would take more to convince Betty, she was telling the truth. She turned her head in concern. Laurona did not know what she could do. Her motherly instincts were kicking her in the guts and she longed to push the button of love she'd rebelliously bottled up for all these years.

When Laurona turned her neck, Betty saw the birthmark behind Laurona's left ear. It was an odd shape, but a familiar one. It was the same birthmark she had on her arm, the same birthmark her mother had on her leg, the same birthmark her aunt had on her back and the same birthmark Shirley had behind her thigh. It was the diamond shape dark mark her grandmother told her was the symbol of the Great Spirit. It was the same shape, color and size. Betty just stared at the mark as if she had reached an epiphany. Without thinking and without saying a word, she rushed Laurona and grabbed her as tight as she could.

Laurona was startled but more shocked. Betty was as tall as she was and their cheeks smashed together in a powerful hug. She felt the salty wetness of tears come from Betty's face, which caused her to cry as well. She reached her arms around Betty and squeezed her; placing gentle kisses on her cheek. Suddenly, the dam holding her emotions burst as she began heaving in hyperventilated cries of happiness.

The other children came from out of the corner and rushed to embrace the new mothers as well. The power from the rush knocked them off balance and they collapsed on the dirt floor, reminiscent of a football pile up.

"Wait! Wait!" yelled Nausona from underneath the pile. "Are these mine as well?"

"No…" Shirley paused. "What shall I call you?"

"Uton…uton," she replied. "It means grandmother in Chaktun."

"In what?" Betty screamed from the other pile.

"Never mind," Laurona insisted. "Can we please get up?"

***

It took a half-hour to quell the commotion. Afterwards, the sisters, their grandchildren and the other children sat, cross-legged, around a lantern on the dirt floor. Laurona and Nausona had handed out their rations, shaped like candy bars, for the children to share. The kids took beaming delight tearing into the paper and chomping down on the crunchy morsels like field soldiers. The younger ones seemed to like the chocolate flavored rations. They'd never tasted anything so sweet and sugary. Their eyes bugged with surprise and satisfaction with each bite.

"There's more where that came from," warned Nausona. "We will make sure you are properly taken care of from now on." Then Nausona looked at Betty, reached out for her hand and squeezed. "I guess you are my great-niece," she beamed with pride. "You look just like my aunt. You could be a younger version of her. I can't wait for you to meet her."

Betty smiled and looked over at her uton. "This has to be one of the greatest days in my life. And a few hours ago, I thought I was dead."

"Yeah, you mentioned something about that earlier," Laurona noted. "We can discuss all that later. You are safe. Those people won't ever bother you again." Then she laughed and shook her head."

"What?" Shirley asked.

"Those people are our sworn enemy, but without their help, we probably wouldn't have found you. They led us straight to you. How ironic?"

"Irony has nothing to do with it dear sister. We were brought here because of someone else. And they are still around."

"Shit! I almost forgot."

"Okay," Nausona continued. "What about your mothers?" she asked the grandchildren.

"They are fine," Betty whispered.

"Where are thcy?"

"Home."

"Home? And where is home?"

"About one-hundred miles from here."

Nausona gave Betty a quizzical look. "Explain!"

"You are already starting to sound like Momma," Betty complained.

"Is that bad?" interrupted Shirley.

Betty let loose with a heavy sigh. She turned around to scan the surroundings she had been forced to live in since they ran away two years ago. The plan to become New York City singers did not work out. They had been living in squalor ever since. Stealing for food, living in deserted sheds and picking up other children who either had run away or whose parents had abandoned them. She had become a mother, not just to her cousin, but also to seven other children. She could not take the pressure of trying to feed and clothe them every day. She was barely eighteen years old and she was a mother to eight other kids. No…it wasn't a bad idea for another to be the momma. She was tired of it. She wanted to be babied. She wanted to be comforted…no matter the cost. She wanted the pressure to be gone. She wanted her mother.

"We ran away two years ago," she whispered with her head down in shame.

"Don't worry about that," Laurona said. "We ran away at your age as well, but we finally found our way back home. Are you ready to find your way back home?"

"Yes uton. I am ready. But what about the others?"

"Well, if we can't find their parents, we will take them with us."

"With us?" The shock resonated in Betty's voice. "I have a brother and sister at home. Momma and daddy won't be able to feed all these mouths."

"Yeah, and I have two brothers at home," Shirley added. "I don't think my mother will be able to feed them either."

"That's fine," laughed Nausona, "but the home I'm talking about, you won't have to worry about food, clothing or shelter any more. You are descendants of a royal family. All your needs will be provided to you."

Betty and Shirley looked at each other in amazement, eyes bulging and smiles electrifying the room. The disbelief in their faces shot to ready acceptance in an instant. For what they had witnessed today in the doctor's office confirmed their grandmother's stories, and to have these two, walk into their lives at this particular moment added more credence.

"Okay kids, who would like to go on a magic journey," Laurona offered as she stood.

The shouts of agreement were deafening, but it conveyed what Laurona wanted to know. The children were ready to get out of there. She pulled her interlink from her coat and pushed the connect button.

"*Star Cruiser Tharen*, Lieutenant Hus," came the voice from the interlink.

The children were mystified, but not scared. One of the younger children, approximately ten Earth-years old, reached out for the interlink. Laurona grabbed the child's hand, held it at her hip and smiled at him. He smiled back with glowing eyes. For the first time in a long while, he felt safe.

"Request gate portal opening for eleven," she said into the interlink. "Have the quartermaster prepare lodging, food and clothing for nine youths, ages five to sixteen," she added, converting the children's Earth age to Chaktun.

"Sire, sending three portals down. We have to step you three at a time, unless you want to move outside the structure," commented Hus.

"No, that's alright. We will send up six, two in each, for now."

"Tiah!"

Then the familiar hum of the gate portal resonated in the room as the air energized and gave way to the light of inner space. The invisible door first appeared like heat rising from the floor. Then three spots of light illuminated as the four-foot wide, seven-foot tall invisible door rose from the floor. The bright white light illuminated the shanty, driving the yellow devilish glow of the lantern into the shadows of nothingness.

The kids cheered with wonder at the light. Nausona was surprised how easily the children took the light. She remembered when she first saw the gate portal activated as a child; it scared her to no avail. She could not sleep for weeks, because she thought the white light was the angel of death swallowing people alive.

"Okay, you and you into this light. You and you, into that one. And you two go into that one." Nausona directed the children with military precision.

"Are we going to die?" the ten year old asked Laurona.

Laurona squeezed his hand even tighter, "No baby. It will take you to a wonderful place. It will take you to my ship in the sky."

The boy's smile grew even larger as he pointed skyward. "Up there…really?"

Laurona smiled at him, "That's right honey…up there!"

"Wow!"

Laurona and Nausona giggled at each other. "Wow is right!" Nausona added. "Are you scared?"

"No ma'am. Not if I can go with her," he answered swinging Laurona's hand.

Laurona's heart skipped a beat as she felt her motherly instinct naturally extend to the child. "What's your name honey?"

"Franklin…Franklin Jones."

"Well Franklin…where are your parents?"

"Dead ma'am…Killed when I was eight."

Laurona felt sorry for the lad and now moved her other hand around his shoulder. "I'm sorry Franklin…I'm very sorry to hear that." She then looked him in the eye. "My parents were killed right in front of me when I was young also. I know how it must hurt. It still hurts me today when I think about it. But let me tell you Franklin. I will be here for you…from now on…I will be here for you."

"Okay children…off you go!" commanded Nausona to the others. The children then skipped into the light and the door closed behind them making them seem to disappear from the face of the Earth. The hum dissipated and the room filled back with the yellowish glow of the devil.

"Wow!" said Shirley. "You are the Great-Spirit!"

Chapter 14—Tuit Encounter

Soon the room electrified again with the hum of gate portals. The noise was so common to Laurona and Nausona; they didn't bother to turn toward it. They continued to study their charges, their grandchildren and Franklin.

Then the door began to lift on three gate portals, but this time sharp red lights consumed the room as the doors lifted. The lights caught the sisters off guard. They turned toward the hum, while reaching for their pagenays. However, it was too late.

Three women dressed in black robe-like uniforms, with pure yellow eyes of evil, looking like the devil's own soldiers springing from the pit of hell, jumped out of the light with rifles drawn and pointed at them. Laurona and Nausona froze, while the children slid behind them. They let the pagenays drop back into their pockets.

Dina, the Command Daughter of the Fireship *Tesle*; Isha the Command Daughter of the Fireship *Snikle*; and Sasha, the Daughter of Defense for the Fireship *Snikle*, stood in front of the Osguards.

"Do not move…raise your hands!" Dina ordered, speaking in Tuit. Neither the Osguards nor the children understood what she said. However, the gesture from her weapon prompted a rudimentary understanding. They lifted their hands.

"Uton," Shirley whispered. "What's going on?"

"I don't know Shirley, but don't make any sudden movements," Nausona directed.

"Shut-up!" Sasha demanded in Tuit. Once again, the words were lost on the intended audience.

"I think she wants us to be quiet," Franklin noted as he moved closer to Laurona.

"Um-hum!" Laurona murmured.

"I said shut-up!" Sasha repeated.

Even though they did not understand the words, the waving of the weapon in her face made the intent very clear. All complied.

***

In the night, above New York City, two new stars hovered. No one noticed and no one cared. If they had noticed, they would have seen something peculiar about these stars. They were not white, and they weren't twinkling. They were grayish in color and pointy, like an arrowhead. Soon, the two stars were joined by a third arrowhead star, flanking the right side of the first star. The full moon's illumination reflected nicely off the three USSTAP star cruisers, almost magically.

Yet on the *USSTAP Star Cruiser Tharen*, the gate portal operator was frantic. Major Modi, an Archer, had attempted to open three more gate portals at his sire's last known location, but the area would not accept a gate portal. He double-checked his calculations once more and then swept his hands over the console for the third time. Again, the red reject light illuminated on his console. Then he scanned the area, like he should have done before activating the portal. He knew he had just activated it and stepped six children onto the pad. The quartermaster, Lt Ell had taken charge of the three boys and three girls in the far corner. They were somewhat scared, but defiantly confident—a strange combination for children to have, especially children so young.

"Mister, where is my uton?" the little girl asked Ell.

"And where is Betty and where is Shirley?" the younger boy piped in.

"Major Modi is trying to get them here now," Ell answered in his best English. Ell had studied it as a child, because he knew it to be the second language of the Osguards and he wanted it to be his as well. Many people from Chaktun learned the language because the rightful heirs to the Chaktun throne spoke it with ease. Many times the sisters would slip into English to hide what they were saying to each other from wondering ears. However, they soon realized, the multitude of Chaktuns learned the language as well in the spirit of respect and honor.

"You talk funny," the younger boy ridiculed.

"Oh! Is that so?" Ell replied, shooting a *'don't mess with me kid'* look at the boy. His dark mahogany skin glistened with sweat and his nose flared as he struggled to pronounce the English words.

The boy stepped back into the shadow of the oldest girl, who was barely nine, in Earth years. He grabbed her arm as if it were a weapon to ward off the mean quartermaster. Ell turned back around, satisfied he had shut the young man up for the time being, and glared at Modi.

"What's wrong?" he whispered to Modi.

Modi had just finished the scan sweep of the intended gate portal opening. "I'm getting an energy disruption—like a chromerion field. I can't see into it at all."

"What?"

"A disruption—like a chromerion field, I tell you. It's not supposed to be there, but it is."

"So what are you going to do about it?" Ell requested as he stepped toward the console.

Modi looked at his console in disbelief. "I never had to do this before," he relented. Then he opened a sealed cover on his console and pushed the panic button. The interlink rang to life. "Alert one…repeat Alert one…emissaries irretrievable…emissaries irretrievable…security detail report to gate portal one…security detail report to gate portal one…extraction measure alpha…extraction measure alpha."

Modi had just activated the most sensitive Alert in the USSTAP system. His voice wavered, but his tone was strong and steady. There was a real possibility that the Osguards were in trouble and they were on a hostile planet without security backup. He had practiced activating the Alert signal in many simulations, but he never thought he would have to actually do it. His position was the only position, other than the bridge, to have access and authority to activate the Alert signals. He had just usurped the Centurion of Engineering, who presently had command of the bridge. He knew he had to act fast, and explaining the details to the Centurion would take time.

Yet the Centurion of Engineering was a trained warrior who knew Modi would not activate the most sensitive Alert without a reason, so he echoed the Alert without hesitation to the other ships, the *Nary* and the *Jessup*. In twenty seconds, the three ships were poised for battle, and their number one gate portal rooms were buzzing with activity. Ecned stepped on the gate portal platform first, dressed in full combat gear, including a pagenay rifle, chromerion face shield and the new self-protection arsenal called the delta belt.

The belt held a quick release holstered coronet side arm strapped low on the side of the thigh at hand level. The gun was a sleek sexy looking eight inch barrel black weapon with a curved handgrip conformed to fit in the owner's hand. The gun shot rapid coronet energy pellets at the speed of light. The impact of anything traveling at the speed of light especially a coronet energy pellet not only put a hole in its target, it ripped through its target cutting clean seared grapefruit size holes. Also the belt contained a palm-size three-button pagenay strapped to the right hindquarter of the belt. The blue button fired the blue beam that quickly and neatly burned its target with high unbearable heat. The red button corresponded to a red beam of energy, which overloaded the human axons and dendrites in the nerve cells with heat, rendering its victim unconscious. Then finally the yellow button corresponded with a yellow beam briefly disconnected its victim's axons and dendrites causing momentary sensory deprivation and momentarily disorienting its victims. The belt housed another weapon called a Mation I. Depending on the sequence the activation button was pushed, the weapon shape shifted a metal liquid polymer into any type blade. It could change from a knife to a saber to a sword or even to a machete.

Outside the shanty in the Tenderloin area of New York City, fifteen white gate portal openings sprung out of the darkness like lightening. Inside each opening stood the silhouette of a USSTAP Sixana warrior, clad in dirty tan pants, shin high black boots, matching tan jacket, a black chromerion charged flack vest covering their upper torso and a black helmet with a chromerion charged face plate. Each carried a short pagenay rifle at waist level. Stealth was not the plan of the day. Mass, economy of force and surprise was the plan of execution.

Ecned and his people dove for the nearest cover. Ecned found a spot behind a giant tree and pulled his PARIT for a sensor and scan sweep of the shanty. Off to his left, six more portal gates flashed open as Alar, Ti and their security team stepped onto the scene. Ecned gave them a slight nod and then pulled his interlink from his belt. The interlink was a round device that fit in the palm of his hand. It had tiny lights surrounding its circumference. The lights turned green when he transmitted and yellow when he received. When the lights blinked red, the attempted transmission or reception was being jammed or monitored from an unauthorized source.

Ecned pushed the activate button inside the interlink, "Chting and Oria…This is Wtong…Chting and Oria…This is Wtong."

"Alar Chting here!"

"Ti Oria here!"

"Take your people around back…cover the back. I'll give you five to get there."

The cloud of dust left by their feet told Ecned they were complying with his orders. Then Ecned signaled for his left flank to cover them and for his right flank to cautiously move toward the shanty. His PARIT read eight life forms inside, two whom he recognized as the Osguard sisters, three who registered from Earth and the last three he did not recognize. He also did not recognize the field that was surrounding the house. It was similar to a chromerion field, but different. Nonetheless, he knew the pagenay stream would not penetrate it. His first order of business was to neutralize the field.

***

Nausona looked anxiously out the window, trying not to let the intruders know that something outside caught her attention. Actually, the white light from the gate portal openings, very unmistakable to her, flashing against the backdrop of the night did more than catch her attention, it worried her. For she knew their situation called for the most extreme of responses. By regulations, any situation where she or her sister might be held captive would call for a full out assault. However with the children in the direct line of fire, the situation was different and more grim than anyone outside knew, and a full out assault would be the most dangerous approach at the time. She just hoped Ecned, Alar or Ti would figure it out and hold fast for a while.

She turned to Laurona, who she imagined also recognized what was going on outside. The gleam in her eye and the nod of her head confirmed her suspicions. Laurona held Frank closer to her with one hand and held Betty's hand tight with her other. Nausona didn't realize it, but she was also squeezing Shirley's hand—almost in a death grip. However, Shirley didn't mind. It told her, her new uton cared about her safety and somehow that made her feel a little more at ease with the situation.

"What kind of monsters are you?" Dina screamed.

Her sudden outburst startled the children, causing the sisters to hold more tightly to their charges.

"What kind of animals are you?" she screamed again in Tuit. "We triangulated on your communication's signal so I could see the faces of such animals. I wanted to make you suffer, like you have made me suffer."

None of the hostages understood her, but they understood she was agitated and they were the center of her agitation. Nausona prayed she had kept her PARIT on and it was recording the language for further analysis.

"You drag us to this unfamiliar space, you attack our ships without warning, you track us down and then you attack a significantly inferior ship orbiting around this archaic planet—again without warning or provocation." Dina's voice trailed to civility. "You are truly evil—children of the devil."

"And like the children of the devil, command daughter, we must eradicate them immediately," Isha commented.

"No...we can't," Sasha pleaded. "They are too strong." She turned back to the hostages. "Even if we kill them here, their ships will hunt us and kill us without hesitation. We need an edge…we need an advantage…until we can become strong enough to attack them and withstand their weapons."

"Spoken like a true Daughter of Defense," Dina observed. "And you are correct…what do you propose."

"I don't know…I'm not sure we should even be here…"

The sharp sound from Dina's interlink device interrupted Sasha's thoughts. Dina tapped the jewelry on her wrist and her interlink bounced to live.

"Command Daughter Dina of Jaywick," she announced.

"Command Daughter," came the frantic voice over the interlink. "We are showing several of the devils surrounding your position. You need to get out of there…quickly!"

Dina looked up in deep contemplation, but something caught her eye. She saw Alar's eyes staring at her from the other side of the window, in a vain attempt at reconnaissance. Out of sheer training, she lifted her rifle and shot at the window. A red ball of energy spit from the rifle, sailed across the small room and blasted the window, the sill and all of the wood surrounding the window. The blast, somewhat dissipated by the wood and glass, slapped Alar and slung him backwards twenty feet.

He landed, unconscious, on his back with glass and woodcuts all over his body and face, and a fist size hole burning into the left side of his chest. Ti ran to him, grabbed his arms and dragged him into a ditch for cover.

Fire erupted from where the blast hit the shanty and began eating that side of the wall. The fire burned like a hungry beast, devouring the oxygen and the dry wood, growing with each lick. The flames rose from three feet to five feet within a few seconds.

Dina was stunned by the suddenness of the fire and stood with the rifle still chest level, wondering what just happened. Her two partners stood with their yellow cat like eyes, covering their faces with their free hand, half scared of the fire and half mesmerized by it.

Nausona reacted. She reached for Dina's rifle with her free hand and pulled her toward her, knocking her off balance. Then she lifted her elbow and whacked Dina's jaw. Dina fell back, unto her butt, letting the rifle loose. Nausona coiled like a cat and jumped onto Dina, landing one foot on her chest and the other on the dirt floor. She swung her balance to her left foot and kicked Dina in the face.

Laurona let go of her charges, grabbed Isha's arm and twisted it down and out. Then she cracked her face with a left cross, followed by a backhand, never letting loose of Isha's arm with her right hand. Then she swung her body left and delivered a gut wrenching roundhouse kick to Sasha. Sasha doubled over in excruciating pain, spitting blood as she fell to her knees. Then she lifted her leg and crashed it down onto Sasha's head, sending her to the blissful darkness of unconsciousness. Laurona turned back to Isha and delivered three more quick blows, satisfyingly feeling the bone crunch under each blow. Isha fell to her knees and Laurona let her go. Then she fell to her face with a hard thud.

The fire now moved to the outer walls, catching the rags and more dry wood for kindling. Smoke filled the yellowish glow in the air, giving it the evil ambiance of Hell. Laurona and her family coughed as their bodies fought for fresh air. Their lungs convulsed, telling them to get out of the fire.

"Run…run girls…run Frank…get out of her," Nausona commanded. The girls and Frank hopped over their lifeless captors and fled outside.

Nausona leaned over and picked up Dina and threw her over her right shoulder. Dina was a tall woman, but not very heavy, at least not for Nausona's Chaktun Omega two-four-four DNA. She turned and saw Laurona had placed her victim over her left shoulder and was attempting to drag the third one by the arm. Nausona reached back and grabbed Sasha's other arm and helped her sister drag her outside.

As if God and the devil played a hand in it, the shack ignited into one big fire, similar to a fire in a fireplace, when the sisters walked out carrying their baggage. Several guards rushed to the sisters and freed them of their heavy burdens. Once relieved of their loads, they turned in search of their family. The search did not last long. Betty, Shirley and Frank came running toward them with open arms. Betty and Frank ran up and hugged Laurona and Shirley ran and hugged Nausona.

Their tiny arms around them felt like heaven's cloud—warm, soft yet strong and reassuring all at the same time. Their arms felt comfortable…they felt good…they felt right, as evidenced by the grin occupying Nausona and Laurona's face.

"Let's go people," Ecned ordered. "I don't want to be around here when the authorities show up. Let's light and step…light and step!"

Chapter 15—Interrogation

The room was dark. The doctor had turned off the lights as the final gesture of respect. It was easy for the spirit to find Jus without the lights of humankind blinding the soul. It was tradition to leave the body in the dark for the first two hours after death. This was the hardest part for any medical professional, because turning off the lights meant defeat. It meant the doctor did not have the knowledge, the tools or the skills to beat death. Every doctor in USSTAP prided himself or herself in defeating death. With the advancement in technology, the pride swelled more and more each day. If the patient came to them alive, there was a ninety-eight percent chance the patient would remain alive, no matter the extent of the injury.

Colonel Jerum Nicallet had such pride—an almost omnipotent pride about his knowledge, tools and skills…until today…until he saw Centurion of Operations for the *USSTAP Star Cruiser Nary*, Alar Chting. Ti and Ecned stepped Alar into his med lab. Nicallet surmised these were his closest friends, for they declined any attention for themselves to ensure Alar got to the med lab.

Alar's vital signs were strong. His wound was bad but treatable—at least Nicallet thought. He was rushed into bay one, where Nicallet removed Alar's clothing and placed the diagnostic Medical Artificial Intelligence, MARIT, on him. At first, Nicallet thought it a simple pagenay burn, until he saw the wound. Then he thought it a wound from the nasty coronet pistol. A device he detested more than anything else in the world. For its use meant almost certain death, when targeted at any vital organ. It ripped, tore and shredded human flesh like a nail through a water balloon. The usual result was messy, terrifying and instant death. If the victim survived long enough to make it to a med lab, minutes counted. So Doctor Nicallet rushed in.

He and his assistants cleaned the wound, stabilized the patient and scanned for foreign objects. The MARIT indicated no foreign objects in the wound or in the patient's blood stream. Then the world crashed on Doctor Nicallet. The patient's blood pressure dropped. His heart, which the weapon missed by inches, slowed, and the patient's brain activity ceased. Nicallet knew he had seconds to react.

His team used several stimulants to wake the heart up. They used several blood transfer techniques to keep the blood pressure going and they used a mind stimulant MARIT to refocus the patient's brain activity. Soon the wound became a secondary project and keeping the patient alive became Nicallet's prime concern. However, after three hours in the med lab and no luck in arresting the situation, Alar gave up the ghost to Jus—seemingly without a fight.

The doctor and his crew left the med lab in such despair. With the final whisper of a soft command, "Lights off," another brave Sixana warrior, an expectant father, the emissaries' favorite, son of a hero of the last galactic war and son of the princesses' savior—left to meet Jus.

The ritual's two hours were now at a close, and Nausona, Shirley, Laurona and Betty were outside the room keeping watch. They were the closest to family, Alar had on the ship. His wife was back on Chaktun ready to give birth to their son. Nausona did not know how to break the news. Alar gave his life to protect her and her family, but somehow died needlessly. It wasn't his time. Yet Jus chose him. *For what? And why now?*

The pain ached in her heart, for her heart was not completely healed over her husband's death. She sobbed as she looked through the glass doorway at the figure laying on the med lab table, draped in the USSTAP flag. Shirley reached out for her uton and pulled her closer. Shirley, the shorter of the two, buried her head into Nausona's bosom, close to her heart—right where the pain hurt the most.

"He was that close to you uton?" Shirley asked.

"Yes my dear. I saw him almost every day from the day he was born. His father is a great friend to us. He saved us from certain death, more times than I care to count. And now I could not pay back that simple debt once."

"It wasn't your fault Aunt Nausona," Betty chimed in. "This has been one hell of a day. I just don't understand why everyone is after us…after you."

"Unfortunately, it is part of our birthright," whispered Laurona, who was fighting back her own tears. "The Kulusks are our natural enemy." She choked back and took a deep wavering breath. "It started from a misinterpretation of an old Kulusk folklore that the descendants of a great king will rise from an uncivilized world and destroy them. The Kulusks think that Laurona and I are those descendants. And the fact that we spent time on Earth, an uncivilized planet according to Kulusk standards, lends credence to that old Kulusk folklore. We are trying feverishly to overcome that misunderstanding now. But the planet Kulusk has cut all forms of communication with the rest of the galaxy. Now I'm afraid we have another misunderstanding—a misunderstanding that brought death to our house."

"It's time," Nausona announced. She placed her palm over the lock and the door split open. The foursome slowly walked to the table as the lights gradually came on, chasing the darkness away and illuminating Alar's body.

"He is gone—spirit—mind—and soul," Nausona chanted.

"All that is left is a warrior's shell," Laurona added.

"I will take him back to the *Nary*. When this is over, he will be buried in the Osguard cemetery, with his wife's permission of course, as a great warrior and an extended member of the Osguard family. His name will be on the wall of warriors in the Steeple—in our home."

She knelt down on one side and her sister knelt on the other side. They lowered their heads and each grabbed on to Alar's hand as if to will him back alive. Betty and Shirley stayed behind their grandmothers, hands on their shoulders to let them know, they had family to support them in their time of grief. They had granddaughters who were giving them instant love. They had family with them now. They remained silent for another hour, meditating and praying. They had lost one of their own.

***

Vid Son walked into the conference room, wearing a large grin. However the other members in the conference room were still in a somber mood. Laurona, Nausona, Ecned with his Centurion of Operations, Paq Ario, and Ti were sitting around the conference table. The Osguards had just finished their family ritual over their friend's body, assuring his place in Jus'

Land. Vid ascertained his mood was inappropriate and his grin dulled to a polite smile.

"Vid, I hope you have some good news for us," shot Ti, whose eyes were red from mourning.

"Considering the circumstances, I think I have," he stated.

"What is it?" Nausona asked, staring off into the stars from her port window and showing her disinterested in his comments.

"Well sire, we put our visitors in the guest quarters on deck five, where I was able to adjust the ARIT to study their speech and language. Well the ARIT has interpreted their language as a strange derivative of the ancient language of the fourth age of the second generation of humankind."

"What the hell are you talking about Vid?" Laurona snapped. "Even in the second generation the fourth age had many languages. No one language dominated—as today—no one language dominates the galaxy."

"I know sire," Vid apologized. "But we have an extensive library of languages, especially since the inception of USSTAP. This language they are speaking is a derivative of the Tuetize early development."

"Who the hell are the Tuetize?" Laurona pushed.

Nausona shook her head, clearing the cobwebs from her mind. She stared at Laurona and Vid, who was now too scared to continue. Laurona had bellowed him into a non-cooperative position. "Laurona!" she called. "Let the man finish. He's only reporting on what we asked him to do." Then she stood and walked over to him. She caught his arm and guided him toward his seat. "Vid, if I remember my history, the Tuetize are believed to be the link between the second generation, the carbon breathers and the third generation, the oxygen breathers. Tuetize is a planet on the outer realm of our galaxy. USSTAP scientist just recently discovered the ruins. But all this is just theory…right?"

Vid nodded.

She then took her seat next to her sister as she pushed her mind back into work to overpower her grief. "But the Tuetize never made it to the second age. They died out, like so many others. So the theory of them being the missing link between the generations was never proven."

"Correct sire," he smiled for the support. "Folklore stated they didn't die out, but the fourth age of the second generation returned to their home world and collected their cousins, the first age of oxygen breathers, and brought them to another dimension."

"And you think these people are related to the Tuetize?" Laurona asked with civility.

"Yes…but we can explore that later," Vid responded. "The ARIT broke their language," he announced with pride shining through his words.

"So what have you learned?" Paq asked.

"They call themselves the Tuits."

"Tuetize…Tuits? A plausible connection," Nausona admitted.

"They are a race of women…warriors really," Vid continued. "They control two star superclusters. I haven't figure out which ones yet, but I would guess Tagot Rowe is one of them, since it is the closest to ours. It appears…and I am surmising here based on our knowledge and what they said to each other…It appears they travel through the other space, the red one…they call it ultra space, like we travel through inner space…and while they were traveling, the zeshion storm hitting are gate portal ripped them into our galaxy."

"They control entire star superclusters?" whined Paq.

"Apparently so," Vid responded.

"Damn, we are just getting out to reach other galaxies, and these women control not just one, but two star superclusters…hundreds if not thousands of galaxies…I dare say millions." Paq looked out the port at the sea of stars, and then snapped back around at Vid. "Are you sure?"

"I can only go by what they say. What they call dimensions I gather are superclusters. But it could be something else. It could be galaxies, or it could be just solar systems…but I doubt it. We are talking star superclusters. These Tuits inherited and maintained the fourth age of the second generation. People we are looking at the fifth generation of the second age."

"Impossible…they are oxygen breathers," Ti shot back.

"True," Vid admitted. "Technically, you are right. Somehow, these Tuits skipped the first, second and third age and shot straight to the fourth age of space exploration and beyond, perhaps even to the unknown fifth age…the age of enlightenment. I dare say in their world we would see members of the water breathers and carbon breathers. I believe wherever the Tuits come from…that is where the first and second generation of humankind went when they left our galaxy."

"Enough Vid," Laurona screamed. "If you are bucking for the Wolbo award, I'll see that you get it. For now…I need help telling these people that this is one big fat misunderstanding…a costly misunderstanding, but still a misunderstanding."

Vid threw a head MARIT on the conference table. "There is your help."

"What?"

"There is your help sire," Vid beamed with pride again. "I have adjusted the MARIT to act as a translator directly to the mind. I programmed this one and another in my lab to take their language and filter it into Chaktun to the wearer. I have fixed three more to place on our guests' foreheads that will translate Chaktun to Tuit. You will be able to speak directly to them. You can tell them yourself about the mistake. And you can tell them they murdered a good man for nothing." Vid's smile turned into a painful look as he stood and walked over to the door. He placed his hand on the lock and the door split open.

He had had enough of the abuse and he was tired. While the others were in mourning over his friend, he was working on a solution to communicate with the intruders. He did not want Alar's death to be in vain. Something good had to come from his friend's death, even if it was another scientific breakthrough. He had been up for over twenty-four hours and his body was about to shut down. His patience was just as thin as the Osguards, but his pride was even thinner. He wanted to go, and he was not about to wait to be dismissed. He did not want to argue. He did not want to teach. He just wanted to leave.

"Vid, where are you going?" Nausona reacted.

Vid turned his neck to face Nausona, "I am going to pay my respects to my friend, Alar. Then I'm going to my quarters to get some rest. I have been up too long and working too hard. Instead of interrogating me, you should be interrogating the Tuits. If it were anybody else that brought you this information, you would be thanking him. I'm not asking you for your thanks. I just want to go to bed. Now if you would excuse me sire." With that, Vid walked out, weary and blurry eyed, but taller than he ever felt before.

He had stood up for himself and it felt good. He knew he was the brain behind USSTAP technology. He had invented the galactic gate portal, he had invented the coronet pistol and his theories led to the building of the fleet's gravogenic engines. Even with that, every time he walked into one of the meetings, the Osguards treated him with disdain, because he was not a true Sixana warrior in their eyes. However, now it didn't matter. Right now, he wanted to go, so he left.

"What got into him?" Ti asked.

"Pride!" Nausona declared. "Simple pride!"

***

The room was spacious, usually meant for dignitaries and heads of state. For now it was a makeshift brig, housing Alar's killers. It had a sitting area, three bedrooms and a common washroom. The sitting area had the latest ARIT accessories; however for the present occupants those accessories were turned off. Also different was the guard placed outside the door wearing a delta belt.

The reason for putting the Tuits in such glorious accommodations was twofold. One, because their motive for attacking the Osguards on Earth was unknown, making their exact status unclear. Laurona and Nausona suspected their appearance in the galaxy was a mistake. And the fact that USSTAP fired on their ship was technically an act of war, which complicated the matter even more. They knew they would have responded in kind if they were fired upon by another ship. So they concluded that treating them like prisoners at this stage before knowing the facts would be dangerously premature. Second, the accommodations helped relax the occupants, made them more talkative and free with their information, allowing Vid Son to work his magic and crack their language. Although, this was technically spying, it was necessary in order to start a dialogue. The hunch paid off. As usual, Vid came through for USSTAP. He cracked their language in twenty-four galactic hours and programmed MARIT devices to act as translators allowing the two parties to communicate.

Laurona and Nausona walked into the room, unarmed, holding the MARITS in their hands. Dina, Sasha and the MARIT-repaired faced Isha were sitting on the couch in the middle of the living area. No one attempted to stand. They just looked off into the distance. Laurona set the three MARITS on the table in front of Dina. By her demeanor on Earth, Laurona knew she was the leader, the commander of the mission.

Dina glanced at the devices and turned her head toward the side, like a kid who just got caught cheating on a math final. Laurona moved around the table to get within Dina's view. Dina turned her head away again.

"This isn't going to be easy," Laurona noted. She walked over into Dina's view again. Once more, Dina moved her head to keep Laurona out of her sight. Laurona then snapped her MARIT into place and signaled for her sister to do the same. "Put it on, so we can talk," she said, repeating the sentence as Vid taught her in Tuit."

Dina snapped her head and stared at Laurona, "You speak our language?"

Laurona shook her head and repeated the words, listening for the echo in her head to say them in Chaktun, "Put it on, so we can talk."

Dina looked at the MARIT on her head and then looked at the devices on the table. She reached for one of the devices and held it in her hand for a few seconds.

"Put it on, so we can talk," Laurona repeated.

At first, Dina showed hesitation, and then curiosity claimed her face. She snapped the device on her forehead like Laurona and Nausona had theirs. Once satisfied the device offered no danger, she ordered Isha to put one on. Yet, she wanted Sasha to remain without one, in case it was a trick.

"Thank you," Laurona said. The message registered in Isha and Dina's brain. Even though they heard the words in Chaktun, their brain registered the words in their language.

"How is it I hear your tongue but understand it as if it were my tongue?"

"That is a mystery to us as well," Nausona giggled. "But we have a great man, who was able to adjust these devices so we can talk. How he did it…only he knows. I doubt if there is another man alive that can do this."

"No man is great…only the Daughters of Fire are great," Isha expressed with authority.

Nausona had forgotten she was speaking to a warrior race, which meant they held men in small regard if at all. She did not want to get into a philosophical debate on the strengths and weaknesses of the societies. She just wanted to get these people out of her space…for good she hoped. She smiled, like her uncle taught her, in an effort to diffuse the situation.

"My name is Nausona Osguard, and this is my sister Laurona. We are the emissaries for the Universal Science, Security and Trade Association of Planets. We are an alliance of nearly one thousand worlds in a mutual support pact to share scientific knowledge, to provide defense and to oversee the peaceful trade of goods across the galaxy. We are not a government. We do not represent any one world or people. USSTAP is a congruent conglomeration of interests, in support of a multitude of governments. It is our jobs as emissaries to ensure these interests are protected. Therefore, we are the duly appointed representatives for these worlds in dealing with these interests."

"I see," Dina nodded.

"And you?" Laurona asked exuding a highly polished diplomatic tone.

"I am Dina of Jaywick, Command Daughter of the *Fireship Tesle*. This is my second, Sasha of Tellwick and she is Isha of Solwick, the Command Daughter of the *Fireship Snikle*. We are from the Tuit Consortium—an organization similar to yours. We provide protection and oversee trade for millions of worlds in two dimensions."

"And where might these dimensions be?" Laurona asked, still deploying her diplomatic smile.

"I don't know," Dina admitted. "It depends where we are. This space is entirely unfamiliar to us. It appears your great gate has brought us to a dimension we know not of."

"Listen, we wanted you to know it was an accident that brought you here."

"An accident?" Dina pushed.

Laurona and Nausona took a seat on the couch opposite Dina, flashing pleasing smiles, but seething inside because of what she had done to Alar. It pulled at both of their diplomatic skills not to let their personal feelings crowd in and take control of the situation. Nausona wanted to exact revenge with her bare hands, choke the living soul from Dina and discard her carcass from the nearest airlock. A similar thought ran through Laurona's mind as well.

She thanked Jus that Vid did not make the devices a mind reading tool. But how handy such a tool would be right now? She was cognizant the intruders were here by accident. Nevertheless, their cold calculated method in the murder—that's how she came to think of it...as murder—their cold calculating method in which they murdered Alar was unforgivable and gave a disturbing insight to their character. Conversely, the diplomat in her yelled for her to give them the benefit of the doubt—to open dialogue and discuss the events in a calm rational manner.

"ARIT," Laurona called. "Play recording Laurona Osguard...four–five–nine...Alpha two!"

A screen shot from the table and the images of the zeshion storm approaching Millmum Station flashed on the screen. It played the entire episode of what happened in the station and what happen on the *Star Cruiser Tharen*. It showed the Fireships that Isha identified as the *Snikle* and the *Tesle*. Dina then explained what happened on her ship after they entered the gate portal until the escaped from the *Tharen's* inadvertent pagenay shots. Beyond that, she was uncooperative.

"So you see...it was an accident," Nausona summarized. "We never intended to fire upon you. We didn't know you were there."

Dina closed her eyes as if in meditation. Isha looked skyward and huffed. Nausona and Laurona did not know what to make of their expressions, or lack of expression.

"Can you leave us for awhile," Dina said with her eyes still closed. "I would like to discuss this with my sisters."

Laurona thought for a second and stood, "Certainly!" She shot a glance at Nausona, who really wasn't ready to leave.

Nausona felt there was no reason to leave. The situation was clearly explained and precisely...no details were expunged...even their weapons capability...a detail she thought was unnecessary to explain. Although Laurona, however doubtful, thought it necessary to explain the hit their ship sustained was not at full power. She had hoped this would be the tiny detail to turn them into favorable allies. Dina hardly blinked at the revelation. In fact neither Dina nor Isha ever gave away their thoughts through body language. To Nausona, this was a sure sign they were dealing with a highly trained military operative. Leaving them alone to discuss their option left a bad feeling in her stomach.

"Let us leave them alone dear sister," Laurona ordered. Nausona stood and registered a protest with her eyes, which she duly noted.

"And please turn off any listening or monitoring devices you have in the room. Now that I know you can understand our language, it would be inappropriate for you to listen in any further to our conversations."

Laurona looked guilty as the words wafted over her. She nodded, "ARIT privacy mode," she ordered.

"And?" questioned Dina with her eyes still closed.

"And give privacy mode control for this room only to Dina of Jaywick." She turned to Dina whose eyes were still closed in meditation. "Please state a privacy code so the ARIT can recognize your voice."

"Dina of Jaywick," she responded. "Will that suffice?"

"Yep, that will just about do it," Nausona stated, failing to hide her agitation at the situation. Her tone brought a slight smile to Dina's face, which further irritated Nausona. She turned to exit the room, followed by an irate Laurona.

Laurona turned at the doorway, "We will give you two galactic hours to discuss your predicament."

"Or what?" Isha retorted.

"Or we will change your accommodations to something more appropriate."

"Appropriate for what?" Dina responded, now with her eyes wide open.

"Appropriate for someone who kills a member of my family without provocation. The man you shot was my godson and my sister's second. You see, our shot upon your ship was an accident and not dangerous. Your shot was intentional and deadly. We came to you in a sign of peace even though our hearts are saddened by what you did, and you sit there like nothing happened. Unless you agree to let us help you get the hell out of our galaxy, your stay here will be most unpleasant…yours and the crews of your fireships. You see ... we had the little conversation on Earth you had with us at gunpoint translated. The language was most disturbing. We came to you to show you, you were mistaken, but you seem bent on violence. I warn you, do not take this offer of help as a sign of weakness." She then turned and let the door close behind her.

Nausona smiled at her older sister, "For a moment I thought you were getting soft on me."

"No sister. I just want those assholes out of my galaxy, shit I want them out of my star cluster. And if they won't go…I want them out of the way."

Chapter 16—The Escape

Her mind was on overload, but somehow Shirley was enjoying the experience. She was frozen, mesmerized by the beautiful view of her planet, sailing in a dark sea of space. The white puffs of clouds washing the face of the planet with the gentleness of God. The blue shine of the sea, spattered with the myriad of brown and gray landmasses hypnotized her into a tranquil fever. Never in her life did she ever imagine what she was experiencing now.

Just yesterday, she was worried about the cut on her hand; she'd received from working at the restaurant. It had grown into a painful infection. Her hand was the reason they searched out the doctor. Then her world turned upside-down in a matter of five hours. She shook her head, trying to wake up from this dream.

She touched her hand for the fifteenth time since the doctor looked at it. Really, he repaired it. He used some type of glowing light that massaged her hand and then he put a cream on it. The infection disappeared almost instantaneously, leaving nothing to remind her of the cut. It was a miracle. The entire episode was a miracle. She was as happy as she could be. She could not wait to see her mother and father's face when she presented all this to them. Her entire family will be so pleased. No…pleased wasn't the correct word. They will go out of their cotton-picking minds. She laughed as she played various pictures in her mind of her telling the family about their adventure and their heritage.

"Are you ready?" Betty asked, startling Shirley. She had quietly entered the room and studied Shirley for a few minutes. Pride swelled inside her, because she knew her cousin deserved more than what she was providing, and she was finally getting it. Betty had always blamed herself for talking Shirley into joining her when she ran away to New York. What a childish dream to run away to New York to seek a singing career, and how stupid she felt for dragging her little Shirley with her. Thankfully, God had worked in a mysterious way and had provided more than she could ever hope for or dream of. She was truly content now.

"Yeah, I'm ready," Shirley gleamed after catching her breath again. "My uton wants me back on her ship," she said. "My uton…my grandmother…it has a nice ring, don't you think?"

Betty nodded; wearing the widest grin Shirley had ever seen on her face. "I know that, dummy. Aunt Nausona already took George, Kelly and Sue over. She's quite taken with them. I think they have a new mommy."

"You think?" Shirley questioned, making her way to the exit.

"Yes, my uton has already fallen in love with Frank, and she has added Bobby, Marcus and Mary to her brew. I believe our family has officially grown."

They both left the room and slipped down the hallway. They had been on the ship for a short time, but they felt right at home. They used the time to check out the ship from bow to stern. Because they were the descendants of the emissaries, they had free reign.

Now they were making their way to gate portal room one, for Shirley to step to the *Star Cruiser Nary*. She had stayed after dinner on the *Tharen* to be with her cousin. She was not ready to leave Betty when Nausona returned to the *Nary* earlier, but now Shirley felt more than comfortable and was ready to spend some quality time with her grandmother on the *Nary* —by herself.

"My uton says that tomorrow we will go home and see our parents," Betty offered. "She said, as soon as this business with the Tuits is done, she would personally take us home. She can't wait to see my mother and I bet Aunt Nausona can't wait to see your mother."

"I know I can't wait," she gleamed, feeling the warmth of love surrounding her heart for the first time in three years. Then she stopped, grabbed Betty's arm and asked, "Why do we have to wait until tomorrow?"

"Uton said it isn't safe quite yet. Tomorrow it will be safer. She is troubled by the Tuits. She doesn't know how to read them yet."

"Read them…what do you mean read them?" Shirley asked.

"I don't know exactly…but I think she doesn't trust them yet."

"Oh!"

***

He didn't know what hit him. All he knew was he was serving the intruders their food, and next he was swimming in a sea of darkness. The guard lay sprawled out on the floor face down with blood dripping from the back of his head where the statue piece connected. Sasha wanted to use her own hands in a simple Tuit maneuver, but the guard, a trained Sixana warrior had made the ladies move away from him. Unfortunately he turned his back on Sasha as he laid the tray on the table. Sasha took the opportunity to throw the statue of the *Star Cruiser Tharen* at his head. She picked it up from the desk and carefully measured the distance. She took aim and with the skill of a major league baseball pitcher, threw a fast pitch high. It slammed into the back of the guard's head, breaking in two pieces from the force. He didn't see it coming.

He only felt the sharp and overwhelming pain of the stone figurine crack him on back of the head. The pain cried for instant relief, and the only relief the brain could offer was instantaneous shut down. He was unconscious before his knees hit the floor. So his mind did not register his kneecaps cracking under the weight of his body crashing down. Then his torso followed, hitting the table and sliding off to the right. His momentum made his body fall on its right side and waddle back to the left, under the table, onto his stomach.

Sasha, Dina and Isha then grabbed the steward and pulled him toward the door. The three of them struggled to lift his body and raise his right hand to the door lock. Sasha pushed his hand into the mechanism and the door split open from the middle, with a loud whoosh. Dina grabbed his delta belt and strapped it on. Then she passed the pagenay to Sasha and the Mation I to Isha. She pulled the coronet pistol from its holster and held it at the ready.

Without any communication, the women stepped out into the hallway, which was empty. It was still dinnertime and most of the ship's personnel were either on duty or in the galley. It was perfect timing, or it was lucky timing. Dina did not care which. She just wanted to get off the ship. She pointed to the left. She remembered the room in which they stepped from the white light was in that direction. Her limited scientific knowledge had already surmised the white light was similar to their ultra space. It was a medium, which allowed travel over great distances. She just hoped she knew how to activate it without killing them.

The trio hugged the wall and measured their steps. They slinked as stealthily as they could, relying on their Tuit training to guide them in the unfamiliar territory. Then Dina, who was in the lead position, stopped and signaled for the others to press against the wall more. They had reached a cross hall and several people were coming toward them.

Two unarmed personnel, a Chaktun male and a Patt Woman, walked across the hallway; so deep in conversation they did not notice the three women in the shadows of the other corridor. After they passed, Dina released a heavy sigh of relief. She stuck her head out to ensure they were gone and no other personnel were in the corridor. Then she hopped across the crossway and pressed against the wall once more. Sasha and Isha did the same. Once they crossed they continued down the hallway.

Soon the trio came to the door leading to the gate portal room. It had a hand-activated lock. Dina studied the lock in disgust. She thought she should have cut the steward's hand off for just this sort of situation. She turned to Sasha and Isha and with her eyes asked if they had any suggestions. The look of frustration occupying their faces answered Dina's question. *Now what,* raced through her mind?

Then the sound of footsteps crushing the soft-carpeted floor grabbed her attention. She looked down the corridor in the direction of the footsteps. Then she heard voices. They were talking in a different tongue. Unlike the Chaktun tongue the MARIT in which they still wore, could interpret. It was the language of the planet below. She then turned in the other direction and pointed down the corridor.

The women raced down the corridor and around the bend. They stopped when they thought they would be out of sight of the personnel approaching. Dina turned and stuck her head around the corner to see who was approaching. She recognized the two young ladies as the girls who were with the Osguards on the planet's surface.

She watched as they stopped in front of the gate portal room. The taller one reached up to the lock and put her hand into it. Dina signaled for Sasha and Isha to follow her. Then she went into a full sprint toward the girls.

Betty and Shirley turned in the direction of the dark shadows racing toward them. They recognized the robes. Shirley let out with a blood-curdling scream that rocked the entire corridor. The door split open and Betty pushed Shirley into the room. The gate portal operator, Major Modi was already reaching for his pagenay in the arsenal draw under the console. However, he recognized the two heirs to the USSTAP dynasty and slowed his reaction. The girls ran into the room, which further confused Modi.

The doors started to whoosh closed, when a hand grabbed one side and pushed. The door opened. The door was programmed to reverse power in case of pressure to halt any unintentional crushing of personnel, who may be too slow in crossing the threshold.

Dina, Sasha and Isha stood in the doorway with weapons pointed at Modi. He raised his hands. However, Sasha took his sudden movement as a sign of deceit or a sign of cowardice. Either way, she took pleasure in boring a red flash from the pagenay into the man's chest. Modi fell backwards as the red beam of energy overloaded his axons and dendrites in the nerve cells with heat, rendering him unconscious. Sasha thought the red button meant a deathblow and was satisfied with the results, thinking Modi was dead. The girls witnessed the blow and also thought Modi was dead. They remained cowering in the corner of the room.

The Tuits walked in letting the door close behind them. As if the ship knew what was going on, as the door slammed shut the Alert three buzzer rang over the intercom, followed by the synthetic impersonated voice of Neraka Osguard, the mother of the Osguards, chiming in, "Intruder Alert…Intruder Alert…Prisoners have escaped…Prisoners have escaped…Alert three…Alert three. Gate portal rooms—shut down…Gate portal rooms—shut down…startram bays— lock down…startram bays—lock down."

Dina looked up as if she could see the person talking. Her mind was interpreting the message, even though she was hearing it in a foreign language. It was freaky and more than disturbing. Nonetheless, Dina had decided to keep the MARIT on so she could understand the enemy. She knew the enemy had the capability of understanding them.

She raced around the console and kicked Modi to the side. She played with the sensor plates for a quick second all the while her heart was racing and she could feel her body temperature rise with nervousness. She had to figure the console out. She wanted to chastise Sasha for being too quick on the trigger. The operator would have been a great help in deciphering the console. They had hostages. He would have had to help them in order to protect the hostages. It was perfect. Well, it was perfect until Sasha overreacted. She made a mental note to speak with Sasha about her hot temper if they ever got out of this situation alive.

Then a yellow light began to flash on the console. Dina didn't understand the meaning of the light, but she knew it was not good. Now her nervousness turned into panic as she pushed and pressed against the console's sensor plates. Sweat streamed down her spine as she fumbled over the console. She really had to talk to Sasha about her quick draw. She hated when things did not go well and the last two days were the most challenging days of her career.

The yellow light began flashing even quicker. Dina didn't know if the light was something she did, playing with the console, or if the bridge was trying to communicate with the operator. Then she heard it blaring over the intercom.

"Major Modi, you have not reported your GPR secure yet…please report," Laurona's voice came over the intercom."

"Uton!" Betty screamed. The voice sent a chill up Laurona's spine when she heard her granddaughter in the room.

Sasha pointed the pagenay at Betty and was about to fire.

"No you idiot. You've already shot the operator. Don't shoot our insurance as well."

Laurona recognized the voice and the chill covering her spine turned into fire in her stomach. "ARIT…Translate!" she ordered.

The ARIT repeated what Dina said in Chaktun. Now the fire burned hotter in her stomach, seasoned with fury and coated with hatred. They had her granddaughter and probably her niece as well.

"Security…to GPR one," she ordered, hopping from her command chair. "Delta belt," she yelled at the bridge sentry.

The sentry unlocked the arsenal cabinet to his right and handed a delta belt to Laurona. She strapped it on, clicking the buckle into place and tightening the leg straps around her thigh. Then she jumped down the two steps and raced down the corridor to the coaster. She hopped into the coaster, "Deck five…GPR section!" she commanded. The circular coaster doors closed and the coaster hummed into life as it raced down the vacuum tube.

Laurona tapped her private interlink to her sister and waited for a response. When her sister answered, Laurona gave her the highlights of what was happening. "Is Shirley onboard the *Nary*?" she asked.

"No!" came the chilling reply.

"Don't worry sister, I will get them both back," Laurona said. "I will get our grandchildren back!" Then the interlink went dead.

In GPR one, Dina was still trying to figure out the system. She was unable to read the symbols the consol displayed, which hampered her progress. She could only guess at what the console was trying to tell her. In time and with many trials and errors, she could figure the system out, but she didn't have the luxury of either. She had to go with her gut instincts. So she pushed several points on the coordinate pad and searched for the activation sensor. She pushed the outside sensor and the familiar hum of a gate portal rang in the air. On the podium three white lights of inner space glowed like the majestic wave of God's ocean.

"Quick, into the light, and bring those brats with us," Dina ordered.

Sasha rushed to the girls and grabbed each by the arm. Shirley began to scream, tears rolling down her cheeks like a faucet. The entire episode was broadcasted over the ship's interlink. Laurona's heart jumped in agony at the sounds she was hearing.

Sasha manhandled the girls onto the podium. She threw Betty over to Isha like a rag doll. Isha grabbed Betty's arm and twisted it behind her back. The pain shot through Betty's arm like a knife. She screamed louder than her cousin for the pain was more than Shirley's fright. However, she knew her one chance at survival was to cooperate, so she tried to quell the scream into a whimper.

Yet Laurona heard Betty's scream all too well. The feeling in her gut now was being turned over by impatience. She needed to get to deck five and she needed to be there already. Finally, as if commanded by her will, the coaster doors flung open exposing deck five. Laurona jumped out and met up with the six-man security detail halfway down the corridor.

"No one moves until I give the word!" she warned. "That's my family in there and we are going to do this right." The nods and hums that followed told Laurona she had made her point perfectly clear.

They reached the outside of GPR One, and the security detail took up positions on both sides of the door. Laurona stood in front of the door with her hand on the lock. She didn't know what she would find when she opened the door. The room had suddenly gone quiet and she feared she would find her family dead on the floor. The image rushed into her mind like a flood, but her determination chased it out. She listened to the interlink, trying to pick out some strategic, tactical or operational advantage from the sounds. She strained to hear what was going on inside. It was quiet, eerily quiet. All she could hear was the sound of… "Damn it," she shouted. "It's a gate portal opening."

She unlocked the door and it split open. She dropped to the floor and rolled into the room, came up on one knee with her coronet pistol in the ready. She turned to the podium just in time to catch the last glimmer of light from the gate portals closing. They were gone.

Laurona's eyes watered with emotion. A tear roared from her left eye and sank down her cheek as the feeling in her gut turned into a feeling of loss. This soon was replaced by rage. She stood, holstered her gun and ran to the podium. She kicked the podium, venting her rage the best she could. The security team who entered after her looked at each other in awe. This was the first time they saw their emissary lose her cool, but they understood. They holstered their weapons.

The team leader saw Modi on the floor behind the console and went to him. The smile on his face told the others Modi was still alive, but Laurona didn't notice. She finally dropped to her knees and lowered her head in despair. She then clicked her private interlink to her sister.

"Nausona…I failed…they're gone."

Chapter 17—Angels of Death

Snuggled away between San Antonio and Houston, about two hundred and fifty miles south of Dallas was small town America, at least what small town America in Texas was like at the turn of the century. The streets of Victoria Texas were dirt roads; horse and buggy were still the main mode of transportation and several remnants of the cowboy era still existed. The sun was bidding its day's farewell to this part of the world, signaling the end of the workday for the farmers and ranchers of this community.

On a small ranch east of town, rancher Jonathan Jackman had finished his daily chores. It was a rugged life, one peppered with hard work, long days and no gratitude. Yet, it was a life he enjoyed, because it brought with it several rewards, an honest day's living and good food on the table and a sturdy roof over his family's head.

Jonathan Jackman, fifth generation rancher, stood tall with broad shoulders and muscles molded by heavy lifting. His face was weather cracked by the hot sun and dry wind that pushed through the territory like a sandstorm during the rough seasons. His hands were hard and calloused from the countless hours of manual labor he had done throughout his thirty-five years of life. Every crack in his skin, every ache of his muscles and every blister that formed was a battle scar of manhood, which he proudly wore.

His wife, Mary, also looked upon him with the pride only a wife could feel. She knew how hard he worked to provide for their two sons, Robert and Brian. Nevertheless, she also was proud of her work. Mary Jackman made sure the house was spotless and there was always a good meal waiting for her man. She made sure the boys were always clean and presentable when guests arrived and she made sure the boys understood and appreciated their father for all he did for the family.

Their ranch was small, but profitable for them. They had twenty-five head of cattle that seemed to need as much attention as their two teenage boys. Luckily, their boys were able to help their father around the ranch after school. For now, his family had finished dinner and had turned in for the night, and Jonathan was about to head out the door to start his busy evening with his neighbors. The blood red moon glowed high above the horizon, like a fiery ember.

Jonathan stepped out onto his porch and took in a deep breath, which was his ritual almost every evening. The taste of whiskey still lingered on his tongue as the cool air from the fall evening filled his lungs. He scanned the night sky, as he made a mental account of what he was about to do this evening. Dressed in a white robe, embroidered with a red cross on the right chest, and carrying a white hood, he stretched his arms over his head walked to the end of the porch and stepped to the dirt ground with a loud thud. He had work to do.

Suddenly, in front of him, three white lights flashed from the ground up. The light appeared pure and angelic. He froze in his tracks, too scared to move and too afraid to speak. The light just bathed him as it wafted over his body. He felt a warm sensation, almost spiritual. In his mind he thought he was dying and the angel of death was coming for his soul. *But how could that be?* He wondered. He felt no pain; he didn't have a heart attack. He didn't slip and fall and he was not shot. *Why was the angel of death coming for him?*

Then from the light, he saw silhouettes. Three black robed beings seem to float from the light. Two of them carrying something—no someone... Now his thoughts went from denial to fearful acceptance. *He must be dead,* he thought. *The angels of death have picked up two people and he was the third.*

The power he prided his life on, left him as his knees buckled and he fell on them to the ground. Panic gripped him as he shook his head. He mouthed the word *'no'* several times, but his vocal chords refused to utter a sound. Finally, he stretched his arms forward trying to ward off the angels of death, but he only managed to shade his eyes from the light. Then the light was gone, as fast as it had appeared, it had disappeared. He dropped his hands and gazed upward. The three blacked robed strangers were ghostly white, with yellow cat eyes that seemed to glow with fire in the darkness of the night. Their dark hair slipped from under their hoods and draped over their chests like a horses mane, solidifying in his mind his first impression.

The image, forever blazed in his memory, caused him to hyperventilate. The taller one shouted something at him in a language he never heard before. Then she pointed her bony finger at him, further convincing him that she was an angel of death. And as if the mighty hand of God commanded him, his body shut down, his mind swelled in the black blissfulness of nothingness. His body crashed to the ground. He lay unconscious at Dina's feet.

Dina looked over the scene in surprise, but the feeling was fleeting. She knew she had to move and move fast. It would be a matter of time before the Osguards filtered through the litany of false coordinates she managed to leave in the console database, and capture the right coordinates to follow them. She wasn't sure she had initiated the machine correctly to hold the false coordinates in the memory bank. If that was the case, another gate portal should be opening anytime. She didn't know whether she should go on the defensive or retreat.

She surveyed the area and saw nothing but darkness. Her gut feeling told her to take the defensive. There was no advantage to the terrain for a tactical retreat. But it also offered no advantage for a serious defensive stand. Before she knew it, she pointed to her right and motioned for the others to follow her. Instinct or fear had overridden her tactical gut sense. She did not question it; she just went with the momentum.

Sasha dragged Shirley by the arm; still keeping it twisted behind her back. A sharp pain shot up Shirley's arm telling her, her captor was serious and she should not resist. She bit her lip to muffle the inner scream her body wanted to release. Isha held the Mation I on Betty, giving her freedom from physical pain, but not from the mental torture of being a victim, once again. She jabbed Betty in the back. The pinch was sharp, but did not penetrate her skin, yet the pain, or the promise of pain was loud and clear. She was to move as well. She took a baby step forward. This was not enough for Isha, another pinch from the sharp metal of the Mation I stung her back. The promise of pain was more realistic than before. She pushed out with a larger step, closing her eyes awaiting another pinch or even harder stab from the Mation I. When it didn't come, she stepped forward again, still with her eyes close, but her face wet from crying. Within an hour the five ladies had disappeared over the small hill, leaving Jonathan Jackman on the ground, unconscious but unharmed.

***

The slap stung his face. However it was painful, which meant he was alive, so he thought in his cloud-filled mind. Then another slap slammed across his face like ice. It was definite pain, welcome and wanted pain. He fought to open his eyes, but he wasn't quite there yet. He wasn't fully aware and not fully in control of his body to perform the simple task of opening his eyes. Then the third and most brutal slap of the three rang across his right cheek.

Strength rushed into his muscles, awareness sprang into his mind and the blood rushed to his head. Jonathan Jackman's eyes opened, his legs sprang underneath him and he hopped up. However, dizziness still owned him. The blood had not settled in his brain yet, he swayed backward as he tried to focus on who was there with him. Then a strong arm grabbed on to him to steady him. He closed his eyes and took a deep cleansing breath. He could feel the awareness of the world return to normal inside his head. He reached out to grab the arm, which was steadying him for more support. As he felt his strength surge throughout his body, he relied less and less on the supportive arm holding his arm. He soon found himself able to stand on his own, so he let go.

Then he cracked open his eyes again and focused on the figures standing in front of him. He could not make them out, but he knew it was not his wife or his boys. He rubbed his eyes with the back of his hand to clear his vision. Then he looked up again. When he finally focused on the figures, he saw two middle-aged light skin black women with hazel eyes and shiny auburn hair, highlighted with gray streaks, pulled back into a bun. They wore tan colored pants and jackets that hung open, with tan ruffled shirts. They wore shiny black boots that came up to their shins. They also wore strange gun belts, with long barreled guns hanging on their hips. However, before his mind registered what he was seeing, he blurted out in disgust, "Niggas!"

The smile on Nausona's face disappeared as the word she had not heard for over four decades penetrated her soul and wounded her pride with the same ferociousness it had so many years before.

"I could have gone two more lifetimes without hearing that word," she commented.

Jonathan's mind then registered he was talking to two heavily armed and maybe highly sensitive colored women. He realized his comment wasn't just unwarranted, but might have been stupid. He was unarmed and they just picked him up off the ground. He needed to remain in control, but he needed to defuse the situation.

"What happened?" he asked staring at the gun belts Nausona and Laurona were wearing.

"We were hoping you would tell us," Nausona said.

"Why should I tell you nig…" he stopped in mid sentence to reevaluate his situation, "Why should I tell you anything?"

Laurona simply pointed behind him toward the porch. He turned to see five more men, two black and three white, dressed in the same outfit as the sisters, standing on the porch with his wife and two sons. His wife had a mournful expression on her face. Robert and Brian stood defiant almost challenging to the men on the porch. Their weapons were holstered, but they gave the impression that that could change, depending on his level of cooperation.

"See sister," Laurona interrupted. "I told you…they would never change. Shirley told me all this last night. This planet has not changed at all. It's the same shit, different day."

"I'm afraid you are correct," Nausona admitted. "I had hoped things would be different, but they aren't. That only strengthens my resolve on getting our children off this planet."

Jonathan looked back at the sisters in confusion. "What the hell are you two talking about?"

"I'm talking about…you better tell us all you know, or I won't hesitate to make you childless and a widower," Nausona strained. The cold callous words rolled off her tongue so easily that it frightened her, but most of all it convinced Jonathan she wasn't anybody he wanted to antagonize any more.

He shook his head in disbelief and turned back to his family on the porch. The men still had their weapons holstered, but he noticed they were closer to his family and his wife and kids had not said a word. Now he was scared—more scared than facing the angels of death. However the more he thought about it the more he began to doubt if the other people were the angels of death.

"Mister, you best start talking now. My patience is wearing thin," Nausona warned.

Jonathan, still looking at his family on the porch, could see fright roll onto his wife's face. Then he saw the defiant look on his boys' faces start to wane.

"You wouldn't dare!" he yelled.

Nausona pulled her coronet pistol and grabbed Jonathan by the throat. The strength in her hand surprised Jonathan. He couldn't turn to face her. His mind didn't even think about challenging Nausona. His hands remained at his side. Nausona then turned his face around to the side of the house. She aimed the coronet pistol and blasted. The side support of the house blew away; sending quarter inch splinters of a support beam flying out, up, and back. The house began to list as it searched for the support on that corner. It didn't find any, so the wall collapsed showing the inside of the house and exposing his bedroom to the outside.

"Try me!" Nausona screamed, throwing him down to the ground. "I won't ask you again."

Rubbing his neck and looking at the damage to his house, Jonathan rose, fully aware the weapon she used on the house was pointing at him now. He then turned to his family, mouth agape looking in their eyes for what to do next. He saw in his wife's eyes fear and a plea for him to tell them what they wanted to know. In his boys' eyes he saw disappointment and confusion. In his own heart he was feeling all these emotions and more. His eyes told the story, and Nausona saw that.

She lifted the pistol to his head, "I would rather kill you first, but I want to see you suffer."

Jonathan turned back to her, "Okay! What do you want to know?"

***

It took a minute for Jonathan to tell what he saw. What he saw was not worth the time the Osguards spent interrogating him. Angry and frustrated, Nausona holstered her pistol and pulled her PARIT. She adjusted the aim several times, clicking the trigger as she made a circular sweep. The readings were weak, but the modifications Vid Son made to the PARIT enabled it to pick up a faint reading of Tuit and Chaktun Omega two-four-four DNA floating toward the east. She then pulled her interlink from her belt clip. It was tan to match her belt, square like a woman's compact. She slid the cover up, exposing the mouthpiece and speaker. She pushed the flat sensor to the left.

"Osguard two to Vid Son…Osguard two to Vid Son," she hollered into the interlink. She waited the few microseconds it took for the ARIT chip to recognize the command and direct the signal to the special encoded interlink belonging to Vid's interlink. Right now she needed his genius, something she always recognized but never personally acknowledge to him.

"Colonel Son," the interlink rang in.

"Colonel Son, I need you to get to the bridge and translate these readings from my ARIT. I am trying to get a read on the escapees. Have the star cruisers move into position in order to employ a sensor and scanner sweep. I want to find them as soon as possible."

"Sire, I'm already there. I am receiving your readings now." The pregnant pause after was excruciating for Nausona. "Take heading…four–four–two…mark zero–seven."

"Tiah! And thanks Vid…you're the best."

"Keep your interlink open…I will monitor. We should be in position in three minutes."

"Tiah!" she responded, placing the interlink onto her belt holder.

Laurona moved over to her sister, "Damn girl, I thought you were going to kill those people."

Nausona looked over her shoulder at Jonathan, who had joined his family on the porch, then turned to her sister and shrugged, "I still might."

Laurona looked for the familiar twinkle in her sister's eye, which usually followed her off color humor. However, there was none. She was not sure whether Nausona was serious or not. "Are you alright?" Laurona asked after studying her for a while.

"Yes, I'm fine."

"You weren't serious back there were you?" Laurona whispered.

Nausona looked away, searching her own soul and conscience and slowly shook her head, "I don't know."

"Nausona! You better know. We can't afford you flying off the handle like that. You are going to be the emissary to an alien galaxy next week. If you lose your temper like that, it could mean more trouble than it's worth. You got to keep it together, or we will lose all we worked for." Laurona then reached for her sister and pulled her in for a hug. "Baby, I love you. We will get our family back. But I need you at full strength and in control. Do you hear me?"

Nausona pushed her cheek up to her sister's cheek, drawing her strength from her soft but sturdy touch. A tear fought to come out of her left eye, but she reined it back in with a deep cleansing breath. "Okay…you're right." Then she pulled away to look into her sister's eyes. "But it worked! It scared the shit out of him."

Laurona cracked a smile followed by a slight giggle, "Yeah, it worked. But it scared the shit out of me too."

Nausona shook her head, fighting a smile, "It did?"

"Yeah, it did."

"Osguards…" Vid's voice called from the interlink. "Just in case you forgot…your interlink is open."

The surprise looks on the Osguard sisters' faces raced to embarrassment. They covered their faces with their hands, hiding from their warriors watching the Jackman family on the porch.

"Don't worry Osguards. I isolated your communication. I'm the only one that heard. Now you should get going."

"Tiah!" Laurona acknowledged with her strongest command voice. Then she turned back to the porch. "Roe and Yad, you are with us. Ahmica, Radix and Toik, fix this mess and then report back to the ship," she commanded.

Roe, one of the black warriors from Chaktun and Yad, one of the white warriors from Patt jumped off the porch and fell in behind the Osguards. Son had initiated a beacon direction, which he passed to Nausona's PARIT. A green arrow blinked on her screen along with numbers written in Chaktun, pointing in the direction of the DNA traces.

Nausona looked at it and nodded in the direction to go. The foursome moved eastward, following an invisible trail, only Son and his genius could pick up.

"Vid…any luck with the sensor and scanner sweep?" Nausona queried.

"No sire," Vid reported. "I don't know why the ARIT isn't picking them up. If it wasn't for the DNA sniffer I put in your PARIT, I would say they were never there."

"I don't like this Vid," Nausona said. "I don't like this at all. Vid, please keep on top of this."

"Tiah!"

Chapter 18—Field of Dead

The sun was high in the sky. The foursome had been walking for almost five hours. Yet they did not see or hear anything. The invisible trail the PARIT was following still remained as faint as it was at the beginning. This made Nausona and Laurona think they were on a wild goose chase. The Osguards were still perplexed why their ships did not pick up any traces of the DNA, especially the Osguard strain of Omega two–four–four. The ARIT was fined tune enough to pick out individuals from orbit, especially when they had the specific DNA to compare it to. The doctor had taken blood samples from their grandchildren upon arriving on the ship. Besides confirming Shirley and Betty as Osguard descendants, it also banked their DNA for quick identification. It should have been a simple task for the ships' ARITs to pick out the DNA and provide coordinates for the Osguards to step to, but it did not. It was like their DNA was being masked, or altered.

The same should have been true for the Tuits. The doctor scanned the three Tuits and recorded their specific DNA. The ships' ARITs should have been able to single them out—especially since the Tuit DNA was alien to the planet. No human on Earth or in the galaxy for that matter, had such a DNA sequence.

Vid was correct. The Tuit DNA showed evidence of the second generation of humankind, the carbon breathers. The Tuits were a hybrid of the second and third generations of humankind. This disproved the scientific theories that the generations were separate and distinct life forms and not derivatives from or linked to one another. The Tuits were living proof. They were the bridge from the second generation to the third generation, but they were also technologically advanced as well. Meaning…what? Were they a danger, or were they a Godsend? Neither Osguard knew or cared at the moment.

The Tuits' existence would have been a great scientific debate for the ages. Vid would have loved to explore the possibilities more, but right now, the Tuits had their grandchildren. They already exhibited aggressive behavior to the point of psychotic. The Osguards knew, the longer their grandchildren were with the Tuits the less likely the chance for their safe return. So with each passing hour, the Osguards became frantic and less sure they would find their grandchildren alive.

It was at this moment, with both Osguards concentrating on the same thought and feeling of hopelessness, when Nausona's PARIT caught it. Her mouth gulped open and her heart beat so hard in her chest that she could almost hear it. She raised her hand for all to stop. Then she knelt to the ground, hiding behind tall grass, as if she were evading an unseen enemy. The others followed suit.

"Vid…all scanners…all sensors about half a mark ahead. What do you see," she asked through the interlink.

"In the name of Jus," was the shocking reply.

Vid's tone of voice solidified what was going through her mind. She then shot a synchronization pulse to her sister, Roe and Yad's PARITS, so they could see what she was seeing.

Laurona's face drew pale as she read her PARIT. Terror struck, as she looked at her sister. For a split moment she had lost control of her training. She reached for her coronet pistol and raised it to the ready. She started to stand, when she heard her inner voice command her to slow down. Listening to that voice, she kneeled back down on one knee. She then shot a glance to Nausona who was at point. It was Nausona's show and Nausona's decision.

When Nausona realized she had everyone's attention, she signaled for Roe to move to the left flank, Yad to move to the right flank and for Laurona to join her at point. The Sixana warriors moved with the stealth and grace of spiders, barely moving a blade of grass. When Nausona saw on her PARIT all were in place she stood and moved forward, with her coronet pistol in her right hand and her PARIT in her left. The others remained covered by the tall grass.

She clicked and moved…clicked and moved until she reached the tree. She looked up at the tree staring, dumbfounded at what she was witnessing. She clicked the *'all clear'* signal on her PARIT. Laurona raced up to her sister and stood next to her, out of breath, not from running but from fear.

The sun was burning hot above their heads but the chill of the scene cooled their bodies as it ran along their spine. Their eyes remained wide, trying to understand, their mouths remained open, wanting to speak, but unable to utter a sound. The horrific scene was worse than any battle and worse than any accident. It was unthinkable. It was inhuman. It was death in its most gruesome and frightful mayhem.

Soon the entire scene sunk into Nausona's spirit as she felt her stomach churning and the burning sensation rise in her throat. She turned and vomited, releasing her stomach acids onto the ground. The sound and sight of her sister's illness, moved onto Laurona, as she too felt sick to her stomach. She kneeled away from the tree to spit up as well. Roe and Yad both appeared from the sides like bookends to witness their Osguards vomit in the tall grass. They turned away, out of shame or out of respect, they did not know which, to allow their Osguards some privacy. Their eyes caught the tree and they both subconsciously followed the tree with their eyes up and out to the limbs. There they saw what upset their Osguards.

The strong and sturdy twelve inch oak tree limb was about fifteen feet off the ground. Around it were five ropes tied into nooses. And at the end of the nooses were five bodies, severely beaten, brutally hung and then callously burned like roasted pigs. Their faces and their genders were unrecognizable. Flies and other bugs had surrounded the bodies, and maggots had begun to infest the open wounds. The heat from the day's sun had accelerated the decaying process, spewing the stench of rotten burnt human flesh throughout the area. The heads of the two on the right were grotesquely leaning on their shoulders, the product of a broken neck. As for the three to the left, their eyes were bulging out, a symptom of asphyxiation. Apparently, they choked to death as the rope collapsed their windpipes.

The Osguards, now relieved, looked back over their shoulders at the scene once more. The image of what had happened began to play in the Osguards' minds as if they were there and they witnessed it. For Nausona, she could feel the pain the people went through. She rubbed her stomach, face and leg in an empathetic but unknowing attempt to connect. She did not know if she was looking at her grandchild or not. She wanted to study the victims to see if she could see a hint of them in their faces, but the scene was too ghastly.

"Vid…please scan the bodies…see if they are…see if any of them are…my granddaughter or niece," she whispered.

"DNA scanners activated," Vid announced.

The next couple of minutes were agonizingly slow, as the Osguards looked on trying to accept the fact that their grandchildren could be hanging from the tree. Rage found its way into their hearts.

"Vid…what's taking so long?" Laurona boomed.

"First Osguard, there are a lot of bodies…or should I say body parts to sweep through," Vid responded.

"What the hell do you mean?" screamed Nausona. "There are only five bodies and although they are messed up, they are basically intact."

"No sire. Those bodies you are standing next to are not your people. But I am wading through the twelve others approximately forty paces in front of you."

"What?"

"I thought you could see them. There are twelve or so more bodies in front of you."

The sisters shot at each other a more horrid look. The feeling of dread swallowed them again. They didn't know if they could live through another examination of dead to see if their granddaughters were among them. Nausona exhaled hard and shook her head. She was trying to choke back tears.

Laurona reached out and grabbed Nausona's arm, more to steady herself than her sister. She bit on her lower lip and closed her eyes in disgust. Then she raised her head and stared off in the direction in which Vid directed. She pulled her PARIT and synchronized once more with the others.

"I'll go first this time, Nausona. You can follow when you're ready." Then with a deep breath she turned to the guards. "You guys, please take down the bodies." She then exhaled. "Please treat them with dignity."

With trepidation circulating in her veins, Laurona stepped forward, pistol in one hand and her PARIT in the other. She clicked the trigger to her PARIT several times, until she received a reading. She stared at the readout, while she crept toward the site. Then something caught her attention in her peripheral vision. She lifted her head and stared at it for some time. She could not make it out, so she switched her direction and moved toward it. She transferred the PARIT to the object and clicked the trigger.

Laying on a rock was a white cloth, torn and bloody, that much she could see. Then when she walked about four paces to it, the scene became clear. It was an arm, ripped from the torso at the shoulder. The ligaments and muscles frayed into shreds. Blood soaked the white cloth. She followed the cloth down toward the hand. The wrist was unnaturally bent backwards, apparently broken. It had the stench of death permeating the air around it. She then turned to visually scan the area. Where there was an arm, there should be a body.

She didn't have to look far. A headless and legless torso lay about ten feet to the right of the arm and to the left was the right arm, and slightly over from that were the legs. The torso was bloody and the white robe, similar to the one Jackman was wearing, was soaked in so much blood that it appeared red. The muscles and ligaments were shredded like some giant ripped the limbs of the body. She coughed from the pungent smell emanating from the body. In some ways it was worse than the burnt bodies hanging on the tree. At least the attempted burning of those bodies had slowed down the decaying process, decreasing the swirl of the death smell. Even though burnt flesh was repugnant in its own right, it wasn't the smell of death. Yet, here, the bodies, or body parts were exposed more to the sun and the heat of the day without the benefit of cauterization. However, she could not believe this one body gave off such a powerful degree of the death smell.

She gazed farther down the field and started witnessing spots of blood on the tall grass. She had overlooked the spots before, but with her new discovery it became more obvious in her crosscheck. She walked over to the next set of blood splatters and saw another torn apart torso; this one still had a head connected to it. The bearer wore a pointed white hood. Its eyes still open, containing the last moments of life in its pupils. What Laurona read in those eyes, sent chills down her spine. The last minutes of life were painful. So painful that the eyes said it pleaded for death to come. When death came for it, the pain still lingered and the lone peace it received was in the soul.

She kneeled down and removed the hood and studied the face more. Again, the open mouth and the horrid expression on it confirmed her suspicion. The last minutes of life were too painful to bear, too ugly to fight for, and too humiliating to want. Death was the only answer and it came slowly for him. It took several minutes, maybe an hour for his soul to give up the ghost. It took time for the blood to leak from the mangled twisted muscle which once held his limbs in place. While the blood leaked, gushed or poured from his veins, agonizing pain racked his body, invaded his mind and crushed his spirit.

The sudden pressure from a hand on her shoulder startled her. Laurona jumped sucking in her fear and reaching for her pistol. She turned to see Nausona staring down at her. Nausona's hazel eyes were red from tears, but her face was solemn, showing the resolve and determination of a warrior. Laurona looked past her sister to see where Roe and Yad were. They were still cutting the bodies down from the tree, not noticing anything they were doing in the field.

Laurona stood and looked out over the field. She squinted and covered her eyes with her hand to block out the sun. "Let's see what else is out here," she suggested. In a short time, Laurona and Nausona found fourteen bodies over a quarter acre area. Each body was ripped to shreds, limbs torn off like sticks and wearing the same blood soaked white robe, embroidered with a red cross on the right chest, like a uniform.

Laurona stopped at the last body in the field and then adjusted the parameters of her PARIT to seek out Omega two-four-four DNA traces. The trace stopped in the midst of the field, similar to the exiting of a gate portal. Then she switched the parameters to search for restion particle residue. Vid reminded her before they left; the Tuits used what they called ultra space to step. It was a restion particle radiation haven. The particles left a residue similar to the benion residue left after a gate portal opening from inner space.

Her PARIT registered several trace amounts in several different areas, suggesting at least fifteen openings. She took in the reading in despair. She shot the readings to her sister, and then opened her interlink to the others in the exploration team.

"It looks like the Tuits have been here. It also looks like they returned back to their ships and probably took Shirley and Betty with them." She did not know how, when or what the scene played out. She did not know if this was an army that met up with Tuits. She did not know if they had something to do with the burnt bodies hung from the tree. She did not know if they were the aggressor or the victims. All she knew was each and every body they discovered died the most horrendous death possible. She had no explanation other than the Tuits. No matter what the story, she knew the Tuits were involved. She closed the interlink and looked skyward. She fell to her knees in the midst of the bloody field. "Jus, we need your help…Jus, please help us," she screamed with outstretched hands. "We want our children back."

Chapter 19—Beyond the Moon

It was a small blip, but a blip just the same. Vid watched his screen to see if it was an anomaly or if something was really there. His gut told him there was something there, but the system wasn't confirming the feeling. He twisted around from the Centurion of Operations chair onboard the *Nary*, which he had been occupying since he stepped onto the bridge and activated his controls to run a diagnostic. The system hummed for several seconds as it checked internally for any problems. Then the screen on the C.O. chair came back —*'Grade A.'*

Vid was not satisfied the blip was an anomaly and the diagnostic just made him more paranoid. He leaped to the defensive system operator's area and pushed aside the disgruntle defensive officer. He then redirected the sensor and scanner sweep toward the blip. He swore it was an energy source, but it was on the other side of the planet, coming from the satellite the Osguards called the moon.

"Osguard two," he whispered into the interlink.

"Yes Vid."

"I am sweeping the system for a possible energy source. The *Nary* will not be covering you for a while, but the *Tharen* and the *Jessup* have full systems on you. However, I need permission to take the *Nary* around the planet to get a better look."

"Okay Vid, you are my C.O. Do what you think is necessary."

Vid's mouth dropped open as the words penetrated his consciousness. He was the Centurion of Operations, or was she being facetious. He thought it strange that Nausona requested his presence on the *Nary*. Now he was wondering if he was to move up to Centurion of Operations for the *Star Cruiser Nary*. His mind flashed at the greatness of such a feat. Then the sorrow of Alar's death overcame his momentary joy. He closed his eyes in a silent thank you.

"Did you hear me, Vid," Nausona asked.

"Tiah!" Vid responded.

"It's already on record. All the ARIT needs is your voice of acceptance."

"Tiah! Inputting command acknowledgement code." Vid moved to the C.O. chair and pushed in his personal code as the new command code. The ARIT accepted it without hesitation.

"Voice recognition," the ARIT announced.

"Centurion of Operations...Vid Son...Command Code Whiskey three...Fox seven...Papa nine...Jules four. I accept second in command of the Universal Science, Security and Trade Association of Planets, *Star Cruiser Nary*."

"Command code accepted."

With the feeling of acceptance so long wanted here, Vid sat back down in the C.O. chair. He pulled the screen around. "Pilot—break orbit and head to a parallel orbit on the other side of the planet. I want to take a look at the moon. Comm…notify the *Jessup* and the *Tharen* we will be taking a little jog to the other side. We will be back in a few minutes."

After the proper notifications and acknowledgements, the *Nary* gracefully separated from her sister ships and maneuvered around the planet, setting up orbit above the Asian continent, where it was now night. The entire trip took less than ten minutes.

"D.O." he called to the defensive operator. "All sensors…all scanners on that satellite."

The defensive operator readily obeyed the new centurion's command, trying to make up for the small show of disapproval he had displayed earlier, when Vid took over his controls. At the time, he didn't know Vid was the C.O., or he would have stepped aside more quickly.

The readings streamed in, heat signatures popped from the sensors, mathematical equations flowed from the scanners, all suggesting something unnatural on the surface of the moon. He narrowed in on the source and changed the parameters of the search. Then the readings blossomed. It was a tribolemincic signature. More specifically, it was two tribolemincic signatures.

"Centurion," he called.

"I see it," Vid notified the young officer. "Comm, call the *Tharen*…secure channel.

***

"Gate portal exits…now!" Laurona ordered upon receiving the news from Ti Oria.

Instantly, four gate portal openings hummed to life, four invisible doors lifted and the majestic white light of inner space shone on the field of dead bodies. For a moment it appeared the gates of heaven had opened up to take the souls of the dead to their final reward.

Laurona stepped to her opening, and then looked over her shoulder at the field of dead. In her heart she promised to Jus one thing—*'revenge.'* Then the USSTAP exploration team, E-Team for short, moved into the light and let the visible spectrum of the day swallow them as the gate portal doors slammed down closed.

Within seconds, on the *Star Cruiser Tharen*, seven openings appeared. The entire E-Team, including Ahmica, Radix and Toik from the Jackman ranch stepped out of the light into the platform of GPR one. It was a trip they had taken a thousand times, but none seemed as important as this trip. They were on the hunt and their prey was on the moon.

Ti stepped forward to greet Laurona and Nausona. Her expression was all business and her spirit pumped for the fight. She nodded to the sisters, "Osguards."

"Status?" Laurona snapped as she brushed by Ti.

Ti turned to fall behind her and Nausona, "Vid has found the Tuit ships. They were on the moon. It appears their portals have a greater range than ours."

"No, Ti," Nausona corrected, as they walked through the parting doors. "Our portals have unlimited range. We choose to limit their range for strategic reasons. Not long ago, the gate portal system was an interplanetary system. But that violated individual planetary sovereignty. The Congress banned interplanetary portals because they did not want it used as a means to secretly land an invasion force on another planet."

Ti regarded Nausona for a moment. She knew all of this. After all she was an engineer and gate portal system was a fundamental system to even the novice engineer. Ti had to catch herself from rolling her eyes.

However, the long pregnant pause caused Nausona to reevaluate her statement, "But you knew that of course."

"Go on," Laurona insisted when they reached the coaster doors.

"Well, Vid had them under surveillance, but they must have noticed the array system. They took off about two minutes ago, at a high MOP rate. Vid is in pursuit."

"What?" Nausona yelled.

The threesome hurried into the coaster and sat down. "Bridge," Laurona commanded. The coaster door closed and then the coaster lifted on an air of invisible coils and sped down the vacuum tubes toward the bow of the ship.

"As soon as you were on board, we went to MOP thirty in pursuit as well. But they have a large jump on us. Vid reports the Tuits are doing MOP forty-five and he can't keep up with them."

"Do we have an idea where they are going? Maybe we can get a ship to intercept," Nausona suggested.

"Yes emissary. We know exactly where they are going. They are going to Millmum Station. At least that is where the trajectory is tracking to."

"Contact Colonel Ke Lee and let him know what's coming his way."

"Already done sire."

"What does he have in the way of defense?"

"Station defenses are Grade A. However, the nearest star cruisers are us and we can't get there before the Tuits."

"How late will we be? What's the delta in ETA's?" Nausona questioned.

Ti turned to her and squinted, while she made the mental calculations. Then she shook her head and squinted again. No matter what technique she used the answer remained the same. That was the drawback of hard science. The right answer would never change; no matter what way you attacked the problem. She always loved that about engineering, but not today. She wished she could give them options, like Vid did with his soft science theories. Yet, even Vid had to depend on hard science to prove or disprove his theories, and so far, Vid was batting one hundred percent. In a way, this irritated Ti. Especially, now that Vid moved up to C.O. of the *Nary*. It wasn't that she didn't like him. She just didn't think a theorist should be in charge of operations. The position called more for a tactician, like herself.

She cleared her mind of her jealousy and recalculated for the third time the scenario. Again, the news was not good. "I calculate a little more than eight and a half hours between their arrival at Millmum and ours," she said. "And that is at MOP thirty all the way. We can't do any better than that."

The coaster slowed to a stop and the doors swung open. The ladies stood, and retreated from the coaster into the corridor. They turned right and walked down the corridor toward the bridge. It was about twenty yards to the bridge door. Laurona placed the palm of her hand into the lock reader and the doors opened. Then she stepped onto the bridge, where the sentry announced her presence. She handed the sentry her delta belt, as did her sister. He locked the belts in the bridge arsenal cabinet to his right.

Laurona went to the command chair and sat in it. She looked at the screen, studying the projected route of flight. Nausona stood behind her sister and to the right also studying the route of flight. Two red dots signified the Tuit ships on the track; one blue dot representing the *Nary* was on the same track but falling behind. Two green dots, representing the *Jessup* and the *Tharen* were farther behind on the track. Usually, a picture was worth a thousand words, but the picture the screen projected reiterated just a few words. They were losing the hunt.

***

The next twenty-five hours were excruciating, but somehow the Osguards survived it with the grace and dignity they were known for. At the seventeen-hour point, Colonel Ke Lee reported "All clear." And for every hour after that, he reported, "All clear."

Finally the USSTAP star cruisers, the *Jessup* and the *Tharen* were flying the approach to Millmum Capitol Station. The *Nary* arrived a few minutes earlier and had already docked onto the station. Laurona was leery that there were no signs of the Tuits. They may have doubled back to Earth once they got out of scanner and sensor range, yet she doubted it. Her gut told her, they were still around, but her gut was fighting with her emotions. Her granddaughter and niece were still missing. She wanted to take one of the ships and head back to Earth. Conversely, in the stratagem of the moment, that was ill advised.

The two ships docked without incident on the main docking ring. The ships had run hard for the past several days, especially pushing MOP thirty during most of that time. The dialairtic crystals needed to be checked. The ships needed a hull check and the engines needed a rest, but they could not rest. Once docked, the ships took on an immediate alert position, ready for immediate launch at the slightest hint of Tuit activity. Maintenance would have to wait.

Laurona and her sister raced to the observation deck, the command center of Millmum station. If anything were to happen, it would come through there first. Colonel Lee had reduced the alert status to Alert Two. Nonetheless, all members of the station still retained their delta belts and essential operations corps remained at the ready. All Alert two did was release the other corps, the security corps, engineering corps, diplomatic corps, economic corps, science corps and the medical corps to their routine stations.

"Incoming message," the comm officer announced. "It's for the Osguards."

"At my chair," Laurona commanded.

Nausona moved to the second chair and linked in with the incoming message. On both chairs a screen rose from the armrest and opened up in front of them. The picture was black at first, and then a strange symbol appeared on the screen. The writing was also foreign to them. Then the ARIT translated the writing into Chaktun—"Tuit Consortium Fireship *Tesle*." Then Dina appeared on the screen.

"My dear Osguards," her voice translated. "I am sorry for the confusion upon our arrival in your galaxy."

Laurona held her tongue. She thought Dina was attempting to set another trap. She knew her diplomatic talents needed to kick in now, over her military yearning for revenge. "We too are sorry, but you have something we want and we cannot get over this misunderstanding until our grandchildren are returned."

"I understand," Dina added. "Your grandchildren are safe, back on that planet. We stepped them home to their parents."

"What?" Nausona voiced.

"We are dropping our shields; we will approach you from the gate portal side. You are welcome to sweep us with your array. You will note we do not have your children onboard."

"Tuit ships approaching from three–four–two, mark three–two," the defensive officer announced. "All scanners…all sensors activated," he announced in anticipation of the next order.

Laurona nodded in appreciation.

"No Chaktun or Earth life form aboard either ship," he reported after several minutes of checking and rechecking his readings. He had used every typical parameter he could think of.

Then again, it was not enough for Nausona. She moved from her chair over to the D.O. position. He moved aside and let the Osguard work. She fingered the controls, quicker and more masterfully than he ever did. He watched in awe as she slipped from one pattern search to another. She entered parameters he never could think of, but it did not matter. The results were the same—no Chaktun or Earth life form aboard.

She nodded to her sister, Dina was apparently telling the truth. At least she was telling the truth about their grandchildren not being aboard.

"Okay, for the sake of argument, let's say you are telling the truth. Where is home? And what happened back there."

Dina looked over her screen as the MARIT interface translated the words. The process took an extra second, because it was not directly connected to her brain like before. When the words were complete, Dina smiled.

"When we escaped we ran up against those men in white robes. They had hung those poor people and they set them on fire. It was appalling. Your grandchildren were more afraid of them than us. They kept calling those poor people niggers. That seemed to upset your grandchildren even more. Well we were outnumbered so we waited in the tall grass. When our ships finally found us, we sent down a present for those white robed animals. I admit, it was kind of brutal, but my kind does not like to see innocent people handled in that way."

"You mean the Consortium?" Nausona chimed in.

"Yes," Dina responded. "And when we saw you attack that ship, well we thought you were attacking an innocent being. I am sorry. I was wrong. And I am afraid my haste has caused the death of a good man. Your godson, Alar…If there was something I could do to bring him back I would. But there is nothing I can do."

"What made you change your mind about us?" Laurona asked.

"We converted one of those MARIT devices to help us communicate with your grandchildren once we got onboard our ships. They told us the person you chased off, tried to kill them. She told us all you told them and we believed them. They also told us they wanted to go home. So we stepped them home."

"Why did you run then?"

"Your anger frightened us. We did not want to do battle with you. We did not want to further the mistrust among us. So we retreated in hopes time would dull your anger."

"Tell us where we can find our grandchildren." Nausona responded.

"Now that I can't do."

"Why not?"

"Although, we believe you, I am not sure you believe us. So this is what is going to happen."

Laurona and Nausona looked at each other for a moment. Dina was about to lay down demands for the information. This was not the sign of trust. This was a sign of a warrior. Then Nausona gave a slight smile to her sister. Dina was doing exactly what she would have done in the same situation. *It just wasn't good when she was on the receiving end,* she concluded

"Our scientist took the information you provided and have figured a way for us to get back to our own dimension. But we need your gate portal. Once we activate your gate portal and see the familiar red of our ultra space we will pass the coordinates of where you can find your family on that planet."

"You mean all you want is to leave?"

"Yes…that is all we want."

"Why didn't you say so in the first place?"

"Remember, you were the aggressors to us. You attacked us. You attacked the Kulusk ship. That type of behavior is what the consortium detests and what we vow to stamp out. You were the enemy. But your sweet granddaughters have convinced us, it was a great misunderstanding. However, I am not totally convinced your motives are still honorable. So I must have a fallback. And this is it."

"I see," Laurona pushed. "You are somewhat right. I am not sure I believe you. What if I want to detain you for a while to make sure you are on the level?"

"You are planning to hold us here and send a ship back to Earth and scourer the area your granddaughters said they were from. I happened to know they didn't tell you where they were from exactly. But your system could search for them and probably find them. I already thought of that. That is why we found your family first. We injected them with a DNA inhibitor that will shield their true DNA from your search array. We injected Shirley, her mother Amanda and her two brothers, Tim and Randy. We also injected Betty, her mother Lilly, her brother Robert and her Sister Susan. I tell you this, and provide you with more information to let you know I did it and I am telling the truth. This inhibitor will pass from generation to generation for the next six generations. And without the code for the inhibitor, you will never find them unless you get a blood sample from every black person within a five hundred-mile radius. Oh…and I told Betty and Shirley that if all goes well you will meet them at the coordinates a day after tomorrow. So, what is it going to be? Us or them?"

All of a sudden revenge seemed too minuscule to Laurona, compared to finding her family. She gazed at Nausona and read her eyes. It was time to let this one go. "Okay!" she finally admitted. "But I want two of my ships off your flank. Just in case you try something. If nothing happens, you are free to go."

"As you wish," Dina replied.

Within two minutes the *Nary* and the *Tharen*, commanded by Vid Son and Ti Oria respectively, sailed out to meet the Tuit ships, which were approaching the gate portal. The *Nary* parked one thousand kilomarks off the left flank of the *Tesle* and the *Tharen* parked one thousand kilomarks off the right flank of the *Snikle*, both with their weapons trained on their respective quarry.

Once in place, Nausona fingered the interlink to contact Dina once more. "Are you sure you don't want our scientist to take a look at your plan…sort of validate it?"

"Your race is too violent. We cannot afford to have you know how to get to us. If what you did was truly caused by the storm, it would be a million to one shot of it ever happening again. Those odds make me comfortable. So thanks, but no thanks."

"Okay," Nausona said shrugging her shoulders. "Gate Portal three activated."

A bright white light illuminated from the gate portal soaking the Tuit ships. Then the Tuit ships both fired a black beam, hardly visible to the naked eye, into the middle of the gate portal. A swarm of different colors engulfed the white light. Then the light pushed forward and turned red.

"We are setting coordinates to our dimension now," Dina said. Don't worry; we do not have the radiation of your universe, or of what you call inner space to make a return trip. We will tell the consortium of our encounter. We just want the consortium to know we may have a friend in this dimension. I hope I am correct in calling you friend."

"If our families are safe, you are correct," Laurona said, placing the veiled threat of revenge back on the table.

"Passing coordinates to you now."

The coordinates began to stream across Laurona's screen, but the sub frequency of the channel Dina chose to send the coordinates bounced in the wake of the red wave that engulfed the ship, intercepting the stream and cutting it from being fully transmitted.

"Dina," Laurona called out. "Please retransmit, the signal was cut." Yet, the only response was static.

"Ultra space is giving off too much interference, I doubt if she can hear us," Nausona observed.

"Damn it, that bitch better hear me," Laurona screamed. "Dina, please retransmit, the signal was cut."

"Still no answer," Nausona cried out. "I'm trying to clear it up. I'm trying to clean the frequency so we can get the coordinates. Recording it now!" she said, hoping to be able to get the coordinates later by putting the recording through a filter. Unbeknownst to her, the signal was not traveling through ultra space; it was being bounced around like a BB in a jar. What she thought was interference was plain static.

Then the heavens lit up as the red light of ultra space that held the Tuit ships, blossomed into a ten-mark mushroom cloud, sending smoke and haze associated with radiation throughout the area. Tiny fissures of normal space and ultra space sparkled in the cloud like lights on a Christmas tree. It was the reverse of a zeshion storm. The *Nary* and the *Tharen* pushed backwards at hypersonic speed to keep their search array focused on the Tuit ships, but the ships disappeared from their arrays.

Vid, who was onboard the *Nary*, switched parameters on the cloud and tried to acquire the ships again. He knew they had not moved into the gate, but he wasn't sure if that was their plan to begin with. The light of ultra space did come forward and snag them. Maybe in the explosion it pushed them to their dimension, although somehow he doubted it. Dread overcame him. He changed the parameters to search for debris associated with a ship that has blown apart. The search array found splinters and slivers of metal, but nothing definitive associated with a ship. At first glance, the slivers and splinters could be associated with normal hull debris that occurs with space voyage. The traces were so minute, that only a trained scientist with his knowledge and speed could have detected it in the first place. Meanwhile, to make sure, he called the young D.O. over to the station.

"What do you make of this?"

The young officer studied the readings for a long period and then turned back to Vid, "Make of what centurion?"

"Never mind…never mind," Vid said in disgust. When he looked back at the scope, the readings where gone, and so was the mushroom cloud. The scope showed normal space, empty, cold and vast, with the two arms of the intergalactic gate portal resonating to a dull white shine.

"Vid…Vid!" Nausona called. "What happened?"

Vid stroked the interlink, "I don't know," he whispered. "I don't know," he repeated after he clicked the interlink off."

Chapter 20—What Next?

The screen blacked out for a moment, and then the lighting grew. Ortho Chting was sitting behind the desk at Millmum station. His eyes were red and his face pale. Jarod could tell he was filled with emotions. The HVP was the most graphic he had ever seen—even more telling than the HVP story about Laurona and Nausona's enslavement on Earth. Ortho had to watch the image of his father's death, a father he never knew, but always admired. He knew Ortho's father died a patriotic death, saving the Osguards. Still, it seemed a wasteful death when observed in the HVP. Jarod knew it was difficult for Ortho to see it. It was difficult for him. He felt a pang in his heart when he saw Alar's death. It was like watching a friend die in front of his eyes. It was a painful reminder that his father was fighting for his life as well.

Ortho's voice cracked as he spoke, "The Osguards, Laurona and Nausona, thought the Tuits made it back to their dimension. However, Vid Son always doubted it. After Laurona's death, Vid Son studied the records in more detail, using special filters and other materials he installed in the ARIT, and discovered the two Tuit ships exploded in the seam of ultra space. Thus Vid was afraid, given the Tuits pension for justice, they would return one day to avenge their companions' deaths. Since you are viewing this, the day must have arrived."

Jarod was intrigued at the simplicity of Ortho's rational. The Tuits saw themselves as the universe's avenging angel, seeking revenge for deaths that happened over a hundred Earth years ago. *Talk about grudges*, he thought.

"My only prayer," Ortho continued, "is that I have fulfilled my destiny and found the Osguard descendants by this day. If I have, ensure they view this HVP. I am sure they will know what to do. However I do regret the emissaries did not receive the coordinates to find the Osguards. The fact that the Tuit DNA suppressor blinded our search array made things worse. The Osguard sisters spent two months searching the area two hundred and fifty miles around New York City with the search array, postponing the indoctrination of Memlan and Minor Man Galaxies. Eventually, their duty to USSTAP took center stage and they went on to recruit five more galaxies into the association. Even though they took in the children Betty and Shirley were watching over in New York City as their own children, they were never the same. Nausona adopted George, Kelly and Sue who at the time of this HVP reside with families of their own on Chaktun. Laurona adopted Frank, Bobby, Marcus and Mary who also reside with their families on Chaktun."

Jarod's eyes lit up at the mention of seven more lines of Osguards. He had no knowledge Laurona and Nausona had raised a family. This was a shock, which enraged him. He clenched his fist and pounded it on his desk. It didn't matter they weren't Chaktun; neither was he. In fact their descendants would be more Chaktun than he or the other Osguards, because they have propagated their lines with Chaktun blood.

Then there was the same old question with a different twist. What happened to Shirley and Betty? Where did their line go? If they could be found, it would give them more lines to train as Osguards and man the galaxy protectors. It would take time to make that happen, and time was a luxury he did not have.

"Although they were raised by Osguards, they are not the true descendants of the Osguards. However, according to my latest instructions passed on by the Osguards before their death, if I can't find the blood descendants when the Tuit DNA suppressor terminates, I am to indoctrinate the descendants of the Osguards' second family."

"Why didn't you anyway?" Jarod screamed at the HVP. "That's bullshit. They are just as much an Osguard as I am, even more. They were raised in this shit. I wasn't, and neither were the others. There's no indoctrination needed. Ortho, you motherfucker—you stupid ass motherfucker!"

Regina slid her chair back at the Osguard's outburst. She never saw him so livid over a HVP. In fact, she never heard him curse before. It was a little bit embarrassing to hear him curse at her dead grandfather, his mentor as well as the mentor for all the Osguards. She turned her face away and looked at the screen, keeping Jarod in her peripheral vision.

"Somehow we must communicate with the Tuits, the actual events surrounding the destruction of their ships and the death of their crewmembers," Ortho continued. "We must display this HVP to them so they can understand that USSTAP had nothing to do with this accident. We must show them it was a misunderstanding that grew out of proportion, but the spirit of cooperation was coming about. Although it was not full cooperation, it was cooperation nonetheless. So I charge the Osguards who are viewing this with the task. You are the last hope for peace."

With Ortho's final plea echoing in the room, the screen went blank. The HVP was over, but the burden of peace had just become harder. Jarod knew they were no longer in a war in which battle plans and strategy would prevail. They were in a war in which statesmanship and diplomacy must take center stage. It was easier when it was us against them. We destroy and kill more of them than they do of us, and whoever has the most at the end wins.

No...Ortho had to put a twist on it. It wasn't a war against an immoral aggressor. It was a war against someone who thinks they are fighting for a righteous cause. Those enemies, whether right or wrong, were always difficult opponents. Jarod knew that is why the Middle Eastern terrorist recruited their people in the name of Allah. Even though the leaders were morally corrupt, their followers...their soldiers were righteously charged. Defeat for them was only a way to heaven, not a measure of failure. With that kind of charge, demoralization of the enemy was impossible. Were the Tuits like that? Were they fanaticals bent on some type of religious fervor? Or were they just crazy? By what he saw in the HVP, it was a mixture of both—a dangerous combination.

Jarod closed his eyes to continue his thought process, but more to cool the wrath that built in him over Ortho's decision not to include the descendants of Laurona and Nausona's adopted children. He had forgotten Regina was in the office with him. He was almost in his own spirit, meditating, thinking and assuaging his soul.

After five minutes of silence, he opened his eyes to see Regina waiting. Her sight shook him a little. When he looked at her, her expression was, *'What's next...tell me what you want me to do.'*

Jarod just smiled at his C.O., "I'm sorry for my outburst. This HVP has just put an entirely different spin on our situation. One I am not sure I like." Then he lowered his head in shame.

He had just cursed the most revered man in USSTAP, Ortho—her grandfather. He reached for her hand, which was resting on her lap. She allowed him to take her hand into his. Her eyes racked with guilt for what she thought was her part in a long running betrayal.

"I'm sorry," Jarod apologized, staring into her green eyes. "I'm sorry I cursed your grandfather. He was a fine man…the best. He brought my family and me into this fine organization. He taught us, trained us and there isn't a day we don't thank God for his mentorship. I was just appalled at what happened with the adopted families. I can't believe my ancestor left such an archaic order. It's reminiscent of medieval times on my planet, where birthright meant more than love. I guess I should have known that though. If the birthright wasn't so important to my ancestors then we would never had been given this opportunity to lead USSTAP. I guess it was acceptable until I found this out. It is too much to take in at one time, and I flipped. I'm sorry."

The worried look in Regina's face did not lift. She still felt the Osguard's anger was partly her fault, and she wanted to make it up to him. But how?

"Sire, I am sorry…"

"Sorry for what?" Jarod cut her off.

"I feel I failed you."

"Nonsense! Girl you may have just saved us. Just because I don't like the news you brought me doesn't mean it can't help us. I just have to figure out how. Or should I say we? We have to figure out how.

A polite smile crossed her lips as the feeling of betrayal burning in the pit of her stomach melted away. The Osguard had diplomatically dismissed her part, or he was tabling it for another day. Either way, she knew she could not dwell on it any longer. She had a job to do. She had to figure out their next move, and as if her grandfather whispered in her ear, the plan flashed in her mind.

"Sire, I have an idea!"

***

It was an ugly looking chamber. It reminded Jarod of a gas chamber in a state prison. It was round, metal and most of all windowless. It sat in the middle of the room like a misplaced statue, a grotesque throwback from the middle ages in the middle of the most technologically advanced spacecraft known to humans. As he looked at the monstrosity, he made a mental note; the conference chamber would have to be cosmetically altered to make it fit its surroundings better. He realized this was just the test model, the beta of the technology, but it proved itself in all testing and now he was about to use it for real. It was time to come out with one that reflected the grandeur of USSTAP technological know-how.

He moved to the door, which was a normal door; one that mechanically swung out and closed which only solidified his first impression that the chamber was just plan ugly. It did not have a modicum of beauty anywhere on it. The rivets connecting the panels looked like the rivets on a suspension bridge. The silver of the tank disgusted him so much, he had to close his eyes and shake his head before entering it.

The seat in the middle of the chamber was somewhat more to his satisfaction. It was a replica of his seat at the Senate Chamber at Millmum Capitol Station. It was meant to look like it. He walked toward it, sat down and placed the corynx crystal containing the HVP into the holder inside the right arm. Then his hands swept across the control panel on the left arm.

Instantly a black light swirled in the chamber, taking all visual clues from his sight. He was disoriented. He grabbed the armrest to steady his mind from giving his body inappropriate signals. He hated this part. It almost made him nauseous, but he swallowed hard to alleviate the feeling. Then as suddenly as the room went black, light invaded the chamber, blinding, painful light. He shut his eyes to the pain. He held them shut for several seconds, and then he began squinting, trying to adjust his eyes to the light. Slowly he was able to fully open his eyes.

Now he saw the Senate Chamber at Millmum Capitol Station. It was set in a deep well type room. With seats and rows of tables situated every two steps. The room was circular and at the bottom of the well sat a holographic projection stage to display briefings, diagrams and schematics. Unlike the real Senate Chamber, this room did not have the balconies shielded by glass for observers. The positions at the tables were numbered. The first row nearest the stage was numbered one through ten. The second row, where he sat, was numbered eleven through twenty-five. The third row was numbered twenty-six through forty-five. The last row was numbered forty-six through sixty. Each number designated where the corresponding Osguard sat.

Around him were his fellow Osguards, some squinting, some still with their eyes shut and some who like him had already allowed their eyes to adjust to the light. He smiled as he surveyed the room and saw the HVP images of his family once more. Each Osguard had done as he had, and entered their respective conference chambers upon his urgent call. The chambers connected to each other through a series of ARIT and gate portal technology allowing the members to holographically project their images into each other's chambers. It was a myriad of signals and electrons flowing between a hodgepodge of ARIT memory and gate portal communication arrays. The Osguards weren't together in the chamber; they were actually in their steel drums on their own stations. While the technology gave the illusion of being there, if they attempted to move from their chairs or tried to touch the image of anything other than the chair the link was broken, and had to be reestablished. It was a concept that took several tries before they became use to it. At first it was difficult. They naturally attempted physical interaction with each other. Additionally, the ride back into reality was just as shocking as the ride there, except it was more jolting when you weren't expecting it. Jarod remembered the first time, when he wanted to get up and see his sister, Osguard fifteen, Rachel and his brother, Osguard twenty-four, Tim. He bent over his seat and rose up slightly and the link was disconnected. The rush of blackness burned his cornea as he tripped back into reality. The sting to the brain was also painful. The MARIT connection ripped from his frontal lobes gave him such a headache; he thought he had been hit in the head with a hammer. It took several minutes before he attempted a reconnect to the chamber.

With his lesson learned, he sat perfectly still in the chair, only moving his neck to catch glimpses of his fellow Osguards. He knew this part had to be updated as well. He should be able to walk around the chamber in reality without breaking the link in cyberspace. The scientist said that was the next step and the chamber should be ready for that improvement in a couple of months. That was before all resources were reallocated for the war effort. He did not know if the project was still on time. He knew he wanted it to be, because the conference chamber would be used much more often than he had planned.

The green light over the stage illuminated, signifying all sixty Osguards had checked in and were ready for the meeting. Michael's face popped up on the screen first. His eyes were red and his face drawn. All could tell the war was taking its toll on him. All the Osguards were under tremendous stress and all showed signs of wear and tear, either physically, like Michael or emotionally like Jarod.

"Osguards, I give the floor to our cousin, Jarod Stone, the Siryman Galaxy Osguard," Michael announced without any fanfare.

Jarod's face replaced Michael on the big screen; so all the Osguards could see him as well without careening their necks and possibly losing the link.

"My fellow Osguards, my cousins, my family," Jarod began. "Something has come into my possession which I know will shed new light on our plight. Rather than me giving a briefing or sending out a report on it, I think it prudent for you to receive the information in the same format and the same way that I did…through an HVP."

The rumbling in the crowd began to grow. Jarod knew the Osguards felt as he did, there was no time to waste watching an HVP. They needed strategy meetings. They needed to plan. The Tuits were destroying USSTAP without the association putting up a fight. They were being slaughtered like cattle. An HVP, no matter how important, should be synopsized and reported through expedient channels.

Jarod raised his hands in a motion to quell them. They soon quieted and allowed Jarod to continue.

"Thank you," he replied. "I know the importance of our time, just as well as you do. And I am not one to waste time, especially during a crisis like this. So hear me out. We as a family— not as Osguards—but as a family need to watch this. We need to feel it and we need to digest it. I tell you this much, it has a direct bearing on our situation. This is not the first time that USSTAP has done battle with the Tuits. The Tuits have been here before. And our Osguard mothers, Laurona and Nausona, had dealings with them that directly involved our lineage, our line and our future. This story has been kept a secret from us, because it is not very pretty. It is not a usual USSTAP triumph over evil story. It shows we have made mistakes in the past as an organization. And unfortunately those mistakes have come back to haunt us as the descendants of the Osguard mothers. We have to correct those mistakes and try not to make any more. USSTAP is depending on us. The universe is depending on us. We need to step up to the plate, swallow our pride and do what is right. You will see what I mean once you view the HVP."

Jarod switched the screen to the start of the HVP. Ortho appeared and the telling of the first Tuit contact with USSTAP played again.

Chapter 21—Let the Healing Begin

He was starting to pant a little. The first bead of sweat began to form on his brow. He was thirty-nine years old pushing forty in a couple of weeks. Age was creeping in on his soul and he was desperately trying to ward it off. He was going on his sixth mile on his morning run, his second trip around the ship's outer corridor. The *USSTAP Galaxy Protector Neraka* corridor was specifically made for runners. The floor had a special shock absorbing quality, which cushioned the feet and took less wear and tear on the knees.

Along the track were twenty strength-building stations to do push-ups, sit-ups, chin-ups, crunches and so forth. Michael usually ran nine to ten miles every morning at the break neck speed of an Olympic runner—sixty-five to seventy minutes. When he felt spirited and if he had the time, he would complete the strength training stations during his last lap.

He knew his lifespan was not that of a normal Chaktun. He had too much Earth blood in him. His strength and stamina, even though greater than a normal human from Earth, was small in comparison to his cousin Reppus. Nevertheless, Michael, along with his siblings and cousins who wore the title of Osguard, vowed to keep in shape and do everything to ensure his Chaktun DNA dominated his Earthling weaknesses.

He still remembered the first time his Chaktun DNA was awakened. It was during the most ostentatious ritual he had ever witnessed or been a part of. It was the first time they arrived on Chaktun, prior to any training and prior to them understanding what was happening to them. Ortho had collected them like the pied piper. Michael remembered being scared, nervous and excited at the same time. They stepped through the white light into the Steeple's East Garden. There the crowd had gathered, cheering and clapping as they approached. The young Osguards wore the red tunic embroidered with the black diamond of the house of Vedar Osguard. The ceremonial hood was attached to the tunic, the first and last time they wore the hood. It covered them like a shroud of darkness, not allowing any of the cheering crowd to get a clear glimpse at them.

They lined up in six rows of ten, which later he learned corresponded to their Osguard number. He was the first one in the first row, signifying him as the First Osguard. Unbeknownst to any of them, Ortho had already assigned them their Osguardian numbers.

They exited the light, marching in the Chaktun style up to the palace steps, where Igna, the Chaktun Maxum, Reppus' father, stood in his red regal attire, similar to the Osguards. However the diamond on his chest was royal blue. Michael learned later, the color was change to discern the difference between the house of Vedar and the house of Akaher. Actually it was to assure the other member planets that USSTAP was not associated with the Chaktun government—it was an entity of its own. However the shape was kept to signify the close relationship with Chaktun.

They stopped in front of the railing separating them from the Maxum. Then Igna said several words in Chaktun, which he was unable to translate then. Later, he gleaned the context of the speech as acceptance back into the family fold.

He remembered Igna saying, "You are of my blood, and I am of your blood. Even though time and distance have kept us apart, you are home now, and I am home now. I am happy to call you cousins in the House of Osguard.

Although your lineage is different, we are the same. This is your home; this is your planet…welcome."

When Igna was finished, the Osguards, pulled out their golden rods of power, pushed a button and the tops flipped down into a seat. They planted the end of the rod into the grass as Ortho had trained them, and took their seats. The seats were metal, hard and very uncomfortable, but it was better than standing, because after that, every government leader in the universe gave an acceptance speech, welcoming the Osguards as the leaders of USSTAP. Even though each statesman was limited to a five-minute segment, the entire proceeding took over four hours. The additional length in time was because most of the speakers did not follow the five-minute rule and spoke longer than necessary.

When the last speaker was finished, Ortho approached the railing and gave the final signal of acceptance. In unison, the young Osguards stood, removed their hoods, reassembled their golden rods, and opened the end of the rods that exposed a chalice. Inside the chalice was a purple sparkling liquid. They placed the golden chalice to their lips and saluted Ortho. Then they drank the ceremonial drink, which Michael understood awakened their Chaktun DNA, giving them greater strength, endurance and agility. Now Michael understood, the drink stripped the last remnants of the Tuit suppressor that clung to their Chaktun DNA. He and the others were the fifth generation…next to the last generation in which the Tuit DNA inhibitor was supposed to effect.

It was an immediate reaction. His blood warmed, his muscles tingled and his mind became clear. It was an intoxicating buzz, but also an enlightening encounter. It was exhilarating like an out of body experience. His vision dimmed and then exploded in bright color. His hearing faded and then sharpened to the point where he could hear the bugs walk on the grass blades. He could now break out the different fragrances of flowers in the garden, where before they were a hodgepodge of smells. Now he had a discerning pallet and was able to taste the difference between different ingredients in the liquid, where before it was a collage of taste exploding in his mouth.

He turned to his right, Jarod Stone, Osguard eleven, was smiling from ear to ear. He knew at once, Jarod was feeling the same sensations. He looked down the front row past Jarod and watched Osguard twenty-one, Kendall Steele, Osguard thirty-one, Clay Trent, Osguard forty-one, Peter Grace IV, and Osguard fifty-one, Brian Nightman Jr. beam the same euphoric grin. He turned around to look for his brother, Shawn, who smiled as if he was in the spirit. He couldn't completely see his sister, but he could see her head sway as if she were in the spirit as well. Michael then nodded his head and slapped Jarod's hand, giving him a soulful welcome into the experience.

That was the day. That was the day they knew they belonged. They knew they had a destiny…they knew they were Osguards.

Well destiny has turned into fate, and fate was dealing them another universal challenge. It was time to shit or get off the pot, as Michael liked to say. He had to make a move and he had to make a move fast.

He had studied his options for almost three hours last night, after the conference chamber. He had put a plan together, but was reluctant to push it. He spoke to Michelle soon afterwards and realized there was no other way. He needed to act and he needed, once again, his brother and sister Osguards to accept it. His mind was made up. *'Operation Expansion'* needed to be put into place.

He rounded the corner to start his trip back to the bow of the ship. Two more miles and he would be finished for the day. He looked up onto the plate glass viewing wall, separating the running corridor from the outer main corridor. He saw his crew going about their day, not noticing him or the other runners who ventured out this morning to run circles around the huge ship. His presence, along with the fifteen other people he had passed this morning, was a common occurrence.

His next stop was the Sixana workout room, where he planned to put in a half hour practicing his fighting skills. However, today was an odd day, a day that demanded his immediate attention. He had to finish his thoughts.

Tirana Ritchen, his new C.O. and the sister of the new Kulusk Maxum, Opel was just ahead of him. Her blonde hair, which she usually wore in a tight bun, waved around her shoulders as she ran. Michael guessed she was doing an eight-minute per mile pace, which he thought was very competitive for a Kulusk. He pulled up to her right side and shot a smile at her.

She turned and batted her blue eyes and flashed a perfect smile at him, "Hello cousin! How is your run this morning?"

The word cousin coming from a Kulusk grated Michael's nerves, but Tirana was wearing him down and he was starting to accept it. At first he wanted her to stop calling him that, but he thought it wiser to see where it led. Was she bucking for an Osguardian position? Was she reminding him of his Pathgo blood? Or was she sincerely trying to break the ice between them? He gave her the benefit of the doubt and settled on the latter.

"Hey Tirana…I'm about to finish up the run," he responded. "I need to see you right away in my office when you're done. Some new evidence came my way last night and I need to run some things by you."

Tirana's eyes brightened with surprise. Up to now, Michael had relegated her to the most mundane operations as C.O. and had not even held a meeting with her. She was going to complain about it this morning, but it seemed like patience finally won out.

"Can you give me a hint?" she asked.

"It's about the Tuits, and the Osguardian mothers."

"What?"

"Yeah, that's what I said," Michael shrugged. "I need my C.O. on this. Do you think you have the hang of the job yet? I mean...I put you out there so the people could see you and get to trust you like I do. So now it's time to put that trust to a test."

"I'm ready, cousin."

Michael's inside cringed at the word cousin again. "Listen Tirana, I know we are distant cousins, but every time you say it, I feel you are trying to stick a knife in me. I'm not Kulusk and the bloodline that binds us is not Kulusk. So just call me Michael when we are among family and Osguard when we are on duty. I think that will make our relationship go a long way…don't you?"

Tirana stared into Michael's eyes to glean any special meaning in his words, but all she saw was his honest attempt to cross a bridge that no other Osguard had dared crossed before. She slowed down a bit to catch her breath, as did Michael to keep up with her.

"Do you accept me as family?" she posed.

Michael stopped running and she stopped running, he turned toward her and grabbed her by her arms, and looked into her blue eyes. "The bloodline between us is one I wish to forget. The hatred between the Kulusk people and mine is another sore subject. But I am happy as well as the other Osguards to call you and Opel family. You saved our lives and there is no other gift one family member can give another than life." Then he hugged her, allowing their cheeks to touch. The sweat between them mixing like the blood of a blood-oath. "You are not Osguard, you are Ritchen, but as long as there is an Osguard alive, the current House of Ritchen is family…Okay?"

She reached around him and squeezed him. It was the first time she felt accepted in the two months she had been onboard. It was the magical charm Michael seemed to exude and it had caught her in its grasps. "Okay, Michael. I guess I just needed to hear that."

Michael loosened his grip and held both her hands. Several runners passed by, but did not give the scene a second look. They knew their Osguard and they knew the new C.O. was a member of his family, no matter that she was a blonde, blue eyed white girl from Kulusk. Tirana caught the runners out of the corner of her eye and saw the implied acceptance. A tear rolled down her cheek, mixing with the perspiration already glistened on her face.

"Oh! By the way, we're going to have another addition to the family in about seven months."

"What?" she screamed, wiping the tear from her cheek.

"Yup! Michelle is pregnant."

"Great news…How come I'm just finding out about it?" she teased.

Michael didn't know how to answer. Even though he knew Tirana was technically his cousin, he had not told her because until now, he had not considered her part of the family. Their relationship stemmed from what he considered far too distant and tainted bloodlines…the hated the Pathgo side of the family.

Phillip Pathgo, the plantation owner who wanted his ancestors dead, had two sons, who had raped Nausona and Laurona, giving them the bastard children in which he and the other Osguards descendant from. Tirana and the new Kulusk Maxum were descendants of Phillip Pathgo's nieces and Efas and Erif, the Kulusk heirs who were sent to Earth to kill the Osguard children. Efas and Erif married the Pathgo nieces and then converged on the single mission to destroy his ancestors. And up until the revelation of Regina's Holovidpic, he had thought they succeeded in at least killing Betty and Shirley.

Now that he knew differently, his outlook toward Tirana had softened…just a little bit. At this moment, he realized how antisocial he had been to her. "Don't know…I guess it never came up in our conversations," he rationalized to her. "But I tell you what. Stop by for lunch and let Michelle tell you all about it."

"What is there to tell?"

"Girl stuff I guess."

"Is she alright with me stopping by?"

"About damned time," Michelle's voice rang from behind them. Michelle had entered the workout corridor to start her daily walk and happened on to Tirana and Michael. She had thought Michael harsh on Tirana, but she didn't say anything. She didn't want to get into his business as the Osguard. Still she had thrown settle hints about having her over for lunch or dinner. *Lord knows Michael always had Eduardo Sanchez over. It was only civil to have the second in command over for dinner once in awhile.* "Please Tirana, come have lunch with us. I need some family to talk to besides him and the kids," she smiled, kissing Michael on the cheek.

Michael feigned he was mortally wounded by his wife's words. Tirana looked over to Michelle and both shot a bright smile that rivaled the stars outside.

"Okay, that's settled. I'm going to shower. I expect you in my office in an hour. We still have a war to fight," Michael grumbled, jetting down the corridor to finish his run.

"Is he always like that?" Tirana asked.

"Like what?"

"Unpredictable?"

"Unpredictable…no, moody…yes, but you'll get use to it," Michelle said, pulling Tirana by the arm. "You'll get use to it. Come…walk with me for a while. Let me tell you about my husband. I think you should know about Talion."

***

Michael finished his run, showered and was now sitting behind his desk conferring with Tirana. In his hand he held the ARIT tablet outlining *'Operation Expansion.'* It was a simple plan, but again it was bold and time consuming. He did not know if he had the time to execute it properly. He was working on the Tuit timetable and there was nothing he hated more than not being able to control his own timing in a conflict. When the Kulusks attacked Millmum Station, he had turned the tables on them, but he was not sure he would be able to pull another rabbit out of the hat with the Tuits. It all hinged on three factors; one, predicting where the Tuits would hit next; two, adapting and refitting the old flagships; and last, finding and training new Osguards to fly those ships. And while he was doing this, he needed to keep the fracturing alliance together. It would take all his diplomatic skills to work that miracle.

"You are very far-sighted, Michael. This is a beautiful plan. But you need some cooperation from the Tuits to make it work."

Michael looked up at Tirana and knew she only spoke out loud what he had been harboring in his thoughts for the last couple of hours. "But I see no other way…do you?"

Tirana looked at her ARIT tablet copy of the plan. "No, I guess I don't," she shrugged. "But let me offer an amendment."

"Like what?"

"Pialairtic crystals and jorelli plugs!" She saw the surprised look on Michael's face. "Hear me out. I know Pialairtic crystals are highly toxic, but they have a low combustibility and a very low fracture rate. Kulusk has been using the pialairtic crystal for over a hundred years. We have several mining operations in the Kulusk Empire that can supply your ships with enough energy to last several years. This way you can give your supply of dialairtic crystals to the alliance and that should keep them happy for a time. Combine this with jorelli plugs to power your weapons and conversion to taonic circuitry. Your ships will be better than new. Plus I want to introduce the Kwainique cannon to our ships. It is the weapon that turned the tide against Kie."

Michael raised his eyebrow in thoughtful contemplation. "Are you sure we can convert our ships to use this new technology?"

"I am reasonably sure."

"That may be a band-aid fix to our problem. What I really want is to get my hands on that triboleminciс crystal."

"Why? That is more unstable than the dialairtic crystal and I can imagine its fracture rate. Look at what happened to the Tuits when they tried to activate the gate. I'm no scientist, but I bet their tribolemincic crystal had a hand in their destruction. No, Michael, I say use pialairtic crystals and jorelli plugs. My brother would be happy to increase production and supply USSTAP with the energy sources. The Tuits won't be expecting it. Then we can use the tribolemincic crystal against them. We can train our search array to pinpoint its special exhaust and signature. It will help us trace them, find them and eventually eradicate them."

"I'm not sure eradication is our objective," Michael moaned. "I'm not sure what the objective is other than to stop them from what they are doing."

"Fine, we will cross that bridge when we get to it. For now, it is simple. We need to survive."

"Okay! Call your brother. Let him know what is up and I will push this to the other Osguards," he relented. "Heaven help us!" He stretched his arms above his head, turned to look at the stars from his view port and sighed. Even the beauty of space could not calm the uneasiness riding in his stomach. He closed his eyes, searching for peace, but turmoil circled his mind. Then he shot up, startling Tirana a little. "Ready for lunch?" he rushed changing the subject. "Call Opel, let him know what we are thinking and then join me and Michelle for lunch. I am starved."

Chapter 22—Battle Lines

Her perky, perfectly round breasts were tantalizing, teasing and ever so inviting. She straddled him like a bareback horse rider. Her thighs clung to his waist, massaging, pinching and squeezing his manhood with every loving stroke. Musoto's eyes rolled back into his head as the tingling sensation of making love to Mona traveled up his spine to his head and back down toward his toes. He could not feel anything but the wondrous electricity her body was sending into his. He melted into her rapture, little by little, with each stroke. His mouth was agape, gulping for air with every movement of her hips. He was helpless to the point of feebleness. She was in control and he did not mind it. In fact he preferred it.

Making love to Mona was a new experience and sensation each time, the same but somehow different at the same time. She had awakened primordial instincts in him, he never knew existed, feelings his body never experienced and needs he never knew he had. Each time was like another step on the stairway to heaven. The feeling became sweeter with each intimate moment. The blinding lust raged in his body with each touch of her finger, each kiss of her lips, and each lick of her tongue. Her body was perfect, her skin was soft, her eyes were tantalizing and her technique was flawless.

He was in the throes of passion, losing all sense of himself, time and reality. His mind was in a pleasure fog of desire in which he wanted no escape. His body was in the grips of intoxicating delight, craving for more but barely able to handle the love she was giving. He was addicted. She was in his system, in his blood, in his soul. Every thought was of her, every moan was of her and every want was of her.

Then if by queue, she arched her back, hitting another erotic pleasure zone, causing his manhood to pulsate as he tried to fight for control. However, it was a losing battle. Control is not what Mona had in mind. Control was the last thing she had in mind. She wanted to feel him explode inside her like a volcano. She wanted to drain him of his lust. She wanted to empty him. She thrust her hips faster and harder to force the issue. With every thrust, the crazed feeling of desperation inched into Musoto. He could no longer hold his manly explosion, and with a lion's roar, Musoto released his love river loose inside of Mona. She stopped, arched more and swallowed the river inside of her with a gleeful scream. When the flood receded, Mona fell forward unto Musoto's chest, letting her long brunette hair cover his face like a blanket.

For several minutes, they lay in the mixture of their own sweat and love, feeling nothing but each other's heartbeat searching for normalcy. Then, while in deep contemplation that comes with the aftermath of lovemaking, Musoto fell into a deep slumber. Now it was time for Mona to go to work.

She rolled off Musoto, being extra careful not to wake him. She reached into the nightstand top drawer and retrieved the piper. It was similar to a USSTAP MARIT used to transform thought into words. However, it had a more sinister objective. The Tuit piper probed the mind for information. It was an informal way of interrogation. However the subject had to be asleep—not just asleep, but in a pleasurable and exhaustive state of sleep. Sex seemed to be the exact tool to put Musoto in this state.

She snapped the circular red device onto Musoto's forehead, slipped out of bed, stood in front of Musoto, and fingered the scanner in her hand. The scanner was a gray cylinder that fit between her trigger finger and thumb. A green light, representing Musoto's thought patterns, flashed between the scanner and the piper. She held the scanner approximately six inches from his head for three minutes. When she was done, she unsnapped the piper, placed the device and scanner back into the nightstand, and crawled back into bed. She peered at Musoto and brushed back his hair from his forehead. He stirred and turned onto his side. She moved closer, pressing her bare body against his back and wrapped her arms around his waist.

For a second, a twinge of guilt pervaded her mind, but her Tuit duty chased the twinge from her consciousness. Yet another feeling, she couldn't quite shake, remained. She didn't know what it was, or how to explain it. All she knew was she was comfortable with Musoto and something about them felt vaguely right. She shook her head to quiet the thought, but it still nagged her. She studied Musoto while he slept, committing every line, spec and feature of his face to memory. Soon peace surrounded her soul. She laid her head next to his and soon joined him in the joyful slumber.

***

Her yellow cat eyes burned brighter fueled with hatred looking for an outlet. She held the picture of her grandmother, Dina in her hand. She never knew her grandmother, her mother, Rena, was a baby when her mother died in the alien galaxy so long ago—killed by the heinous territorial aggressor known to the Consortium, the Osguards of USSTAP. So many times her mother recounted the story of her grandmother's ship snatched from ultra space by some devilish technology, attacked and eventually destroyed, only to have the pieces sent back through ultra space like chunks of vomit. The recordings found on the ship weren't intact, but they provided the majority of information needed to reconstruct the entire episode.

Since that day, the Consortium's goal was to annihilate the organization that dared cast an unprovoked attack on the peace loving sisters of the Consortium. It was appalling at best, but it was even more treacherous to find out that it was two females, sisters in the spirit, who committed this dastardly action against the Consortium. If they were men, it would almost be understandable, but they were females, who allowed men in their presence—another sin against the Consortium, who were responsible for the deaths of their sisters.

Before the time of recorded history, the men who were once Tuits had spread so much war and destruction that they threatened to annihilate the entire planet. That was when the consortium was founded. The first Daughters of Fire adopted a constitution banning all acts of aggression which, no matter how small, were punishable by death. After the first couple of centuries of rebellious factions trying to overthrow the Consortium, peace reigned within its boundaries. Then the Consortium spread out onto other galaxies and other star clusters, eradicating men, the lolwes of society, for they were natural aggressors and punishing all those, whether female or male, who followed the path of aggression. It was a simple rule, one that every sister learned to live with. It brought peace and harmony to the Consortium, until her grandmother's death.

She put the picture back on her desk, still staring into Dina's eyes as if she could read her thoughts in the picture. The picture caught Dina's warrior demeanor. In her eyes her soul shone through like a royal robe. She wore the furl on her forehead like a crown, exuding regality with a simple twist of her head. She was the First Daughter of Fire, the chairwoman of the Consortium, the leader of her people, and she was snuffed out like an animal for no practical reason. Even if there were a reason, it would not be a good enough reason for the death Dina experienced.

It was Rina's sworn duty to avenge her grandmother's death. Her mother Rena tried several times to put a plan into action, but the Consortium said they had to study the enemy more. They could not go in without any intelligence. Well it has been almost a century of studying the enemy and she was tired of it. She had trained for almost forty years for this moment, and now she was more than ready, she was hungry, she was trained, she was equipped and most of all she was willing. She obtained the most powerful position in the battle and she was not going to blow it. She wanted to taste the blood of the First Osguard on her lips as she twisted his head from his dead body. She wanted to kill all the Osguards with her bare hands, but the First Osguard was the symbolic kill, because it was a First Osguard, Laurona, who set in motion the plan that killed Dina. It was the First Osguard who had to die first.

She wanted him to suffer. She wanted to ruin USSTAP, make it a poor shell of the mighty organization it thought it was. Then she wanted to shame the Osguards, discredit them in the face of the other governments. Then she wanted to kill the Osguards, one by one, starting with the First Osguard. Finally, she wanted to destroy all the governments associated with USSTAP, kill their men and usurp their women into the Consortium, like her ancestors did so long ago.

It had been eons since the Consortium indulged in such action and she was on the cutting edge of it now. She knew her grandmother would be proud. She knew her mother would be proud. She wanted to pass on more to her child when it came time for her to bear one. She was nearing the upper age limit, the age a warrior puts down her sword and begins a life of rearing a child. She purposely chose not to rear a child during her warrior age. She wanted no hindrances blinding her on her quest for revenge. However, soon she would have to pay her obligation to the Consortium and propagate her line.

The gene splice cloning procedure with surrogate lolwes the Tuits adopted to propagate the race was almost too neat. It was a medical procedure involving artificial insemination. She would have to carry the child for eight cycles. Then raise her to be a productive member of the Consortium. Then her service would be ended and she would be offered her choice of euthanasia methods. It would be her final duty to the Consortium, to not be a strain on the system. Once her usefulness was complete, so was her life. Therefore, she realized this was her last chance to avenge her grandmother's death. The taste was so bitter sweet in her mouth. She licked her lips several times rejoicing in the spirit of the warrior realizing her last battle.

The buzzer rang. She turned toward the door as if she could see who it was through the door. She took a deep cleansing breath, and then pushed the button on her desk. The video screen showed it was the First Daughter of Fire, her rival since childhood and Isha's granddaughter, Tisha of Solwick. Tisha and her mother, Esha had always secretly blamed Dina for the incident. Dina was the Command Daughter in charge of the mission and her mother told Tisha that if Isha were in charge, they would have found a way back home. However, the evidence was so overwhelming that Dina did everything properly; they decided to keep their suspicions to themselves.

Unfortunately, Tisha managed to be promoted to First Daughter, and Rina knew it was her who pushed for the challenge she suffered earlier. Moreover, she also knew Tisha was against her becoming a Daughter of Fire, but was either outvoted by the other daughters or it was a condition of the challenge. Either way, she knew Tisha's visit was not social.

Rina buzzed her in. The door vanished allowing the First Daughter to walk in. Once she was in, the door appeared again, closing the two rivals in the room. Rina knew she still had to pay the proper respect to the First Daughter, even though it sickened her to her stomach. So she stood in front of her desk, waiting for Tisha to speak first.

"Well sister, how are you doing?" she opened with a smirk.

"Fine First Daughter…I am doing just fine," Rina faked with a smile. "And to what do I owe this visit?"

"The first cycle is almost up, and it will be time for you to use the rhetonic cannon once more as we agreed. I have come to speak with you about the necessity of such a maneuver."

"First Daughter, you yourself said I must have the Consortium's best interest at heart and the Daughters blessed my use of it. Why now do you come and try to change the ruling?"

"I am not trying to change the ruling. No Daughter can change the ruling of the Consortium, not even the First Daughter. All I ask is, are you sure it is necessary?"

"Yes, First Daughter, it is necessary. The original plan was flawed for two simple reasons. One, the Daughters of Fire were not at the helm, we left that to the Kulusks. And two, we had no bite. Last meeting solved both flaws. I am in command of the invasion and the rhetonic cannon provide the bite. Rina, the Sixth Daughter of Fire, stepped closer to Tisha, so their eyes would meet. She wanted her message to be clear. "Yes, First Daughter, I will use the rhetonic cannon in three days and it will provide the necessary punch we need to succeed in five cycles."

"Oh…I see!" Tisha exclaimed, lowering her hood and allowing her shiny blond hair to drape over her shoulders in a regal way.

“Are you sure?” Rina challenged. “Because if you aren’t, I can provide an addendum to the strategic plan the Consortium has approved.”

“No, sister. That won’t be necessary. I understand the premise to your strategy. And I must say, it is a very optimistic premise. I hope you can deliver.”

Rina recognized the threat in her words and in her tone. She started to react, but thought it not wise. She had already pushed it as far as she wanted to push with Tisha. She stepped back around to her desk. Looked up at Tisha and smiled, “Kiza, I can…I can deliver a victory and I can deliver it on your timetable.” Then she changed from a light-hearted expression to a quizzical expression. “First Daughter,” she called.

“Yes!”

“Now that I am a Daughter of Fire, I wonder if you can answer a question that has been plaguing me for a while.”

“I will try!”

“Why after all these years of our reconnaissance and planning, the Consortium places a strict timetable for victory? I mean it has been almost a century since the incident. Why rush now?”

“Precisely the point, sister…precisely the point. It has been too long. We need to put this to bed now. No more wasting of time. We need our revenge while we are still alive. Neither I nor the other daughters are willing to push this off to our children. I am sure you feel the same way.”

Rina lowered her head in contemplation. Yes, she too wanted a quick resolution, but she was not too sure on the timetable the Daughters had set. “Ahem,” she mumbled. Then she picked up the con tablet from her desk, containing her plan. “Well First Daughter, if that is all, I have some work to get to.”

“Oh, of course. I see!”

Rina opened the door, giving Tisha a more evident clue. She turned toward the door and looked out into the hallway. She was not moving yet, which irritated Rina more.

“Is there anything else?” Rina asked.

“Not now, but maybe later,” Tisha huffed. She placed her hood back on and then exited the room, allowing her golden robe to drape behind her like a cape.

When the door appeared shut, Rina sat back at her desk and began mulling over the plan, flipping through the electronic pages on her con tablet. However, her concentration was not on the tablet, her mind was focused on what just transpired between her and Tisha. Soon she found she had flipped through eight electronic pages without digesting a word. She closed the tablet lid and shook her head. Then with a burst of rage, she threw the con tablet against the door, shattering it into three large pieces.

"Maug! Maug! Maug!" she screamed, calling the First Daughter a bitch in Tuit.

***

Her broad luscious lips framed her sweet, attractive and sexually inviting smile. The mahogany color of her skin uniquely highlighted her light brown eyes. Her dark black shoulder length hair, with a bang curled over her forehead framed the smooth round features of her face. Recently promoted USSTAP agent, Lieutenant Stelana Rican, walked down the sidewalk on Connecticut Ave in Washington D.C. like she owned the town. Her confidence washed her like a halo of light. Her tight black pants hugging her shapely waist and hips, along with her red cotton sweater that highlighted her broad shoulders and muscular torso exalted her beauty even more. Heads, both male and female, subconsciously turned and followed her as she passed.

However she did not notice the stir she was causing. She was walking on a cloud. Her mind was focused on one thing. In her young career, she had met and worked personally with one Osguard, Juanita Genesis-Clark, and now she was working directly for Michael Genesis. His marching order was what was on her mind. She also was on a high from his visit.

The First Osguard, the Protector of Millmum Galaxy, the Chairman of the Osguard Senate, the undisputed leader of all of USSTAP, came to her apartment in Richmond Virginia to speak to her. When all he had to do was summon her and she would have traveled the universe to attend an audience with him. He was so impressed with her performance during the Kulusk invasion of Osguard Gardens and her work for Osguard fifty-five; he knew she was the one to handle this assignment as well. Of course it was on Juanita's recommendation, but it was still a pleasure to have such a reputation so early in a career.

She sashayed across the street into a little coffee shop. It was like an old movie. All heads seemed to turn her way as she stepped across the entrance threshold. The normal murmur of voices seemed to quiet down and she seemed to become the center of attention. She looked up and dismissed the phenomenon as her imagination going wild. She moved to a table near the outer window and started perusing the menu. It took several seconds, but once Stelana allowed her Sixana training to kick in she realized the coffee shop was not so little. It was quaint, but not little. It was a high profile shop, where politicians, lobbyist and all sorts of special political makers and breakers seemed to hang out between making the world stop and go.

She now knew this was not the right place to conduct the business she had in mind. She felt a bit ashamed for not checking it out when he suggested they meet there. She wanted to meet in a neutral place. However, she did not know the city that well and she did not have any suggestions, so she deferred to his judgment. *First mistake!* Suddenly, Michael's paranoia did not seem so out of place. This didn't feel right.

So she took out her PARIT, shaped to look like a cell phone, connected the wireless earpiece to her ear and pretended to make a phone call. In actuality she was using the PARIT's search array. It reported several hits of electronic ease dropping devices and acoustic gain devices in the area. Someone knew about her meeting and had an array of spy devices to capture her conversation.

She felt foolish. She had urged Michael to give him another chance. Upon her urging, Michael decided to include FBI Agent Anthony Musoto's services in this little endeavor, but his gut told him it was the wrong thing to do. He had warned her to be careful, which she did not heed until now. The fury of betrayal swelled inside her. Her Chaktun blood boiled, making the palms of her hands sweat.

She jumped up and moved toward the exit. She felt the eyes of several patrons watching her. Now she knew it was not her imagination. There were people watching. She shook her head in disgust. When she reached the exit, she turned around to do a visual search of the area. She wanted to mentally record the patrons in the room, in case she ran up against them again. This way she would be ready. She stepped backwards, swung around and bumped right into Musoto entering the café.

She looked up into his eyes and searched his soul. She could feel the deceit flowing from his eyes. This only raised her ire even more. Her smile changed into a shear look of repugnance.

"You bastard!" she growled. Then with the pain of betrayal and the fume of hate, she slapped Musoto across the face as hard as she could. Her Chaktun strength soared in the slap, pushing Musoto across a table, like he was hit with a right cross from a heavyweight boxer. "Michael was right! You can't be trusted." She grunted and then rushed out of the café. Leaving Musoto somewhat dazed and nursing what would later become a swollen cheek.

In the corner of the room, behind a large pair of sunglasses and a scarf woven around her blonde hair, the Republican Representative from Texas, the House Majority Leader and the Tuit Commander of Earth's evasion force, Joyce Thelma Eldridge, smiled. *This was too simple,* she thought.

A smirk developed on her lips as she stood and moved toward the exit. The clamor from the patrons talking about what they had just witnessed still buzzed in air. It was like applause to her. The scene she directed was so perfect so ideal she could not believe it. She always thought humans were easily manipulated, but she never figured a USSTAP agent would be. She walked up to Musoto, whose embarrassment was still showing on his face and gave him her must sympathetic smile. “Lover’s quarrel?” she smugly asked.

Musoto looked up at the seemingly compassionate patron, trying to hide his shame and still massaging the sting from his cheek, “No ma’am…not at all. I would call it a simple misunderstanding.”

“Hmm!” she responded. “That’s what all men say.”

He jerked back from the response and shook his head. Immediately, he knew this woman was not the compassionate soul that she originally appeared to be, but she was a male hating busy body that found some perverse pleasure in his situation. He studied her up and down, not seeing pass her big round sunglasses or the floral scarf wrapped around her head. Something about her was out of place. She seemed like a woman straight out of the fifties or sixties.

His gaze made Eldridge uncomfortable. Her senseless bravado had just made her a standout in a nondescript crowd. Now, she feared Musoto might recognize her, even with her face partially covered. After all she was no stranger in Washington, and very recognizable by the media. Why would an intelligent FBI agent not recognize her?

She lowered her head and raised her hand to her mouth. “Well…if you would excuse me. I have things I need to do,” she lied, pushing her way pass Musoto. She scampered out of the café and turned right, out of sight.

Musoto’s gaze remained fixed on the last spot she was visible from. There was an uncertain familiarity about the woman that caused a chill to run down his spine. He couldn’t put his finger on it, but it was there. Then he turned back around. Most of the patrons had finish gawking at him and had returned to their personal business. However, a few patrons, with nothing more interesting to look at, still watched him like they were watching a soap opera on T.V., wondering what would happen next and afraid to turn away, because they may miss something.

Musoto had an urge to flip them off, but stopped as his elbow bent forward. He just nodded at the few spectators and proceeded out the door. He turned to the left to see if Stelana was in view. She was not. Then he turned right to see if the strange lady from the past was still in view. She was gone also.

“Damn!” Musoto growled.

***

Outside the coffee shop, and across the street, two figures stepped from the building’s shadow. The first figure, an Asian Pacific female, stood about five feet, two inches, with black shiny full shoulder length hair, wearing black slacks, blue top covered by a white mesh wool pullover sweater, held a cell phone connected to a wireless earpiece, similar to Stelana’s. The second figure, another Asian Pacific female, with long hair that flowed over her shoulders like a blanket, was a little taller and thinner than her partner, wearing a black mini-skirt, knee high black boots and a white button down shirt. She also carried a cell phone with an earpiece.

"Kim, you take the woman. I'll stay with Musoto."

"Tiah!"

Chapter 23—Searching

The Steeple, the home of the Chaktun Maxum, was a large forty thousand square foot, six-story, one hundred-room stone palace sitting on forty acres of prime green grass. Gardens littered the landscape, displaying an assortment of brightly colored flowers. The East Garden, the famous escape route, Laurona and Nausona took when they escaped the Kulusk attack, which now contained the prominent USSTAP wall of honor, greeted the huge orange sun, known as Gen. Gen was about one third bigger than Earth's sun. Chaktun, almost twice as big as Earth, was the third planet in the Gen Solar System.

Even though USSTAP was not a sovereign state, it enjoyed the amenities of one. It had political stature, economic power, social status and a strong military. However it lacked a true natural territory. Its territory was all of outer space. The mass of nothingness, that somehow became the lifeline of the entire universe. However, this solar system, this planet, this palace was the hidden heart of USSTAP's power. It was the only natural landscape, the only God-made territory the Osguards could call home.

Their dead were honored here, no matter from what planet or what galaxy. When the Kulusk attack endangered Capitol Station, the Osguards evacuated all noncombatants, including their families to Chaktun's Steeple Palace. And when hostilities ceased with Kulusk, it was at the Steeple where USSTAP signed the final peace accords. Holding the ceremony at the Steeple was a political gesture, because everyone knew USSTAP was a natural extension of the Chaktun Republic. Of course the Chaktun Republic had no control over the association.

This fact annoyed the current Chaktun Maxum, Reppus Osguard. Even though he enjoyed the special relationship Chaktun had with USSTAP, he was aware of USSTAP's dominating supremacy, which he thought should be Chaktun. It was like having the child parenting the father. It wasn't natural…it wasn't right.

Now Michael Genesis, his Earth born cousin, the leader of USSTAP was here to visit him and talk to him about something important to both of them. It was a favor he was calling upon due to their blood relationship. Michael had never called upon him in that fashion before. So he was now intrigued, intrigued enough to rearrange his business for the day and see the First Osguard.

Reppus looked out of his office window, gazing upon the setting sun. The mastery of the orange fiery glow, especially at sunset, made this part of the day the most beautiful. The yellow clouds seemed to dance in the sky, almost in celebration of the sun's retreat. The sun's rays sparkled in the atmosphere like diamonds in the sky. The heat from the day was dissipating, allowing the cool breeze from the east to ride through carrying with it the fragrances of the eastern garden flowers. The fragrance was similar to a balanced mixture of lilacs, roses and magnolia blossoms.

The beep from his ARIT rocked him from his daily cleansing ritual. He glanced at the monitor and saw it announced Michael's arrival in orbit. It will be a matter of minutes before he would step to the conference room. He acknowledged the signal and sat down in his chair with his hands folded under his chin. Curiosity ruled him, but he also had to play the diplomatic game. No matter how comfortable the leaders of USSTAP felt at the Steeple, it was still his home and his domain. He was going to make Michael wait on him.

However, as soon as he made up his mind to have Michael wait on him, the familiar hum of a gate portal filled the air. The magic door lifted and the white light of inner space poured into the office. He forgot that he had passed the code to drop the chromerion field around Steeple when he acknowledged the signal. Michael had taken the opportunity, used the search array, pinpointed Reppus' location and fed those coordinates into the gate portal to step to. Thus Michael stepped out of the light and into Reppus' office, much to Reppus' irritation.

"Reppus!" Michael greeted as the gate portal closed behind him.

Reppus stood, "Michael? I thought we were going to meet in the conference room?"

"I know, but I needed to speak to you right away and in private," Michael responded taking the seat right across from Reppus. "Besides, this is personal, not business and I don't have time to go through the pissing contest you always make me go through when I visit. I have a universal war I'm fighting…I mean we are fighting. Besides, you know, I'm not one to stand on ceremony."

"But I am," corrected Reppus. "I am the Maxum of the Chaktun Republic and there is a certain protocol to follow, especially between heads of state."

"Well Reppus, you are correct. You are a head of state. As for me, I have no state to head. I think of myself as sort of a CEO to a large business conglomerate. Therefore, time is money and money is time. I can't waste either. Speaking of which, let me tell you the real reason I am here."

Reppus huffed in dissatisfaction, but the insult Michael had levied on him was done privately and in his mind did not need a response…for now. He just tacked it on the back of several other issues he had with USSTAP for discussion at a later time.

"What do you want dear cousin?" Reppus put forth, trying to defuse his own anger.

Michael handed him the corynx crystal. "I want you to view this first and then we can speak."

Reppus took the crystal and without hesitation, put it into the HVP slot in his desk. His HVP screen slid from the ceiling in front of the desk and Ortho's image appeared once more. It took about two hours to view the HVP. It was Michael's third time viewing it. The first time was about a week ago, when Jarod brought it to the Holographic Senate Conference. The second was when he assigned Stelana Rican the task of finding Shirley and Betty's lineage and now.

When it was over, Reppus looked at Michael with genuine shock. Michael watched Reppus throughout the showing and concluded Reppus was just as much in the dark as he was about the entire episode.

"Did you authenticate this?" Reppus challenged.

"It came from a reliable source…it came from the House of Chting."

Reppus knew his challenge of the events had just died, because there was no other house that held such honor in both the Chaktun Republic and USSTAP than the house of Chting, except for the House of Wtong of course. He smacked his lips and sighed. "Interesting HVP," he commented.

"That's all you have to say?"

"What else can I say? It gives us some insight on what we are dealing with."

"Forget that. I want to know what happened to the kids."

"What kids?"

"The ones Laurona and Nausona adopted."

Reppus rolled his eyes to the left and sighed once more. "Why?"

"First of all they are Osguards. We are legally bound to offer them their rightful place in USSTAP."

"I don't think so," Reppus snapped back. "By Chaktun law, adopted kids are banned from inheriting stature prior to bloodline. You are the bloodline; therefore, they are not entitled to any seat as an Osguard for USSTAP."

"As you say, dear cousin, that is Chaktun law. I am not Chaktun…I'm American. And USSTAP is not Chaktun either. Therefore your archaic law does not apply."

"But your laws were founded based on Chaktun law."

"Founded yes…copied no. The senate last week overwhelmingly approved Jarod Stone's bill to amend the inheritance law. Under USSTAP law, the descendants of George, Kelly, Sue Frank, Bobby, Marcus and Mary are rightful heirs of the USSTAP dynasty."

The words, *rightful heir of the USSTAP dynasty*, bristled at Reppus' nerve. In his mind, USSTAP was not a dynasty like the Maxums. However, now he was throwing around the word as if he was a statesman representing a sovereign state.

Michael read his face and realized he was getting nowhere fast. He needed a subtle and quick change in strategies. "Reppus, we need more Osguards to train, to take over the battle if something happens to us. The next generation of Osguards is not ready to train. They are too young. We are in a war!"

"And this has never occurred to you before today?"

"We never faced an enemy like this before today."

"Well the Akaher Osguard line is ready to fill those shoes. And we are of the same blood. Akaher and Vedar were brothers."

"Reppus, you don't have to recite the family lineage to me. I know all that. But the agreement Akaher made with Laurona and Nausona was his line will rule the Republic and their lines would run USSTAP and neither the two shall mix. I have no claim to your throne and you have no claim to USSTAP. Besides, placing your line into USSTAP would blur the line of government intrusion."

Reppus stood and stretched his arm. Michael remained seated, but kept his gaze on his distant cousin.

"I know that," Reppus muttered, "but you can change that as well. As long as the direct line is not involved—I mean me and my children—then it should be alright."

Michael feigned thought on his words, but he was thinking of a way to say no. "I see your point," he began. "You mean like your uncles' or aunts' children, Osguards who will never have a chance to rule the Republic."

"Yes…yes…exactly!" Reppus snapped.

"But don't they still have allegiance to you?"

"They can be released from that allegiance, just like Laurona and Nausona were."

For a moment Michael considered the offer. It was sound on the surface, but he knew the Parliament would reject it. The main balancing chip that USSTAP held was that it had no allegiance to any government. The Osguards came from a barbaric world that knew little of their existence, which made the others feel safe. It wasn't always like that. Chaktun natives ran USSTAP until they accepted power fifteen years ago. So Reppus' suggestion rang of merit to him for a second.

"Reppus, it's not me or the other Osguards you have to convince. It will be the Universal Parliament you'll have to convince," he countered.

"Did you get their approval on the adopted Osguards?"

Michael took a deep breath and let it out a slow sigh. "No, not as of yet."

"Good, when you present your case, I will present mine."

"Fair enough," Michael agreed. "Now do I have a case?"

Reppus opened his left desk drawer, pulled out an ARIT crystal and handed it to Michael. "These are the living adopted descendants."

Michael took the crystal and shook his head. "You've known all along."

"It was no secret. It just wasn't widely publicized. Besides, every Maxum since my grandfather has kept an eye on them. We aren't total barbarians. The mother Osguards left them monetarily well off, because there were no bloodlines around. They just could not inherit the throne of USSTAP."

"This makes no sense!" Michael exasperated. "Why were we kept in the dark?"

"It seems Ortho already answered your question on the HVP."

"Fine, why did you keep it a secret?"

"I don't know," Reppus said with a smirk. "I guess it was because I knew something you didn't and it gave me a feeling of…"

"Power?"

"Maybe!"

You bastard, Michael thought, shooting a challenging stare at Reppus.

Chapter 24—Defensive

At its height, the D'Ardin Empire spread over a third of the Siryman Galaxy and covered fifty thousand light years of space. However, since the inception of USSTAP as the galaxy's vanguard, the D'Ardin Empire shattered into small planetary states with collective ties to one another. The D'Ardin king, the Kinsile, still controlled the governmental affairs of D'Ardin Prime and D'Ardin Two. Two thousand, one hundred and ten inhabitant planets he once ruled were now independent, but still answered to the Kinsile's sphere of influence. The people of the empire were originally appalled at the Kinsile's decision, but once the economic prosperity the Osguards promised came to fruition, the rhetoric died.

Now for the first time in three universal years, the flagship of the Osguard presence in the galaxy sailed in the heart of what was once called the D'Ardin Empire. The *USSTAP Galaxy Protector Gentry*, flanked by the galaxy protectors *S'Coril* and *P'Togi* along with eight galaxy cruisers scorched through the heavens at MOP sixty toward the D'Ardin solar system in sector ten. On its bridge, Jarod sat staring at the ARIT track displayed between the navigator's position and the pilot's.

He massaged his chin in an awkward attempt to wash his worry away. It was a long shot in his opinion, but it was a shot they had to take. Michael's *'Operation Expansion'* was either a house of cards, ready to fall and take the known universe with it, or it was a brilliant strategic plan, formed out of insightful deduction, grit experience, and divine intuition. Michael was batting one hundred so far and if it was his character or luck, he liked the odds with Michael. However, the knot in his stomach was still tightening with each parsec of space that ticked by.

He knew the other fifty-nine Osguards were doing the same thing in their galaxies, rushing to protect the most influential government under their care. For most, the decision on which government fit the category was easy, but for Jarod, it was a tossup between the D'Ardin Empire and the Yo Republic. Even though the Yo Republic was the home to USSTAP Siryman Galaxy Academy, and the USSTAP's unofficial home in the galaxy, like Chaktun was USSTAP's unofficial home in the Millmum Galaxy, Gail French, his Centurion of Security and the most tactical sound mind he has ever met, convinced him the D'Ardin Empire was the most likely target.

She had hypothesized the Tuit's intelligence was limited and could only make decisions based on charts and space traffic. From that perspective, the D'Ardin Empire made an attractive target. It once owned the largest real estate in the galaxy, and it still had a powerful influence over that real estate. So if Michael's thoughts were correct, and the next target was to destabilize and splinter the governmental allegiances to USSTAP in the galaxies, then the D'Ardin Empire was a prime target. If it seceded from the alliance the other two thousand one hundred and nine planets would follow suit. If it were destroyed, the governments of those planets would blame USSTAP for not protecting the empire and secede to form their own defense.

In theory, it made perfect sense, but in practice, there were too many variables. What if the Tuit's intelligence was not as limited as they thought? It still baffled Jarod how the Tuits knew of the dialairtic crystal mines? And how the hell did they contact the Kulusks? They must have spies in the organization. *But where?*

Michael had thought of that as well, and had ordered a full DNA scan in all USSTAP facilities in Millmum Galaxy and suggested the other Osguards do the same. The scan would take some time to complete on all facilities, but the initial reports from the capitol stations reported negative for the unique Tuit DNA. Right now, Jarod's thought was the Kulusks provided much of the intelligence to the Tuits, if not all. With the Kulusk threat eliminated, the Tuit's intelligence should be dated and unusable. The one question was, how much did the Kulusks know about operations outside the Millmum Galaxy? *Apparently enough to be a threat,* he concluded.

"D'Ardin Solar System…dead ahead," reported the navigator.

"Signal the fleet…slow to standard approach speed," Jarod chimed. "Once within range, signal the Kinsile of our approach."

"Tiah!" the communications officer responded from his right.

Regina, who was sitting next to him, stood and walked past the navigator to the ladder leading to the control bridge. She turned and stepped down the ladder. She then walked behind the last row of controllers, in charge of the long-range search array. "All sensors…all scanners," she ordered. "We are looking for any surges in trachion, restion or benion radiation. Also I want one of you tracking for triboleminicic exhaust." The flurry of nods told her she did not have to repeat the order. Her troops knew the importance of the mission and each had their eyes glued to their screens.

Outside the USSTAP fleet slowed through the speed scale, stepping through MOP, hyperlight, hypersonic and finally sonic speeds, as they entered the solar system. The D'Ardin Solar system contained eleven planets, but the first two planets, D'Ardin Prime and D'Ardin Two were of equal distance from the sun, just on perpendicular orbits. Because their rotation and orbital travel were almost identical, the planets never crossed. It was one of the mathematical miracles of God. However, this miracle made it difficult for Jarod to defend the home planets.

"The Kinsile has responded," the communications officer announced.

"On bridge viewer," Jarod ordered, standing and moving between the pilot and navigator station.

As soon as he reached the screen, the Kinsile's image appeared. He was a gray-haired man, about eighty Earth-years old. His face was winkled from time or from the strain of rule. Jarod did not know which one, nor did he care. He studied the Kinsile for a few seconds, giving him his most charming smile.

"Osguard," the Kinsile called, "To what do I owe the honor of your presence?"

"My dear Kinsile, I am sorry for the intrusion, but security demanded it."

"Security?"

"Yes, security. It is our contention that your system may be the next Tuit target."

The Kinsile's smile told Jarod he had just received a diplomatic barb. Yet his smile remained unchanged. His prejudice against the perceived lifestyle of these people had caused him to neglect his diplomatic duty of visiting the Kinsile. Like B'Kailine, the Kinsile never made it a point to question his actions, or lack of action when it came to the D'Ardin Empire.

The remorse in his heart begged for forgiveness. However this was not the time or the place to recant his diplomatic history. "We are here to see that does not happen in accordance with our treaty," he announced in hopes it would confirm his sincerity to the situation.

"Well Osguard, I am sorry it took a threat for you to visit our fair system. Yet, I do appreciate your concern. What makes you think we are the target for the next attack?"

"We have our sources, in which we really don't have time to discuss," he lied. "I implore you to go to your highest self-defense posture and be ready for anything. We will park our ships in stealth ten in a protective barrier surrounding your system."

"I see," the Kinsile whispered, "How long?"

"As long as it takes, Kinsile…as long as it takes."

***

Gate Portal Room One, onboard the *USSTAP Galaxy Protector Neraka*, beamed again with white light as the invisible door opened. Michael's six-foot, two-inch boxer built shadow seemed to consume the light. It was like an angelic aura surrounding him, but also highlighting him. He stepped through the light onto the portal. The door closed behind him and he stepped down onto the floor.

Tirana greeted him with a nod, "How was your trip, sire?"

"I guess I got what I wanted, but I didn't like how I got it."

"Explain?"

Michael looked at her and started to let his frustration spill out, but he was aware of the gate portal operator in the room. He shook his head. "I'll explain it over a Jack-n-Coke later this evening."

"It's a deal, but I'll have a Kulusk scotch."

"Tirana, I don't think we have stocked up on many Kulusk items yet. I'm not sure the bar has Kulusk scotch."

"If it is alright, I'll bring my own. My brother sent some over with the last shipment of my things."

Michael shook his head in disbelief, grabbed his C.O. by the shoulder and led her through the doors. "Tirana, you are a trip girl!"

"What?"

"Nothing! Yes, it's okay. You are the second in command. If you want Kulusk scotch, then you shall have Kulusk scotch."

The two walked down the corridor and boarded a coaster. "Command Bridge!" Tirana ordered. The two sat down on the red cushion circular seat that ran along the wall.

"So Tirana, how does it feel to be the first Kulusk to orbit Chaktun and not be attacking her?"

Tirana took a deep breath, debating how to answer the question. She looked into Michael's eyes, trying to hide the pain from the unintentional insult. She considered the remark bordering on prejudicial. "Michael, I am a Kulusk wearing a USSTAP uniform. I am a Kulusk who just pledged my allegiance to USSTAP. I am a Kulusk outsider in a USSTAP universe. Therefore everything I do will be new, strange and awkward. I would hope I had your confidence and your support in making the transition. Questions like that do not help."

Michael stared into her blue eyes and saw the hurt his innocent question had produced. He did not quite understand it, but he made the analogy. Her situation was comparable to Jackie Robinson breaking into Major League Baseball, or the Little Rock students walking into an all white high school. Being the first at anything, in the face of deep prejudices was not easy, and without family support it was damned near impossible. Her family support system was on Kulusk. Michelle, the kids and he were the only family she really had. So acting like a stranger, asking discriminating questions only alienated them from each other.

"I see," he responded. "I'm sorry, Tirana. I wasn't thinking. I was just curious about how you felt. I thought it would be an emotional experience and I just wanted you to know I am here, if you need to talk. I know being the first Kulusk in USSTAP has to be trying. But I am here to make it easy. I'm your sire and your mentor. Actually, you have many mentors. All of us want to see you succeed. You and I have the same blood flowing in us. Even though it is not the bloodline I wish to recognize, it still exists. And these few weeks of us working together has made me realize, it isn't the bloodline that makes us family. It is our common belief, our common needs, our common wants, and our common love for peace that makes us family. All of USSTAP is a family. You are part of USSTAP. You are part of a big family, not just my family, and not just the Osguard family, but the USSTAP family. So don't feel like you are a stranger. You are now USSTAP."

Deep down Michael was getting tired of being Tirana's cheerleader. He, as well as the other Osguards, had accepted Tirana and her brother almost immediately after they provided the antidote to the Terinolice virus, and helped destroy Kie Ritchen's reign. However, for some reason, Tirana still felt uncomfortable, despite his best efforts. "Listen Tirana," he announced before he knew it. Now he had started to speak his inner thoughts and Tirana was very attentive. He didn't know whether to continue or not. Then his instincts told him to continue.

"Tirana, I know this is new to you. I have opened up all that I can. But it's time for you to step up to the plate. Stop second-guessing my intentions. You are my second in command. You are my Centurion of Operations. You bypassed several training schedules, skipped USSTAP academy indoctrination because you've proven yourself in battle. No one has ever done that before. It took a unanimous vote in the Osguard Senate to approve that…and it was accomplished on the first vote. I am happy with that. But what I'm not happy with is the constant maintenance you seem to need. You are my family, distant I agree, but still family. But most of all, you are USSTAP. You are like us. Most of the Osguards, I wouldn't consider family except for the fact we are Osguards. So under that same umbrella, the USSTAP umbrella, we are family as well. I can live with it. Can you?"

Tirana's eyes tightened as the words washed over her. She didn't know what to expect. She didn't know where the Osguard's outburst was going to lead. She just listened and tried to refrain from speaking anymore.

"I have cousins, I have Osguards. And like I said this morning, I am happy to welcome you into my family circle. But what I need is a competent C.O. and a competent friend. I want you to be that more than my distant cousin. Understood?"

Tirana nodded, as a strange feeling burst inside her. She did understand. What she was searching for was acceptance. She thought it was acceptance as Michael's family member, but that wasn't it at all. What she was searching for was acceptance as Michael's second in command. What Michael just said constituted that acceptance. It was her first chewing out, but that was what she wanted. It showed Michael cared and wasn't stepping around her. He wanted her to succeed.

The door opened to the command bridge corridor. They stepped out and turned right. They walked up to the stairs separating the command bridge from the control bridge. Then Michael stopped, turned toward his office door. "Tirana, I want you to organize the fleet for the protection of the Chaktun Republic. I will be in my office executing the second part of Operation Expansion."

Tirana wanted to ask if the Osguard was sure, but decided against it. She nodded, "Tiah!"

Michael disappeared into his office and Tirana moved up the stairs to the command bridge. She stepped through the doors, handed the sentry her delta belt and moved toward the Osguard command chair.

Timothy Mann, the Centurion of Engineering was at his position to the left of the Osguard command chair. He looked up at Tirana and gave her a small smile, "What's next?"

"We take up the defensive," she replied. Then she pulled out her ARIT tablet and read it. She had four galaxy protectors, ten galaxy cruisers and several small scout ships. She flipped through Michael's battle plan that she helped build and studied it for several seconds. Then she put the tablet down, and took a deep breath. "Comm…deploy the fleet, stealth ten, baker five-five defensive position. All sensors…all scanners…full spread," she ordered. "We are looking for any surges in trachion, restion or benion radiation. Also I want every ship searching for tribolemincic exhaust."

"You're getting the hang of this," Tim whispered.

Tirana regarded Tim for a moment, shot him a smile and picked up the tablet once more. Then she turned to Tim, "How's the new weapons upgrade?"

"Your Kwainique cannon has been uploaded onto all ships. It was a simple upgrade. I especially like your taonic circuitry and the unique use of jorelli plugs as a power source. Do you think the jorelli plugs can be used for other weapons?"

"Eventually, but after the Kwainique cannon proves itself, your coronet guns and pagenay will become obsolete."

"Lord knows we have been relying on the pagenay for over two centuries. I feel it is time to upgrade to another system," Tim admitted. "I thought the coronet gun and the Asher torpedo would replace the pagenay. But the versatility of the weapon has kept it as the USSTAP weapon of choice."

"Those who fail to change with technology will die with history," she quoted from a Kulusk historian.

"Well I sent the specs to all ships with instructions on how to add the weapon to the arsenal. So now we have fore and aft pagenays, forward coronet guns and Asher Torpedoes and fore and aft K-cannons. They are all tied into the Defense Officer's console. It was easy to replicate and easy to install. But how much do you want to bet the pagenay will still be our mainstay."

"You sound upset about that, Tim."

"Not upset, just a little annoyed. We are getting our butts kicked by women with some planetary killing weapon of mass destruction and we want to fight them with a two hundred year old weapon system. It reminds me of the Indian wars in the United States. The Native American used bows and arrows against rifles and bullets. The Native Americans became a force to be reckoned with when they switched to rifles. The pagenay is our bow and arrow in my opinion."

Tirana smiled, "Even a bow and arrow can kill, if used correctly."

Tim was taken aback a little. "Didn't you say, *'Those who fail to change with technology will die with history?'* Whose side are you on?"

She turned back to the view port screen showing the Chaktun's northern hemisphere, never losing her smile but adding a slight twinkle in her eye. She placed her hands on her hips, and with the pride of a mountain lion answered, "USSTAP's side, centurion…I am on USSTAP's side."

Chapter 25—Surveillance

She was tired, cold and a little bit frustrated. She had followed Musoto the entire day, since the coffee shop incident. She was not sure she had obtained any useful information. Now it was dinnertime, and Musoto was on the road, traveling on I-95 South. It appeared he was heading toward Richmond...but why? Or was he heading toward Osguard Gardens once more? According to Stelana's report, Musoto had already visited the gardens and found it empty. For the second time in four months, the inhabitants of the gardens were evacuated to Millmum Station. The First Osguard called it a precaution after the assassination attempt on him in Connecticut.

However, for Lieutenant Gloria Magma of USSTAP Security Corps it was more than a precaution, it was a strategic move. She knew the family was more important to Michael than USSTAP. She also knew the Osguard family was USSTAP, so they were just as viable a target as he was. Therefore, he had to remove them as targets. Conversely, Michael couldn't keep evacuating the gardens every time the universe threatened USSTAP. Osguard Gardens was starting to be a liability.

Ever since Earth General Wang Lo recruited her, along with Lieutenants Kim Salmot, and Sheri Filgo from the Philippine Islands seven years ago, her being had been expanded pass any thought or imagination she had as a kid. They were the first from their island to join the secretive organization. Once they did they were able to pull their extended family out of poverty, gain the respect of many people and travel throughout the galaxy.

Growing up in the Philippines was not easy. Money was scarce and job opportunities were even worse. Tourism was the official business of the Islands, and catering to strangers was somewhat appalling to her. She worked hard in school to make top grades, because she wanted to be more than a waitress or cashier for some foreign corporate hotel.

To her dismay, she witnessed many of her sister Filipinos turn to the sexual entertainment industry. They either stripped for money or walked the streets and worked the bars and hotels, selling their bodies to the highest bidder. Stripping or prostitution was not in her future. Every day she would see men from all over the world visit the Philippines and during their stay they would seek out a young Filipino woman, barely of age to satisfy their sexual needs. It was like a quest for some of them to sleep with a Filipino girl. The young women were beautiful, exotic, mysterious and willing to do anything for money—a sad combination for her culture.

It got to the point where she resented anything that was not Filipino, especially the foreign men who came to her country and thought they owned it. She knew they looked down on her like she was less than human, just a sex toy to barter for. They would smile at her as part of the game she was not willing to play. She wanted to scream, *not every woman in the Philippines was a whore,* but she knew it would fall on deaf ears. Because, there were enough women that were prostitutes to dispel her objections.

Then one day, when she was out shopping with her friends, Kim and Sheri, a Chinese gentlemen, she assumed was from Hong Kong approached her. First she thought he was another foreigner looking for a conquest thinking she was in the game. It would not be the first time it happened. Gloria was very pretty. Her round face, full lips and large breasts always caught the men's eyes. Her sexy hips and strong thighs, which were unusual for a Filipino woman, also made her standout in a crowd.

She turned away; laid the skirt she was looking at back on the rack and walked out of the store. Kim and Sheri saw this and followed her. Once outside, she told them about the old Chinese man who approached her. She swore, she saw right through the façade. He was an old geezer wanting something he couldn't have. Sheri and Kim turned and saw the man walk out of the store and head in their direction.

They spun around and scurried down the crowded street, bypassing street venders, and other people trying to do their daily business. Two blocks of walking, and the gentleman was still following them and gaining. Gloria's defiance now was melting away into fright. Usually a simple brush off would discourage any foreigner, because there were more than enough women around who would gladly sell their dignity for a couple of dollars. However, this man was persistent and it was scary.

Kim and Sheri began to panic as well. They looked to Gloria for guidance. Even though Gloria was not the oldest, she was the leader by default of the small clique. She had convinced them to strive in school. She had convinced them to apply for college in the United States. And she showed them how to apply for scholarships.

They were to start at the University of California, Berkley in the fall. It was a dream, come true. For once they were going to be the foreigners in another land. For once they would be the ones people would serve and wait on. She could not wait. However at that moment, being chased…that was the right term…chased, by an old man in the middle of the day, made going to America seem like a dream that would never come true. Nothing but bad things could come from any confrontation with a foreigner, especially a wealthy tourist, and this guy looked wealthy.

He was impeccably dressed, with Italian shoes, silk shirt and tie, and an Italian suit. His hair was gray with a businessman cut. His smile was perfect as were his teeth. He wore expensive sunglasses and held a mahogany cane with a gold tip and a gold handle. Yes, he could be someone's sugar daddy, but not hers. Yes, someone else with a morbid lack of self-respect would have taken the infatuation from a rich middle age man like this, and turned it to their advantage. However, that was one of many things her father instilled in her—self-respect.

Then like an angel, he touched her shoulder, and called out her name, "Gloria…Gloria Magma."

Half startled and half curious, she turned and answered, "Yes,"

"And you must be Kim Salmot," he said pointing to Kim, "and you must be Sheri Filgo."

The ladies sheepishly nodded.

"Don't be frightened. My name is Wang Lo. I represent some people who are interested in hiring you and sending you to school. We saw your test scores, and I must admit…they were pretty impressive, considering the conditions you have endured here."

Gloria did not know if she should take Lo's comment as a compliment or an insult. The confusion on her face was more than evident to USSTAP Earth General Wang Lo.

"Please, let me buy you a cup of coffee or tea. If you give me a few minutes, I am sure I can clear up any confusion you may have."

"Thank you, but no," Gloria insisted.

"Ms. Magna, you will be missing out on the opportunity of a lifetime…I assure you."

"I don't think so," Sheri chimed in.

"I'm so sorry you feel that way, Ms. Filgo. I assure you, my intentions are honorable. If you feel any different later, here is my card." He handed each a card that read USSTAP, a toll free number and the words… *'Isa Pa Po'*…One more please.

Lo turned and disappeared into the crowd, without saying another word. Gloria thought it odd the man was not more persistent. She was also relieved it was not what she imagined it to be. Then a shutter blanketed her body. If it wasn't what she imagined it to be, then the man might have been offering them a job and an opportunity to go to school. She stared at the card once more, studying the words, *'Isa Pa Po.'* Something about the words caught her interest. She didn't know what, but her interest was aroused.

Later that night, Gloria decided to call. It was the phrase "One More Please" that still intrigued her. The lady on the other end of the phone answered in English. Gloria transitioned to her best English. She asked for Mr. Wang Lo. The lady at the other end asked her name. She politely gave it. Then there was a long pause, in which Gloria began to become nervous. Then the operator came back on, repeated her name, and gave her address. Now Gloria was panicky, but she confirmed it was the right address. Then the operator asked her to move away from the north end of the room. Gloria didn't know which side was the north side of the room, or why the lady insisted she move, but she moved to the far corner of the room.

Then the lady asked her not to be nervous, but she was about to witness a bright white light in the middle of the room. Gloria now was scared and wanted to hang up the phone, but something kept her from doing it. She wanted to scream for her parents, but they were out. She was all alone and cursing for making the phone call. Then as the lady promised, the white light of inner space illuminated in the middle of the room. Inside of it was a man's shadow. Gloria cowered in the corner, praying and trying to scream. Then Lo stepped out of the light. This time he was dressed in a black jumpsuit with a blue turtleneck; he wore a black jacket with markings on it. The invisible door of normal space closed behind him, taking with it the angelic light.

Wang called her name. His voice was strong and almost vibrating like thunder. Gloria thought she was witnessing a miracle, a messenger from God. He told her his offer was only for this one time. He would take her to see the universe, to touch the stars, to swim the deepest oceans, to sail the unknown seas and to learn what cannot be taught in a class. He was here to take her to her destiny. His voice still thundered to the point her soul vibrated when he spoke. The fright melted, as her interest surged, but she still was uncertain.

He reached out his hand toward Gloria. He said if she came with him now, there was no return. She would forever be changed. She asked if she would be able to see her parents again. Lo laughed. He assured her she would. The no return he was speaking of was a return to innocence. She was about to learn the mysteries of man. Once she learned that, she would have grown past her own potential. She would grow into the potential that destiny had laid out for her. Gloria didn't want to, but something compelled her to stand and grab hold of Lo's hand. Within ten minutes of making the phone call, she was within the white light of inner space on her way to Lilly Station.

When she stepped out of the white light, onto Earth Station Lilly, her eyes took a second to adjust. Her heart was beating erratically, but she was no longer afraid. Something about Lo's presence comforted her. Lo showed her all he promised. He took her to the deepest part of the ocean in the *USSTAP Sea Cruiser Neptune*, a variant of her sister the galaxy cruiser. Then they traveled in a startram, hugging the ocean and finally departing into space. They circled the solar system, visiting the atmospheres of Venus, Mars, Saturn, and Pluto before spending the night on Moon Station Set. The station resided on the dark side of the moon, but she still remembered her first glance at Earth from space. How magnificent the blue marble with white whispery clouds was to her. At that moment she was sold. Whatever Lo was selling, she was buying.

After a day with Lo, she retrieved her friends and brought them into the USSTAP fold. They spent three and a half years on Chaktun, going through the USSTAP Millmum Galactic Academy, learning everything from quantum physics to spiritual science. They learned Chaktun and the Sixana warrior way. When the women completed their training, they reported for their first tour of duty—security officers on the *Galaxy Cruiser Scriptanal*, Osguard thirty-five—Barnard Grace's first ship. That was how many ships were referred to, as an Osguard's old ship, if they had the luxury of such a distinguished history. They served under the leadership of Centurion Richard Keyes, one of the handsomest, toughest and greatest men she ever met—next to the First Osguard, she thought.

Lo came to them last week while they were on leave in the Philippines and asked them to help Stelana out with this assignment. Yet Stelana was not to know they were there. Lo figured their experience as security officers, made them perfect for this covert operation. He stated Michael had reservations about Stelana's objectivity and wanted the best people the general could find to back up Stelana. It was such an honor to be asked, they could not refuse, even if it meant cutting their vacation short.

A slight tone went off from the CC receiver implanted in her ear, signifying someone was trying to contact her through her CC. She tapped the front of her CC, making sure she kept a steady hand on the steering wheel. "Magma here," she responded.

"Gloria…it's me…Kim."

"Tiah!"

"I just want to report to you that the woman I am following is House Majority Leader, Republican Representative Joyce T. Eldridge from Texas."

"What the hell was Eldridge doing at that coffee shop?"

"The more interesting question is why is the House Majority Leader, Republican Representative Joyce T. Eldridge from Texas, registering as a Tuit on my PARIT."

"What? I scanned her earlier. She didn't show any abnormal DNA patterns."

"Yeah, I know. But I grabbed some food she discarded and ran a biological separator scan. What I found was DNA inhibitors, similar to what the First Osguard sent us last night. I stripped the DNA inhibitor and found the weird DNA that registered as Tuit."

"Damn girl, why didn't I think of that?"

"You think Musoto is Tuit as well?"

"I don't think so. So far, according to the Osguard's report, the Tuits seem to be an Amazonian race. No men. But just because we have not seen any male Tuits, doesn't mean there aren't any. I guess I'll have to try your trick." Gloria scratched her head, trying to think of the next move to make. "Report to Sheri what you found out. Have her go into this woman's history and find out how the hell a Tuit got to be a politician in the United States. And find out what the hell she is doing. This is getting weird, sister…really weird."

***

Stelana read the message for the third time. It still shook her to the core. She didn't know what it meant, but she had a feeling it meant she messed up royally. She put her ARIT tablet on her kitchen table and placed her head into her hands. Tears started to form in her eyes. Her body started to tremble. It was a personal message from the First Osguard. The kind you didn't want to see. It was alarming and somewhat disorienting. She peered up at the ARIT again, as if she was reading it for the first time. *"Lieutenant Stelana Rican, you are hereby immediately recalled to Millmum Capitol Station. Please, proceed on the earliest transport."*

The tear rolled down her cheek. She saw her career in USSTAP over before it started. Just this morning she was patting herself on the back for having such a sterling career at such a young age. Then Musoto screwed it up in five minutes. She hardly got her report in, before the Osguard's message came through. *'Immediate Recall!' Damn the luck.*

***

Gloria pulled her USSTAP modified SUV up to the curb. She watched Musoto pull into the driveway, get out of the car and walk up to the front door. When the door opened, a vivacious brunette skimpily dressed in a see-through silk nightgown covering a sheer teddy appeared. Obviously, she did not mind letting her neighbors get a good look at her, because she stepped outside and planted the longest, hottest and sexiest kiss Gloria had ever seen. It was so intense that Gloria felt embarrassed watching and averted her gaze from the show. After the kiss and a few whispered words, the couple disappeared into the house. Almost immediately all the lights went off and Gloria knew she was parked for the night. This was a booty call.

Pangs of hunger began wrenching Gloria's stomach. She realized she hadn't eaten since she left the Philippines earlier that morning. She laid her PARIT down and opened the glove compartment. Inside she found several candy bars and a box of USSTAP rations. "Thank you, Wang Lo," she whispered knowing Lo had the food placed there for just this occasion. She knew if she checked the back, more supplies would be there, probably a blanket and small toiletries. She smiled as she ripped open the chocolate covered coconut candy bar. No matter how hungry or cold she got this night, it was still an easy assignment compared to some of the assignments Centurion Keyes sent them on.

She took several bites from the candy bar, then wrapped the remaining portion back up and slipped it into the glove compartment. She checked her watch. It was 11:30 PM local. Her body had barely adjusted to Philippine time after leaving the Scriptanal. Now she was on Eastern Standard Time in the United States. Her body was all messed up and her sleep cycle was in an uproar. She picked up the PARIT, set the scanner to pick up Musoto, pointed it to the door, placed the sensor for motion, and placed the earpiece in her ear. Then she pulled the flap from the steering wheel, thumbed the controls, setting the holographic emitters on the window to make it appear as if the car was empty. Once she was satisfied anyone passing by would see an empty car, she reached in the back, felt for the blanket, grabbed it and curled up in the seat.

Before she closed her eyes, she checked under her coat in the passenger seat for her delta belt. She knew it was there, but she needed to reassure herself of its position. If she needed to grab it or a weapon from it, she did not need to waste time fumbling for it. She patted each weapon, the coronet gun, the pagenay and the Mation II. Then she pulled the PGP from its spot and placed it in her hip pocket. She thought she should do the same with the pagenay.

She was on Earth. Stealth was a major factor during her operation. Using the pagenay to knock someone unconscious would probably be the preferred method of self-defense. She shook her head, because she never liked the pagenay. It gave your position away to the enemy, and it was not always reliable, depending on distance and atmospheric conditions. Again, she was on Earth. Atmospheric conditions like she encountered on some of her E.T. missions would not be a factor. She reached back under her jacket, clipped the pagenay from the delta belt and placed it inside her boot cuff.

She took one more look at the house. The lights were still off, confirming her earlier assumption. She knew as long as the trip took to get here, Musoto was in for the night. He may not be sleeping, but he was in for the night. So she closed her eyes to give her brain and body the required recharge they needed. Soon the playful spirit of slumber enveloped her and took her to her private dream world. The last thing in reality she saw was the house and the first thing in her fantasy world she saw was Centurion Keyes on the bridge of the *USSTAP Galaxy Cruiser Scriptanal.*

Chapter 26—Crap Hits the Fan

The automatic alarm rang on both bridges. It was loud, scary and sobering. Regina jumped from her chair and flew down the railing to the control bridge. "What is it?" she yelled.

The chief controller was surprised to see the centurion on the control bridge. Usually, all information he gathered was automatically pumped to the command bridge through the communications suite. However, for some reason Regina was downstairs and wanting to know firsthand what had set the Alert one alarm.

"Ma'am," the chief controller responded, collecting his thoughts. "The search array is picking up a large concentration of restion particles, one hundred thousand kilomarks off our port bow."

"Show me," she demanded.

He stepped aside and thumbed his control panel. She leaned over, reading the screen. Her eyes reflected back off the dark smoky glass. And if she had noticed the reflection of her eyes in the glass, she would have seen the fright that engulfed them. "If these are benion particle readings, I would say there are ten gigantic portal openings happening."

"Tiah!" the chief controller swallowed.

"Wake the Osguard. Notify the *S'Coril* and the *P'Togi* to set an intercept course. Vega two formation, hyperlight speed in five seconds."

The chief controller was barking her orders as fast as she was saying them into his headset. The orders went to the communications suite and spread out to all within a split second.

Satisfied she had seen enough and had put the counter-attack plan in motion, Regina stepped back up the ladder. When she reached the top, Jarod was racing through the entry door.

"Status?" he asked racing to his seat.

"They're coming, ultra space openings one hundred thousand kilomarks, heading two–three–zero decimal three–two, mark four–four. Us, the *S'Coril* and the *P'Togi* are on an intercept course, Vega two formation. E–T–A twenty-five point nine seconds."

"Very good…battle stations…arm all weapons," Jarod ordered. It was a needless order, but he needed to get the words out to help him focus. He had just awakened from a deep sleep and the situation was still a dream to him. He had to fall back on the familiar."

Regina looked around to make sure his orders had already been complied with. "Complete," she announced taking her seat next to him.

"Damn, he was right again," he whispered to no one in particular.

"You mean Michael?" Regina interrupted without looking up from her chair's ARIT screen.

"Hell yeah, I mean Michael. That motherfucker is always right," Jarod joked, pulling his own chair's ARIT screen, preparing for battle.

"Is that bad?"

"No…it's just frustrating at times. But I'm glad he is on our side."

"I think we all are, sire. I know I am."

"It sounds like you like him more than you like me."

"No sire. It's not that. I think he carries a tremendous burden being the First Osguard and he is wearing it well. I know if you were First Osguard you would do the same excellent job. You all would. Remember, he was the first found and the one that looks like Vedar the most. His title is happenstance and not a sign that he is better than you or any of the other Osguards. Michael is just doing a damn good job."

"You know that's why I love you. You always know the right things to say."

"Don't tell anyone, but I think you're the bomb too."

"Ultra space openings, ten of them, dead ahead," announced the Defensive Officer.

"Slow to fighting speed, all ships," Jarod commanded. "On screen," he added.

The view port screen filled with the tapestry of space. In the middle, red ovals of light grew from nothingness, to spot this area of space like holes in Swiss cheese. Soon the white cone ships formed inside the light. Every fiber inside his being, told Jarod to send Asher torpedoes into the fiery holes of hell, and blow the crap out of the Tuits. That was how he would have handled the situation, until he saw the HVP. Nonetheless, now that he understood this entire war might have been an unfortunate result of a misunderstanding, he had to attempt contact with the Tuits and clear things up.

So far the Tuits were responsible for the deaths of billions of lives under the USSTAP protectorate. He did not want any more deaths of USSTAP personal under his watch. Michael did not dictate how to confront the enemy. All he suggested was to protect our interest at all cost and attempt diplomatic contact. He left it up to the individual Osguard how to perform those tasks. Michael knew his sphere of power did not reach into other galaxies, but he knew his sphere of influence did. Therefore, he suggested the ends, not the means.

"Should we send the prescribed hail?" Regina asked.

Jarod hesitated for a split second as he watched the last of the Tuit ships enter normal space. "Chromerion field up…send the damned hail. Train Asher torpedoes on the lead ship. Lord, I hope I didn't make a mistake letting those bastards come through."

"Hail away," the communications officer responded.

Over the hail channels, a pre-recorded message, which Jarod prepared and translated into Tuit earlier in the day played.

"Tuits fireships, this is Osguard one-one, Jarod M. Stone of the Universal Science, Security and Trade Associations of Planets. You have entered USSTAP protected space. Based on your previous actions in USSTAP protected space, we consider your intent hostile, and we will be forced to use lethal means to halt your actions. Please cease your actions. We believe your hostile activities are based on a misconception. Your Fireships, Snikle and Tesle were destroyed in an unfortunate accident. We have proof and we are willing to share with you how they met their demise.

Again, I request you cease all actions and stand-down. This does not need to go any further."

The communications officer waited several seconds for a response that never came. He shook his head, "No response sire."

"Just as I figured," Jarod pushed. "Well Michael, you aren't always right. But I wish you were this time…Boy do I wish you were."

"Sire, they are charging weapons!" screamed the Defensive Officer.

"Evasive maneuver J–3, fire Asher torpedoes…send them back to hell," he growled.

The *Gentry* dove forty-five degrees nose low and turned forty-five degrees to the port side, the *S'Coril* split sixty degrees to its starboard and the *P'Togi* split ninety degrees to the port side and ascended ten on the galactic plane. Each ship spit out two Asher torpedoes. The twenty-five foot missiles sailed through space so fast they looked like streaks of light whipping from the bows of the dark black birdlike galaxy protectors. The orange and red plum that made up the torpedoes' wakes spread like ripples in an ocean.

The *Gentry*'s first torpedo hit the lead ship, mid section under the belly. The ship rocked like it was caught in an earthquake. The weapons fell off line and a purple mist vented from the spot of the explosion. Fragments of the ship ripped, tore and shredded off like flakes of snow, littering the area with metal fragments. The *Gentry*'s second missile homed in on the tribolemincic exhaust, as the targeting scanners had programmed it to. The exhaust led to the last third of the ship, under the belly to a rear glass-like enclosure attached outside the ship, hanging like an appendage. The missile connected and the glass frame exploded with the force of an atomic bomb. A faint orange mushroom cloud made a brief appearance before being erased by the vacuum of space.

The torpedoes from the *S'Coril* illuminated a colorful trail that hit the second ship to the left flank of the lead ship. However the Tuit ship had energized its deflectors and began evasive maneuvers to the right. The missiles hit the ship's port deflectors, exploded and pushed the ship, making it slide off glide path toward the first ship, which was now pinned between the lead and it. The first ship dove sixty degrees nose low trying to escape the impending carnage. The second ship clipped the tail cone of the first ship and ripped a one thousand-foot chunk of the tail cone off. The first ship continued to descend, leaving a trail of debris like blood in its wake. The second ship regained control and maneuvered over and behind the lead ship's right flank.

The missiles from the *P'Togi* curved at a sixty-degree arc and pushed toward the first ship to the right of the lead ship. This Tuit ship raised its deflectors and spat out several blast from its shockdel plasma cannon. The bright yellow melenai ionic plasma balls of energy spread through space like a spider web. Four of the balls slammed into the newly modified slitanium-chromerion field surrounding the *P'Togi*.

After the first battle with the Kulusks where the slitanium hull in stealth mode ten became invaluable in deflecting the shockdel gun's melenai ore, combined with the intelligence garnered from Centurion Vezec's confrontation with the Tuits, the engineering corps modified the chromerion field to contain slitanium radiation. Like the K-cannon, it was a slight modification and easily completed. The chromerion field ripped the ionic plasma energy encasing the melenai ore, exposing the ore to the slitanium radiation in the field. The ore's energy harmlessly dissipated like a static discharge around the ship and off the skin.

***

Rina, in the crippled lead ship, saw the ineffectiveness of the shockdel plasma cannon and for the second time in a few short minutes, fear gripped her heart. She tried to call out to her ships, but the damage to her ship was so severe, only life support and intercom remained. Blue and purple smoke filled the air, causing her to cough. Her ship was slow to raise its defensive deflectors, while her sister ships automatically raised them upon seeing the USSTAP welcoming committee. She instead, elected to power her weapons first. This in hindsight was a deadly mistake. She thought since USSTAP was outnumbered and outgunned, they would hesitate upon opening fire first.

She underestimated the military thoroughness of USSTAP. She underestimated this galaxy's Osguard. The offer of peace that was sent in his primary hail was either a rouse or a decoy. Either way, it relaxed Rina to the point in which she was counting the victory before the first shot. Now she was out of the fight and hoping her sisters would bring the victory home. *Only if I could contact them,* she thought. "I need communications to the fleet. Get me some damn comm to the fleet…now!" she hollered.

Her comm officer looked at her with awe. She wondered if the Sixth Daughter was crazy, because she was working as hard as she could to reestablish comm service. She just shook her head in disbelief. She already did not like Rina of Jaywick, and this incident made it abundantly clear, Rina of Jaywick was an egotistical, power-hungry incompetent warrior, who by luck or sheer determination rose from the deprivation chamber onto the seat of power with the swing of a blade and over the body of a sister warrior. Not the most honorable way to win a seat as a Daughter of Fire, but it was worth notice.

Outside, the Tuit ships completed a bomb burst, spreading to the four winds of space. The two far right ships climbed to thirty on the galactic plane, the next one descended to escape a possible collision with the inner two ships. On the left, the last three ships ascended five to ten above the galactic plane and separated by one thousand kilomarks. Rina could only helplessly watch her fleet haphazardly disperse. For all intents and purposes, she was dead in space. Her power source, the tribolemincic crystal was destroyed. She was running on battery power.

The USSTAP ships swung around for another attack. The *S'Coril* ascended up the galactic plane and let loose with two more torpedoes. The torpedoes scorched the blackness of space, split and homed in on the two Tuit ships respectively. The first torpedo found its mark on the front deflector. The energy wave pushed the invisible deflector inwards, sending a compression wave of energy toward its bow. The Tuit ship rocked and skipped backwards from the force of the explosion. Several bulkheads buckled and internal fires were noticed on several decks.

The second missile missed wide left of its intended target. Sensing its miss the warhead self-destructed fifty kilomarks behind the Tuit ship. The Tuit ship stopped maneuvering and pointed its bow at the approaching *S'Coril*. Then from the four points of the Tuit ship's cone bottom, beams from the rhetonic guns shot out forward. Two were red and two were blue. The beams converged into one spiraling color twisted ray two thousand meters off their bow. The mixed ray shot toward the *S'Coril*. The *S'Coril* shifted to a sixty-degree hard right turn. The spiral color beam of death twisted through the slitanium-chromerion field like a knife, hitting the port engine. Instantly the ship fractured as the immense heat changed the physical properties of the hull. Fissures and cracks erupted in the hull, causing the atmosphere to escape and the ship to collapse onto itself, like a crushed beer can. Death was instantaneous for the two thousand and five hundred-member crew. Then the ship imploded, sprinkling tiny metal shavings, blood, and body parts onto a permanent grave of cold nothingness.

Jarod watched his scanner in horror. The sight was heart wrenching. The *S'Coril* was the first galaxy protector destroyed in battle and it was under his watch. He'd just witnessed the instantaneous death of twenty-five hundred USSTAP members. Fortunately, his mind didn't have the time to fathom the destruction, before his training kicked in.

"Reset…Reset!" *P'Togi* …reset!" he ordered. "Second wave attack!" he screamed into the interlink.

The *P'Togi* fired two more torpedoes and scrambled to complete its one hundred and eighty-degree turn, to rendezvous at the reset area. At the same time, the eight galaxy cruisers, screamed down from above the fight raining pagenay fire, coronet guns and Asher torpedoes. The five Tuit ships that used the upper galactic plane as a haven caught the anger of USSTAP weapons. Their deflector shields shook, rattled and gave way onto the onslaught of energy weapons. The ships crumbled, cracked, and snapped like a chicken's neck. Mercy wasn't their intention now. The weapons onslaught continued even after the ships were visibly out of commission. At first,

Jarod's objective was to cripple the ships and take the Tuits alive, but that was no longer the objective. Death was the objective and Osguard one-one's silence tacitly condoned and blessed the change in strategy.

Revenge sunk into his heart and every heart on his ship. They were losing the war, but by God, they weren't going to lose the fight. A message had to be sent and it had to be sent with emphasis. "You fucked with the wrong people!" Jarod whispered. He turned to his weapon officer, "Let's give the K-cannon a try. Target the Tuit ship at three–three–three, mark three–four…fire at will."

The weapons officer flipped the cover to his new toy, a blue crystal like multifaceted, eighteen-barreled weapon—ten feet long, four feet thick and three feet wide. It also was constructed of taonic circuitry and powered by jorelli plugs. Unbeknownst to him, it shot invisible beams of energy more destructive than coronet pellets or melenai pulses and with a devilish grin; he ran the targeting scanner to the coordinates. The lock was instantaneous due to the taonic circuitry. With a silent prayer for revenge, he fingered the firing switch. A whining, high-pitched sound rang through the bridge just a split second prior to the beam tearing a two hundred-foot hole in the Tuit ship sending white chunks of its hull into space with a violent explosion. Metal, blood and fuel strewn over the area like colorful balls of hail, dissipating in light as the coldness of space engulfed them. Then he fingered the cannon a second, third and fourth time. And finally on the fifth shot the ship exploded, lighting the surrounding space with a tremendous fireworks display—making vibrant, but gruesome, spherical designs.

Jarod smiled, a victory was in hand. He turned to Regina, who was calculating something on her ARIT. He glanced at his ARIT tablet and clicked it to repeat her screen. She was searching for the last three Tuit ships. Somehow they had escaped the fight when they descended. Then in horror, Jarod saw the energy surge shoot on his tablet. It was coming from two hundred below on the galactic plane. "Hyperlight…now!" he yelled. Instantaneously, the hyperlight engines engaged, skipping the usual speed schedule, and the *USSTAP Galaxy Protector Gentry* flashed across the heavens, unseen by the naked eye. The *USSTAP Galaxy Protector P'Togi* was not so lucky.

She was moving to the reset point at hypersonic fighting speed, still spitting coronet and pagenay blasts from her rear weapons array onto the carnage the galaxy cruisers were creating on the shells of the five helpless Tuit ships. Her search array did not extend to below the zero galactic plane. Like the devil's own fist, the twisted red and blue beam of the Tuit's rhetonic cannon reached out of the darkness of hell and hit the *P'Togi* in the belly. In an eerie repeat of the *S'Coril*, the ship fractured as the immeasurable heat cooked the hull. Fissures and cracks erupted, again causing the atmosphere to escape and crushing the ship. Once more USSTAP experienced the abrupt death of twenty-five hundred personnel as the ship imploded, giving the nameless grave of space more souls to call it their final resting place.

Jarod's search array recorded the destruction, as the numbers raced down his screen; this time his mind had time to register the event, along with his anger. He pounded the arm of his chair in sheer frustration. "Turn this bitch around," he yelled. "Weapons Officer, take that motherfucker out, fire everything we have at it. Pilot! Get us within fighting range. If that thing thinks about spitting that beam at us, maneuver at will."

The *Gentry* turned and reverse course still traveling at hyperlight speed. Within one hundred and twenty thousand kilomarks, the *Gentry*'s search array registered several gate portal openings to ultra space. Jarod read his ARIT screen and his heart jumped into his throat. They were escaping.

"Don't slow, until we are within firing range!" Jarod ordered, letting his anger control his training.

The restion particles of ultra space began to overload the *Gentry*'s sensors. She lost the three remaining combat capable Tuit ships in the static. The pilot had to slow to hypersonic fighting speed. The galaxy protector pulled within the visible light spectrum, one hundred kilomarks away from a red gate portal opening. The last of the Tuit ships was barely visible inside the light. The red light of ultra space had swallowed the other two ships.

The pilot turned around and looked at Jarod, who was studying the scene and mulling over something in his head. "Orders?" the pilot requested.

Jarod remained still, studying the scene and digesting the possible courses of actions at computer like speed. He stood and walked over to the pilot. He put his hand on his shoulder, as the pilot turned forward once more. "Follow them…fighting speed…take us in."

"Tiah!" the pilot responded showing no emotion, but deep down inside his heart had jumped into his throat and his stomach turned sour. The Osguard had just ordered their certain death, and every survival instinct in him begged him to disobey the order. His Sixana training overcame the instinct and he glided his hand over the control, pushing the ship forward into the red light of ultra space."

"Weapons, if you have a clear shot…take it. Pilot! Be ready to hit the reverse engines. But if we have to go all the way to make the kill…we will."

The *Gentry* swam into the red light, following her prey, with weapons ready. However the restion static played havoc on the ARIT targeting systems. Jarod remembered the destruction of the Tuit ships recorded almost a century ago on the HVP. He surmised firing weapons in ultra space was not a particular good idea. His training finally overpowered his thirst for revenge. "Belay firing order. Reverse engines now. Pilot—get us the hell out of here," he screamed.

The pilot fingered the reverse button, but the engines could not grab onto the restion particles, like it did with benion particles of normal space.

"Change to thrusters!" Regina ordered, standing and moving next to Jarod, with her eyes fixed on the view port screen showing nothing but red space.

The *Gentry* screeched, pulled, popped and hummed as the thrusters pushed backwards. The opening was slamming close behind them. Jarod closed his eyes chastising himself for putting his crew in danger and praying for God to let him have a miracle and let his ship make it back to normal space. His prayers went unanswered. God either did not hear him or the answer was no. Either way the light engulfed the ship and then shut. The *USSTAP Galaxy Protector Gentry* was gone.

Chapter 27—The Search

The beep woke Gloria from her slumber. She lifted her head, barely remembering who she was, let alone where she was. The beeping sound, which started like a little bird chirping, was pounding her senses like a church bell, snapping her from her pleasant dream state like a tornado. She shook her head, trying to induce reality. Then she brushed back her hair and opened her eyes. The flood of sunlight penetrated her dark world, painfully and without remorse. She blinked several times, while attempting to shield her eyes from the light with her hand.

Then as if someone turned on a switch, her brain engaged and the situation flooded into her mind. The shock of reality jolted her upright behind the steering wheel. She wiped her eyes and gazed out the windshield just in time to see Musoto and the glamorous brunette hopping into his car. She watched for several seconds with her hand on the ignition key, wondering if she should follow or if she should stay.

Musoto's black late model sedan pulled out of the driveway, turned up the street and disappeared. Gloria remained in her SUV, still pondering if she should follow. After a few more seconds, she let go of the key and stepped out of the SUV. She closed the door, looked around for any activity in the area and then sauntered toward the front door of the house. While she was walking up the walkway, she pulled her PGP from her pocket and without looking, fingered a point-to-point step for a two-foot end point. She didn't know the layout of the house, but she figured there should be clearance two feet beyond the front door. When she reached the door, she took one last look around to make sure the coast was clear. Once she was satisfied, she activated the PGP in the shadow of the front door, stepped into the white light as if the front door was open and stepped out in the foyer.

She scanned the area with her PARIT, searching for any source of DNA to analyze. She thought her best option would be in the kitchen. Maybe the duo had a meal in there before they left. So she pushed toward the kitchen. It was spotless, the food had been disposed of in the garbage disposal; the dishes were washed; and the floor was swept. She could probably find tiny bits of DNA from fingerprints or food material in the refrigerator, but it would not be enough to complete a full analysis.

Her next stop was the master bedroom. She knew she would be able to find hair follicles, a used toothbrush, or samples in a make-up kit. She was rushing, for she didn't know when the couple would return, or if they would return. She swept the bed first. The PARIT indicated several deposits of DNA from male semen and vaginal fluid, further confirming her assumption of the reason for the visit. "Booty call," she whispered, shaking her head in judgment.

She clicked through her PARIT menu to *'Analysis.'* A blue light beam shot from her PARIT disguised as a cell phone. She held it on the spot on the sheets indicating the largest deposit of DNA. The semen registered as Anthony Musoto's DNA, which they had on file. She ran a spectrogram, searching for the DNA inhibitor and found nothing. Then she ran the analysis on the vaginal fluid. The DNA information appeared human, belonging to a female with A- blood type, which was very rare. She then ran a spectrogram, again searching for the DNA inhibitor. This time she found it. She clicked it once more to start the process over again and the results remained the same.

She then stripped the DNA inhibitor from the sample and allowed the PARIT to construct the DNA sequence without the inhibitor. The word *'TUIT'* flashed on the PARIT view screen. Her mouth dropped as she read the word. She never expected this. She thought Musoto was conspiring with the United States government to expose, capture or to destroy USSTAP. Now there was a different player in the game—The Tuits.

Her mind raced as she tried to grasp the possibilities of the new development. *Were the United States government and the Tuits working together? Was Musoto double-crossing the president as a double agent for the Tuits? Were Musoto and the president unknowing pawns in the Tuits' plan?*

She had to steady her mind, because she was gathering information, not deducing a hypothesis from it. Other people were paid to do that. However, armed with this new information, she had to alter the course of her search. The main objective of the search had now shifted from Musoto to the girl and the congresswoman. However, Musoto's involvement was still a mystery that needed to be solved.

Gloria clicked through her PARIT menu for full search for power sources. She then circled the bedroom, pointing the PARIT at various angles so its span could reach every corner of the room. A strange reading registered on her screen, coming from the nightstand. She moved closer, trying to narrow the focus of the PARIT. However, the PARIT could not identify the source. She clicked the PARIT off and stowed it in her pocket. She reached down and cracked the nightstand drawer open. Then she retrieved her PARIT once more and tried to get a reading. Still the PARIT could not identify the source.

This time with the PARIT in her hand she used her free hand to pull the drawer completely open. She scanned the inside of the drawer, while watching the PARIT. The PARIT's reading didn't change. Whatever the source was, it was beyond the PARIT's ability to identify.

Gloria then pushed record and transmit, sending her findings straight to the lab on Lilly Station. The process took exactly forty-four seconds, but it seemed like an hour to Gloria. She kept peering out the window, wondering where Musoto and the strange girl went, and wondering if they were returning soon. She wondered how she would play it off if she were caught. She would be considered a burglar, arrested and placed in jail—if she was lucky. If she were not, the Tuits would recognize her as part of USSTAP and execute her. Which scenario would play out? Finally, she decided she would play it by ear. She would not tip her hand; she would allow them to tip theirs. Her main objective was not to be caught.

The PARIT chirped it was done. She packed it away in her pocket and began searching the room for more information. She needed to know who this person was, where she came from and what she was doing on Earth. She went to the closet and picked through the clothes—mainly business suits, expensive shoes and silk blouses. *Well, she wasn't a waitress,* she concluded. The closet inferred a businesswoman, maybe a politician's aide or lobbyist. That would fit right in with Eldridge. However, nothing else out of the ordinary or out of this world could be found in the closet.

Gloria huffed, closed the closet door and turned toward the dresser bureau. She searched the five-drawer bureau, making sure to put each item back as she found it. Again, she found nothing. She closed the last drawer and moved to the make-up table. There she picked up the empty contact lens case and examined it for a minute. It was a simple disguise, but effective. The contact lenses hid the Tuit natural yellow cat-like pupils. She replaced the contact lens case and turned in frustration.

She then searched under the bed, the bathroom, the living room and the kitchen once more, again nothing—at least nothing in the open. The bills on the living room desk were addressed to Mona Richards. At least she had a name, whether an alias or not, it was a start. She wanted more, she wanted plans, Tuit technology—she wanted the smoking gun. She stood in the middle of the living room pondering; where she would place that kind of stuff if she were Mona. Then she remembered, when she is home, she would hide her delta belt in the wall of her closet. *Could it be that simple?* Then she raced back into the bedroom, opened the closet and started knocking on the walls, listening for a hollow sound.

In the back right corner, the sound of her knocking changed. It was hollow. She knocked several times more to make sure it wasn't an anomaly. Then her nimble fingers searched for a hidden switch, she pressed and pulled at the spot. Then she pulled her PARIT once more and scanned the area. The PARIT found a power switch hidden in the wallpaper pattern. It was DNA activated. Even if she did push the switch, it would not activate the panel. Gloria mumbled a few choice curses. All she could do is scan the contents, so she did.

Several pieces of equipment, including two types of energy weapons registered on the PARIT that could not be identified, but one piece was identifiable—a high-powered rifle, with a scope. It was professional, broken down and placed in a case, surrounded by velvety foam to keep in clean and protected. Now Gloria was amazed. Why would such a sophisticated organization bother to have an archaic weapon like a rifle? Again, she reminded herself to just collect the evidence.

Just then a noise at the front door grabbed her attention. It was the sound of a key turning the lock. They were back. She replaced the clothes in the closet and activated her PGP for emergency retrieval. She stepped into the light and disappeared just as Mona walked into her bedroom.

Mona stopped and looked around the room. Something wasn't right. She stared at the bed, the nightstand, her dresser bureau and then her make-up table. She rushed to her closet and peered inside. She knew someone had disturbed her closet. The hangers weren't spaced as she placed them, and the string on the far wall, she used for tamper detection, was detached from the last hanger. The hanger had been moved. She then moved to the make-up table, reached underneath, flipped a switch and watched the table flip upside down, exposing a command console. She sat down and strummed the console. In the view screen, Mona witnessed Gloria's search. Step by step, Mona's security system recorded the entire episode.

Mona smiled, "About time!" she whispered. "This was becoming too easy. Now the game really begins."

***

The red light was intense. If traveling through the white light of inner space was like trespassing in God's backyard, traveling through the red light of ultra space was like running for your life in the devil's front yard. The eeriness surrounded the command bridge like an ultra violet lamp. A strange purple aura encircled each crewmember, radiating like heat from their bodies. Jarod looked at his hand, but he did not recognize it. He looked over at Regina and was almost captivated by the aura she was emitting. In some strange way it was beautiful, but it also was scary. He just stared at her as she did at him, studying and memorizing the phenomenon.

"Life-support?" screamed Gail French. Her words vibrated like a kettledrum.

"Life-support is grade 'A', the young technician replied.

"Weapons?" she bellowed next.

"Weapons are all on line," the offensive officer answered.

Kelly Sterling then moved to her station and thumbed her panel, requesting a diagnostic on all engines.

"Ship is running on thrusters," the ARIT announced after several seconds. "Hypersonic drive is at one hundred percent. Hyperlight drive is at one hundred percent. Mass Orbital Projection drive is at one hundred percent. Intragalactic Port Gate drive is at one hundred percent. Medium of this space is not trachion based. All engine drives will not function. Thrusters only!"

Kelly stood and looked at the red light emanating from the view screen. She turned back to Jarod, "It appears the same rules of travel that apply in inner space, apply here as well."

"Good," Jarod announced. "Stealth mode ten…full thrusters. Follow that Tuit ship, but don't let them know we are here." Then he patted his navigator on the shoulder. "Get all the readings you can. We need to know how to get back. I want you to record and decipher everything. Try to put a coordinate system to this. Start with inner space coordinate system."

"Tiah!" the young Mexican from San Antonio replied with enthusiasm. Lieutenant Gene Arroyo loved a challenge and Jarod had just handed him the biggest challenge of his career. A challenge he did not really fathom the importance of. His fingers flew across his console and he started his analysis from the point of entry to his present position. "Permission to drop Bishop Buoys?" he asked.

Bishop Buoys were space markers used to chart open space. Upon a special encoded interlink signal, the buoys would activate giving the ship position and distance. Thus dropping them would be like dropping breadcrumbs marking their journey.

"Agreed," Jarod concurred. "Drop them dead…standard distance…USSTAP encryption three…alpha…six."

Jarod knew the standard encryption would allow any USSTAP ship to activate the buoys and follow their trail. That is if any USSTAP ship was able to activate a gate portal opening to ultra space.

"Tiah!" Gene responded with a twinkle.

Jarod saw the gleam in young Gene's eyes and concluded he was the sole person happy about the situation. He looked at the ceiling in disgust. He realized it was his need for revenge that put his ship in this danger. He rolled his eyes back to his command chair and chastised himself for losing his composure. He needed to regroup.

"Centurions," he bellowed, "my office now!" He looked to the comm officer, "Chief controller to command bridge to take the con."

Jarod went around his chair stepped up to the back door followed by Kelly, Regina and Gail. The sentry opened the door for them. They stepped down the two stairs and turned into Jarod's office. He took his seat at the conference table in the corner of his room, and the ladies took their respective positions.

"First, I must apologize for getting us in this situation," he said, trying to fight the red light and the aura floating around them.

"No apology necessary," Gail said. "You did what you had to do. Those yellow-eyed bitches just blew five thousand of our people out of space. As your chief tactician and security officer, your moves were prudent and warranted. I would not have done anything different."

"I bet Michael would have," he whispered.

Regina looked up in shock, "What the hell did you say?"

Jarod bristled at her tone. As long as he had known Regina, she never used that tone with him, especially in front of the others. "What?" he sighed, trying to defuse whatever it was that was bothering Regina.

"You heard me," Regina continued with the same fervor, "I don't like that. And I'm sure Gail and Kelly don't like it either. You are our Osguard and self-doubt, self-pity or jealous statements like that one have no place coming from any Osguard; especially our Osguard."

Jarod looked at the three and saw the damage his statement did in their faces. He didn't realize he had said it aloud. It was a continuous nagging thought he harbored for years, more of a fear, that he could not live up to the reputation Michael had obtained as the First Osguard. He had never voiced it until now. And his *'Angels'* were giving him hell for it.

"Look," Kelly announced. "I understand this situation, this war, and all the deaths we've seen in the last couple of months would make any man doubt himself. I am sure Michael is full of doubt now. He isn't the god you make him out to be. I know for a fact the Talion incident took a lot of steam out of Michael. He was a brash arrogant son-of-a-bitch before then. He believed his own publicity. He thought he was invincible, the next thing to God Himself. Then he lost a third of his crew at Talion. He never thought he would lose anyone. It was the first time he had to deal with deaths on his crew. You remember how long it took him to get back to work and he was never the same. Michael learned a lesson, I pray, you will never have to learn. He learned he was mortal…he was human…and his decisions effect more than just him."

"How do you know this?" Jarod asked.

"He told me."

"How? When? Why?" Jarod stuttered.

"He wanted to know if he could have done anything different. To my surprise, he chose me as the best tactician in the fleet to use as a sounding board. After weeks of correspondence, analysis and reenactments, we concluded he did the only thing he could do. Any other option would have destroyed the *Justice*." She stood and walked over to Jarod and placed her hand on his shoulder. "It helped, but it took time for him to get over the feeling that he should have died at Talion with his crew. He had the time to recover. You don't. So let me tell you now. Considering the information you had, you did the right thing. The *S'Coril* and the *P'Togi* went down fighting, like true Sixana warriors. There is no more honorable death for a Sixana warrior. You know that and I know that. So let's not forget them, but let us concentrate on our next step." She peered into his eyes as if she was trying to reach his soul. Neither blinked, but a warm forgiving feeling flowed between them.

"Fine…consider it done!" he replied.

"Fine…next step is to find out where the hell we are and then where the hell are the Tuits taking us," Gail suggested. "Because wherever we end up, I bet there's no USSTAP station where we can park the ship."

***

His eyes widened with every word he read. His heart sank as well. The initial report did not take long. Approximately two universal hours after the engagement ended, the initial report was streaming through the USSTAP communications net.

'Siryman Galaxy USSTAP Forces encountered the enemy in space near the D'Ardin Solar System. USSTAP force consisted of three galaxy protectors and eight galaxy cruisers, little more than half-strength, because other packages were assigned to cover other assets in the Siryman Galaxy. Ten Tuits fireships encountered in ten-minute battle. Five destroyed two captured; three escaped. USSTAP forces lost: Galaxy Protector S'Coril, destroyed, all hands lost; Galaxy Protector P'Togi, destroyed, all hands lost; Galaxy Protector Gentry, missing, all hands presumed dead. Osguard Eleven, Jarod M. Stone—missing in action ... presumed dead.'

Michael gave the dispatch tablet to Tirana, and then lowered his head. With his eyes closed he searched his soul. *Could I have done anything different?* His mind flooded with doubt. It felt like Talion all over again. He was in a no win situation like he was at Talion, but he refused to see it that way. His overconfidence caused the deaths of more than a third of his crew at Talion. And now that same attitude has caused the deaths of over five thousand more, and the loss of Osguard Eleven…his cousin Jarod.

"I'm sorry Michael," Tirana offered. "It's a shallow victory, I know…but it is a victory none the less. We stopped them."

"I know, Tirana. I know. I keep telling myself we saved billions of lives yesterday. But it still hurts to know we lost a lot of good people."

"I know the feeling. I never thought I would see the day an Osguard would be killed in battle."

Michael looked at Tirana, his eyes brazen with angst. He reached across his desk and picked up the coin representing the House of the New Osguard. He flipped it to Tirana. She caught it in her right hand. "Jarod isn't dead," he rebuked. "Jarod isn't dead," he repeated softer. "If he was, I would feel it. I would know it in my gut. I am going to wait to see the full report, before I can tell you what happened to him. But I'm sure he isn't dead. I am as sure he isn't dead as I am sure you are holding my coin."

Tirana opened her hand and studied the coin. The black diamond encased by two orbits shone vibrantly on the side she had face up. Around it was a red shiny surface, radiating, almost pulsating with beauty. Somehow it seemed to beam power into her hand. She placed it back on the desk. "I pray that you're right sire. I pray that you're right."

"Haven't you been around me long enough to know by now? I'm always right."

She regarded Michael for a short moment, because his arrogant statement surprised her. Then she saw a slight smile beam on his face."

"Sometimes, I'm always right," he joked. Then the seriousness bounced back into his demeanor. "But I am right about Jarod. We Osguards have a sixth sense about each other. It is sort of a psychic net. We can't read each other's minds or anything like that. But we know when one of us is no longer connected to the net. And Jarod is still connected. I can feel him."

"Sire, are you sure that's not wishful thinking? I mean…you haven't really lost an Osguard before to test this theory."

Michael sighed and looked skyward. "No, it isn't wishful thinking. It is my instinct; my gut that tells me it is true. And if you ask any Osguard, they will tell you the same…Jarod is still alive…and I'm going to find him."

Chapter 28—Games People Play

Musoto's office in the Hoover Building, also known as the concrete mushroom, had become the talk around the water cooler. His new corner office on the fourth floor enclosed for privacy, overlooked the corner of Pennsylvania Ave and 9th Street NW, and seemed to elevate speculation on who he was and whom he worked for. The other agents were aware Musoto did not answer to any supervisor and when asked, all the supervisors would shrug and suggest Musoto worked directly for the Director. It seemed Musoto's importance shot up over night and that made some of the agents edgy and suspicious at best. Trust was a hard thing to come by in the agency.

The bureau had now become more political than capitol hill. Ever since the terrorist attacks, the FBI was under fire, which pushed an already fragile system even more. Agents were afraid of losing their jobs; afraid they were being watched and afraid the brass was second-guessing their decisions. Backstabbing, character assassination and double-dealing had become the norm of operation in the bureau, as people moved up and down the promotion ladder. Then to witness a young punk field agent who messed up several times in his short career establish himself as a player in the bureau overnight, quite frankly upset the bureau's political network.

Musoto's plush corner office, facing the west side, was somewhat smaller than the director's office. He also had a secretary, who by all Washington standards was a knockout. Angela Santos was twenty-nine years old and from Austin Texas. She stood about five feet and five inches tall with dark shiny hair with red highlights that flowed down to the middle of her back, and bronze skin like a goddess. She apparently worked out, because her strong muscular build was evident even in a business outfit. She had high cheekbones, radiant eyes and a smile to kill for.

Many of the male agents would alter their daily travel to their offices just to stick their heads into her office and say hello. Angela knew this, but she didn't mind. They were polite and friendly and not bothersome. However, the daily parade of men, stopping by and trying to strike a conversation with her was somewhat interruptive to her work. So in the past several days, her smile and demeanor became less and less friendly. This curtailed a few of the gawkers, but the majority still made their daily trek to her office for small talk.

The government selected and trained Angela as a CIA field operative, due to her Spanish speaking ability. She served two years with the station chief in Colombia South America, secretly fighting the war on drugs and gathering intelligence about certain unsavory elements in the Colombian government. The cold war was over, but remnants of it still existed. Rogue elements, the last bastion of Soviet dominance still roamed the Earth looking for upheaval to upset the United States. Most of the elements ran with the Russian mob, trafficking in weapons, drugs and prostitution. There were some who catered to the Middle Eastern terrorist network, attempting to sell weapons grade biological and nuclear elements.

Angela was able to stop such a sale during her first assignment in Colombia. Her surveillance and reports allowed the CIA to profile the entire episode and use certain counter techniques to turn the factions against one another, while capturing the five grams of weapons grade plutonium.

Her reward for such an excellent job was a Washington post. However, she never figured the Washington post would be an undercover job in the FBI. Posing as a secretary for Musoto seemed benign at first. She had read all the reports on USSTAP and Musoto's exploits with them and was amazed. She felt like she was playing Scully to Musoto's Fox Maulder on an episode of the X-Files. It was unbelievable, but it was true. At least it was true enough for the President of the United States to take note.

Thus the constant interruption from the sex-deprived degenerates who frequented her office was becoming a nuisance. She knew Musoto needed all the help he could get. However she began to notice most of the small talk now became focused on her, Musoto and their particular job at the bureau. She was trained well enough to evade direct questions without seeming to. However, the talk still appeared more pointed than ever. She soon realized it was not her they were interested in. It was information they were interested in.

Well today, she decided to end the run of men parading through her office. It was time to put the fear of God into them. It was 7:00 A.M., and the building was just coming alive. Angela was wearing a black pinstriped skirt; blue silk blouse and matching jacket. Her one-inch high heels sculpted her calf muscles, highlighting her sexiness, which is what she wanted to do. She had made it through the security checkpoints as normal, and now stepped off the elevator. The traffic in the corridor was light. A few agents were moving, while slurping down their morning wakeup call of coffee.

She sashayed pass them, allowing her perfume to waft in the corridor like a cape, behind her. The male agents took notice and careened their heads as she passed. The smiles that beamed across their sour business-like faces showed the morning pleasure of watching Angela walk by them. The three female agents, who were privy to the show, also turned their heads and watched, but the frowns on their faces highlighted their displeasure or their jealousy. Even they did not really know which.

Special Agent Thomas Ward was one of the agents who enjoyed the morning show Angela gave. He also was the number one guest in Angela's office who tried to pump her for information. He would always find a reason to stop by the office around 8:30 A.M. However, something about the way Angela passed by him this morning made him want to move his timetable up just a hair. He stuffed the chocolate cream donut in his mouth, wiped his hands and changed directions to follow the vivacious young Mexican American.

"Angela," Tom Ward called out.

Angela stopped and turned like a model on a runway. The vision was almost captivating, as the morning sun coming through the corridor windows seemed to beam on her like a spotlight. Tom almost choked as he swallowed hard.

"Yes Tom," Angela delivered with deliberate coyness.

Tom picked up his pace as he race to think of what to say. His actions were immaturely instinctive, like a high school boy going through puberty. He reached Angela, but all he could do was stare into her bright and beautiful sparkling eyes.

"Yes Tom," Angela said again with her most sexy voice.

"Well Angela…I…I…I," Tom stuttered.

"Yes Tom, I would love some coffee. I take it black with a blue packet of sugar," she said, giving him an out.

"Black with a blue packet," he stammered. "Coming right up. I'll bring it to your office."

"Thanks Tom. I'll be waiting," she said with a wink.

The wink caught Tom by surprise. Until then, Angela had been friendly but civil. No hint of any sexual attraction. And he read the wink as a sign that he could pursue her in a sexual manner. He smiled as he watched her turn and continue the parade toward the cross hall and disappear to the right going to her office. He stood there dumbfounded for several seconds, drinking in her perfume and remembering the smile and wink that went with it.

"Yes!" he whispered, clinching his fist in victory. "She wants me!"

Five minutes later, Tom entered Musoto's outer office. Angela was sitting behind her desk in front of the door that led to Musoto's office. Her legs were crossed and her skirt hiked up a bit more than usual, showing the muscles in her thighs. Tom placed the coffee mug he had in his left hand on the desk in front of her, never letting go of his gaze upon her crossed legs.

Recognizing the fog of fantasy that Tom fell into, Angela cleared her throat to bring him back. "Thanks Tom."

Tom shook his head, clearing his thoughts and moved to the opposite chair. "You're welcome," he croaked out. "Anytime," he added with more force. He sat down with his cup of coffee, took a sip and let out a satisfying whimper, "Um…Um. No one makes better coffee than our own cafeteria, don't you think?"

"Oh you went to the cafeteria for this? Why thank you. That's so sweet. But then again, you are a sweet man, aren't you?" she said laying the trap while reversing the tables. His boyish giggle let her know the hook was in. "So Tom," she started, while uncrossing her legs allowing Tom to see more of her thighs. "How are things?"

"Things are fine," he rattled, never losing sight of her legs.

"How's the case coming?" she threw in.

"Case is coming along fine," he said without thinking.

"Oh!" she almost shrilled. "I heard different."

Tom's eyes darted from her legs, to her eyes with an unusual pause at her breasts. "What do you mean, you heard different?"

"Well, rumor has it that you're behind and don't know where to look next."

"Behind! How can you be behind on a simple surveillance job? We got the wiretaps in place and we have teams watching the house around the clock." Then he paused and cocked his head to the right. "What do you know about my case?"

"Maybe it is my job to know," she teased.

"What do you mean maybe it is your job to know? What is this place…some type of internal affairs? Are you spying on us? Is that what Musoto is…a snitch to the brass?"

"I didn't say that," she gasped.

"Wait a minute…is that why I see every agent from around the building coming in here? You are interrogating them, watching them, and reporting on them…aren't you?" Tom's voice rose in anger.

Angela tried to hide her smile behind the cup of coffee she raised to her lips. She closed her eyes as if she were caught in a lie. Once she regained her composure, she put the cup back on the desk, crossed her legs again, giving Tom another taste for his eyes and male libido.

"Tom, I didn't say that…please don't go spreading those rumors…as I told you yesterday, Special Agent Musoto is no different than you."

"If that's true, then why the big office? Why the special secretary? No…there are rumors out there on what you do. And now I think I can confirm most of them. Musoto is working for the brass all right. He is spying on us and reporting our every move. And we idiots have been coming down here and giving you the information like little schoolboys. Shit…weren't we stupid?"

"Now Tom, calm down. It isn't like that…I swear."

"Tell me you don't work for the top man?"

Angela looked away, fueling his suspicions and telling the truth. She knew Musoto worked directly for the President of the United States, and they don't get any more top than that.

"Shit, I knew…I knew it!" he screamed, as he stood. "You aren't anything but trouble. And I will make sure no one comes by here anymore…at least anyone who wants to keep his job. I hope Musoto finds out you let the cat out of the bag. We'll be watching you."

Tom regarded Angela with dispassion instead of the special attention he had in his heart when he walked in. Now her beauty had faded and he saw a threat to his livelihood, which made her uglier than the devil in his eyes. He turned and rushed out the door, slamming it with such a fury it made Angela laugh.

"Mission accomplished," she giggled. "No more uninvited guest trying their mind games on me anymore. Now I can get back to work."

***

President Peters regarded each of the men with contempt. He did not feel he could trust them, but he had to. Something was amiss with his plans with USSTAP and he had no way of telling if any of them had anything to do with it. Peters called the special meeting in the Oval Office to discuss what he knew, or more of what he didn't know. He quietly but attentively sat at his desk. National Security Advisor, James Hall; Vice President George Willis;

Secretary of Defense Paul Thompson; and the Chairman of the Joint Chief of Staff, Army General William Oliver sat across from him. Unlike the first two times, each man seemed alert, contemplative and vigorous. One of them had to be the traitor; one of them had to be the one who was intentionally sabotaging his efforts to communicate with Michael.

General Oliver voiced his objections to Peters' plan last time. Due to his military training he could not acknowledge the prospect of a force superior to the U.S. Military. He thought USSTAP the enemy, who needed to be spied on. Oliver wanted to use Musoto as that spy. However, Musoto was no longer in a place of regard to be used as a spy. Peters studied Oliver and realized that fact did not seem to bother him. He was wearing the shit-eaten grin of a cat.

Then there was Vice President George Willis. His Alabama blood revved up in him, once he found out African Americans led USSTAP. He sounded like he thought it was an overpowering extension of the NAACP, which he never hid his disdain for very well. Peters could never forgive himself for picking a racist bigot as his running mate, but political expediency called for it. That choice cost him the black vote, as Willis so amply and repeatedly reminded him almost daily. According to Willis, this administration should not cow down to the pressures of any self-serving, self-appointed minority leader. This administration was about the business of government, not paying off blackmailers. Peters hated it when Willis got on his tirade about minority and civil rights ruining the backbone of America. Peters had already decided to drop Willis from the ticket during his bid for re-election. However, this little trinket of information may cause him to have to keep him. Was Willis smiling because he knew that, or was he smiling because he is the mastermind behind the sabotage?

Then there was the Secretary of Defense, Paul Thompson, who hadn't had an original thought in his head since birth. All his papers and speeches were soliloquies of past generals and Defense Secretaries. He was a play it safe type of man. Offensive strategic thinking was not his forte. A type he needed in that position during times of peace, someone to keep the dogs of war on a leash. Peters always knew if war ever broke out, he would run things and not Thompson. However, Thompson was another appointee who the media constantly berated, which cost him the respect of U.S. service men and women, here and abroad. Peters shook his head. He had made some political bombshells for decisions in choosing his cabinet. However, Thompson had grown a backbone recently, as evident when he pitched reservations on the Peters' plan. However slight, he still showed personal disapproval with his plan. Could the sheep have sprouted horns? Could he have been mistaken about Thompson's ability to take on a fight?

National Security Advisor, James Hall was the only one Peters knew he could trust. He and Hall grew up together in Iowa. Hall had been with him throughout his entire political career, through his stint as senator and governor for Iowa. Hall had even been his campaign manager during the presidential race. He knew Hall had a good head about him, when it came to international relations. Hall had been a professor at the University of Michigan, before he swooped him up to join his political team, twenty years ago.

"Mr. President?" Hall called, shaking Peters from his mental evaluation of the foursome.

Peters cleared his throat and careened his neck around; cracking the stiff muscles with loud pops the guests could hear. He was tired. He had been up most of the night preparing his speech for the news conference he had to take on the Strategic Armament Reduction Amendment he bully tracked through Congress. The political media had become very suspicious of the spirit of cooperation that seemed to take over the Hill about this amendment. Peters had met no opposition during the entire process. The Republican Party folded on the issue, thanks to the pressure brought to bear by Senator Bass and Congresswoman Eldridge.

"Yes James," Peters replied with red tired eyes.

"Again, I am unsure what our next step should be," Hall continued. "I mean the Kulusks are no longer a threat to USSTAP; therefore, they are no longer a threat to us. USSTAP has flown the coop. We lost our only insight to them when they alienated Musoto. I see business as usual. Well, I see your original agenda back on the plate. We need to build our conventional forces, upgrade Homeland Security and Intelligence Agencies. We do not have the power, money or time to chase a phantom organization that appears to be our allies."

"I don't agree," Oliver interrupted. "Just because they did us a favor, does not make them our allies. Shit, we have been working hand-in-hand with Russia, but I still don't consider them allies. I still consider them the fucking enemy." He sat up in his chair as if he was silently beating his chest. "This USSTAP is a foreign army on our soil. That, in itself, constitutes an invasion. They have invaded the sovereignty of this nation. And it is our job to regain that sovereignty. I want to build up our nuclear arsenal again. I want to kill the band on biological testing. We need to pull out all the stops. We need to be ready when these bastards decide that they just don't want to watch any more, but they want to take over. Shit, Mr. President, we are like sheep ready for the slaughter, where we were once a nation of hungry wolves. We need to become wolves again."

"Thank you general," Peters dismissed. "Your sentiments are noted, but I am the Commander in Chief, and I feel the bigger threat is from the piss ant third world dictators and terrorists circling our country like vultures. I want to become partners with USSTAP. I want their technology working for us. Imagine a wing of Asher missiles, or our troops equipped with pagenays and coronet pistols. Can you see the power we would hold? No country; no terrorist; and certainly no piss ant third world dictator would dare confront us again." Peters turned to Oliver. Their eyes met in a moment of confrontation. The gauntlet was dropped and Peters had the mantle. "We had nuclear weapons and that didn't stop them. We still have our SLBM's and nuclear bombers and that won't stop them either. General, the world knows the United States is reluctant to use weapons of mass destruction for small upheavals. So why do you think building a larger arsenal would change things. We have to have big guns we aren't afraid to use. We have to have big guns that won't give the liberal idealists fodder to criticize us with. These weapons are clean, effective and accurate. Collateral damage will be a bygone term. We hit whom we want. We destroy what we want, when we want and how we want. General, get your head out of your ass and think outside the box. A new age has dropped into our laps and we have failed to grasp it. We need to grasp it. Don't you understand? I am trying to make the military stronger, but in a different way. Think about it general…think about it!"

"Mr. President," Thompson interjected. "What makes you think USSTAP would share their technology with us? It appears their dummy corporation is worldwide. They even have satellites in Moscow and China. That tells me that they are in bed with enemies of the state."

"We have fast food restaurants, soda companies and gym shoe companies in Moscow and China. Are you telling me they are in bed with the enemy as well?"

"No sir, they are bringing capitalism to them, weakening them from the inside. Letting them know how a democracy works."

"Thompson, you dumb ass," Peters snorted. "Democracy is a political system. And democracy is what this Republic practices, to the fullest extent. Capitalism is an economic system. The cold war was about capitalism versus communism, more than democracy versus communism. Democracy just happens to be the perfect forum for capitalism to thrive and communism to die. The problem is bringing capitalism to our enemies only makes them economically stronger to fuel their war against us. It is their political ideology that is the heart of the matter. It is incompatible to us, especially those ideologies that condemn our freedoms. Again, I ask you to think. You have to separate the two. Our enemy has changed. They are no longer threatening our economic survival; they are threatening our basic survival. They have adapted our type of economy to fund their wars against us. So look past your cold war books and catch up Thompson. There is a new world out there and it doesn't like us for some reason."

Thompson shook his head at the lecture, with disbelieving eyes. He didn't understand where Peters meant to go with his logic, but in his opinion, Peters failed to get there. He wanted to shout, *Are you insane!* Luckily, his political savvy kept the outburst in check. He just let Peter's words hang in the air, as if he were truly contemplating them, giving Peters the satisfaction of him being the teacher and he the student. He had to come at it from a different angle, because Peters was now obsessed in owning USSTAP technology and was blathering incoherent political diatribe to justify his wants.

"I understand that sir," he lied. "But let's look at this from a different perspective. According to Musoto, USSTAP has unified thousands of world governments. They shy away from nation states like ours. They also have satellites all over the world ... which means they have a stake in other countries, not just ours. Finally sir, I don't see them supplying one country to dominate the others. From all reports, they are equal protectors. I mean we say we are friends with Russia, but do you see a Russian sitting as your vice president. The First Osguard took a Kulusk as his second in command after the peace accords were signed."

"But they are Americans…they have to…"

"Sir, you told me yourself, not too long ago," Willis interrupted, "and I quote, *'these people are so far removed from what is happening here on Earth. Shit man, they are fighting for sixty galaxies, and they seem to be losing. Get your head out of your ass. You have to think bigger than that.'* I would take that a step further, and say, they are so far removed from what is happening here on Earth, they don't consider themselves Americans anymore. They probably consider themselves citizens of USSTAP…of the galaxy…shit, of the universe, before they consider themselves Americans."

Peters looked at Willis with ire in his eyes. He hated his words being thrown back at him—especially when it made sense. He looked to Hall for help.

Hall took the queue and shrugged his shoulders, "Sorry sir, I have to agree. Searching out the Osguards for what you want is like pissing up a rope. I just don't see it happening. But what I see happening is you and President Repustinov bringing this to the Security Council of the United Nations. In a joint, but secret session, you can acknowledge USSTAP's presence and superiority, hinting at the close relationship the United States shares with them. The word will get out and those piss ant dictators and terrorist may think twice before kicking sand in our face, knowing we have a big brother who is a heavyweight boxer per se."

Peters rolled his eyes skyward. He couldn't believe Hall said that. He wanted to ask if he was crazy, but decided to leave him his dignity. He huffed and lowered his head, "What good is that going to do? Once the word gets out, USSTAP loses its secrecy and we are to blame."

"It won't matter who is to blame sir. Once word leaks out, you can claim plausible denial, because you only told the United Nations Security Council, and that was done with Repustinov."

"So?"

"So…what do you think the world reaction will be to USSTAP once the world finds out that cures for cancer, AIDS, and other life threatening illnesses are available, and because of some stupid code, the people of Earth were not allowed access to it? Public opinion will turn on USSTAP. They will look like Hitler. They will be the most hated organization in the world. They would have to respond and whom else would they come to, to help them form a response? You, that's who they will come to…they will come to you!"

"James, you devious son-of-a-bitch! It's so simplistic, but brilliant. It will also give our enemies another target to hunt, besides us." Peters shuttered at the thought. The entire episode played in his mind within a few seconds. "But what about what I've done with the START amendment?"

"Easily explained away as a decision made to protect the country. Everything you did was in the best interest of the country. And no one will care after they find out what a tyrannical organization USSTAP really is, allowing children, mothers and fathers to needlessly die from something they could've cured. That is the angle we slip to the media once the ball gets rolling. Think about it, all those people in Africa need not have died, droughts need not have happened, famine need not have occurred. The powerful USSTAP had the ability to help, but chose not to. The public will ask, *'why?'* And you will look like an innocent bystander, caught between a rock and a hard place, working for the people like no other president has. We will also slip the fact you where chasing USSTAP down for their technology…their medical technology. And they refused to meet with you. All these reports from Musoto could substantiate that as well."

"I like it," Oliver laughed.

"I must agree, Mr. President," Thompson chimed in. "It is a brilliant plan. I see it as a win-win scenario. I say, let's do it!"

"How about you, Willis?" Peters boomed.

Willis sat still, reflecting on the suggestion. Then a small smile grew on his face. He then nodded, "I can live with it," he replied. "It will expose them for what they really are."

"What is that?" Peters asked.

"Street thugs!" he quipped.

Peter's sighed in disgust. Then he turned to Hall, dismissing Willis' comment with his body language. "James, let's set it up. I will call the Russian president today and propose we speak to the U.N. Security Council. I want you to call Musoto, and see if he can get us some concrete evidence I can present to the council."

***

The door chime broke Michael's concentration. He placed the ARIT tablet on the desk and peered into the viewer to see who dared interrupt him while he was working out the details of USSTAP's second offensive operation of the war. The first had ended with the demolishment of the Kulusk military. The second he hoped would produce a situation in which he could sue for peace with the Tuit Consortium.

The face of the last person he wanted to speak to now, Ambassador Agna T'Mock, the Prime Ambassador of the Association's Parliament, was smiling in his viewer, like a cat that ate the canary. T'Mock was the ambassador from D'Ardin and the unofficial mouthpiece for the Kinsile who still covertly ruled over the two thousand and one hundred planets of the D'Ardin Empire in the Siryman Galaxy. In Michael's haste he had not observed political protocol in personally offering his condolences to the Siryman Ambassador for the loss of the galaxy protectors *S'Coril* and *P'Togi* —a genuine oversight of enormous proportion; especially now that he needed their support in gathering the largest deployment in USSTAP history.

He huffed and buzzed T'Mock in. The doors parted and T'Mock stood in the archway with his hands on his hips like a comic strip superhero, letting his brown cape sway off his elbows. His pale green face, beaming with victory, was highlighted by the twinkle in his golden eyes.

"Osguard!" he announced with obvious false platitude.

"Prime Ambassador," Michael greeted, while standing and motioning for T'Mock to take the seat opposite his desk. "What can I do for you?"

T'Mock entered and the door closed, signaling to Michael the beginning of what he considered a boxing match—a heavyweight championship fight to be more precise.

"Osguard," he said, "it is what I can do for you." He took his seat never turning his gaze from Michael's eyes. "Or more precisely, what the parliament has already done."

Michael sat, feeling his heart pounding in his chest. He knew T'Mock's unannounced visit was not going to be good. He was wrong, it was worse. T'Mock was here as the Prime Ambassador, and not here as the Kinsile's mouthpiece, as Michael thought. "Go on," he beckoned.

"Well Michael...can I call you Michael?"

"Please do, Prime Ambassador," he said, although he wished he wouldn't.

"Well Michael, after I received the news about what happened in Siryman Galaxy, I called an emergency session of parliament."

Michael wanted to ask why, but he knew why. "Oh!" was all he could manage to say.

"That's right Michael. It seems I was not the only one concerned about the safety of our home worlds."

"Are you suggesting I or the other Osguards aren't concerned about your safety?"

T'Mock broke his gaze from Michael's eyes to look out the window port. He motioned to the stars, "We aren't sure if the Osguards care about any particular planet, other than Earth, more than they care about their legacy."

"And what is that suppose to mean?" Michael shot back.

T'Mock turned back toward Michael, connecting with his eyes once more, losing his smile, "It means neither I nor my fellow ambassadors think the Osguards are worried for our planets. These Tuits seem to appear without warning and destroy planets as easy as you or I squash bugs on the floor."

"You're not telling me anything I don't know, Prime Ambassador," Michael warned trying to control his frustration.

"Well, here is something you don't know," T'Mock said, allowing his smile to grow wider across his face. "The parliament voted last night and by an almost unanimous resolution decided to execute article one hundred and one of the Association Constitution."

Fury flowed through Michael's veins as the words sunk into his mind like a jackhammer. Article one hundred and one of the Association Constitution allowed, under the declaration of Martial Law, the reconstruction of the republics, the empires, the federations, confederations, and all of the former domains, which had previously dissolved to make up USSTAP.

Michael shook his head, "But the Osguard Senate has not declared Martial Law."

"And I doubt if the Osguard Senate would ever declare Martial Law," he goaded. "However, the provision to call Martial Law is also the purview of the parliament, with a four-fifths majority vote. And like I said we had more than a four-fifths majority vote."

"You mean to tell me, you achieved a near unanimous vote from 50,241 members of parliament authorizing complete secession from USSTAP charter, and it was ratified by all sixty congresses?" Michael recounted, knowing he was facing a referendum against Osguard rule.

"Yes," T'Mock said, producing an ARIT tablet from his cape pocket and throwing it on the desktop. "Here are the results and the stipulations for article one hundred and one. Basically it says the domains will call back any and all ships assigned under their command for the protection of their area."

Michael's eyes blossomed with rage, the anger rose in his throat and his muscles twitched in disgust. He felt like jumping over the desk and strangling T'Mock. In his younger days when emotion ruled his actions he might have. But today, this very minute he had to be the First Osguard, a diplomat, a politician and a statesman rolled into one very neat package. But all he could concentrate on was the political knife T'Mock just shoved into his back.

The D'Ardin Empire had always wanted to rule the universe, not as the Osguards, but as an Empire. That is why they didn't receive galaxy protectors. The compromise was to hand them Siryman Capitol Station. But Michael now realized that was not enough to appease the Kinsile. They wanted more. And somehow this move that T'Mock orchestrated will give them the upper hand. *But how?*

Michael viewed the ARIT tablet, soaking in the intricacies of the article's provisions. T'Mock summarized it correctly. The article would only leave Michael the sixty galaxy protectors flying under the Osguard flag…well fifty-nine now that Jarod was missing.

"This is unacceptable," Michael shot back. "How am I to go on the offensive with only fifty-nine galaxy protectors?"

"Not my problem," T'Mock huffed. "You are the great and almighty First Osguard…you figure it out."

"I need more than fifty-nine galaxy protectors," Michael found himself pleading.

"No!" T'Mock jeered. "The ships are to go back to the domains immediately."

"Fine," Michael sighed. "The ships can go back as soon as you arrange for their transfer."

"Transfer? What do you mean transfer?" T'Mock laughed. "You will order all crews to return to their domains immediately."

Michael smiled as calm washed over him. "No, you must arrange for their transfer. You see, my dear Prime Ambassador, the provision of the article states all ships assigned to the domains will be called back. It doesn't say anything about their crews. Article one hundred and one, paragraph twenty-four states only the presiding Osguard has authority to release the crews from USSTAP responsibilities, not parliament. I get to keep the crews. So my dear Prime Ambassador, all you've seemed to achieve is to obtain the ships. You will have to man them. USSTAP personnel will remain with USSTAP."

T'Mock squinted as if he were trying to summon heat waves from his eyes to sear the Osguard. Then he huffed, "Fine…if it's going to be that way…so be it."

Michael thought he would back down and would terminate the articles execution, but realized T'Mock's back was truly against the wall. Now he had to give him an out. He ran his fingers over his chin, thinking of what to do. He then suggested, "T'Mock…I will allow a combat crew, not a full crew, but a combat crew to fly the ships to their respective domains and stay to protect the domains, on a couple of conditions."

"What are they?"

"One…upon the completion of hostilities, and when victory is assured, the domains dissolve once more and give full authority of USSTAP ships back to the Osguards. In other words, upon the end of Martial Law, all must revert back to normal. Two…we put that clause into article one hundred and one. Three… I want you to propose that both the parliament and the Osguard Senate ratify article one hundred and one in the future before execution. I don't want every time members of parliament get scared they run off and secede from USSTAP, taking our technology and building up their empires. USSTAP was conceived to end empire building, not to encourage it."

"Isn't USSTAP an empire in its own rights?"

Michael stared at him, showing no emotion. USSTAP had never tried to govern or rule in sovereign territory. All planets ruled as they saw fit, even when their rule was contrary to USSTAP's doctrine. USSTAP may have applied economic or technological embargoes to worlds whose rule was diametrically opposed to USSTAP, but never ever did we use force. *If they want to believe what the Osguards have built is an Empire so be it,* he thought. *But it isn't T'Mock's place or any other ambassadors' place to challenge me on this right now,* he concluded.

"Take it or leave it," Michael persisted. "Either way, I don't have the ships. Unmanned and waiting for your crews to transfer them, they are sitting targets. At least in my proposal they will aid somewhat to the cause." Michael threw the ARIT tablet back at him. "At least my way will make you look like a hero. You have challenged the authority of the First Osguard and won. It is a win-win situation for you."

T'Mock shook with trepidation. His plan would backfire if Michael was successful in defeating the Tuits without the ships, but that would be impossible. And when Michael loses, it won't matter if the domains exist or not; the Tuits will attack them next. The other domains will be looking for another unifying entity to save them. And who else but the D'Ardin Empire could unite the fragments of a splintered USSTAP. Yes it was a winnable situation. There was no way Michael could defeat the Tuits with fifty-nine galaxy protectors.

T'Mock began to grin once more. "You drive a hard bargain, Michael. But I guess that is why you are the First Osguard."

"Losing my entire fleet and those of the other Osguards doesn't constitute a bargain in my mind," Michael huffed. *But I had to keep USSTAP united and this was the best way. Now I know how Abraham Lincoln must've felt.*

The two men stood and shook hands. Michael watched T'Mock leave his office; feeling like he had just spent eleven rounds with the devil and came out battered and bruised. As the door closed behind T'Mock, he couldn't help wondering if T'Mock felt the same way. All in all...Michael concluded the event ended in a political stalemate.

He sat back down, took his ARIT tablet and pushed the attack plan he was working on into the save file. *I may need it someday, but not today.*

"Well like mommy says, *'sometimes you have to fight fire with fire,'*" he told himself. Then he picked up the last communiqué from Jarod. He read the filename 'Starguards'. "B'Kailine, this better not be another ploy for the D'Ardin Empire's rebirth. I have enough enemies to contend with."

Chapter 29—Arrival

B'Kailine stepped onto the observation deck of the Siryman Capitol Station. In front of him, Commander Toevph was directing the docking of the *Galaxy Protector Maji,* carrying Osguard fifteen, Rachel Stone from the Miopsolan Galaxy, and the *Galaxy Protector Hestia,* carrying Osguard twenty-four, Tim Stone from the Breilon Galaxy. The ships filled the view screen as they sailed closer to the docking ring. B'Kailine's heart sank to the pit of his stomach.

It was bad enough to send the report about Jarod being missing in action and presumed dead, but now he had to deal with Jarod's siblings overseeing the operations in his galaxy. By USSTAP law B'Kailine was now the acting Commander in Chief for the Siryman Galaxy, until another Osguard could be appointed. However, there were no more Osguards, at least none of birthright. He began thinking, he would be the first Osguard appointed not from bloodline. He was hoping Rachel and Tim were here to officially recognize that fact, but he knew otherwise.

Their reply suggested they were coming to oversee the operations and search for their brother. It was insulting, because it suggested B'Kailine was either indifferent to the operations or incompetent to carry out the operations. Either way, he took it to heart. It said much about the arrogance of the Stone family, if not the entire Osguard clan.

"Don't take it personally," whispered Toevph, as if she could read his thoughts.

"Take what personally?"

"They are here because Jarod is their brother. They had to come. They have to do everything they can to find him. It's called being a family. It has nothing to do with you."

"How can you be so sure?"

"Because that is what I would do."

"Seriously?"

"Yes!" She then gave final docking instructions to the ships. When she finished, she turned to B'Kailine. "If it was my brother, and I had the ability to help out in the search and rescue effort, nothing and no one could stop me—not even you."

B'Kailine looked at her in surprise. He never counted on sibling love to be so strong as to defy established protocol. "You don't say?" he responded.

"Tiah! And if I may be so bold to advise you sire, I would keep that in mind while dealing with the Osguards. They are between rage and grief. Their minds and their mood will not be normal. You may see them act a little rash and inconsiderate at times. You need to be patient with them."

'Hmm!" B'Kailine expressed. "Well it seems like I will need someone who is versed on the subject to keep me out of trouble. Will you accompany me to the reception deck?"

"Tiah!"

Toevph signaled for someone to take her station and she followed B'Kailine from the observation deck into the bowels of the station. Several minutes later they emerged onto the reception deck just in time to see Rachel and Tim slip onto the deck from the main gateway. They both favored Jarod. However, Tim was more muscular, shaped more like a running back; where Jarod was thinner and sleeker looking, like a wide receiver. Rachel was strikingly beautiful. She wore her auburn hair tied back into a ponytail. She was tall, about five feet, ten-inches tall and very shapely. She had a sprinter's look about her physique. Long but muscular legs, strong long arms and a tiny waist. Her hazel eyes, another trademark of the Osguards, shot through and seemed to make love to your soul when she looked at you, and she was definitely looking at B'Kailine.

B'Kailine, all of a sudden, felt a warmness surrounding him. It was uncomfortable, but delightful at the same time. Toevph and B'Kailine approached the Osguards.

"Welcome to Siryman Capitol Station. I am sorry it is under these circumstances," he greeted with a half smile.

"Thank you, admiral," Tim responded, shaking his hand. "We appreciate all you have done and we appreciate you letting us come."

"No problem." He reached for Rachel's hand. "I understand. If it was my brother, I would be doing the same thing," he lied for the D'Ardin race did not nurture such feelings for siblings. All in all, the D'Ardin race discouraged emotional attachment—of any kind. Nonetheless, he had noticed how much emotional attachment meant to other races during his space voyages, especially during the last eleven years dealing with USSTAP. Most of their decisions were blinded by emotions—gut feelings, Jarod would call them. He didn't approve of such a risky way of doing business, but Jarod always seem to come out on top. So he had to deal with emotions, as Toevph so eloquently reminded him on the observation deck.

Then he noticed he had forgotten to introduce the commander. He stepped aside and waved Toevph to step closer. "Osguards, this is Commander Toevph of the Yo Republic. She is the Chief of the Observation Deck and Head Traffic Controller. She docked you today."

"A wonderful job, I might add," Rachel stated extending her hand.

"You know my brother has spoken so much about you and the admiral in his communiqués with us," Tim said as he shook her hand next. "Especially in the last communiqué, he said he had a nice conversation with you admiral," he continued as he started toward the exit. Since all capitol stations were identical, the Osguards knew the layout of Siryman Station. The one difference would be the mosaics and collages of pictures representing stories of the galaxy. Usually Tim would stop and ask about the stories on the walls, but he had several pressing issues he needed to attend to and had no time for sightseeing. "I think it is only proper we let you know. Our father is back from the hospital and is on Chaktun with his lover. He knows about Jarod being missing."

B'Kailine stopped. Emotions aside, he knew how torn Jarod was about his father.

"That's good news," he whispered. "I thought he could be saved."

"We all did," Rachel chimed.

"Your mother, how's she taking the news about Osguard Eleven?" Toevph interjected.

"I hadn't the nerve to tell her," Tim replied, sending a note that the subject was closed.

"Oh!" was all B'Kailine could manage to say. Then they moved to the coaster and piled in. Now B'Kailine was starting to wonder where they were going. He had lost control of events when Tim moved to the coaster.

"You have several prisoners, including one who you believe was the leader of the Tuit attack," Rachel questioned.

"Tiah!" B'Kailine responded. "But they haven't said anything under interrogation yet."

"Do you mind if my sister and I give it a try. We just want to talk to the leader and see if we can get her to talk."

B'Kailine bristled at the implied insinuation; he was not able to conduct a proper interrogation. Rachel saw the wound his pride took with her brother's request and decided she needed to soften the blow.

"Admiral," she called while laying her hand on his arm. "It is not that you aren't doing a great job. My brother had every confidence in your ability to get the job done. But we have to try. These people do not like the Osguards, and maybe we can use this in our favor. They really have no quarrels with you, so you may not be able to elicit an emotion that could trigger the response we need."

Her touch more than her words calmed B'Kailine's pride. He stared into her eyes, that still seemed to see through his soul and manipulate his body and mind, and nodded. "As you wish!" He turned to the ARIT control, "Gate Portal Deck" he ordered. The coaster doors closed and the circular glass tube sailed on a cushion of magnetic coils at a speed of one hundred and sixty miles per hour. The prison station was several thousand kilomarks and negative one on the galactic plane from capitol station. They had to use the gate portal to step to the station. It was twenty decks with no windows, ports or any view of the heavenly stars outside. It was temporary lodging for prisoners, awaiting trial or thus being sent to a prison planet, similar to what Earth was four hundred millenniums ago.

"Admiral," Tim bellowed. "We are simply your guests. Until we find Jarod or the Osguard Senate appoints another Osguard, this is your show."

"Thank you, Osguard. I understand your position…and I understand mine."

"Not really, admiral," Rachel interjected. "I can tell from your initial report, you think Jarod dead. Well, we the Osguards feel differently. We have a sixth sense about one another. It is sort of a link. A link we weren't aware of, until our indoctrination so long ago. We can feel each other, and when one is lost, we would feel it. What we feel when we concentrate on Jarod is distance, not death. I suspect Jarod found a way to chase the other ships back and he followed. I feel he is in danger, but he is alive. If we can get something out of their leader we may be able to bring the fight to them and save Jarod."

"How?" Toevph asked.

"Our Science Corps thinks they have discovered a way to use our gate portal to open up ultra space. They have given their findings to the Engineering Corps for validation. If this works, all we need are coordinates. I want our top engineers, yours, mine and Tim's to go through that ship of theirs and find out all they can. But I am most interested in finding the coordinates to transverse ultra space."

"How come I didn't know about this before?" B'Kailine asked.

"It's Osguard level only," Rachel said with the voice of an angel. "And you are now the acting Osguard…so you are privy to the information."

"What about me?" Toevph asked in surprise. "I'm just a commander."

"Jarod said you were the admiral's sounding board. So whatever the admiral knew, you had to know," Tim responded.

"I didn't know your brother was that insightful," B'Kailine mused. "Until recently, I thought he didn't care for the way I ran the station."

"He told us all about that," Tim continued. "When we get him back, you two will have much to catch up on. And that is too bad. Jarod should have let you know how he felt earlier. But at least he did let you know."

"Tiah!" B'Kailine replied, wondering how much of that conversation Jarod shared with his siblings or with other Osguards.

The coaster slowed to a stop and the doors flung open. The foursome stood and exited, moving to Gate Portal Room One in silence. B'Kailine gave the operator instructions and within seconds, four gate portal lights appeared on the platform. They stepped into the light and instantly appeared on the prison station gate portal platform. The station's sire, a rugged looking Yo, with sapphire eyes and mocha colored skin, slipped through the door just in time to greet the Osguards as they stepped off the six-inch platform. Colonel Torade stood six feet tall and had a stern granite-like face.

They exchanged pleasantries and exited the room. Torade escorted them to the main prison floor. They entered a long corridor, lined with electronic cells enclosed by chromerion fields, making it seem like they were open study alcoves in a library. Inside the alcoves were some of the Tuits taken in the battle of D'Ardin. They wore the black robes of the Tuit soldier, but one, in the middle cell, wore a golden robe, markedly different than the black robes. It had several white braids around the arm, suggesting a high rank and she wore a gold belt with a strange emblem on the buckle, showing a strange star pattern.

Torade ushered them to her cell, clicked the DNA lock reader. The chromerion field dropped and the white noise humming from the doorway disappeared. "Osguards! Let me introduce you to the Sixth Daughter of Fire of the Tuit Consortium, Rina of Jaywick."

Rina stood, her eyes narrowing as she focused on the foursome. She recognized the characteristic auburn hair and hazel eyes on Rachel and Tim as that of the Osguard lineage, and rejected B'Kailine and Toevph as flunkies. She lunged with cat like precision toward Tim. Tim slipped to his right, raised his left knee and crushed it into Rina's stomach. The wind rushed from her lungs with a loud whoosh, as her forward momentum stopped like a car hitting a wall. Then Tim slammed his left elbow down on her back, sending her crashing to the floor.

"Nice to meet you too," he conveyed in an authoritative but calm voice. Then Rachel picked her up and slung her like a rag doll back to the bed.

"Now Rina of Jaywick, Sixth Daughter of Fire of the Tuit Consortium, let's have a little chat," Rachel stated with the same calm demeanor.

"Admiral, colonel and commander," Tim addressed, "if you please give us some privacy…we would like to have a talk with Rina."

Torade turned to B'Kailine and Toevph for confirmation. B'Kailine sighed and then shrugged. "As you wish," he murmured. "Try not to get any blood on the walls," he added, half joking and half serious, while handing Tim an interrogation MARIT.

"I'll try to remember that," Rachel mused, patting a dazed Rina on the cheek.

Upon hearing this, B'Kailine, Toevph and Torade exited the cell, replaced the chromerion field and disappeared from sight.

***

"Mom…Dad!" Stelana shouted from the corridor.

She had just arrived at Millmum Capitol Station and was directed to the auditorium by one of the security guards. When she saw the two figures standing near the back row of the auditorium, she thought them familiar. As she stepped closer, she recognized them as her parents. She ran toward them like a little girl, aching for the hugs and warm embrace.

Her mother, Misiana, grabbed her first, holding her tight like only a mother could do. Stelana sunk into her arms, feeling the warmth generate around her like a chromerion field. For this second, she was in heaven. Whatever lay ahead was nothing, now that she had her parents here to help her face it.

Her father, Vijari, collapsed his arms around both of them and laid his head over his daughter's head. His embrace added to the feeling of warmth swelling around them. Tears floated from his eyes, salting his cheeks and winding down to Stelana's hair, but he didn't care. He was also in heaven. He had his family in his arms, safe and sound—the first time since the war started. It was an unexpected surprise. He didn't want to let go. He wanted to hold on to the moment for eternity. So he just held on, as tight as he could, letting the feeling dissipate on its own.

A few seconds passed before Vijari let go of his embrace. He grabbed Stelana's hand to keep the warmth alive in the circle. "What are you doing here?" he asked.

"The First Osguard summoned me."

"He called for your father as well," Misiana replied.

"What do you think it means?" Vijari questioned to no one in particular.

"Look!" Misiana exclaimed. "At the door…isn't that your brother Rikar?"

Vijari turned and squinted. He waved to the person in the doorway, who waved back. "Tiah! That's Rikar."

"I thought he was on the *Gemdi*?" Stelana perked.

"I thought he was too," Vijari noted.

"What the hell are you doing here?" Rikar roared as he shook his brother's hand. Then he leaned over to kiss Misiana and Stelana on the cheek.

"Don't tell me…you were summoned by the First Osguard?" Vijari asked.

"Yes, I was. And so were my two sons."

"Are Tomi and Chiki here?" Stelana inquired.

"Yes, they just arrived. They will be here shortly."

"Great, the mystery thickens." Vijari added.

The lights shifted to red, then normal, indicating the speaker, whoever it was, was about to start. They had five minutes to take their seats. Tomi and Chiki, walked in escorting their mother, as the lights went to normal. The brothers and their family sat down after exchanging more pleasantries.

Worry now started seeping into Stelana's heart. She didn't know what this was about. And she didn't like not knowing. It was a sign of weakness or a sign of not being prepared. Either way, it was a position she did not like to deal from. All her Sixana training told her to be on her guard, but her common sense told her otherwise. She was in the heart of USSTAP, Millmum Capitol Station--the stronghold of the universe. She was among her peers, and now her family. Caution need not be a prerequisite for the evening, but caution still lingered in her thoughts.

Michael walked onto the stage, without fanfare or an introduction. The audience recognized him and stood at attention. Michael smiled and asked them to take their seats. He walked to the glass podium in the center of the stage, sporting his boxer-built muscular frame like a model. His walk was confident, strong and sturdy, exuding the mantle of leadership with each step he took.

It was a mantle he held for over fifteen years, taking USSTAP from a strong economic power to one of almost sovereign proportion. The last thirty galaxies were installed under his watch, and the treaty assigning an Osguard to watch over each of the galaxies also came under his watch. Until then, only the three galaxies in the local group had Osguard oversight. The other galaxies were satellites under the USSTAP flag. It was Michael who united USSTAP and who kept the peace for the last eleven years.

To the audience, they were looking at their George Washington, a man whose deeds have overshadowed the man, placed him not just *in* history, but *as* history, while putting him on the pedestal of fame that no other man could live up to. Even with the present danger of universal war, Michael still radiated the composure that made him a legend.

When Michael reached the podium his eyes swept the room in long glances. He took several breaths as he thumbed his room control PARIT to secure the room. A low hum and a change in light color washed the room as the ARIT searched for listening devices and unauthorized personnel in the room. His PARIT blinked the words *'ROOM IS SECURE'* on the screen. Michael placed the device down. Again he looked around in long drawn out glances.

"Good day!" Michael opened with. "I'm sorry for the mystery surrounding the summons calling you all here today. But it was necessary for security reasons. What I am about to share with you is very important for the future of our universe." He paused to study the faces of his audience. He saw determination in their eyes. At that moment, he knew anything he asked of them, they would gladly do.

He clicked his PARIT once more, and the latest HVP displaying Laurona and Nausona's adventure on Earth played for the audience. It needed no introduction, because its existence had been rumored throughout USSTAP for the last couple of days. For Stelana, it was the second time she watched the HVP, but she watched in silence anyway.

Two hours later, the HVP ended and the audience remained silent as Michael re-entered the auditorium. He stepped onto the stage and gazed over the crowd once more. He saw the same determination in their eyes, but he also witnessed curiosity surrounding their looks. He expected it. His opening statement didn't satisfy the main question, *'Why were they summoned?'*

"Okay," he began again. "The main gist of me calling you today is this. The Universal Parliament, in a special session, held by interlink, looked at two propositions for additions to the Osguards. The first proposition was to add those of the Akaher lineage who would not inherit the throne of Chaktun. As I suspected, the Universal Parliament rejected it. The second proposal was for the descendants of the Osguard Mothers' adopted family to enter the Osguards. This proposal was accepted. I am here to tell you, there are forty-six living descendants who have just been nominated as Osguards."

Michael flashed a family tree chart listing the descendants of the adopted Osguards. Stelana eyes searched the chart until she saw her name. It branched from her father, Vijari, who through her grandfather, Stelanar, branched from Mary, the adopted daughter of Laurona. Obviously, Mary was her great-grandmother, but she did not know her as Mary. She thought her great-grandmother's name was Ari—at least that is what her grandfather Stelanar called her. Stelana did not remember her. She passed when she was still a baby.

She turned to her father, "Dad! Did you know anything about this?"

"No baby, I didn't. As far as I knew, she was a descendant of the House of Sailon. I had no idea she was raised by an Osguard Mother—especially Laurona. My grandfather served under Laurona just before she died. I suppose that is how they met."

"Dad, do you know what this means?"

"No…baby…it is still a lot to take in."

"It means, we have been voted in as Osguards...Daddy, we are Osguards."

Vijari regarded his daughter for a moment, and then turned to his younger brother, who was beaming with so much pride, he was about to pop a button. Stelana's words sunk in and his heart went from dread, to neutral, to exhilaration in a split second.

"I know none of you suspected the lineage," Michael continued after the clamor subsided. "It was hidden from you because of Chaktun law. Once the Osguard Mothers passed, the adopted children had to give up all claims to the Osguard name. They were wealthy, but without a name. They were listed in the books as orphans. But, I am happy that all the descendants found their way into the USSTAP family. It must have been instilled in each of you since birth to follow in the steps of your parents and grandparents. It seems all of the adopted children entered USSTAP and served in many capacities. And their children, some of you, followed and your children followed. Therefore the transition to Osguard should be fairly simple." Michael paused, took a deep breath and exhaled. "But because of the war, we do not have the time to properly train you as Osguards. I am hoping your Sixana training will carry you forth. I need you to be Osguards without the formal training. I need you to train yourselves. I am not asking for USSTAP...I'm asking for the universe. Are you willing to take the step and accept the vote?"

Michael looked onto the crowd and saw many heads nod. He needed verification. The parliament required it as well.

"Those of you, who have been elected Osguards by the parliament, please take the PARIT at your station, enter your personal code and vote acceptance or not," Michael ordered.

In the audience, Michael heard the scramble of them reaching for the PARITs and the musical strokes of its keys being tapped. He watched the screen on his PARIT as the results rolled in. Within forty seconds all forty-six members had answered. All forty-six had answered yes. USSTAP had increased the number of Osguards by forty-six.

"Welcome cousins," Michael gleamed. "Now this is what I need you to do."

Chapter 30—Centaurus Supercluster

"Normal space off the starboard side," Lt Gene Arroyo announced.

Jarod stood from his command chair and walked to the front edge of the command bridge. He peered at the giant view port screen covering both decks of the command and control bridges. The opening looked like a blue hole in the fabric of red space. The Tuit ships were scrambling toward the hole like flies toward manure.

"Steady as she goes," Jarod ordered. "Can you get in tight without being detected?" he asked the pilot.

"Tiah!" the young ensign replied.

"Do it!" he commanded.

The ensign adjusted the thrusters and shot off larger bursts. The *Gentry* picked up speed and pushed toward the last Tuit ship. The pilot adjusted pitch and roll to slide the galaxy protector to within one hundred kilomarks of the port aft of the ship. Here, the ship's thruster output would feed back like a scanner echo, as long as the young ensign matched the maneuver inch by inch. It was a game he played in pilot school, mimicking his lead ship so well under stealth mode ten conditions that he could get lost in the sensor echoes.

"Weapons at ready," Jarod ordered. "Defensive posture only," he added to calm the crew.

The three Tuit ships eased into normal space, spun on their axis to match the north paw space and immediately jumped into light speed. The opening began to close and the *Gentry* pushed forward. The opening stabilized as the *Gentry* exited ultra space. Once she was through, the opening collapsed and the red light of ultra space disappeared.

"Can we get a track on the Tuit ships?" Regina asked from her chair.

"Tiah!" replied Arroyo. "Plotting and setting. Pilot, track is set."

The ensign nodded.

Jarod looked over to Regina, Kelly and Gail, holding his breath. Then he blew it out hard. "Do it!" he ordered. "Follow, but do not overtake…match speed and track."

The pilot moved his hands over his controls and the ship lurched through hypersonic, hyperlight to MOP fifty, simultaneously spinning on its axis to match the north paw space. Outside the ship moved from stealth ten-mode to the regular light spectrum, and then it stretched from the light to the invisible spectrum.

The *Gentry* followed the track Arroyo laid out for ten minutes, covering fifty light years of conventional space. The Tuit ships slowed to hypersonic speed and entered an eight-planet solar system.

The Defensive Officer reported the Tuits maneuvers to Jarod.

"All stop!" Jarod ordered. "Stealth mode ten! All sensors…all scanners!"

The *Gentry* came to a full stop, a half light year outside the solar system, and then faded into the tapestry of normal space. Her search array filled the heavens, searching for tribolemincic energy dispersal emanating from the ships or any of the planets.

"Sire," the defensive officer called. "I'm reading major civilizations from the fifth planet. Over eight hundred billion life signs—mostly Tuit."

"Do you think it is their home world?" Kelly speculated aloud.

"Perhaps…" Regina answered.

"Defense systems?" Kelly asked.

"I'm reading several different energy readings—none I recognize," he reported. "My guess is it is a combined shielding grid."

"Can we penetrate?" she asked

"Unknown!"

"What's next?" Regina questioned Jarod.

"Recon…baby, recon." He turned to Regina, Kelly and Gail. "Are you guys ready?"

***

"My sisters," the First Daughter of Fire greeted the crowd. She was in the Hall of Fire addressing the full consortium. Five hundred Fireholders, representing five hundred and nineteen thousand planets in five hundred galaxies stretching over five star clusters were assembled to hear the latest report on how the war was going. "I'm sorry to report to you, our invasion force was severely defeated by our foe in the latest attack stratagem. We lost seven fireships, including Rina's ship, the *Jayle*. Our losses are seven thousand sisters, presumed dead or missing. The Fireships, *Catle, Sasle and Pitle*, returned several hours ago with the report. It appears the enemy was laying in wait and had developed a new weapon that sliced through our energy deflectors. It seems Rina of Jaywick underestimated our foe."

The First Daughter, Tisha of Solwick, daughter of Esha, granddaughter of Isha wanted to smile, but knew it would be in bad form to smile while announcing the demise of seven thousand of her fellow sisters. The sweet feeling of revenge was eating at her soul, while she savored the taste on her lips of Rina's demise. However she was not sure Rina met her death. The three ships reported losing contact with the *Jayle*, but they could not confirm its destruction like they could confirm the *Solle*, the *Ishle*, the *Dinle*, the *Eshle* and the *Sinle*. The *Jayle*, the *Comle* and the *Misle* were just unaccounted for and presumed destroyed. Each ship had a crew of one thousand sisters of fire. It was a large price to pay to rid oneself of an enemy, but it was done.

Rina was gone, and her memory was soiled. Unlike her grandmother, Rina would be blamed for the deaths of her sisters. Tisha would make sure of that.

"The Sixth Daughter, Rina of Jaywick, daughter of Rena, granddaughter of Dina was too rash, too impudent, and too uncontrollable to lead our revenge on the fourth level. Her heart was raw and her courage was wavering. Her spirit was flawed and she was too inept to carry out this task.

Yes, my sisters, she had us fooled. She had us all fooled, including me. But the death of our sisters should awaken our eyes to the truth. Rina of Jaywick came from a cursed line. Her grandmother was cursed and probably the cause for the demise of the *Snikle* and the *Tesle*. We have been prosecuting a war for years based on speculation. I say…"

"…I say the First Daughter has lost it!" shouted a voice from behind her.

Tisha turned to see who dared cut her off. When she looked, she saw the Second Daughter, Miam of Solwick, with the look of the devil beaming from her eyes.

"How dare you interrupt me," Tisha corrected.

"Interrupt you…interrupt you," Miam said in exasperation. "I should have interrupted you years ago." Miam pulled out a control tablet. "Rina gave me this, just in case she didn't come back. In here, she outlines every roadblock and obstacle you have thrown in her way during the prosecution of this war. To tell the truth, I find it very interesting. I also find it interesting how you and your mother seem to reject the official report on the destruction of the *Snikle* and the *Tesle*, and came up with your own version. It appears you have been conducting yourself based on your own personal version of events, and not the official version like the rest of us. This in itself is treason!"

Tisha's eyes widened and her mouth went agape. Her mind raced for a comment to counter the charge. She never thought Rina so thorough. She never figured Rina would find an ally in the daughterhood to listen to her. It was pure and simple. If she did not return from a battle, she had an out to preserve her character—that damned con tablet. How long had she been working on it? How much information was in it? What evidence could it contain? Tisha was sure there was no evidence to collaborate the charge.

"All lies…all lies!" she countered. "There is no evidence to support this claim. It is preposterous that you even bring her claim to light." The whispers in the hall echoed in her ear. She knew confusion rang in the whispers. She had to turn the tide her way. "What do you offer in support of Rina's claim?" she pushed, seeing a way out.

Miam stood and walked to the center stage, sharing the light with Tisha. She gazed upon the audience and saw the same confusion Tisha heard hanging over them. The whispers started to ring louder in the Hall of Fire.

"The other Daughters of Fire have viewed the charges," Miam continued. "And though I admit the evidence is circumstantial, it is overwhelming still. I invite the Consortium to view the charges and the evidence and come up with their own opinion. I call for a Vote of Confidence within three days."

The clamor again rose to an audible level within the auditorium. A Vote of Confidence had not been called for any Daughter of Fire in over a century. It was a drastic approach to dethrone an icon, but an effective way if successful. The entire Consortium had to vote whether they had confidence in the way the First Daughter was running the Consortium or not. It had to be a unanimous vote either way. If the vote was inconclusive, meaning a unanimous vote could not be reached Tisha had the Right of Challenge similar to what Rina faced in the Hall several cycles ago. However her challenge would be against whoever called for the vote—in this case, Miam. This was one of the reasons the call for the vote had not been used in so long. A unanimous vote for five hundred members was impossible to achieve. The Right of Challenge was almost a certainty to happen.

Miam peered into Tisha's eyes, like a prizefighter preparing for a fight, searching for fear in the soul. The search turned up empty. Miam saw defiance in Tisha's eyes.

"You're making a deadly mistake," Tisha pushed. "Your only hope is the vote is unanimous for me, because if isn't, I will surely kill you."

"That's strange," Miam mused, "I was about to say the same thing to you."

***

Under the darkness cloaking space, the *USSTAP Galaxy Protector Gentry* sailed under the Tuit solar system negative five on the galactic plane, using hyperlight speed. They parked on the outer edge of the system and went to stealth mode ten. Several seconds later, the two-mile long ship flew out from under the solar system, undetected and undaunted.

Hours later, in the midst of the night in the Tuit capital, in the market place amongst the geometric buildings of pyramids, spheres, cones, and cylinders towering into the night sky, trying to kiss the twin orange moons, three strangers to the area watch the challenge over a large view screen displaying the proceedings. One of the strangers had a familiar strong chin and shoulder length hair. One had brunette hair falling below her shoulders, and the third exuded confidence just in her posture alone. Regina, Kelly and Gail had stepped to the planet when the *Gentry* penetrated the solar system to get within gate portal range. Reconnaissance was their mission.

They were wearing yellow cat-like contacts and green robes with hoods to allow them to blend into the population. Under their robes, they carried a Charlie Belt combination, containing a PARIT, Pagenay and a PGP. The PARIT was set for translation with an earpiece that they hid under the hoods and attached to their ears. It was a pure guess on what color robe to wear, but they knew from the HVP the Tuits dressed in hooded robes, and gold robes meant command and black meant soldiers of their military. To their surprise, the streets were full of women of all colors, shapes and sizes, wearing multiple color hooded robes, some with designs and some plain.

Except for the characteristic cat-like yellow eyes, the women were exact replicas of humans.

Regina leaned over to Gail and Kelly; "It looks like we may have an ally in the Tuit Consortium. The First Daughter doesn't accept the Consortium's version of events surrounding the *Snikle* and the *Tesle*."

"Yeah, but how does that help us?" Kelly asked.

"Maybe if we give her a look at our HVP it will help confirm her suspicions," she answered.

"I don't think she wants her suspicions confirmed in that way," Gail added.

***

"Sire," the defense officer called, "an approaching ship, heading four–four–five, mark zero–zero."

The *Gentry* was parked several light years outside the Tuit solar system, at negative fifteen on the galactic plane, in stealth mode ten. The blackness of space shrouded them, while the black slitanium skin absorbed, bent and refracted light and energy, making it almost invisible to search arrays and difficult to see in the visual spectrum.

"Run silent," Jarod ordered, making sure the stabilization thrusters keeping them in place and the search array were off. The thrusters would leave energy patterns for the Tuit ship to pick up, and the search array could be traced back to them. Passive detection was all that was required to chart the approaching ships path.

The defensive officer complied with the command and switched to passive detection mode, collecting data on energy output coming from the Tuit ship and plotting the course on the star map, which was depicted on the left screen between the pilot and navigator position.

The Tuit fireship sailed at hypersonic speed overhead, all the while the crew of the *Gentry* held their breaths, hoping and praying the Tuits did not have the technology to penetrate the USSTAP stealth equipment. The dots clicked on the screen at an unnerving slow pace, because the crew, especially Jarod was experiencing temporal distortion—similar to watching an accident happen before their eyes. Their brains recorded every microsecond that passed, making it seem like minutes. Every dot that clicked on the screen seemed like an eternity.

When the dots correlated to a ship directly above their heads, perspiration sprang on Jarod's forehead, as he felt hot all of a sudden. His gaze focused on the screen as his mind imagined the image of the white cone ship floating in space above them. No one moved. All were frozen in place, as if a sudden movement on the ship would somehow signal their presence to the enemy.

Then after several agonizing seconds, another dot plotted on the screen, signifying the ship had passed them. Then another dot and another dot, placing the ship one thousand kilomarks in front of them, heading toward the Tuit solar system. Jarod began to breathe normally and his pulse slow down. He was starting to feel better, thinking the danger was passing.

Then when he calculated the next dot should appear it didn't. He waited a split second before turning and shooting a quizzical look to his defensive officer. The defensive officer shrugged his shoulders.

"It appears they stopped, sire," he followed up with.

Jarod rolled his eyes, "Gees…how far?"

"Approximately two thousand kilomarks."

"Well within their weapons range," Jarod noted. "Do you think they detected us?"

"Tiah sire, they are turning around and descending," he replied.

"Shit…shit…shit!" Jarod cursed. "Alert one…battle stations…chromerion field up…weapons on line."

The command decked hummed with activity as Jarod's orders came to life. The Alert one buzzer whaled like a police siren in the air. The weapons officer activated the K-cannon first. Then he activated the other weapons. He was confident the K-cannon made the difference last time and that it would be his first weapon of choice this time. When all systems showed ready, he nodded to Jarod.

"One thousand kilomarks, negative five on the galactic plane," the defense operator reported. "They are powering up weapons."

"Decoys away…thrusters to maximum…reverse direction…ascend to match galactic plane."

Several circular two-meter diameter energy balls, wrapped in finely polished glass flew from the stern ejector pods. The glass amplified the energy balls and gave a faint signature of a full size ship in quiet mode. The *Gentry* then ascended on the galactic plane, still in stealth mode.

The Tuit ship continued its descent toward the decoys. Then from the four points of the Tuit ship's cone bottom, beams from the rhetonic guns shot out forward. Two were red and two were blue. The beams converged into one spiraling color twisted ray two thousand meters off their bow. The beams obliterated the decoys into nothingness. Jarod thought of running, but his energy signature would give him away. He had to neutralize the threat and then escape. Jarod shook his head thinking of the word neutralize. It was euphuism for killing, and he was about to kill a large number of people in the name of war.

The huge white cone ship soon filled the large view port screen. Jarod swallowed hard, while looking at his crew. He knew they were waiting on his orders. They would be the instruments he would use to commit this act. Was it murder? Was it justified? He didn't know and for a split second, he didn't care. That split second was all he needed to clear his conscience and give the order.

"Lock on and fire!" he commanded. His voice was a stranger to him. He did not recognize the voice coming from his own throat, but they did. He heard the words, he even understood the words, but he heard them and understood them like he was a spectator on the outside, watching the action go on without his input. He sat back in his chair, praying to God to bless the souls he had just condemned to death.

The *Gentry* popped out of stealth mode, respecting the laws of physics once more. The black ship of death rang out five quick shots from the K-cannon, splicing space with the awesome Kulusk weapon. The shots punched, pounded and cracked the Tuit ship's port hull—from bow to stern. The hull ripped apart like an orange peel, slicing off big chunks. The Tuit ship listed to port and then to stern. Fire was evident throughout the ship.

Jarod looked on with horror. He saw the ship fighting for its life. He would usually stop the battle here and offer the occupants a way out, but he was not in familiar space. He was in enemy territory. Taking prisoners was not an option, or was it? He hesitated a moment while he pondered the question, knowing his weapons officer had his finger on the K-cannon trigger, ready to deliver another blow. He was trained to sustain life whenever possible. It was the Osguard code…Guardian of all…Protector of all.

"Hail them for survivors," he commanded.

"Tiah!" responded the communication officer to his right. He flipped the switch and recorded a hail in the Tuit native language. Then he began to flip the switch to send, when a bright explosion filled the giant view port screen. The Tuit ship exploded with such a force, the scathing light rivaled the distant sun. The tribolemincic core had sustained too much damage and sent explosive shocks throughout the ship. Pieces of white metal, blood and body parts sprayed space and littered the *Gentry*'s chromerion field.

The explosion was so bright; Jarod had to shield his eyes with his hands. Training took over. He had to get away from the scene. It would take the Tuits sometime to figure out what happened and by then he should have a plan in place to execute. For now, he could not be discovered. He set coordinates into his ARIT pad on his command chair. The coordinates then flashed on the navigator and pilot stations.

"MOP ten…get us there now!" he yelled.

The *Gentry* flew into the speed schedule and challenged the laws of physics once more, disappearing into space faster than light, leaving in its wake another one thousand dead Tuit sisters of the Consortium.

Chapter 31—Hit or Miss

The door crashed to the floor with a loud thump. The windows blew out, shattering in a thousand pieces. Five black clad soldiers, carrying sleek gray rifles stormed through the front door and three stormed through the back door. Two soldiers bordered each of the now glassless windows. Silver laser range beams shot from their rifles, and dotted the darkness. No patches were visible, just a black silhouette outlining the bodies could be seen. Their helmets, gloves, and flak jackets appeared connected, making them look like robots in one-piece armor suits.

The house alarm rang, breaking the silence of the quiet neighborhood. One soldier hurried to the alarm control box, pulled an instrument from a thigh cargo pocket and ran it in front of the box. The alarm shut down.

The other soldiers scurried to the bedroom door, where the instruments inside their helmets indicated the subject was located. The readout displayed range and bearing of the target in the lower right and left corner of their helmet view screen. The lead soldier dropped to a knee, lifted the rifle and shot a blast into the door. The door shattered into splinters, blowing out like a swarm of bees in every direction. The two standing next to the soldier, rushed into the bedroom, visually sweeping the area. Their readouts directed them to the bed.

On the bed lay a small five-inch long box. On the front, red lights were flashing in a steady rhythm. The lead soldier's head cocked to one side. The subject wasn't in bed. Even though the readout indicated the subject should be in bed, the soldier only saw the small box with lights flashing. Then in a moment of clarity…a frightening epiphany where reason met fact ... the soldier's eyes widened inside the black glassless helmet.

"Evacuate…emergency evacuate!" she screamed.

White ovals darted in and out of the house as the soldiers ran, dove and rolled into the safety of inner-space. The scramble took less than three seconds from the time Lieutenant Gloria Magma called for the emergency evacuation. A split second after Gloria was safe inside the chromerion field inside inner space, Mona Richard's house exploded with the force of a Kulusk Torko bomb. Splitting the roof into three and sending the pieces a hundred feet in the air. The walls shredded like paper and blew out, raining metal, wood and cement over a one hundred-yard radius. The blast rocked the ground and spread to the neighboring houses, piercing basketball size holes throughout. Instantly sirens rang through the air, searching for the fastest route to respond to the explosion.

Gloria's handler, on Lilly Station was monitoring her every word, along with her vital signs for stress. Each soldier had a specific contact, a handler, back on Lilly Station, listening, watching and seeing all through a remote access PARIT in his or her battle dress suit. In case of emergency, the handler had the full authority to pull their charge out.

When Gloria called for emergency exit, the order rang over all interlinks and each handler pushed the emergency gate portal, which activated within a foot of his or her personnel. They scrambled into the white light without hesitation, as they were trained to do. This trained reaction allowed the fifteen-man team to return to Lilly Station, unscathed.

On the portal stage of Lilly Station gate portal room five, Gloria rolled out of her white opening and fell to the floor followed by a half dozen of her crew, slipping, sliding and rolling from the light and crashing to the floor. Gloria rose to one knee, the black sparkle of a micro portal shining around her head, chest and hands. Two-seconds later her helmet, gloves and flak jacket faded away in the midst of the sparkle. She stood, holding her coronet rifle, wearing her delta belt and dazed by the last few seconds.

"Shit!" she swore to no one in particular.

Around her, the rest of the crew was shedding themselves of the additional armor as well.

"Call Kim!" she shouted. "Tell her to pull back…it's a trap. The bitches knew we were coming. Emergency evac…repeat…emergency evac!"

The portal operator signaled the control deck through his console and forwarded the *'Emergency Evac'* call.

Gloria ran through the doors, barely clearing them as they opened. She needed to get to the control deck. She wanted to see what was happening with Kim. Her feet glided over the carpet, barely touching but almost flying. Her heart filled with dread. She knew it was sheer luck she deciphered the flashing lights on the box as a countdown. She was unable to read the lights, but the lights were too steady, too rhythmic to be anything else. She was not sure if Kim would figure it out in time.

Kim was leading an extraction team to pick up Eldridge at her apartment in the Watergate Building. If Mona had set a trap, so would Congresswoman Eldridge. If not, it would be safer to assume she did and find another way to extract her from the planet.

Gloria turned a corner, hopped on a ladder and slid two levels down. She jumped off the ladder and cut to her right and sprinted twenty-five yards down the corridor. When she hit the door, her breath was labored, but not exhausted. She put her hand in the DNA lock reader and it slid opened to the right. She ran into the room.

The room was circular with control consoles littering in some mosaic pattern throughout. Behind each cylinder console sat a controller with an earpiece clipped to one ear. She didn't know who was controlling Kim. She didn't know who to go to. She scanned the area until she caught sight of a young man waving for her to come to him in the middle of the thirty-console room. She made her way through the maze of consoles to the man.

As she got closer, she could hear his accent as he spoke into the console microphone. He was English or Australian. She could never quite discern the difference between the accents. He stood six feet tall, with dirty blond hair. He sported a small mustache and wore ensign's rank.

He put up his finger, signaling for her to hold on for a moment. Then he spoke into the microphone again, "Thank you…Ensign Jones, out."

Gloria rounded the console and peered into the view screen. She saw the top floor of the Watergate building ablaze. Fire engulfed the floor, shooting up fifty to sixty feet in the air, devouring everything in its wake, like a hungry rapture.

"What happened?" she whispered, fearing the worst.

"It was a trap, just like you feared. The team had just entered when they received the *'Emergency Evac'* call. They got out just in time. The apartment went up four seconds later. It was a close one."

"Then Kim and her team are alright?"

"Yes lieutenant…they are fine," he said with some satisfaction. "They just stepped back. They are in their retrieval gate portals." Then he pointed to the screen, "But we think about ten to fifteen people were killed in that explosion. And more may die…it's hard to tell."

"Can we get to any of them?"

"No, the flames are too intense and besides," he paused and took a deep breath. "We aren't registering any life."

Gloria bowed her head upon hearing Jones' cold words. The extractions were supposed to be quick and tight. No innocents were supposed to get hurt. If things went off like planned, no one would have notice they were there, but something went wrong.

"How many in Richmond?" she whispered without looking up.

"Last count…four," he replied. "The neighbors' houses took a pounding."

"They knew…those bitches knew we were coming. But how?"

"Don't know, ma'am."

Jones pulled his earpiece off his ear and studied the screen more. Then he turned to Gloria, who still had her head bowed. "We need to rethink our tactics. I suggest we hold off in extracting Musoto."

Gloria's eyes shot up and she squinted like the devil was in her sight. "No…we will still extract Musoto. But you're right. We have to rethink our tactics. Tell Sheri…Lieutenant Sheri Filgo that is…to acquire visually before extraction. Open extraction authorized."

"Is it?" he queried. "I mean only General Lo can authorize open extraction."

"I know that ensign," Gloria growled. "I am working on the general's full authority. I will make sure he is briefed before we do it. Just tell Lt. Filgo to prepare for an open extraction. I will signal her with the go ahead."

"Tiah!"

***

His eyes were red from lack of sleep. Circles formed under his lids. He rubbed his face with both hands, stealing a couple of seconds of shut eye that seemed to lull his body more into a need for sleep. He had been up for thirty universal hours straight, creating once more a miracle for the ages. Michael stood from behind his desk on Millmum Capitol Station and strolled over to the kitchen area. A pot of regular coffee had just finished brewing. It was his third pot, or was it his fourth? He had lost count. All he knew was that he needed another hit of the old caffeine, his drug of choice right now.

He filled his coffee cup and reached for the sweetener. It was empty. He had used all of it in the past thirty hours. He clicked his CC, "Galley this is the Osguard." He waited for the protocol to connect him.

"Prichard here."

"Prichard, can someone send more sweetener and coffee to my office."

"Tiah!"

Michael slipped back behind his desk and picked up the ARIT pad and thumbed through his latest brainchild. Halfway through his eyes began to close and his mind drifted. He was reading the words, but the words no longer registered in his mind. Soon he found he had read three pages and not retained any of the information.

He put the pad down, shook his head and then took a deep breath. He picked up the pad and tried to read it again. This time he reached the first paragraph before he succumbed to the cloud of tiredness. He threw the pad down on his desk, knowing he needed to get some sleep soon. He also knew he needed to execute his plan as soon as possible. However, he wasn't sure the plan was complete.

The door chime broke what little concentration he had mustered. He pressed the release button on his desk and the door swung open to the right with the characteristic whoosh sound. Michelle and Tirana stood in the doorway. Tirana had another coffee can and Michelle carried his sweetener. Michael was too tired to speak to them. He just nodded.

"We ran into Prichard in the corridor," Michelle beamed.

The ladies walked into the office, putting the coffee and sweetener in the kitchen area. Michelle then picked up Michael's coffee cup from the desk and added his sweetener to it and shoved it underneath his nose. Michael just looked on, unable to say a word, or most likely unable to come up with anything to say.

Tirana picked up the pad and began reading. Michael first tried to object by reaching for the pad, but Michelle grabbed his arms and held them down. "Rest you fool. Let Tirana read it," she ordered, ushering him to the brown leather couch next to his desk.

Tirana sat down at her seat at the conference table, crossed her legs and paged through the ARIT pages at a rapid rate. When she was finished, she read it again. Both times she showed no facial expression nor did she give any verbal comment. She simply read it…quietly and fervently.

After the second time, she passed the pad to Michelle. Michael now had his eyes closed and was in that sweet land between slumber and being awake. His mind was trying to stay awake, while his body was commanding him to sleep. Michelle read the pad. Her eyes widen at times and her head shook at other times. When she was finished she laid the pad in her lap and stared at Tirana.

"Will it work?" she asked.

Tirana looked at Michelle, whose pregnancy was starting to show, and then looked at Michael who now was in a deep sleep. "Yes, it can work. But let's not kid ourselves; Michael is taking a big gamble on the second part of his plan."

"I know that."

"If the stars aren't aligned…"

"Yes, I know that too," pushed Michelle, fighting back the tears. "I can lose him forever." She turned back to Michael almost content watching him sleep on the couch. "There must be another way?"

"There might be, but no one has thought of it yet."

"But why him…we are about to have our third child. He needs to be around for that."

"Don't you think he knows that," Tirana chided. "He has been up here for over thirty hours, racking his brain, trying to figure another way…but he couldn't." She pointed out into space, "All the Osguards have been racking their brains trying to come up with an alternate plan. Time is running out. We need to do something and this seems to be it."

"I don't like it," Michelle pouted. "It's so unfair. This shit isn't supposed to happen."

"I know…but it has," Tirana pointed out. "And to tell the truth, Michael is the only one that can pull this off…at least in the eyes of the parliament. Besides, he won't be alone. I'll be with him as well as the other Osguards."

"But I will be alone. Since I'm pregnant, I won't be allowed into combat," Michelle shrugged. "Life really stinks!"

"I know. Life is a hit or miss proposition." Tirana turned toward Michael. "But in the short time I've known your husband; I have seen something almost magical in him. He is blessed with outstanding instincts. I mean, who else would take in an enemy and make her his number one ally. Just a few months ago, the Kulusks and USSTAP were at each others' throats—a rivalry started long before anyone could remember. And now he has the sister of the Kulusk Maxum as his number one. That took guts. The angels are watching him. It's like he was born for greatness and we are fortunate enough to see him on the journey." Tirana reached down and tapped Michelle's hand. "Life is a gamble and all my money is on your husband. He has what it takes. And no matter how dangerous this plan is, he will find a way to execute it and come back to you. I'm sure of that; just as sure as I'm Kulusk." She then grabbed the pad from Michelle's lap. "I guess I better put this on the street. We have to modify our ships. It's time for us to take the offensive now."

"What about Michael?" Michelle asked.

"Let him sleep. By the time he wakes up, I will have the plan approved by the other Osguards and on its way to becoming reality."

Chapter 32—Face the Enemy

A large horn trumpeted throughout the night air, sending a chilling and ominous tone. The metal and concrete streets of Solwick were already emptying before the wavering horn blasted the silence of the night. Upon hearing the horn, the few sisters left outside in the Tuit capital city scurried inside as if they were running from some unseen insect about to sting them.

"It must be curfew," Gail guessed.

"And if you're right, there will be guards searching soon for those who violate the curfew," Regina added. "We need to get off the street."

"Yeah, but where?" Kelly wondered, trying to hold her fear in check.

"I say we step to the outskirts, make camp and come back in the morning."

"Sounds good, Regina," Kelly replied. "But we have to find some cover to do that as well. As dark as it is, the light of inner space will surely give us away."

"It may be a chance we have to take…I mean no one is around to see. They are all inside."

"Yeah, but they have windows," Gail pushed looking around. "Here, the alley over here. We can step from there," she added pointing across the wide street.

Without further conversation, the three USSTAP agents scrambled across the street between two cylinder-shaped buildings that stood about forty stories tall. The space between the buildings was about two feet wide, allowing just one person at a time to push into the crevice, unless they turned sideways.

Kelly entered first, followed by Gail and Regina. They ventured further into the alley, pushing their way in the darkness, not able to see more than a couple of inches in front of them. Kelly groped at the wall on both sides, using them for support and as a guide at the same time. The texture of the walls was cold and smooth, almost like ice. It was finely polished and well maintained, even in the small cramped space between the buildings. She felt the walls convex as she moved farther into the alley. Then she hit it. The buildings became one, or they touched. Either way, they could not go any further.

"Well that's it. Dead end!" she reported to the others.

"We can turn back," Regina huffed, "or we can stay here. Either way, we can't activate the PGPs in such a tight fit. The obstruction will throw off the coordinate path, and there will be no telling where we'll end up. I'm not sure I want to take that chance."

"Yeah, I know that," Kelly sighed. "And you're right; it isn't a chance I'm willing to take. If we were in friendly territory, it would be worth the risk. But with our luck we would end up right in that Hall of Fire we saw earlier."

"How are you guys at sleeping standing up?" Regina joked. "It seems we are bedding down here for the night."

At that point, the wailing stopped. The streets were quiet again. Regina peered down the alley back into the street and saw what few lights that dressed the streets were now turned off. The area was dark, except for the orange moons, one half and the other full, trying to light the sky.

"Follow me." Gail suggested. "I think we can chance a step now."

The ladies pushed back toward the street until they reached a spot that afforded them some space. They then put their backs against the wall so they could face the other wall.

"That's about enough space," Gail surmised aloud. Then she pulled her PGP, set the coordinates for the drop zone in the woods, and activated in front of the wall.

The opening appeared a half-inch from the wall, making it look like a window letting the light from inside the building shine out. Kelly and Regina did the same. Soon three lights highlighted the structure, shining like the pearly gates of heaven. They stepped into the light and vanished.

Twenty-five marks to the east of Solwick, there stood a forest of mighty trees, stretching into the sky like the Giant Redwoods of America, providing cover and solitude for anyone who entered them. In the midst of the forest, about two marks in, there was a small clearing. At one time a structure, perhaps a house of some sort, occupied this spot. For now it was a clearing, indicating that a human was once here, but not here anymore.

Inside this clearing, three white lights of inner space pushed the night away, glowing, sparkling and illuminating the area like a powerful torch. Gail, Kelly and Regina stepped out of the light like angels from heaven. When the light closed behind them, they remained still, giving their eyes a chance to adjust. The travel ruined their night vision, and the darkness seemed even more foreboding.

It took almost sixty-seconds before either of them felt comfortable enough with their vision to proceed. It was a small change. Their complete night vision had not returned yet, but they knew they had to move on, in case someone had seen the light and came to investigate.

Gail once again took the lead, letting her security and tactics training kick in. She was the best in the entire fleet when it came to tactics—all in the Osguard Senate recognized her skills. Jarod counted his lucky stars each day that he was the one who had her. She had garnered numerous awards and distinctions, including the highest award achievable—the Star of Osguard—similar to the U.S. Medal of Honor. Just thirty people in the medal's sixty-year history had ever won it—five since the present Osguards came to power, and she was one of the honored five. Therefore, the leadership during this phase of the mission naturally fell upon her shoulders.

They pushed east into the forest, away from town and perhaps any wanderers that may filter from Solwick. Gail used her PARIT to pick a secluded spot amongst the thickest bushes and tallest trees. She found a thicket giving a small clearance of four to six inches off the ground. She picked her way under it, using it for a blanket and camouflage at the same time. It matched their green robes, hence the reason for the color. It blended in with the surrounding forest. It was a great escape and evasion color.

Challenged, but undaunted, Regina and Kelly followed Gail into the thicket, paying particular attention not to cut or scratch themselves, thus leaving blood particles and a DNA scent for search arrays to discover. The robes provided additional protection in this aspect as well, protecting them from the sharp thorns populating the thicket. They were covered from head to toe, leaving only their hands and faces exposed to the elements.

The ladies settled on the cold ground, but were warmed by their robes' internal body temperature regulators, similar to their uniform coats, keeping their bodies warm enough to ward off any chill or hypothermia.

"I'll take first watch," Regina offered, pulling her PARIT and putting it on alert. She pushed the earpiece into her ear so if the alert went off, it would not signal strangers as well.

It was difficult, but after several agonizing moments of trying to get in some type of comfortable position, Kelly and Gail closed their eyes and dozed off to sleep.

The morning sun popped up in less than four universal hours. It was glowing blue, giving the entire day a twilight tinge. This tinge was the reason thc Tuits developed the cat-like eyes. The optic evolution was necessary in developing visual acuity in such a low light environment. Gail had surmised earlier the Tuits had extremely good night vision, based on her study of their eye pattern. Therefore, she had given the contact lenses infrared ability. Thus, they were able to see heat signatures in the dark. Even that ability did not allow the three USSTAP officers to see what was about to happened.

In a matter of a fifth of a second seven red ovals grew from nothing. A half-second later, the same time it took for Kelly's PARIT to register the event, seven white-robed Daughters of the Fire Guards, carrying firestaffs popped from the light of ultra-space and charged the thicket. They pointed their firestaffs into the thicket, seemingly right at the USSTAP women.

Gail, Kelly and Regina wanted to move, but stayed still, clinching their pagenays. There was no escape route. Moving further in the thicket would cause the bush to rustle and give their position away.

"Get out," the lead guard said in Tuit.

The translation came through their earpieces. Gail could feel Regina's hand next to hers and she felt the tension flow from her to Regina. They were caught, now the question was, were they going to make a fight out of it, or were they going to surrender? Their death in a firefight would murk up what were already muddy waters. If she were captured, she might have a chance to explain and convince someone she needed to speak to the First Daughter and maybe…just maybe…explain and convince her, the war was an unnecessary byproduct of a misunderstanding that happened almost a century ago.

The tension left her fingers, translating to Regina a decision had been made. Calm came over Regina's grip and she too began to relax. Gail moved forward, burrowing through the thickets toward the opening, leaving Regina and Kelly behind. When the guards saw the movement, they trained their firestaffs unto it. As soon as her hand made it to the opening, a guard grabbed her and pulled her the rest of the way out. They propped her in front of the lead guard, who's cat like demeanor reminded Gail of a lion, ready to pounce on her like a piece of meat.

"Where are the others?" she asked.

Gail understood the question, because of the translation matrix in the PARIT, but she did not know how to answer in Tuit. So she shook her head, hoping the lead guard understood it to mean there was no one else.

"Where are the others?" she asked again.

Again Gail shook her head.

The lead guard huffed, for she was getting frustrated with Gail. She then signaled the other guards to fire into the thicket. Before Gail could object, two guards leveled their firestaffs at the thicket from which she had just emerged. The two-barreled firestaffs glowed red and the weapons fired two beams, blue from the right, and red from the left, that merged into one spiraling beam. The beams exploded in the thicket, popping pieces of the thicket, the ground and tree roots into the air in a uniformed distribution. Without hesitation and with cat like agility, Gail pounced. She jumped and flipped in mid air, kicking her legs and slamming her feet hard into the backs of two guards. She landed on her feet bent over on one hand. She turned and held her breath, as she faced the other four guards surrounding the thicket. The guards swung their firestaffs toward her and she witnessed the glow of the barrels a split second before they spat their deadly rays. She rolled right as the ground to her left exploded, creating a four-foot wide by six-foot deep crater. The percussion strewed the dirt up like a volcano and rocked her off balance as she slammed face first into the ground. The dirt rained all around her, as she tried to spring to her feet. Mud caked her mouth. She spit the mud out. The raining dirt blinded her vision as she attempted to locate her opponents.

Then she withdrew her pagenay and fired toward where she thought the guards last stood. The echoing sound of the blue ray told her the ray hit nothing. Then the sound of the firestaffs erupted from her left. The guards shot another barrage of the deadly rays into the thicket, tearing the thicket apart and clearing the area like a bombsite.

My friends, she thought. *Kelly and Regina were in that thicket.* However, there was no sign of them. They were dead and she wasn't. Sadness and grief grabbed her heart. She turned to the lead guard, aiming her pagenay at her head. Revenge would not bring Kelly and Regina back, but it sure would make her feel better. She knew it was suicide, but at least she would bring this bitch down with her.

As soon as her thumb touched the firing button, another hand grabbed her arm and pulled it behind her back. Then the other arm was yanked behind her and a handcuff device was thrown on her. Then without warning, her face hit the ground, cutting and bruising her entire body. One of the guards had slammed her to the ground with such a force; the wind was knocked out of her. Then the guard ripped her pagenay from her hand and frisked her and found her Charlie belt. Her PARIT and PGP were ripped from her waist. She was now deaf, dumb and defenseless.

The guards pulled her to her feet. The lead guard slammed her fist into her gut, making Gail cough up blood. She didn't have time to nurse the pain before her Sixana training kicked in. She switched her balance against the guards holding her up and swung her right leg around crashing her heel unto the lead guards jaw. The solid sound told Gail, she'd just broken her jaw. Then she pulled forward rocking the guards holding her off balance. She spun, breaking loose from their grasp and leveled the same crashing high kick to the one on the right. The sound wasn't as solid, but it was enough to drop the guard. The other guard tried to lift her firestaff, but Gail switched her footing and delivered a left front kick into her stomach. The guard bent over screaming in pain. Then Gail dropkicked her in the face, sending the guard back onto her butt.

When Gail turned to face the other guard, a sharp pain crashed her skull. The blanket of unconsciousness clouded her vision. She fell to her knees, dazed and fighting for clarity—one word in her mind fighting for attention—*Revenge*. Nonetheless, that word failed to keep her awake. Her mind, body and soul fell silent, before her face smacked the ground.

The guard who slammed her firestaff on Gail's head stood over her, inwardly smiling but outwardly concerned over the other guards lying motionless on the ground. Gail's lightening quick reflexes and powerful kicks astonished her and took her by surprise. However she was able to collect her wits enough to sneak behind Gail and smash her weapon down on her head.

She began to kneel down to check Gail. Then a red light pierced through the trees, hitting the guard and setting fire to her axons and dendrites in her nerve cells, rendering her unconscious. She fell with a hard thump, her body cashed to the ground like rocks.

***

Regina and Kelly stepped from behind parallel trees and the end of the thicket clearing. They had slid from under the brush while the guards were busy collecting Gail. They made it to the other side of the thicket, barely missing the barrage of fire meant to kill them. They then hid behind the trees watching and wondering what Gail was up to. When they saw the battle, they knew Gail had changed strategies because she thought them dead. They retrieved their pagenays and held them in the fire ready position, wavering between using the kill or the unconscious setting. However the battle ended before they could decide to fire their weapons. Once Gail was down, the ladies fired their weapons, choosing the unconscious setting.

The women rushed around the debris, of what once was the thicket that provided them cover toward their fallen comrade. Regina leaned over holding her PARIT over Gail. The readings indicated she was unconscious, suffering from a slight concussion. A smile slipped across her lips, because she had feared Gail dead or severely injured.

They revived her with a concoction of stimulant and pain reliever from their Delta Belt med kits. Kelly placed the MARIT injector on Gail's shoulder. It diagnosed the dosage and delivered it into her bloodstream within seconds.

With a cough and a deep breath, Gail lifted up on her elbows. She fought the fog clouding her vision and her memory. The low light environment didn't help her visual acuity either. She shook her head, fighting the pounding ache that crowned her dizziness.

"Gail…Gail…Are you okay?" Regina called.

The voice was like an angel calling to her. In fact she thought it was an angel. Her last memory was the death of Regina and Kelly, and now she was hearing their voices. Therefore she thought she was dead also. The pain throbbing in her head told her a different story.

"Regina?" she questioned.

"Yeah honey, it's Regina," she comforted. "And Kelly is here as well."

Gail's eyes focused on the ladies leaning over her. A broad smile of acceptance framed her face. The pain ringing in her head was subsiding, thanks to the MARIT injection. Regina helped Gail to her feet and cut the restraints from her wrist with her pagenay, while Kelly retrieved her Delta belt items from the lead guard.

"Now what?" Kelly questioned, giving Gail her equipment.

Gail turned and surveyed the carnage. None of the guards were dead and they would awaken within minutes. Their retrieval time was not for another eight universal hours. They could not afford to stay in the area any longer.

"I say we follow Regina's suggestion," she offered.

"What suggestion?" Regina exclaimed.

"Let's go visit the First Daughter."

"Are you crazy?" Kelly whispered with angst.

"Yup, I'm crazy," she replied ripping a small round device shaped like a tennis ball from a Tuit guard's belt. "According to Osguard fifty-five's report, this looks like their version of our PGP."

"Yeah…so what?" Regina frowned. Then the thought rang clear in her head. "You're not thinking of using that thing. We don't know how to work it or where it would take us."

"I'm sure it has a return feature just like our PGPs," Kelly chimed in as she started to change robes with one of the unconscious guards.

"What the hell are you doing?" Regina questioned.

"Well we can't go like this. I figure we go as the guards. It will be less conspicuous—don't you think?" Kelly smirked.

"Your minds are made up?" Regina asked.

Both Kelly and Gail nodded.

"Fine! I always wanted to commit suicide," she huffed as she starting switching robes with one of the guards.

When they were dressed in the white robes, they stripped the remaining guards of their weapons and equipment, essentially stranding them in the forest. They each took a firestaff and an ultra space portal device and placed the remaining weapons and portal devices in the hole that once was the thicket. Gail raised her newly acquired firestaff, aimed it at the hole and clicked the trigger. A spiraling red and blue beam sprang from the weapon and hit the hole with such force the equipment exploded into thousands of pieces, spewing into the sky like rain.

Gail looked at the firestaff in her hand, not hiding the awe that fluttered inside of her about the power it held. "Pretty nifty weapon," she sang.

"No kidding," Regina snapped back. "Now that that's done…let's get the hell out of here!"

All three women held out the spherical portal devices and clicked the one button with their thumbs. A spherical light grew in front of them, illuminating the area in a devilish glow. The women looked at each other and huffed in unison. Then they stepped into their individual lights, with a prayer on their lips and a hand on their borrowed firestaffs. The daylight disappeared behind them

Inside the light, a protective bubble formed around them. Then unlike their PGP gateway, their bodies floated up. They were weightless, frozen unable to move, hovering upwards with the current of ultra space. Fright started to envelope the ladies. The experience was not what they imagined. They thought they would step into the light and instantly be transported to another area as with their PGP. However, this was not so. They had stepped into the light and found themselves floating helplessly for what seemed like minutes.

A break in the red light appeared over their heads as they floated toward it. Then like an elevator ride, they stopped and the light rotated in front of them and then past them. Instantly pushing them out of ultra space and inside normal space, into what they learned later was the gate portal room in the Hall of Fire building.

In front of them stood another white robed woman at a control panel. The woman looked startled as she peered at the three women. She tilted her head, showing her confusion. However, as soon as her confusion was evident, so was her resolve. She snapped forward reaching for a button, but she never reached the button. Gail's red pagenay beam slammed into her, jerking her as her body convulsed to fight the burning energy ripping through her nervous system, disconnecting her axons and dendrites. The pain was so unbearable but quick, not giving its victim a chance to utter a sound before the nervous system shut down. The operator crashed to the floor, hitting her head on the console, not feeling the pain from either hit.

"Well, what's next?" Regina pushed.

Gail pulled her PARIT and tapped into the keyboard of the computer on the console. She than adjusted it to give a schematic of the building by using its limited search array program. She read it, frowning at times and smiling at others. Then she pushed a button to synchronize it with Kelly and Regina's PARITs.

"Follow me," she ordered walking toward the door. The door vanished as she approached and they stepped into the corridor. The door reappeared after they were through the archway. All three looked at the door as it reappeared in place.

"Neat!" Regina commented in awe. "Totally awesome! What other tricks do you think they have?"

"I don't know and frankly, I'm not sure I want to find out," Kelly added.

Chapter 33—Open Extraction

Rizza's Place was the hottest spot in the D.C. area. The first floor was a lovely seafood restaurant; with a deck that overlooked the Washington Channel that emptied out into the Potomac River. Above the restaurant were several floors for dancing, which featured live bands trying to make a name for themselves. The first floor was set for urban music, the second floor entertained rock music, and the third floor boasted of alternative rock on the weekends and country and western during the weekdays. On the fourth floor, where a special elevator led, listed another exclusive restaurant with classical music alternating with the big band music of the forties. In this plush and elegant setting the social elite of Washington often spent their evenings. Senators, congressman and those special lobbyists trying to corner them frequented the fourth floor.

Rizza's was an international chain of clubs that had franchises in every major city in the world, throughout Europe, Asia, the Middle East, Africa, Australia, South America and North America including the United States—Boston, Richmond, Atlanta, Dallas, Los Angeles, Seattle Washington , Chicago and Washington D.C.—seventy-six cities in all. In her research she noticed an uncanny coincidence between the upstart of Rizza's and the location of Unlimited Association offices. It was a long shot that there was a connection, but it was worth checking out and she had convinced Musoto of that as well.

"You won't believe this!" Lieutenant Sheri Filgo said into her CC.

"What is it?" rang Gloria's voice.

"Musoto and his secretary are pulling up to Rizza's."

"Say again," Gloria responded, not hiding her surprise.

"You heard me. They are pulling up to Rizza's place."

"Oh this guy is good!" Gloria praised.

"Do you think he knows?"

"He may not know how, but he sure knows something," Gloria surmised. "This guy is real good!"

"Instructions?"

"Follow them…extract on your judgment," Gloria replied.

"Tiah!"

Musoto's rented blue Mercedes 220I pulled into the valet parking drop off. He stepped out, wearing a black three-quarter length suit, and a white half-collar shirt with gold metal studs, and imported black leather Italian shoes. He was dressed for the part. He stepped to the passenger side, where the valet had already opened the door for his date.

She stepped out showing her long muscular leg that seemed to invite all to watch, her other leg swung around and out, and with the valet's help she emerged from the passenger side, wearing a red hip hugging dress that seemed to stop just below her voluptuous buttocks. The V-cut of her dress left nothing to the imagination about her bust size. It covered her chest with an X pattern, hugging and clinging to her breast as if the cloth were glued on. Her rich shiny shoulder length dark hair danced as the wind sailed through it and her light eyes seem to radiate, giving her bronze skin a regal appearance. Angela Santos was looking exceptionally well and she knew it, as evident by her glowing aura and beaming smile.

Musoto snatched her hand from the valet, showing his male bravado and somewhat marking his territory. Angela was with him and him alone. He passed the keys to the valet and stepped onto the red carpet leading to the palatial five-story structure with pillars that rivaled those of the White House. His eyes grew as he gazed on the enormity of the building. He had seen it from I-395 off the Francis Case Memorial Bridge several times, but he never fathomed the building was so large.

"Keep your mouth closed boss—act like you've been here before," Angela warned him.

Musoto closed his mouth and shot a daring glare over to Angela. He was a little embarrassed his awe was so evident and a little ashamed he did it in front of Angela. He rolled his eyes back toward the door. "You better be right about this place, because it is taking a big chunk out of our expense account. And it wouldn't look right for me to be spending this money taking you out to such lavish digs as this."

"Gee boss; you sure know how to talk to a girl on a first date."

Musoto closed his eyes and shook the words around in his head. It didn't come out like he meant it. "You know what I mean Angela. I just hope your hunch is right…that's all."

"Yeah boss, I know what you mean," Angela said letting him off the hook.

"Oh, by the way, did I fail to mention how gorgeous you look in that dress."

"Yeah boss, you've failed to mention that," she smirked. "Thanks!" she said after a pregnant pause, which shot into Musoto like a bullet.

"Again, I apologize for not telling you earlier," he pushed as the doorman opened the door for them to enter. "I've just been on edge because I couldn't reach Mona today. It seems like her phone has been disconnected."

"Did you try her at work?" Angela suggested.

"No, today's Saturday. She wouldn't be at work."

"Oh yeah, I forgot. Working for you, one loses track of time," she shot. "Anyway, your mind needs to be on this."

Musoto turned and looked into her eyes. He didn't know if she meant the assignment or her. For the first time he noticed how beautiful she was. His mind had been so wrapped up with Mona for the past several months; he hardly noticed any other female. But tonight his eyes were on Angela. Her skin looked so soft and inviting he wanted to rub his hands against her cheek, but decided not to. He just stared into her bright eyes and winked after several seconds.

"My mind is here, with you and on this assignment," he said turning to the maitre D', knowing he had sufficiently and covertly covered his bases in case she wanted his mind to be on her as well. "Musoto…we have eight o'clock reservations for two."

The maitre D' nodded, pulled out two menus and asked them to follow him. He scurried through a maze of tables, where couples seemed to be enjoying quiet candlelit romantic meals, and placed them on the deck about three rows from the banister overlooking the channel. The sky was exceptionally clear, the stars bright, not obscured by the city lights. The quarter moon was resting between two clouds, shinning its light on the water, and giving a masterful quixotic display.

Several minutes later the maitre D' seated a slender dark haired pacific islander, wearing a plain black skirt and white silk blouse at a single table off toward their right. Sheri Filgo had run downstairs to one of the secret USSTAP subterranean floors and changed in order to fit into the crowd.

Rizza's Place was another front for USSTAP operations. Below each one existed several subterranean floors, where guests visiting Earth from other worlds stayed. Many times the guest would venture upstairs to mingle with the local populace, immersing themselves in the culture and the dance of the area. Washington D.C., as with the other nation capitals, was a particularly popular area with many of the representatives from the Millmum Galaxy. Their popularity was mainly due to the political influence, which inhabited those areas.

In the galaxy as well as the known universe, there was a marked difference between politics, diplomacy and statesmanship. However on Earth the lines were blurred to the point the three entities were synonymous and each nation played the game differently. Only in Washington, could one see the hodgepodge of political ideas and styles tangle together to make such a convoluted web of issues. Representatives from other planets attempted to capture a breath of that while mingling with them on the private fourth floor.

Now Musoto was sitting in the middle of the Washington D.C. hub. No one, including Sheri, believed it was a coincidence. She had reservations about attempting an extraction of any kind with Musoto. Before, she wasn't convinced of Musoto's complicity in the Tuit factor, but now his presence at Rizza's Place had convinced her, Musoto had some role to play. Whether it was covert or overt still needed to be determined. Extraction was the way to establish what part Musoto really played. Now the question was who was the lady with Musoto? Would an extraction include her as well? Should it include her?

Well she was here, with Musoto and as far as Sheri was concern, any woman could be a Tuit agent. Therefore the extraction would include her. First, Sheri knew she had to find out what exactly Musoto was doing at Rizza's. So she decided to observe them for a while, before making her move.

Musoto cornered the waiter for several minutes, attempting to interrogate him about the restaurant behind a hail of small talk. Sheri was able to pick up on the conversation through her PARIT, which she used as an eavesdropping device. The questions were simple enough, but to a trained security agent they could have been damaging if the waiter was a part of USSTAP instead of some kid working his way through college.

"Where are you from?" "How'd you get this job?" "Do you like it here?" "Do you know the owners?" "Did you know there are seventy-six Rizza's Places throughout the world?" "Have you ever worked at any of the others?" "What's the pay like?" "Do you get benefits, pension plan or anything like that?"

The poor kid was working for two dollars more than minimum wage, plus tips. He had no idea why this person was so interested in his private business. Frankly, it made him a little nervous. All, the young waiter wanted to do was wait on tables, and earn a decent tip. So he put on a friendly smile and tried to answer what he consider intrusive questions with evasive answers, which made Musoto more curious and fueled his passion to ask more.

"Where do you go to school?" "Do you have family in town?" "Do you have a girlfriend?" "Have you ever seen the owners?" "Who usually comes here?" "Are the owners black?" "Have you ever heard the name Michael Genesis?" "Do you know a Stephanie Rikes, or Stelana Rican?"

Unto which the poor waiter replied, "No, I don't know," or "I'm not sure." This infuriated Musoto, scaring the kid enough to call the maitre D'. The maitre D', who was a member of USSTAP, assured the youngster, it was simply a case of someone being over friendly and that there was nothing to worry about. However, the young man still regarded the couple, especially Musoto as someone he didn't want to be around.

Musoto and Angela soon finished their dinner, mostly in quiet observance of the others in the room, after scoring nothing with the waiter. Sheri recognized this as a surveillance operation and chuckled to herself. Because when she announced their presence in the restaurant, all residence staying in the subterranean levels were locked down. They were not allowed upstairs to mingle and possibly give Musoto something to report. So the people in the restaurant were those innocent people who came to the restaurant to enjoy a pleasant meal.

Musoto and Angela got up from the table after some small chat and moved to the east side marble stairs leading to the dance floors above. The crowd on the stairs was a mixture of people heading to the different dance floors; some sharply dressed like Musoto and Angela, and some comfortably dressed for a night of dancing. Sheri fell in behind the couple, keeping a respectable distant.

They got off on the second floor, and entered through the ostentatious double doors leading to the music. The music was pumping, vibrating against the walls with its heavy bass and drumbeat. The singer's sultry voice rang through the speakers so vibrantly; it seemed to reach into your soul and jump-start your feelings to get on the dance floor.

Inside the room, the bar lined the walls on both sides all the way around up to the stage, which sat four feet above the dance floor. In back of the large forty by thirty foot dance floor sat several rows of circular tables, some chair high and some stool high. Floating around the room were several waitresses and waiters dressed in black slacks, white blouses and checkered vests. The bartenders behind the bar passed up the vest and wore just a white shirt with a bow tie. The bar wall was mirrored all around, giving the spacious room an even larger appearance.

The dance floor was crowded, as well as the room. It appeared the room was already at maximum capacity, but the doorman, who was in charge of crowd control, knew the exact number of people the room could hold. Every patron had a place to sit, to rest or to lay his or her coat. That was the rule of the house. There would be no standing room only. The house would rather turn back people than have them fight for standing room. The doorman pointed to a stool table off to the left for the couple to sit.

Musoto took the hint and escorted Angela to the table, turning and bumping people as he pushed their way through. A waiter took their drink orders; scotch straight up for Musoto and a cosmopolitan for Angela. Sheri snuck around them and found a seat at the bar behind them. She ordered a diet soft drink, hoping to blend into the crowd.

When the waitress returned with their drinks, Musoto went into his small talk barrage of questions, which was uncomfortable for the young lady who thought Musoto was actively hitting on her, with a girlfriend in tow. She was less friendly toward the conversation than the waiter at the restaurant and politely excused herself to wait on others. After the initial barrage, the waitress avoided their table all together. The other waitresses and waiters took a round robin approach to checking up on them, none staying long enough to engage in conversation.

This was enough observation, Sheri concluded. Musoto was on a fishing expedition and didn't have much to go on. He somehow deduced the connection between the entertainment franchise and USSTAP. That alone was worth a look. Yet, for now it was time for the extraction. She pulled out her PARIT disguised as a cell phone, pushed several numbers and watched the screen. She had entered the go ahead code for the extraction. Now it was a matter of waiting for the most opportune moment. She did not have to wait long.

The several drinks Musoto slammed back had started to affect him. He stood to go to the men's room. He waded through the crowd toward the back of the room, through the double doors, passed the doorman and into the corridor. He slipped into the rest room and found an empty urinal to relieve his bladder. When he entered, four men were in the rest room accomplishing the same task, but when he finished, one man remained. He was at the basin washing his hands. Musoto zipped up and started to walk out the door.

"You don't wash man?" the individual at the basin challenged.

"I don't piss on my hands," Musoto shot back, implying that the man did.

"You're one nasty bastard," the stranger scolded turning to face Musoto.

The stranger looked like a body builder; his neck was thick and bubbled like rock. His sleeves seemed like they were about to bust at the seams and his tight tucked silk shirt clung to his washboard stomach like jelly. Musoto knew he had made a mistake smarting-off to him. He didn't want to tangle with this behemoth, but his rhetorical comeback, *'I don't piss on my hands,'* indicated otherwise.

"Listen man, if it will make you happy I'll wash my hands," Musoto placated.

"I don't care what you do," the man said as he pushed by Musoto. "I just hate to think of all the times I shake someone's hands like yours…of all the nasty things…think of the germs…shit!"

Musoto giggled at the man's paranoia and moved to the sink. He turned on the water and lathered up. It was the last memory he would have of

Rizza's Place. The familiar pain of a pagenay pierced his spine, heated his nervous system and shocked his soul. He was unconscious before his body slammed onto the tile floor. Then a white light flashed and Musoto and the man were gone.

Back in the dance area, Angela was watching several couples display their athletic ability to the sound of the beat. One couple, especially the young lady was so surreal in her dance. The woman stood about five-five, with short blonde hair and mesmerizing wide blue eyes that seemed to grip your soul and shake your heart when she gazed at you. She swayed to the music as if she were making sweet passionate love to it. Her hips moved slowly and rhythmically as she floated on the floor like a butterfly gallantly parading its beauty. The flashing lights in the room caused colors to ripple in her movement, giving a majestic appeal in her dance.

The man she was with was taller with broad shoulders and a strong chin. His dancing was tentative, almost shy. His movements were short, jerky and not very well coordinated, but it didn't matter. The lady drew all the attention to her and no one noticed her partner's awkward display.

Another couple next to them heated the dance floor with their movements. They were fast, furious and full of life. The lady was a brunette, with definite Latin features. She moved like fire. Her hips beat with the drum and her feet clicked with the sound. She had confidence with every step. She moved forward, backward and side-to-side, slipping, gyrating and throwing her hips into the dance.

Her partner, a younger man, was just as animated. He held the young beauty in his arms almost like a rag doll, throwing, spinning and tossing her in perfect harmony to the beat. Watching them was exhilarating, entertaining and unquestionably exciting.

It was amazing to Angela, that two couples would physically interpret the high tempo beat of the music in different ways. She knew it was the culture, the environment in which the couples grew up in that allowed them the freedom to interpret music and dance differently and still be able to enjoy it.

She wanted to hit the dance floor and let loose with her own rendition of physical elucidation. She wondered if Musoto knew how to dance. No it didn't matter if he knew how; she wondered if Musoto would be comfortable dancing...period. The dance was ultimately all about one's comfort zone. From the Waltzes of Europe to the Two-Step of Texas, it was all about how relaxed you were with physically expressing yourself in the open, letting other people watch, comment and enjoy your quiet but physical understanding of music.

The band finished the song, decided to end the set and take a ten-minute break. The crowd from the dance floor eased their way back to their seats at the tables and bar, sweating from a good workout and ready to quench their thirst with more liquor. Others decided they needed air or to take a break in the rest rooms. As the sea of people swirled around her, Angela checked her watch.

Musoto had been gone for ten minutes. Worry started to pierce her reality. She looked around the room to see if he had stopped off at the bar to talk to someone in his sad attempt of informal interrogation, but she didn't see him. She stood and pushed her way through the crowd, surveying the room as she moved back toward the double doors. She still didn't see him, but she did notice something else. A strange feeling came over her as she fought to remember her training.

She asked the doorman if he had seen her date. He shrugged and pointed to the men's room. "He's in there…I think."

"Fine, I guess I will use the little girl's…" Angela saw the line outside the women's bathroom in the opposite corridor and shook her head.

"Ma'am," the doorman called. "There is another restroom around the corner and to the back. It's for the staff, but if you really need to use it, I can show you the way."

"Thank you," Angela agreed.

The doorman escorted her past the men's restroom and around the corner. He opened a door with a key and pointed her down the hall. She nodded and followed his directions toward the restroom.

The doorman held the door ajar until Sheri arrived. He winked and slid the door open allowing Sheri to slip through. Sheri then hurried to the rest room. She pulled her pagenay from her purse and ensured it was set for knockout. Once she was satisfied, she swung the door open and stepped in ready to fire her weapon.

The door didn't get fully open before Sheri felt a backhand smash her in the nose. She fell backwards dropping her pagenay onto the tile floor. Blood spurted from her nostrils as she grabbed her nose. She shook her head fighting the dulling sensation trying to overcome her sense of reality. That is when she noticed Angela going for the fallen pagenay, just as the door swung back close.

Sheri gathered her senses and rushed through the door. The door slammed open with a loud thud, diverting Angela's attention from grabbing the pagenay for a split second. Sheri then stepped over to Angela and let loose with a vicious kick that caught Angela in the gut. Angela rolled over and slammed her back against the wall. She slid to the floor with her head next to the sink cupboard.

Sheri went in for another kick, but Angela grabbed Sheri's foot in mid air, twisted it counterclockwise, pulling Sheri off balance. Sheri stumbled against the sinks, looking for room to maneuver. She balanced her hand on one of the sinks, lifted her other foot and crashed it down onto

Angela's head. Angela let go of Sheri's foot as her face hit the floor, splitting her lip and giving a path for a stream of blood to flow.

Sheri reached down and pulled Angela's face up and drew back to let a right cross go, but Angela spit blood onto Sheri's face, distracting her enough for Angela to head butt Sheri. Sheri's head recoiled back from the pain and a gash formed over her eye. Pushing the pain away, Sheri let loose with a right cross, slamming her fist into Angela's jaw. The blood from her lip, spurted out and sprayed the stall and the walls

With animal reflexes, Angela grabbed Sheri's arm that she was using to hold herself up with, and twisted it clockwise, breaking the hold. Then she pushed Sheri back onto her butt, swung her legs up and over and delivered a crushing kick to Sheri's jaw. Sheri's head hit the porcelain sink, sending her body into riveting pain.

Angela sprung to her feet and rushed to the pagenay still on the floor. Sheri scissor kicked, catching Angela's legs and tripping her once more. Angela crashed to the floor back on her butt, her head hitting the wall she just sprung from. Stars formed in her eyesight and the world became smaller as her vision started to fade. Sheri leaped up on one knee and dove for the pagenay. She fell several inches short of the weapon and began to belly crawl to the instrument. Then all of a sudden she felt Angela's dead weight slam onto her back, knocking what breath she had out of her.

Angela straddled Sheri's back, grabbed Sheri's hair and pulled her head up. Then with a mighty effort she slammed Sheri's face onto the floor. The dense fog of unconsciousness was forming in Sheri's head. Her vision was blurred and closing. She felt her head being pulled up once more. She knew what was coming next and she couldn't let that happen. She reached around, grabbed Angela's hand on her head and dug her nails into Angela's flesh. Then she twisted her hips, knocking Angela off balance, making her let go to grab something else for balance.

Now they were face to face, with Angela still on top. Sheri reached above her, searching for the pagenay while Angela struggled to control her arms. Then Sheri lifted her leg and with uncanny flexibility known to a Sixana warrior, she twisted it around and in front of Angela's neck. Then she straightened the leg, ripping Angela off her chest, and into her crouch. She squeezed, cutting the airflow off, choking Angela. In reality, she would have completed the maneuver with another blow from her leg to break her victim's neck, but this was not a fight to the death. This was a fight of containment.

With Angela struggling for air, Sheri inched her way backwards, clawing for the pagenay. She reached it, palmed it and rose up on her butt, which put more pressure on Angela. The gurgling sounds were slowing down to a trickle. Sheri didn't want to kill her, so she released the pressure and kicked Angela away from her.

Angela scurried to the back wall holding her throat and gasping for precious air. Her eyes were wide and her face flushed from lack of oxygen. Her hair was loose like a wildcat and her tight dress was now loose. Blood foamed around her mouth and horror ruled her demeanor.

"Damn, you really pack a wallop," Sheri huffed, wiping the blood from her face. "You must be one of those damned Tuits."

"What the hell are you talking about?" Angela coughed.

"Sorry sister. You don't get to ask the questions…I do."

"Fuck you!" Angela protested.

"Thanks sister, but you're not my type," Sheri smiled and then hit her with the red beam from the pagenay.

Sheri looked around the bathroom and noticed it was so bloody; it looked like someone had been murdered in it. She contacted the maitre D' downstairs to ensure someone cleaned up the restroom before any of the staff noticed. Until then, she placed an out of order sign on the door and locked it. Seconds later the bathroom was adorned by the white light of inner space. Open extraction was complete.

Chapter 34—First Daughter

The First Daughter, Tisha of Solwick, daughter of Esha, granddaughter of Isha sat at her desk reading the report for the fifth time. The *Fireship Crinkle* had blown up during its entry into the solar system. It was one of the few remaining Fireships in the mother galaxy. Tisha had suspected foul play, but the report blamed a triboleminic power surge. The power chamber somehow became contaminated and exploded, killing the crew. The question was how did it become contaminated? No one had suspected enemy involvement this deep inside Tuit territory, so it was ultimately the command daughter's fault. Any search for enemy weapons fire was dismissed…Except by Tisha.

She had sent her special investigator to the scene and asked her to keep an open mind. Tisha wanted the scene thoroughly tested, and that is what she received. Within eight hours, evidence of an alien weapon signature streamed in. Then an hour from that, the ultra space sensor grid, which monitored all activity in ultra-space, had recorded an anomaly of benion particles, a subset of ultra space, which the Tuits could not master, but the enemies of the fourth dimension had. They were here, in her galaxy, in her solar system, on her planet and worse, in her city. Rina had somehow led the enemy to the home world.

This would exonerate Tisha during the challenge. However she knew she needed more than circumstantial evidence. Everything in the report could be explained away. The explosion of the *Crinkle* could have caused energy anomalies in the area that did not necessarily suggest an enemy energy source. There was not enough of a reading to establish one claim over the other.

The benion anomaly could also be a happenstance of normal travel. Benion particles have been known to leak into normal space as long as several hours after an ultra space portal had opened or closed. Although rare, it had been documented several times by respectable scientific minds. A benion leak could explain the recorded anomaly.

No! Circumstantial evidence would not suffice. She needed hard evidence to present. That is why she sent her guards to track down the anomaly and see if there was something to it—to see if there was someone behind it. And if there was, they were to bring whoever was responsible to her as soon as possible.

The guards had been searching for almost four hours. Their last report was almost an hour ago. The lead guard thought she was on to something, but had not reported back since. Tisha was starting to worry. She placed the report down and stood, stretching her arms, cracking her muscles throughout her body. Her knuckles popped, her elbow snapped; even her back cracked, all in a twisted rhythmic serenade of sounds. However she did not hear the sounds her body was making. All she heard were her thoughts—her fears rattling in her head.

What cost was it to be right, if the enemy was on her home planet? Did she wish she were wrong for the sake of the Consortium? If she were wrong, her very life would be sacrificed. She was in an untenable situation. She knew the Consortium members would not reach a unanimous vote. It was preposterous to think five hundred Fireholders, representing five hundred and nineteen thousand planets in five hundred galaxies stretching over five star clusters could vote alike. There were personalities that need assuaging, and she was not one to pacify anyone, especially the Fireholders from other worlds, other galaxies and other star clusters. Even though all the sisters were descendants of the Fire Tribes who salted the heavens eons ago, they contained more differences than similarities—now, more than ever.

The acceptance of a female dominated existence was about the only similarity the sisters shared. The quest for power, the language, and the culture seem to be the dividing factors separating the sisters from the ultimate goal of unity. No matter how many planets, how many galaxies or how many star clusters were brought into the fold, the infighting still continued, as evident by Miam's enthusiastic challenge.

Sometimes Tisha wondered why they went to a female dominated society, because all the ills they blamed the men for were still prevalent in their system. Wars, famine, sicknesses still raced through their society like a plague. She wanted to steer the sisters away from war, but for over the last century the one thing keeping the Consortium together was their shared focus on revenging the annihilation of the Fireships *Snikle* and *Tesle*. Some innate drive pushed the Consortium to self-destruction over this issue. It seemed she was the only one who saw it.

If she was right, it was her own deeds that may have brought the enemy to them, and assured their very ruin. The Tuits had not fought an enemy on their own soil for over three centuries now. The taste of battle was foreign to the civilian populace. They had never sacrificed, never gone without, like their ancestors, to assure a military victory. The question now was, were they ready? Were they ready to fight an uncommon enemy? They had been ruthless in their pursuit so far, but that was on someone else's territory. Could they show that same tenacity, that same brutality when the fight was brought to them? Would the civilian populace accept the challenge?

Tisha tried to force a smile as the questions rolled around in her head. *It didn't matter if they were ready or not. The fight was here and the fight was now. The populace would have to be ready and the Consortium had to stop their inner bickering.* She plopped back into her chair, staring with her yellow cat shaped eyes at the door, willing the guards to walk in and present her with something she could take to the Consortium. Time was running out.

The buzz from her communications suite broke her concentration. She switched the toggle. "Yes, what is it?" she barked.

The voice coming from the speaker seemed urgent and frantic at the same time, "This is transfer chamber four…we have a breach!"

***

"Where are we going?" Regina whispered to Gail.

The three women pulled to the side. The corridor was made of smooth white polished polymer, almost reflective, bestowing a sterile vacuum-sealed appearance. Due to the low intensity lighting, their white robes blended into the background, almost making them invisible, similar to the camouflage concept behind the USSTAP stealth technology—a definite advantage for a guard to have. The floor was also white, made up of a rubber like material, giving under the pressure of their weight as the girls walked, sucking, absorbing and eating the sound of their feet stepping across it—another stealthy advantage for a guard to have.

Several groups of sisters, in red and black robes sailed through the corridor in eerie silence, moving to and fro. Gail looked around and saw a bend in the corridor, providing a crevice in which to retreat and talk. She scanned the area for listening devices with her PARIT. When she was satisfied they were clear, she ushered Regina and Kelly into the area.

"According to the PARIT search, that Hall of Fire, or at least what I think should be the Hall of Fire is this way," she said pointing down the corridor.

"And why on Earth are we heading there?"

"Do you know another place where the First Daughter would be?"

"How about her office? How about her quarters? How about at whatever they call a command and control center?" shot Kelly. "Who do you think sent those goons after us?"

Gail stopped in her tracks and peered at her comrades. "You know, I really didn't factor that in. How the hell did they find us anyway?"

"Our PGP's probably set off some type of sensor," Regina surmised aloud. "Inner space is not the medium of choice for this society to step with. I figure the benion particles alerted something. Just like we can scan and tell where a portal opened or closed. We left a footprint and they followed it."

"So, you're saying they know we are on the planet and the First Daughter sent her goons to capture us?" questioned Gail.

"Capture or kill!" Kelly almost shrieked.

"Then we could be walking into a trap?" Regina added.

Gail mulled the possibility over in her head for a time, rubbing her chin, and giving the idea some serious thought. "I kind of stepped in this like a bull in a china shop, didn't I?"

"We all did," Regina said. "We want to sue for peace more than anything, but, we are leaving our common sense behind. We aren't thinking like Sixana warriors."

"But the edict," Gail argued. "We are supposed to look for opportunities to negotiate."

"Well as Jarod always said…it's better to negotiate from a position of power," Regina responded. "And sister, this ain't it."

Just as she finished her retort, a loud crisp warning horn blasted throughout the corridor. The low intensity lighting suddenly turned violent, and the sisters throughout the corridor stopped in their tracks, reminiscent of manikins in a store window. Then a voice boomed through the loud speaker. It took the PARITs a microsecond to translate the words. A chill wrapped around the ladies as the translated words repeated through their earpieces.

"Intruder alert…intruder alert! Prepare for DNA scan. Once captured, bring the intruders to the Hall of Fire." The words continued to repeat in a steady non-emotional way. It was their version of an ARIT directing the action.

Regina's heart jumped into her throat. She realized the guard in the portal room must have revived and sent the alarm. At that moment she wished they had killed the operator. However, the USSTAP rules forbade any killing of an enemy who already was incapacitated. Osguardian law considered it murder and no longer an act of self-defense or of combat. That rule implied you were able to take the incapacitated person as prisoner. Sneaking around in enemy territory did not present the opportunity to take prisoners. No, the proper thing was to have had the pagenay set for kill in the first place. Osguardian law would have protected that action, but once the operator was down she became the subject of the law and nothing could be done about that. Conversely, it would have been difficult to persuade the First Daughter their intentions were honorable if they had killed the operator.

Apparently, the operator was awake and setting the entire Tuit military on their back. Now the question was, do they make a stand and fight or let things happen? If they stood and fought, the sincerity of their position would be in doubt. If they let themselves be captured, they would lose the necessary position of strength needed in such delicate negotiations.

Red beams jetted from the wall and swept the hallway like miniature searchlights. The dozen or so lights hit the sisters in the corridor, slowed to a stop and then swung away to the next person. Regina knew the lights were some sort of DNA scanner. It was not as covert as the DNA readers they had, but in this case it did not have to be. Regina pushed her hands out, gesturing for the other USSTAP officers to remain in the crevice of the corner. It appeared this was a gap in the search array field of view. The red lights did not fire into the corner.

Regina was hoping they could somehow avoid the scan and when it was over move on with their plans. That idea was shot down when another white robed figure approached them, motioning for them to step from the crevice. The translation humming in their ear validated what the white robed woman wanted. She was ordering them to step into a clear spot so the scan would have an opportunity to hit them.

Regina swallowed hard, trying to think of something to do. She knew, once they stepped into the middle of the corridor and the search ray hit them, they would be discovered. Now several white robed maidens with firestaffs at the ready filled the hallway. She knew these ladies were the elite of the Tuits, the special guards…the security police of the Tuit society. And being that, she knew a confrontation with them was a death sentence. So the option of making a stand faded. There was one option left…or was there?

She peered at the figure whose gestures and words were becoming more animated and urgent. Then she peered further past her to the left and then to the right. The entire white robe army seemed to be coming from the agitated guards left. Maybe they could run! Try to escape? The thought took root in her mind and she could not shake it. Even though it was a split second from the time she first saw the guard and the formulation of an escape plan, it seemed like an entire day had passed.

Temporal distortion had occurred. It always happened in times of high anxiety, stress and most definitely fright. Every second seemed so distinct, so clear and moved ever so slowly. The guard looked like she was moving in slow motion. Her words seemed drawn out and almost incoherent, especially with the translation. That was because her mind was working at a super accelerated speed. Her mind was calculating possible escape routes faster than the normal speed of thought. Her adrenaline was fueling it, energizing her thought patterns, making her senses sharper. She saw and processed the minute details of every guard's position, distance, speed, demeanor, searching for possible reaction times, weaknesses and coming to a conclusion.

"Follow me girls…pagenays to inhibit…not knockout…inhibit."

Then with lightening reflexes, which called upon her Chaktun blood, she pulled her pagenay and shot a yellow beam at the first guard who called them from the corner. The beam smacked her in the chest. She dropped her firestaff and shook in place as if electricity was coursing through her body. Then she fell to her hands and knees, unable to move and fighting to control her breathing, but cognizant of her surroundings.

Then Regina swept to the right and smacked two more guards, who were confused on what was happening to their captain. At first they thought the DNA beam somehow malfunctioned and stopped in their tracks. They weren't in position to see the yellow beam dart out of Regina's hand. After their captain fell, they saw three yellow beams dance through the violet air, crossed by several dozen pencil red DNA search beams. The entire episode looked like a 1970's disco scene…very disorienting, even to the cat like vision of a Tuit.

With the lead four soldiers down, coughing and fighting for breath, Regina, Kelly and Gail, shot past them and turned left. As they made the turn, the ominous sound of firestaffs firing sailed through the air. One of the blasts caught the beam holding the corner wall up. It tore through, breaking the support. The substances making up the ceiling and the wall crumbled like a curtain, covering the path the USSTAP officers used.

Regina looked over her shoulder and grinned. She had calculated the miss shots because of the disorientation, but she never counted on the debris field it would create. Even though it did not close them off from the pursuers, it hampered their progress. The three officers scampered the corridor firing their pagenay over their shoulders, and at any moving target in front of them, no matter if they were wearing white, red or black robes…armed or not. They left in their wake a stew of coughing and wheezing Tuits on their hands and knees.

In front of them and halfway down the corridor, five white robed Tuits sprang from the red light of ultra space, with their firestaffs in the firing position. Now the USSTAP officers had six Tuit guards on their tail and five in front. They skirted right, turning into a corridor, nearly missing the onslaught of energy spikes flying to meet them. The screams and large thumps they heard painted a picture of a deadly crossfire. *The Tuits had just taken each other out!*

Before the thought could take root in their conscience, Gail, Kelly and Regina crashed into an invisible force field. It was like hitting an electrified brick wall. The instantaneous stop crumbled, banged, and pushed their bodies with such force that pain and dizziness swept through them like lightening. Then the energy bolt sizzled through their bodies like fire, snapping and slinging them backwards, slamming them hard on their rears and on to the soft but sturdy white floor.

Pain racked their bodies, fighting for attention as their brain activity gave the signal to collapse into unconsciousness. Disorientation hovered over them as they grasped for breath to fight off the pain and the dizziness. Gail rolled her head from side to side, trying to keep her mind rooted in reality. Kelly wheezed and coughed, keeping her eyes shut as if to shield her mind from the pain her body was experiencing. Regina moaned as her Chaktun blood raced through her veins to fight off the cloud of unconsciousness descending on her. It took several minutes for the ladies to regain reality, each fighting the pain and shock in different but similar ways.

Regina was the first to recover. She pulled herself up onto her elbows and surveyed the area. Several Tuits stood on the other side of the force field, and behind her, past what she gathered was another force field, stood more Tuits, pointing and gazing at her and her partners. Regina then reached over and shook Kelly, pushing her into reality, helping her to capture the rhythm of breathing once more. Kelly opened her eyes and nodded to tell Regina she was fine.

Then Regina crawled over to Gail and nudged her. Gail's head had stopped rolling from side to side and she was now straining her lower abdomen to push the blood to her head, to fight off the dizziness. After a few seconds, she too opened her eyes and rejoined her partners.

"Hello," a female voice came from the speakers around them in Chaktun. "I am the First Daughter of the Tuit Consortium, Tisha of Solwick, daughter of Esha, granddaughter of Isha. And who are you?"

Regina stood, helping Kelly and Gail to their feet as well. She then looked toward the speaker and gulped. "I am Centurion Regina Dawson of the *USSTAP Galaxy Protector Gentry*." She then nodded to her right, "This is Centurion Gail French," she then motioned to her left, "and this is Centurion Kelly Sterling."

"I know you realize you are trespassing on Tuit sovereign land," Tisha responded in a stern voice.

"Yes First Daughter, we understand!" Regina answered, noticing Tisha used the criminal terminology *'trespassing,'* instead of the military term '*spying*.' She did not know if this was a problem in the translation matrix Tisha was using, or if it was intentional. If it was intentional, Tisha had just opened up the door for negotiations. “However,” she continued. “We come on a most urgent cause.”

“Oh! And what may that be?”

Regina looked to Kelly and Gail with promise in her eyes. She licked her lips and took a deep breath. “First Daughter,” she began. “The hostility between our peoples is a product of an age old misunderstanding.”

“How so?”

Regina reached inside her pants pocket under her robe and pulled out the corynx crystal containing a copy of the newly acquired HVP. “On this contains the record of the first contact between our people and the fate of your ships in our Millmum Galaxy. Even though it was not a sterling example of diplomacy…it is a true account of events. And once you view this HVP, you will realize the entire episode was caused by a terrible happenstance and dreadful set of miscommunications.”

“Oh!” Tisha feigned. “And I suppose this dreadful set of miscommunications is responsible for the lost of one of my fireships.”

“What are you talking about?” Regina shouted.

“Several hours ago, only a few short light years away from here, the Tuits fireship *Crinkle* was destroyed, by what I can only surmise was your ship, this *Galaxy Protector Gentry*.”

Regina shook her head in disgust. She did not know what happened, but she knew whatever Jarod did, he did to save the life of his crew and ship.

“One thousand of my sisters were onboard her,” she continued. “One-thousand!” she yelled. “That is a strange way to sue for peace…by killing an entire fireship of Tuits.”

The words echoed in Regina’s ear. She knew the false hope of negotiation was sliding away. Her mind switched into military overdrive, spotting and surveying the area. The guards behind both force fields stood with their firestaffs at the ready and their weapons still lay on the floor. She calculated by the time they retrieved the weapons and fired them; Tisha would have deactivated the force field, and ordered the guards to fire.

“We’re screwed,” she whispered to Kelly and Gail.

“Emergency-evac,” Jarod’s voice sliced through their earpiece. His voice resonated like a heavenly choir, presenting an option from heaven. “Emergency-evac,” his voice rang again.

Regina threw the corynx crystal to the ground, diverting the Tuits’ attention for a split second. The crystal bounced several times on the white floor, and came to rest against the corridor wall. Then three white inner space openings formed in front of them. They dove inside and the doors closed shut before Tisha could deactivate the force fields.

***

Regina, Gail and Kelly slid onto the gate portal room stage onboard the *USSTAP Galaxy Protector Gentry*.

"We have them," the gate portal operator reported to the bridge.

"Great!" Jarod replied. Then he turned to his pilot, "Get us the hell out of here!"

"Tiah!"

One-half light year and negative fifteen on the galactic plane, the USSTAP *G.P. Gentry* moved up the speed schedule from hypersonic to hyperlight speed, disappearing from light in a puff of energy, and then flashed into MOP speed sailing across the unknown heavens in an unknown and uncharted galaxy of the Centaurus Supercluster.

Chapter 35—The Interview and Interrogation

Lilly Station, the home of the Earth Forces of USSTAP, sat on the Atlantic floor of the continental shelf, once known as Atlantis. The old Kulusk station was the spherical hub, housing the command section and gate portal rooms. Several wings extended from the hub like spokes of a wheel, housing different corps. Extending at the end of the wings were concourses where the sea cruisers docked when in port, and where the startram catcher was also housed.

Inside the main hub, Sheri Filgo stepped from the white light carrying Angela over her right shoulder. She stayed on the platform, bloody and tired, staring at the operator.

"Step us to the medical bay," she gasped.

The operator nodded and input the coordinates into the system. An invisible door slid up and opened behind her, shining the heavenly white light of inner space. Sheri swung around, stepped into the light and the door closed again.

She emerged from the light inside the medical bay on deck four of Lilly Station's east wing number three. A med gurney floated toward her and she dropped the unconscious Angela onto the bed.

"Check her DNA...see if she is one of those damned Tuits," she ordered. "Lord knows she packed a punch like one."

The gurney floated into medical alcove four. A pod lifted from the floor and attached to the gurney, turning it into a medical bed. Then the MARIT flashed a red light from the overhead, and swept it up and down Angela's body. The MARIT ran billions of calculations and instructions within a nanosecond, searching, deciphering and coding the results. It scanned her blood, skin, hair follicles and fingerprints. Then it used micro portals to extract samples of her blood, urine, fingernails and toenails. Meanwhile, Doctor Erlic ushered Sheri to the opposite alcove.

"Broken nose, gashes over the right eye, left jaw, another cut across the forehead, maybe a concussion…it looks like you went ten rounds with Tyson," he commented as he motioned for her to sit on the med bed.

Sheri pointed across the bay, "If that's Tyson, call me Hollyfield and check my ears."

Erlic giggled, picked up his stitching MARIT and began closing her cuts. The stitching MARIT was a pencil shaped, four-inch silver thin rod. It shot a green beam that cleaned the blood and closed the wound as it slid across the cut. Then he motioned for her to lay back. He switched to the bone mending MARIT, a circular black device with several micro port openings. He placed it over her nose while watching the x-ray through a MARIT screen above the bed. He manipulated the device to move and then fused the bone in her nose. Then he moved to her left rib, which was cracked, and manipulated and fused the bone in place as well.

After he completed the repairs to her rib, he gave Sheri a sedative mixed with medication to repair her concussion. In most cases, sleep would be dangerous for a concussion, but the medicine he injected worked better with the subject relaxed and was most effective when the subject was asleep.

Sheri fell asleep almost immediately. Erlic watched the MARIT screen above the bed as it displayed the path of the medicine to her brain. He saw the medicine attack the area of the brain that was bruised, relieving the pressure and easing the pain. The entire repair time would be about two hours and Sheri would feel almost as good as new, except for a little stinging in her rib and in her nose, where he fused the bone together.

With that in mind, Erlic walked across the bay to Angela. He studied the output, which the MARIT recorded. His eyes widened with shock. He then pushed the button to repeat the DNA scan, using all parameters.

The first test came back negative for Tuit properties, but other factors sprung up—puzzling factors, which not only confused him, but also scared him. Erlic called his second over to look over the testing because he was not satisfied he was doing it correctly. He set up a battery of tests, manually checking every body fluid, secretion and hair follicle to include blood, saliva and urine once more. When those test showed the same results, the medical team then moved to manually checking skin, fingernails and toenails clippings, hair follicles and tear duct samples. Again the test turned up negative, but that wasn't what was bothering him.

He pulled up his databank of existing forms of human and crosschecked the DNA sequences against Angela's. He found a match just where he suspected. He nodded to his assistant who still wore the face of bewilderment.

"ARIT compare subject DNA against Alpha One and Alpha Two source," Erlic commanded.

"Processing," the ARIT voice responded, as Erlic pulled his stitch MARIT and proceeded to close Angela's wounds.

"Comparison complete," the ARIT interrupted.

"Proceed," Erlic responded with anticipation. He already thought he knew the answer. He just wanted scientific confirmation to prove his theory.

"Subject DNA comparison to Alpha One is negative one and six degrees." The words made Erlic smile. "Subject DNA comparison to Alpha Two is zero and six degrees." With those words ringing from the ARIT speaker, Erlic's smile turned into a gleeful laugh.

"Got ya!" he whispered while clinching his fist. "Lord, I don't believe it," he added while shaking his head in disbelief. His heart started pounding and he felt the blood rush through his body. He was invigorated as if he had just won the lottery. In his mind, he did win the lottery. He clicked his CC, "General Lo…This is Dr. Erlic." He waited for the split second it took for the signal to clear.

"Go ahead doctor," Lo's voice rang inside his ear.

"I think you better come to the medical bay right away."

"On my way!"

***

The fog was lifting, but the ache was streaming through his body. His muscles were sore and stiff. He remembered this feeling. It was how he felt after the first time…thanks to Stelana. Musoto was waking up from another encounter with a pagenay. He tried to open his eyes. His brain commanded his eyes to open, but his eyelids failed to obey. He wanted to turn his head, but again his mental commands went unheeded. All he knew was that he was lying on his back on something hard, probably a floor.

This was different than last time. When he awoke after Stelana shot him, he was laying on a soft bed in deluxe quarters resembling VIP suites at the most luxurious hotel. However now, he was laying on the floor, or worse a steel bed, like a prisoner. He could feel the restraints around his wrists and ankles. He knew he was not a guest of whoever had him. He knew he was a prisoner.

"Mr. Musoto," a gentle feminine voice called.

He could hear her and he wanted to respond, but once again his mind had no control over his physical movements. Next, he felt a pin prick on his neck and then a hissing sound, and then the pin prick was gone.

"Mr. Musoto," the voice called again.

"Yes," Musoto whispered to his own surprise. His voice was shaky and weak, but he was able to speak. "Yes," he said with more force, trying to clear the frog in his throat. He opened his eyes, but he was unable to focus.

All he saw was a spot; he imagined was the person speaking to him. He blinked several times, training his eyes on the figure above him.

"Mr. Musoto…I'm Lieutenant Gloria Magma, USSTAP Security. I have some questions I need to ask you."

Musoto moaned as he tried to form an answer to the statement. He rolled his head to the side and tried to lift his arms. He pulled against the restraints, confirming his initial thoughts.

"Why the restraints?" he moaned

"Until I'm satisfied with your answers to my questions, it is a necessary precaution—both for your safety and mine."

"I don't understand…I thought we had an agreement?"

"Like all agreements, it is time for us to renegotiate the terms," Gloria snapped back.

"What for?" Musoto chimed, focusing on his interrogator. He saw a round-faced, pretty young Filipino with short-cropped hair. She was wearing the black uniform he had come to know as USSTAP. "Where's Stelana?"

"Called away for now," Gloria answered.

"Called away! Where? Why?"

"All in due time, Mr. Musoto…all in due time, but for now, you can talk to me. I am Lieutenant Rican's replacement. You can say I am your new liaison."

"This is not right! You've kidnapped me!"

"No, Mr. Musoto. We are detaining you for a time. It is very imperative that we receive your full cooperation."

"Why should I?"

"It would help in redefining our association."

"What association?" Musoto snarled.

"So you don't think we have an association of sorts with you?"

"No!" Musoto replied, letting his anger show.

"So when you were working with Lt. Rican in Shreveport, you didn't consider that an association?"

"It was," Musoto answered. "But something happened…somehow what I thought was association dissolved. You guys started treating me like the plague."

"Go on," she urged.

Musoto's feelings flooded throughout his essence. His feeling of inadequacy, one that he had harbored for so long pushed to the forefront of his mind. His fear of failure, which drove his actions, circled his thoughts. He felt he failed to maintain a solid relationship with USSTAP, he knew he failed to obtain the information his president required and he understood he fell short of becoming the top agent he wanted to become. Here, he had the career-making detail of a lifetime, and he could not turn it to his advantage. He just continued to screw it up.

His one saving grace, the only success he knew he had accomplished was his relationship with Mona Richards. Yet, now even that was in doubt. He had not spoken with her since Friday afternoon, and that was the longest he had not spoken to her and the longest he had been away from her. For a moment, his mind drifted to the last time he was with Mona. The blissful peace he felt with her washed over him and calmed him.

"Next question," he spouted.

"No more questions, Mr. Musoto…not now anyway," Gloria whispered as she patted his hand.

The metal restraints snapped off and released Musoto's wrists and ankles. He lifted his arms and began rubbing his wrists. They were not hurting, but he wanted to massage warmth back into them after having the cold steel of the restraints harnessing them for so long.

Musoto rose up and swung his legs off the table. At that moment, something drew his attention to his forehead. He reached up to feel his head and to his surprise he felt the rectangular device he knew was the MARIT attachment that allowed USSTAP to read thoughts. He hung his head down in shame as he realized Gloria had read all his thoughts and all his feelings. He tried to pull it off, but it would not budge. The more he tugged the more the pain shot through his entire head, like a migraine. He stopped and pounded his fist on the table.

"You bitch!" he roared. "You've been reading my thoughts all this time."

"Get some rest, Mr. Musoto," Gloria suggested as she turned toward the door. The door split down the middle and swooshed open. She snapped her head over her shoulder, "You'll need your rest for later." Then she walked out and the door slammed closed, signaling to Musoto, he was indeed a prisoner.

***

The clamor in the Hall of Fire was enormous. Voices rang throughout, echoing off the deep stone walls and mixing together, making a soup of sounds. In the center of the hall, hanging precariously above the forum in a large black caldron, held by electromagnetic forces, was the eternal flame, the fire of life, which the consortium worshiped like a god. The flame, fueled by the strange mixture of gases that swirled in the hall, burned hot. Its blue flickers of light were uniform in its dance and gorgeous in its spirit, variously spreading from four to ten feet high, covering a five-foot circumference. The flame was hypnotic and breathtaking, mesmerizing to all who dared study it. Legend had it, that life first sprung from this fire eons ago, breathing its hot flame of existence into the lungs of the first Tuits, a man named Thun and a woman named Thyn.

The legend told a story in which Thun was arrogant and abusive to Thyn, tricking her several times into doing monstrous deeds against the fire—dousing water, shoveling sand unto it, and once even closing the fire within the walls, now known as the Hall of Fire. Yet, the eternal flame lived. Not only did it live, but it also thrived.

Then one day, while Thyn was executing one of Thun's plans to kill the flame, it spoke to Thyn. It spoke with a feminine voice, telling Thyn that she was her mother and for her to resist Thun…for her to fight Thun. She then told her the secrets of fire, how to start a fire, how to maintain a fire, but most importantly, how to burn things with fire, including Thun.

Thyn did as she was told and while Thun was asleep one night, she set him ablaze, sending him back onto the eternal flame from whence he came. The eternal flame rewarded Thyn with another man for her consort, but this time, Thyn had dominion over the man. Soon Thyn and her new companion, who was never named in the old achieves, populated the planet. However, the distrust between the genders, no matter how veiled was always evident, as the eternal flame kept watch, looking for the time in which she would rid the planet of men—the necessary evil.

From this distrust the Sisters of the Tuit Consortium arose, and over the centuries demeaned man in their presence, reducing them to lolwes…sperm and organ donors.

When one looked into the eternal flame, the entire story flooded into the consciousness like a tidal wave, pushing the emotional buttons of hatred for men, while assuaging the emotion of love for all their sisters. The eternal fire was a constant, an all-consuming reminder of their undying pledge to the sisterhood.

Now today, there was a challenge to that sisterhood—a Vote of Confidence, which was going to turn into a Right of Challenge. Miam, the Second Daughter of Fire's eyes were full of passion and fury as she soaked in the atmosphere. She stood with her hands outstretched from the command portico overlooking the hall. Her red robe catching the blue reflection of the fire burning above her, gave her the devil's look.

"Sisters!" she screamed. "You have had an opportunity to look over the evidence, and now it is time for your vote."

"Not so fast!" Tisha shouted from behind her.

Her voice quelled the noise that was hovering in the chamber. Now you could hear a pin drop as Tisha walked to the perch of the command portico. She stepped past the other Daughters of Fire, who were seated in position.

"You say my tactics were traitorous?" she roared at Miam.

"I do," she shouted.

"But you say my actions didn't stop Rina in any way?"

"No, I didn't say that," Miam countered. "I said your actions made it difficult for Rina and may have caused the failure of her latest mission."

"Then I put to you," Tisha yelled. "Then who is responsible for leading the enemy to our own dimension, where they attacked and destroyed the *Fireship Crinkle*, where they attacked my elite guards outside our city, where they attacked sisters inside the Hall of Fire, and escaped without a trace?" she said raising her voice like a Baptist minister preaching to a congregation, trying to elicit more of an emotional response than a intellectual one. "Whose fault is that?" she yelled. "Whose fault is it?" she repeated in a lower tone. "Is it mine?" She paused to read the members eyes. "No!" she said. "Is it yours?" Again she paused. "No, I don't think so!" "How about Miam, is it her fault?"

Miam's eyes lit up with fear, thinking Tisha was going to blame her. Her mind raced for a quick rebuttal. She was losing the initiative. Tisha was going on the offensive. She needed to put her back on the defensive. She opened her mouth to begin her rebuttal.

"No, it isn't her fault," Tisha interrupted, knowing she shot a spear into Miam's strategy.

Miam closed her mouth, not knowing how to respond now.

"No, my sisters, the fault does not lay with us," she said. "I'll tell you who…I will tell you exactly who did this to us. "It was Rina of Jaywick. Our sister in the order…our companion in the spirit…she failed us. She let the devils from the other dimension in here to take what we have created and what we've accomplished. It's Rina's fault. She's the one. It's her incompetence. It's her inexperience that has us facing our enemy in our own territory." She gulped, feeling the pressure swirl inside the hall. "Maybe, I am to blame," she admitted, looking for sympathy. "Maybe I gave her too much responsibility?" she continued. "I thought I was mentoring her, guiding her, showing her the way." She paused and took a deep breath, playing the timing like a concert conductor.

"This is the first time in centuries we've had to face an enemy in our own territory. And if you look at what Miam presented you, you will see this is what I feared. That is why I did what I did. That is why I was so hard on her. This is why! That is why I did all these things Miam has brought to your attention. I don't deny it. I just wish I had done more. But she had me fooled. I thought she was listening. But she wasn't."

Then she looked up at the eternal flame, "How many more of our sisters must go back to the flame before their time?" She then looked at the Consortium, her gaze sweeping across the hall as if she was looking at each and every member. "We are at war people. We don't have time for this. Cancel this vote and let me get on with the business of the Consortium. Let me get back to killing the enemy!"

***

Musoto sat back in the recliner, huffing in disgust. It had been nearly two days straight of interrogation, or as Gloria called it, a friendly interview. Musoto recognized it for what it was—an interrogation. Gloria had clipped the MARIT that read thoughts onto his forehead. He had seen Stelana use it before, and he realized for some reason he was now considered a threat or at least non-friendly. There was a marked difference in his status from the last time he was here, but none of that matter now.

Musoto was tired and upset, but most of all he was angry. His kidnapping solidified in his mind the dangerous aspect of USSTAP. His former admiration of the Osguards had now turned into bitter distain.

Musoto looked at his watch. It was 5:00 A.M. He closed his eyes and wished he could fall asleep. His adrenaline was pumping and every time he felt himself about to doze off, Gloria or one of the other women would pop in. Although he was intrigued to see Filipinos involved with USSTAP, it did not deter the vile feeling brewing in his soul that USSTAP was founded on the principles of bigotry, racism and ethnic purity. Although these were strong words, he could not shake his conversation with Osguard fifty-five, Juanita Genesis-Clark, in Shreveport from his mind. Her views were astounding, outdated and an ill fit for someone of her stature and position. Yet, she uttered, what he considered, reverse discrimination and highly inflammatory diatribe.

The door swished open and Gloria walked in, erasing Musoto's thoughts from his mind. It was time to play the game again and he was ready. However, this time she was smiling. Her smile was more than alarming to Musoto; it was eerie as well.

"Well Agent Musoto," Gloria opened. "It appears you don't trust us anymore."

Musoto started to lie, but realized the MARIT would tell his inner thoughts anyway. He had been trying to hide his feelings from the MARIT, but obviously he failed. So he nodded.

"Well Agent Musoto, I am not going to get into a philosophical debate with you. I can see your environment and your personality will not accept us…and to tell the truth…that is the main reason our organization remains secret…because of people like you." Gloria pulled up the seat next to Musoto, never losing eye contact. "So let me tell you why we pulled you in."

Musoto's eyes lit up with interest and Gloria knew it without looking into her PARIT monitor. "I know you are familiar with the MARIT on your forehead…and I know you know what it is doing. I apologize for the intrusion on your thoughts, but this is serious. I needed to know if you were working with them or not."

"Working with whom?" Musoto blurted without thought.

"The Tuits…Mona…Congresswoman Eldridge!"

"What the hell are you talking about?"

"Musoto," she continued. "Since you left, we have been at war with the Tuits. They are an Amazonian race from another star cluster. They were behind the Kulusk uprising and we think behind the incident in Shreveport. They have been on Earth for quite some time, trying to exact revenge for a perceived wrong done to them almost a hundred years ago. We have lost about a dozen solar systems and countless lives. Musoto, we are losing the war and Earth will fall if we don't stop them. My job was to ferret out the Tuits on Earth. So far, I have only found two. And you led me to both of them."

"I say again, what the hell are you talking about?"

"Mona Richards and Congresswoman Eldridge are Tuit spies," she stated.

"No fucking way!"

"I'm afraid so," Gloria persisted, laying her hand on Musoto's knee as a show of compassion and comfort. "I know this must be tough, but it appears Mona was using something similar to our brain MARIT to siphon thoughts from you in your sleep. It's not clear how, but we figure she gathered information about us through you. When we realized there was a leak, we suspected you; therefore, you were isolated and followed. Frankly, it was purely by accident we stumbled onto Eldridge when she played that little game between you and Lieutenant Rican in the coffee shop."

"I don't believe you!"

"I figured you wouldn't. And I really don't care. I just thought I owed you an explanation…I mean, since you've been exonerated in our eyes. However, this is the last contact we will have with you. And if you and the president persist in tracking us…well, let's just say don't!"

"Are you letting me go?"

"Yes, we are…both you and Ms. Santos are free to leave."

"Angela…you have Angela too?"

"Yes, we have your CIA partner."

"She isn't CIA," Musoto protested. Then he pushed closer to Gloria,

"Is Angela okay?"

"She's fine," Gloria assured him. Then a voice in her earpiece grabbed her attention. Gloria's eyes widened as she gazed at Musoto.

"What?" Musoto questioned.

"The president is planning on exposing us to the U.N. Security Council?"

Musoto's mind focused around his last telephone conversation with the National Security Advisor, James Hall. And he knew any attempt at deception was futile. He obviously had given some indication that the MARIT picked up in a fleeting thought.

"Well I can't lie to you with this thing on my head," he complained.

"Whatever you say," she said reaching over and unsnapping the MARIT from his forehead. It seemed so easy for her. Musoto had tried all night in vain to detach the gadget from his head. She just touched it and it dislodged with a slight sting. "Now I'm going to trust you."

"Why should I trust you?" Musoto bristled.

"I just told you, Mona and Eldridge were Tuits. Their plan is falling apart at the seams. General Lo thinks they are trying to drive a wedge between the people of Earth and USSTAP. If the president is mysteriously killed on his way to exposing us…I think that would fit the bill. I need to know what you know…no MARIT…just you and me. You have a chance to save your president. Please Musoto, tell me what you know."

Musoto huffed and blew out hard. His feelings were turning left and right. His intuition was testing his loyalty. What if she was correct and the president was in danger. It wasn't just the United States president; it was also the Russian president. He lowered his head. His gut was telling him to cooperate but his brain was saying no!

He again huffed and turned around. He sat back in the recliner and looked out the port window at the pitch black water of the sea. The view reminded him of all the technology USSTAP had at their control. If they wanted the president dead, they would not need his cooperation. They could find him and do it without his help. Right now, he was being tested. They wanted to know what side he was on. They wanted to know if he could be trusted. It was a gamble, but he knew he couldn't play the game any longer. Because Gloria removed the MARIT from his forehead, this was the first time he could mull over any course of action.

It wasn't just the U.S. president. The Russian president was flying to New York today as well. They both would present evidence of USSTAP existence to the U.N. Security Council. His loyalty had to be to his country first and his country only. He looked back up at Gloria with strong resolve, "No! I won't help you. If you want to stop Peters, you have to do it on your own. I will not be part of it."

Gloria sighed and shook her head in disappointment, "I figured that," she responded. She walked over to Musoto and gazed down at him with disfavor. "You know Mr. Musoto…you're an asshole. I offered you a chance to do the right thing and you fucked it up—again." Then she turned and walked out of the room, leaving Musoto to linger in his own bravado.

Chapter 36—Defense or Offense

Ninety-five light years from the Tuit main solar system, on the dark side of the third moon orbiting the sixth planet in an isolated and uninhabited solar system, the *USSATP Galaxy Protector Gentry* hovered in a crevice. The ship remained in stealth mode ten. Her energized sleek, black slitanium skin bent and refracted light and energy allowing the ship to blend in with its background like a chameleon, making her invisible to the naked eye and almost undetectable to any known search array system.

It had been almost three days since Jarod rescued his officers from the Tuit Hall of Fire. Kelly, Regina and Gail had spent most of that time in the medical bay, recovering from the injuries they sustained during their exploration mission. The reports and debriefs revealed little.

Jarod sat in his command chair on the command bridge studying the reports, searching for a weakness he could exploit. However, he realized the little hope expressed in Regina's report about Tisha was dashed when he destroyed the fireship. He knew his actions had turned any compunction over the war Tisha might have had into revenge. He played the short battle in his mind several times, wishing he had decided to run instead. He had attacked to keep his presence in the area a secret, but that objective was blown long ago. Now he regretted the entire episode. His actions and the death of over one thousand Tuits were unnecessary.

Tisha and now the entire Tuit Consortium were well aware of his presence and were now on the hunt for him. He was deep inside enemy territory, with no hope of getting home, and little hope of survival. Thus, he had decided it was time to stop trying to forge a truce and deliver as much destruction as he could while he had the opportunity. He had decided his mission had turned from diplomacy to sabotage. He had to use hit and run techniques of guerilla warfare, and disrupt the Tuit military operation from within. Unlike any other organized clandestine operation, he had no intelligence to begin with. He had no star charts of the area and he had no idea of the Tuit influence.

The command bridge door swung open, which caused Jarod to turn around. Regina, Kelly and Gail stepped onto the bridge and took their seats. Jarod nodded to each one, giving a quick smile.

"Welcome back ladies," he greeted.

Each responded with a nod and a smile, uncharacteristically quiet for the threesome. The air of confusion still hovered over the bridge. Regina opened her PARIT screen and started reviewing several documents on it.

"We need to go on reconnaissance," she offered, keeping her eyes on the screen.

Jarod turned toward her and studied her features. He realized she had come to the same conclusion he had reached, but he wanted to explore her thoughts more. “Reconnaissance…for what?”

“We are at war, Jarod,” she huffed turning toward him. “Peace negotiations are no longer an option. I’m not sure the HVP I left behind could dissuade the Tuits from embarking on their road of revenge. The First Daughter has to push for our destruction because of the *Fireship Crinkle*.”

“Are you blaming me, Regina?”

“No sire. I read the reports and to tell the truth, I don’t think you had any other option, dealing with the facts you had on hand. You had no idea we had compromised our presence in the system. Running would have left our distinctive engine signature mark, which would have told them we were here. I would have done the same thing, hoping the destruction would buy us some time as they investigated. Who knew they could decipher the damage so thoroughly and so fast? No sire, I am not blaming you. It just seems like fate is against us on this one.”

“So the next step is guerilla warfare,” Gail interrupted. “We need to hit them hard and fast as many times as we can, before…” her voice trailed off because she didn’t want to finish the statement. However, everybody knew what it was, *‘before they get us!’*

“Defense,” Jarod called. “Have you tracked any lines of travel?”

“Tiah sire, I am tracking a L.O.T. ten light years from here. It appears to be a repair or maintenance station of some sort.”

“How certain are you?” Gail asked.

“I’m reading five Fireships in varying states of maintenance.”

“If we can take that out, it would delay their military infrastructure…especially if it houses any upgrades or research and development,” Gail surmised aloud.

“Navigator, set a course. Take us point five light years positive twenty on the galactic plane. I want to get a closer look at this. Tell intelligence to begin analysis.”

“Course set, sire,” the navigator responded.

“Pilot, take us out, MOP thirty,” he ordered.

“Slitanium de-energized…engaging on course sire,” the pilot announced.

Outside the ship reappeared in the visual spectrum and lifted up from the crevice. It hovered above the moon and then slid into MOP thirty on the course the navigator set, once again disappearing from the naked eye.

In twenty universal minutes, the *Gentry* came to a full stop at Jarod’s designated spot, point five light years positive twenty on the galactic plane. The ship went into stealth mode ten, energizing her slitanium hull attempting to blend in with the fabric of space.

"Intelligence Corps…start analysis," Jarod said into his interlink. Then he turned to the navigator, "Record and map the area," he ordered. "I want to know this space just as I do my own galaxy. I want to know the planets and the star systems and what they can offer us," he added for emphasis.

Then the piercing sound of the Alert One buzzer snapped on. Jarod turned to his monitor as the ARIT began streaming information on it.

"Sire," the defense officer beaconed. "Ultra space event openings to the port, starboard, aft and bow, below and above." He swallowed hard, attempting to hide the fear that was creeping into his voice. "Nine…no, ten openings!"

Outside, ten large ovals of red light perforated normal space, shining their ghostly light as if hell, itself had opened up.

"Pilot, get us out of here," Jarod ordered.

"Unable sire," the pilot announced. "The events are distorting the gravitational particles. The engines are useless until the events are complete."

"Ten fireships entering normal space," the defense officer announced, still trying to control the fear in his throat. The white cone-shaped fireships, reflecting the red restion particles, sailed through the light, slithering into normal space like spikes of fire. "Events are closing now."

"Okay pilot, get us out of here now!" Jarod pushed.

"Unable sire," the pilot announced. "The gravitational pull of a light speed maneuver will suck one of those ships right into us. I have no clear path to take. We are surrounded."

Jarod checked his monitor and did a mental calculation of the fireships' distances and placement around the *Gentry*. He knew the pilot was correct. The suction causing the push and pull of the trachion gravitational particles would cause a gravitational well, sucking anything within one hundred marks toward the ship, and the Tuit ships were in tight formation in which an escape route would take them too close to one hundred marks to attempt.

"Obviously, they know we are here," Regina speculated. "Do we stay in stealth or put the field up?"

Jarod lifted his head in momentary thought, "Field up, battle stations, weapons on line!"

Regina repeated the orders and the ship returned to the laws of light and appeared in the midst of the Tuit ships, trapped like a mouse in an alley full of cats.

"Oh…this shit's going to hurt!" Jarod whispered to Regina.

"Well boss, let's make it hurt for them as well," she replied.

***

The docking ring around Millmum Capitol Station was empty. No ships, not even the flagship, the *Galaxy Protector Neraka*, were docked on the ring. In the tip of the diamond, on the observation deck, Admiral Toneilk, the station's sire, and Commander Terilela, the station's controller, stood watch. The station's search array system was feeding trillions upon trillions of bytes of data per second to the ARIT, clearing a thirty light year area around the station, searching and scanning for restion events and or Tuit ship engine signatures.

"Anything?" Toneilk questioned.

"Nothing yet, sire," Terilela announced.

"I hate it when the Osguard takes off on one of his wild hair schemes and leaves me here to defend the home front."

"So far, his wild hair schemes have panned out," Terilela reminded him. "And you have done a great job in protecting the home front."

Toneilk smiled, remembering the first time he tasted battle, several months earlier against the Kulusk invasion. He knew he was not in danger as were those who flew the defenders, galaxy cruisers and galaxy protectors. However, he still felt the heat of the battle that raged a few light years from the station, sweating and thinking it was only a matter of time before the battle did reach the station.

However, now if the Tuits attacked, he could very well be the first line of defense. The station was newly equipped with perimeter starguards containing K-guns. He had mentioned a thousand times how he thought the K-guns were nasty little buggers. That kind of destruction could only come from the mind of a Kulusk, but he was glad USSTAP had adopted the gun in its battle against the Tuits. Because that was exactly what was needed to fight the Tuits—a nasty little bugger.

Then a chirp grabbed his attention. "What is that?"

Terilela listened to her headset, catching one of her controllers' voices describing the anomaly that caused the ARIT to chirp. Then she tuned her monitor to repeat the controller's screen. The monitor's mathematical equations abruptly changed under scanner mode. She changed to sensors, allowing the ARIT to interpret the mathematical stream and displaying it onto her monitor. The process took a split second as the screen jumped. Soon the screen focused on forty ultra-space openings dotting the area about thirty-three light years in sector hotel at positive one hundred on the galactic plane.

"Well here we go," Terilela announced.

"Alert One...Defense starguards to operate...Notify Red Osguard One...fight's on!"

***

Admiral B'Kailine stepped onto the observation deck of Siryman Station and plopped into the command chair. He twirled the chair around, affording his senses the luxurious view of space through the three hundred and sixty-degree glass panel, characteristic of all capitol station. His heart pounded with exhilaration. He had not felt this good since before he donned the USSTAP uniform—not since he was the military leader, the Kushcan, of the D'Ardin Empire.

Michael thought that Siryman Capitol Station would be a prime target for attack since it was where they were housing the prisoners. Their sense of loyalty would not permit any survivors to remain in an enemy's prison. So the trap was laid. He was ready and willing to take on the Tuits in battle, especially since the station's starguards were equipped with the lethal K-gun. He had all the armament of three galaxy protectors at his beck and call.

The starguards were satellite stations that patrolled the area grid. The starguards were spherical slitanium balls stapled with the USSTAP characteristic engine pods, capable of stealth mode transformation. Each starguard was twice as large as a defender, carrying one coronet cannon, one pagenay blaster, one K-gun, one pair of Asher torpedoes and a stealth mode generator. B'Kailine knew with the addition of the K-gun, the station became the most powerful entity in the galaxy. He had the firepower at his command. B'Kailine was no longer just a babysitter to diplomats or a butler taking care of the Osguard's house. He was now a full-fledged combatant commander, responsible for the protection of USSTAP's most prized possession in the universe.

The starguards were his idea…his brainchild, that he offered Jarod when he returned to the station. Jarod did not seem that enthused about it, but he took the idea to the Osguard Senate anyway, where it met with resounding favor. Additionally, Jarod gave B'Kailine credit for the idea. He had no idea that the starguards had gone into massive production, where thirty were produced for every capitol station, until Jarod's brother and sister came to deliver them personally to him last week.

A team of engineers spent several days transforming a section of the observation bridge into a defensive command counsel. The test proved promising…so promising that the approval for normal operation only took several hours. Then again, the entire war was cause for any proven weapons system to be fast tracked. The scores of bodies the Tuits left in their wake was unconscionable, even to a warrior race like the D'Ardin Empire. Therefore anything and everything was fair game in the war to stop them.

After Tim and Rachel interrogated Rina, Michael turned to a more aggressive strategy, realizing then that negotiating was a failed objective. There was too much hate, too much animosity and too much contempt in the Tuit society for USSTAP to hope for a congenial conclusion to hostilities.

B'Kailine knew this from the beginning. He knew the type of destruction the Tuits left behind. The number of deaths they caused made them more than a formidable enemy, and it made them evil in human form. There was no way to deal with evil except to exorcise them.

Commander Toevph was watching and listening to her operators as they searched the heavens for signs of Tuit activity. Her sapphire eyes and caramel skin radiated in the light of the observation deck, making the beauty of the situation more pleasant for B'Kailine. His mind transcended the situation as he floated in his own self-styled pleasantness. He was at ease. He was happy. If he was lucky, he was about to enter battle.

"Activity in sector 4–F," Commander Toevph announced, placing the search array results on her screen.

B'Kailine stepped down from his perch and stood behind Commander Toevph to interpret the results for himself. He counted forty restion events, meaning he was about to face forty Tuit fireships. His blood ran hot in his veins. His mouth salivated with anticipation. He turned back to his chair, sat down and activated his monitor.

"Alert one…Activate starguards…Notify Blue Osguard One…fight's on!"

Chapter 37—Air Force One

At thirty-five thousand feet over the northeastern seaboard of the United States, Air Force One, a gigantic Boeing 747-200B modified to carry the president of the United States, flew escorted by two F-15s. Lt Col Ronald Karen flew two miles in lead at thirty-seven thousand feet, clearing Air Force One's path for any intrusive traffic, while Major Sharon Boscoe flew off the plane's right wing. Each fighter carried a full complement of air-to-air missiles. Lt Col Karen carried four AIM-7F/M Sparrow missiles under the lower fuselage corners and four AIM-9L/Ms on two pylons under the wings. Major Boscoe carried eight AIM-120 AMRAAMS. Along with the plane's internally mounted 940 round M-61A1 20-mm, six-barrel cannon, these missiles made Lt Col Karen and Major Boscoe formidable opponents for anyone foolish enough to engage Air Force One with any type of hostilities.

Inside Air Force One's four thousand square feet of interior floor space, Peters sat back in his recliner chair in the office area, wondering how his speech would be received in the U.N. Security Council. He had worked all weekend on it and every time he read it, it sounded like a bad science fiction movie. He attempted to listen to the speech with an objective mind and a disinterested attitude. He even recorded the speech and played it several times, but each time he heard his voice explain USSTAP's existence he felt he should be committed. Now he wasn't sure this was a good idea. He had no hard evidence other than Musoto's reports and the old letters from President Truman and Kennedy.

He and the Russian president, Sergey Repustinov, agreed to keep the depletion of missile warheads secret for now. They both knew if they admitted the loss of their nuclear warheads, their status in the world community as well as their national interest worldwide, would be vulnerable to attack from every third rate dictator and leader. They both feared China's wish to become top dog in the world community, and this would give them the excuse to run roughshod over them. Proving USSTAP's existence was next to impossible, without disclosing the near destruction of Earth that precipitated USSTAP's discovery.

He wanted Musoto to find something more concrete for him to take to the U.N. However, Musoto, as usual, failed him. In fact, Musoto was nowhere to be found, which irritated Peters to no end. He wondered why he agreed for Musoto to stay involved in the situation. He decided when he returned he would assign another, more capable agent to head the search for USSTAP.

***

High in the sky at sixty-five thousand feet, flying over the northern Atlantic at hypersonic speed, two cone shape single-seat Tuit firefighters raced to their designated targets. The woman known as Congressional Representative Joyce T. Eldridge was in the lead firefighter. Mona Richards flew a close second off her starboard wing. On her monitor, she was tracking Air Force One. Intercept time was ten minutes.

"Arming weapons now," she announced into the interlink to Mona Richards. She flipped her targeting array on, energizing the two firestaff cannons silhouetted under the belly below her seat. She could feel the vibration humming through the skin and into the cannons, assuring her the cannons had come to life.

"Kiza ... weapons on line," Mona replied over the interlink.

Eldridge watched the miles tick down like the second hand of a watch. Her mouth watered with anticipation as she drew closer to her objective.

"Are you sure you don't want me to go after the Russian president, while you take care of Peters?" Mona asked.

Her voice broke the silence of the cockpit, pulling Eldridge out of her mental ritual. She shook her head in passionate disgust. "No! I've already told you. Let him live. He will be the witness we need to incite the U.N. Security Council after news of Peters' demise reaches them. He will blame USSTAP and that will place fear into their hearts. Once that is accomplished, the foolish earthlings will undoubtedly pursue military action against

USSTAP, ingratiating them as the incarnation of evil that they have to eradicate."

"I know that!" Mona exclaimed. "However, if we don't attack Repustinov, he may wonder why. I think we should make it look like a synchronized attack to stop both of them from addressing the council and he somehow survived it. This way the motive will take root and be more believable."

Eldridge rolled her head back, looking at the wisdom of Mona's words. It couldn't hurt to spice things up and put a scare into Repustinov. In fact, Mona made sense in her tactic. She thumbed her control to search for Repustinov's airplane. It was fifteen hundred miles outside of New York, scheduled to arrive one hour and forty minutes after Air Force One. She sighed, pushing the air from her lungs in a decisive manner.

"Okay Mona…you can engage, but do not take down, Repustinov's plane. I can handle Air Force One myself."

"Kiza!"

The second firefighter veered right thirty degrees and disappeared. Eldridge reacquired Air Force One in her monitor and continued on her intercept course, wondering if she did the right thing by allowing Mona to go off on her own. She decided it didn't matter; she wanted to be the one that killed Peters. If Mona screwed it up and somehow killed Repustinov, she would just have to adjust her plans a little. Either way, the death or deaths would be blamed on USSTAP. She laughed as the thought of how many politicians would jump on the bandwagon and accuse, torment and outright vilify USSAP played in her mind.

***

Musoto was sitting in the reclining chair staring out the window, mesmerized by the undersea life swimming so effortless in the dark murky waters. Last time he was here, he stayed in a room that did not afford him a view of the ocean. In fact he never realized he was in an underwater complex until Stelana told him. Even though he was more confused and more scared, the first time seemed less stressful and less frightening than now. He admitted to himself that it was because last time he was more curious and was more apt to be in a reconnaissance frame of mind. Now he was more furious and in a defensive frame of mind.

The door swung open and an upset Gloria stood in the arch. "Musoto, get up. You're coming with me."

Musoto turned toward Gloria, "What for?"

"Get up now!" she commanded.

Musoto recognized the tone in her voice as one in which he shouldn't antagonize. He took a deep breath and stood. "Where are we going?"

Gloria's hand moved to her coronet pistol on her delta belt. She rested her palm on the pistol's grip, assuring Musoto she was prepared to use the weapon if need be.

"You'll see," she said.

Musoto was well aware the weapon, unlike the pagenay, had no other purpose than to kill. He felt his heart pound inside his chest. He knew he had pushed too hard and now he was no longer considered a prisoner, but a threat—a threat Gloria would not hesitate to eliminate.

He walked over toward her. She stepped aside and motioned for him to step through the door. On the outside, two guards were waiting. He recognized one as the one who jumped him in the rest room at Rizza's Place. Something about his stance told Musoto that he was eager for him to try to resist. He knew the guard had no reluctance on taking him out. Both stood with one hand resting on their coronet pistol and the other resting on their belt. Again, Musoto read their body language as one of distrust, especially the first one from Rizza's Place.

Gloria pushed him through the door. "Move Musoto," she ordered.

They traveled through the plush carpeted corridors toward the inner workings of the station. As they moved deeper into the belly of the station, the corridors narrowed and the carpet vanished into metal plates and walkways. They were now walking in what Musoto knew was the old part of the station, the original Kulusk station. They maneuvered up several ramps. On the side of the ramps were ladder steps for those who chose to use the more rigorous route. Since he was under escort, the ramp was their circuitous path to wherever they were going. They reached the top deck. He estimated they had walked the equivalent of six flights of stairs. The complex was much larger than he expected.

They moved forward toward a sealed door, which he knew had to be the control center to the entire complex. The smoked doubled glass doors had alien writing on them. He did not know if it was Kulusk or Chaktun, he just knew it was not English, which again confirmed his suspicions about their loyalty.

Gloria stepped from behind him and placed her hand in a device to the right side of the doors. The doors opened, sliding apart into the doorframe. Then Gloria motioned for them to enter the room.

Musoto stepped in first. The room was circular in shape. Three chairs sat in the middle of the room facing each other. The chairs had a control ARIT attached to each of them. There were two stair steps up to get to the chairs. On the outer walls were several ARIT ports with chairs situated in front of them. Musoto saw the same style writing as on the door above each station. In the chair with its back to the door, sat a figure—a woman with long shiny black hair with auburn streaks racing through it. Something was familiar about the figure, but Musoto could not quite put his finger on it. In front of the chairs on the wall sat a large chart of the Earth, where General Wang Lo was standing.

"You know, Mr. Musoto," Lo started without turning around. "I spent ten years on a star cruiser, logging thousands of light years of travel. I spent eight years commanding a sea cruiser on the ocean planet of Thurlan in the Creman system. I fought space pirates, sea creatures and things I still have nightmares until this day about." Then Lo turned toward Musoto. "This is supposed to be my retirement job…easy going…no pressure. But since you and Peters have caught wind of our existence, this job has become a pain in the ass. I don't know of any other planet general going through as much hell as I am right now."

"Well, thank you," Musoto scoffed.

Lo's face crunched up with anger as Musoto's words rang in the room. "Musoto, you are a damn fool."

"I've been told that before."

Lo shook his head in disgust. "Why do we even bother?" he asked to no one in particular.

"I've been asking myself the same question lately," Musoto pushed.

Lo turned back to the screen. "Amplify," he ordered.

The screen changed to a picture near the northeastern seaboard of the United States, around New York City. Several tracks highlighted the screen.

"Musoto," Lo called. "You are looking at the tracks of Air Force One and the Russian president's airplane. They are going to New York to address the United Nations Security Council. Now if we wanted them destroyed, it would take a simple push of a button and puff—they would be gone, with no trace and no evidence."

Musoto swallowed hard. He didn't know how to take the statement, but it sounded very much like a threat.

"But that's not our style," the general confirmed. "Add the intercept tracks," he ordered. White tracks popped up on the view port screen. "Do you see the other tracks…the ones in white?"

Musoto looked more closely and saw the white tracks, one on an intercept course to Air Force One and the other on an intercept course to Repustinov's plane. He swallowed hard as confusion started to dwarf his senses.

"Those I suspect are Tuit fighters. The fact that they are traveling at hypersonic speed lends credence to that. Those tracks don't belong to USSTAP and I doubt you have anything that can fly that fast."

Musoto shrugged. He wasn't sure what to say or do. So he decided he should just listen.

"Now I have the unenviable job of making a tough decision," Lo said, while turning and walking toward Musoto.

Musoto took the sign and moved out of the doorway and moved toward Lo. They met on the side of the command chairs.

"I have to decide whether to let the Tuits complete their job and then capture them, or try to capture them before they get there." Lo stood shorter than Musoto, but his stature made him seem taller, somehow scaring Musoto as he spoke. "What do you think?"

Musoto tilted his head to the side and out of his peripheral vision he caught a glimpse of the familiar figure sitting in the command chair. He twisted his head toward her and felt the cold clamminess of betrayal stab him in the heart.

In the seat, Angela sat. She was wearing a USSAP jump suit, albeit, she was not wearing a delta belt. It was at that moment he realized no one was wearing a delta belt except the sentry at the door, who was at that moment taking Gloria's and the others' delta belts and storing them in a locker off to his side. Confusion still reigned in his eyes, as he stood amazed at Angela's presence in the command center.

"What are you doing here?" he managed to choke out.

"The same as you," Angela answered, "but they had to beat the hell out of me to get me here."

A shot of guilt mixed with embarrassment caused him to lower his eyes to the floor. "Are you alright?"

"Yeah, I'm fine. They have one hell of a medical facility here. They fixed me up as good as new."

"Are you sure?" he asked, finding the nerve to look back at her. This time he noticed she wore four green thunderbolt emblems on her collar, a color and symbol he never saw before.

"Yeah, I'm fine."

"Well Mr. Musoto," Lo interrupted. "What do you think I should do?"

Musoto turned back to Lo with his heart pumping so hard; he could hear the blood rushing through his ears. "I don't give a damn what you do. This whole thing is a bluff. There is no such thing as a Tuit. You are playing some type of game with my head," he shouted.

"Musoto," Lo called. "I said it before, and I will say it again. You are a damn fool." Then he turned to Angela, seemingly exhausted from speaking to Musoto. "Osguard, can you get through this thick headed baboon?"

Musoto snapped his head toward Angela. His mouth was agape and his eyes wide with surprise.

"No," Angela admitted. "I knew it was a waste of time, but I wanted to see for myself." She then stood and walked to the screen in front. "General, the decision isn't really that hard…is it?"

Chapter 38—Surrounded

"The fireships are energizing weapons," the defense officer of the USSTAP *Gentry* reported.

"Offense," Jarod called. "Pick a ship…any ship. Aim for the triboleminicic power source." Jarod stood and walked up to the view port screen, standing behind the navigator and pilot. He saw the instruments of his death hovering all around him. "Hell, make it wide spread…multiple weapons!" he said trying to hide the ever-growing disparaging feeling from his tone.

"Sire," the offensive office called. "Our weapons are targeting two ships at bearing zero–four–zero decimal nine–seven–four, mark zero–zero."

"Fine!"

"No sire," he stated. "The weapons are targeting, not me!"

"What?" Regina responded, moving toward the weapons station. She moved the offensive officer away from the station with her body language as she thumbed the controls.

"Sire, the weapons are targeting from an outside source. Code recognition says it is ... Holy shit…it's the First Osguard."

"Quick set a course…heading zero–four–zero decimal nine–seven–four, mark zero–zero!"

"Tiah!"

"Fire all weapons…Michael wants to clear a path for us."

The *Gentry*'s weapons array spat a reign of death, launching four torpedoes, two beams of pagenay fire, coronet cannon fire and K-gun beams, all at the two fireships off her starboard bow. As soon as the *Gentry* fired, the USSTAP fleet of fifty-nine USSTAP galaxy protectors popped out of stealth mode and into the visible light spectrum. They had covertly surrounded the Tuits, leaving a hole at decimal nine–seven–four. They engaged all weapons, reining the same deadly combination of fire on the other eight Tuit ships.

The two ships the *Gentry* targeted exploded in a gigantic fireball, looking like the finale of a fireworks presentation. She then slipped into hyperlight speed and rushed through the tiny opening she had just cleared, sucking debris from the Tuit ships' carcasses.

The other eight ships were not as lucky during their demise. They were outnumbered seven to one. First, the USSTAP ships cracked their hulls like eggs, allowing the air and atmosphere to ooze out. Then fires erupted, sending stray and untamed energy throughout the ships. Blue static encased the ships as they caved inward, decreasing their size by an eighth. Implosions and explosions had befallen the doomed Tuits. Soon the heavens lit up like a supernova, spewing the lifeless souls of ten thousand sisters of the Tuit Consortium in embers of red, blue and white light.

The USSTAP fleet jumped to hyperlight speed, straining their engines by skipping the normal speed schedule and escaped the unfathomable deadly energy the carnage was spitting out into the universe.

The entire death scene occurred in an instant. Split second timing prevailed in allowing the USSTAP fleet to achieve their objective. Michael had produced mass of forces, tactical tempo and surprise. He sat back in his command chair mentally patting himself on the back, wondering how proud Ortho would be of him right now. He had completed a tactical strike with Sixana precision, just like Ortho had trained him.

Conversely his upbringing, as always, nagged at his heart, because he had just wiped out the population equivalent of a small town. Deep in his mind he knew he had just killed and had somehow altered the lives of a parent, child or sibling. His inner voice quelled his glee and a frown swept over his face.

Tirana, who was sitting next to him in her chair, noticed Michael's mood swing. Michelle had warned her about these mood swings and for her to watch out for them. She leaned over and whispered, "No matter how many Tuits we kill today, they still have us beat on the body count. Remember, they've annihilated complete races, innocent civilians, women, and children that never raised a finger against them. They've murdered…we've killed. It is a small distinction, but it is a distinction. It is the distinction of war…and we are at war."

"Yeah I know that," Michael responded, "but it still doesn't make it any more palatable."

"It should!"

"Incoming message from the *Gentry*," the communications officer interrupted.

"Visual," Michael commanded.

The large view port screen covering the two decks switched over to a visual of the *Gentry*'s command bridge. Jarod, Regina, Kelly were sitting in their command chairs and Gail was standing behind Jarod's chair.

"Michael, you crazy bastard. How'd you get here?"

"Nice to see you too, Jarod," Michael smirked. "I'll answer your questions in due time…but suffice to say, we pumped the prisoners from your battle for information, and we interrogated their ships' databases. Then we modified a gate portal to open an ultra space event, used their coordinate system and your Bishop Buoys, and voila…here we are," he explained. "For now, we are sending our battle plan to you. Now cuz, it's time for you to take your place in the formation. We have work to do."

"But now we are all stuck in this galaxy," Jarod shot back.

"Now do you think I would doom us to such a fate?" Michael laughed. "We have a transport ship with a gate portal projector hiding in stealth mode, ready to open an event for us to get back when we are ready…but for now, it's payback time."

"Tiah!" Jarod replied.

***

Terilela ran her fingers over the smooth smoky glass console, inputting course corrections and directions, driving thirty new starguards toward the invading Tuit force. She maneuvered them into position, five hundred marks from the station on a direct intercept of the Tuit ships. She arranged them in two rows of fifteen, separated by five marks and ten on the galactic plane. Then she activated their slitanium hull, placing them in stealth mode ten, hiding them in the darkness of space.

Toneilk watched her like a teacher proctoring an exam, almost with distrusting eyes. He wanted to know her every move, not because he didn't trust her, but because it was new to him and she already seemed like a professional at it. She was able to maneuver and coordinate the starguards with no difficulty. He was a little more than impressed, he was somewhat jealous.

Then on the outer edge of Terilela's monitor, Toneilk saw the images of the invading ships. They were moving at hypersonic speed, well within the visual and sensor acquisition range of the station. The force appeared to be divided into two formations of twenty. The signatures of the first twenty ships were smaller than the last twenty. She placed alphanumerical designators on each enemy image on her screen.

Toneilk moved to his command chair and activated his monitor. He pickled on one of the smaller signatures, designated as number T–5, and activated a database read. The ARIT then compared the signature to data retrieved off the captured Tuit ship. The screen flashed several times with different configurations of ships as the ARIT went through its comparison procedures. Then it stopped on one configuration. The configuration displayed was a cone shape figure, one-third the size of a fireship, with an armament of shockdel plasma guns only. The ARIT identified the ship as a firestar—a close-range combatant ship, built for quick surgical strikes. It was also built as an escort for its big sister, the fireship. Obviously, the firestar was coming to do both.

"We need to take out the fireships first," he opined aloud. "The station wouldn't be able to take one hit from the rhetonic cannon, but it looks like we will have to deal with the firestars first." He then pickled several of the ships in the center of the formation. "Commander, target these ships first. Punch a hole in their formation and then destroy as many of those fireships as you can."

“Tiah,” Terilela responded. “Two minutes until intercept,” she then announced as she used maneuvering thrusters to collapse the starguards into a tighter formation.

She waited, almost holding her breath, only breathing when her lungs told her she needed to. Quietness covered the observation deck, as if a sound made there would be heard by one of the Tuit ships. Mentally, Terilela put herself out there onboard each and every starguard. She was their pilot and their sire. She was devoid of her physical surrounding, unaware and oblivious of anyone around her. She only heard her own thoughts. She knew what she had to do and she was ready to execute the plan. The one voice she would hear would be Toneilk as he relayed his battle strategy to her.

“Five marks,” she announced. “Four…three…two…one!”

“Open fire!” Toneilk ordered.

The words were like a jolt of lightening to her. This was the first time her immediate actions were part of combat. She was about to push the opening salvo in a battle she hoped would turn the tide in their favor. Her fingers slid over the controls, applying pressure at certain points.

Under the ships, Toneilk had pickled, starguards one through ten flashed out of stealth mode and released three quick K-gun burst onto T–5 through T–15. The K-guns ripped through the ten ships, blasting holes through their hulls so forcefully, the energy busted out the opposite side, spewing the inside of the ships out into space, like a full metal jacket bullet. The ships stopped, twisted and listed onto their sides, wounded but not dead.

Their targeting array picked up the starguards and reacted with uncanny timing. Each ship powered weapons and shot a blast from their shockdel cannons toward the starguards that fired upon them. Terilela was not concerned, because she had activated the chromerion-slitanium field generator. She expected the chromerion part of the field to rip the ionic plasma energy encasing the melenai ore away, and expose the ore to the slitanium radiation in the field. Thus allowing the ore's energy to dissipate like a static discharge around the starguards’ hull and bounce off the skin. However, the Tuits had completed some modifications as well.

The energy bolts smashed into the fields, crushing, pawing and tearing the field, pounding so hard it knocked the starguards for a jostle resembling two point five on a Richter scale. Then in a split second, the melenai ore punched through the hull, rupturing energy pathways and overloading the field generator. What followed was a cascade of explosions, lighting the darkness of space like flashbulbs…blinding flashes resembling inner space openings dotted the line, pulverizing the starguards into tiny embers of black dust.

Terilela pushed back from her console and mentally suffered the punch as if she was onboard the starguards. She blinked several times as Toneilk’s voice rang in her head.

"What the hell just happened?"

"I don't know sire," she whispered. "They must have compensated for our fields," she surmised aloud.

"Great!" Toneilk shouted. "Then we take one out of the Osguard handbook," he pushed standing from his chair, and looking out in the direction of the fight. "Let's play hide-n-punch then seek," he taunted. "Genesis-Toneilk starguard maneuver D–1," he ordered. "Finish those ships and proceed with targeting plan."

Terilela jumped back to her console, activated starguards eleven through twenty, ordered full pagenay spread and fired. The starguards popped into the visible light spectrum and shot several burst of blue pagenay beams connecting on various points on the fallen Tuit ships. The burst lit up the ships like a roman candle, resulting in blue, red and white explosions as the ten ships disappeared from the heavens.

She then put them back in stealth mode, activated starguards twenty-one through thirty and fired K-gun blasts at T–1 through T–4. Then she put those back in stealth mode, and moved starguards eleven through fifteen with thrusters. When satisfied she activated them and fired at targets T–16 through T–20. However, now the Tuit firestars had activated their energy deflectors and the K-gun blasts were bouncing off the Tuit deflectors leaving a momentary red blotch, like red muzzle flashes.

Toneilk saw the ineffectiveness of the weapons on the deflector shields and grunted as his mind raced for an alternative. "Switch weapons, concentrate on the tribolemincic core…repeat, target the tribolemincic core," referring to the energy converter that hung on the ventral side of the ship on the last third like a male appendage. The core needed the extra coldness of space to keep it within operating range. Anywhere inside the ship's hull would contaminate the artificial atmosphere with abnormal radiation.

Terilela nodded and began randomly alternating her weapons selection but keeping her target point concentrated on the energy converter. Her starguards were dancing and flashing in space like fireflies on a summer night, each time releasing a different set of weapons, K-guns, coronet cannon, or pagenay beams. Each time a red blotch would momentarily appear and disappear where the Tuit deflector absorbed the energy.

Terilela was moving as fast as she could, moving, targeting and firing the twenty starguards she had left; trying to keep them out of the reach of the Tuits' shockdel cannons. The cannons would fire at the last known position of the starguards, which made Terilela's job harder in moving them out of the line of fire as quickly as possible, but the odds were against her. In a moment of indecision, a shockdel blast found a target. Starguard fifteen exploded like her sister starguards earlier, in a great white ball of fire, which the vacuum of space extinguished.

The explosion disoriented the commander. She stuttered in her next command, breaking the random rhythm, she had adopted, enough for firestars to destroy starguards 22, 25, 27 and 30. Now she had unraveled. She had lost half her force without any more damage to the enemy.

"Commander…All starguards in stealth," Toneilk commanded.

Terilela activated all remaining starguards into stealth and sighed in disgust. They were losing, but they had at least slowed the enemy's advance.

"I've calculated something, commander," Toneilk continued. "Hit them all at once, K-gun, then pagenay and then coronct cannon. While the red blotch is there, while the shield is absorbing the energy, it is weak. Then you fire Asher missiles right into the tribolemincic converter."

"What?"

"Just do it!" he yelled.

Terilela had never seen Toneilk angry, and she had never heard him raise his voice before now. He was adamant in his orders. So adamant it jolted her into action without thought.

She activated the rest of the starguards and targeted the ten firestars in the lead and five of the fireships as the admiral instructed. The starguards popped into normal light and spewed out the onslaught of hell as Toneilk commanded. The red blotch grew in size as the energy sank into the deflector shields, momentarily weakening them.

"Missiles now!" Toneilk ordered

"Tiah!" Terilela responded, hitting the missile fire button on all starguards. Two missiles flew out of each starguard, punched through the red blotch on the deflectors and connected to the targeted ships' energy converter core. The missiles hit with such an impact, exploding with a detonation equal to a thousand kiloton nuclear blast. Mushroom clouds dotted the heavens, engulfing the ships, swallowing metal, flesh and blood in a horrendous meal of death.

A smile crossed Terilela's face, because since the opening salvo, this was the first time she felt she had the upper hand. She turned to Toneilk, who was also smiling. Then she turned back to her monitor. Words need not be said between them. They knew their job was not done. She turned back in time to see the remaining fifteen fireships spit out their shockdel energy pellets and connect and destroy the fifteen starguards.

Terilela's heart sank into her stomach. She realized her fleeting second of celebration caused her not to place the starguards into stealth and move them out of the way of the remaining ships. Now they were gone, and Millmum Capitol Station was defenseless.

***

In sector 4–F, Siryman Capitol Station starguards lay in stealth mode, making a barrier from zero on the galactic plane up to twenty-five on the galactic plane. Toevph took over the defense console operation and was constantly adjusting the starguards to narrow the field of coverage, based on the search array display of the intruders' path and course. She labeled the intruding ships as I–1 through I–40.

B'Kailine pointed to her screen and signaled for her to place the starguards at a certain range. He arbitrarily chose one thousand kilomarks as the line of defense. He wanted to engage the butches as far as he could away from the station, and in his mind, this was far enough.

"Butches coming into weapons range," Toevph announced.

"Fields activated, charge all weapons," B'Kailine commanded.

As if by magic, thirty starguards entered normal light, peppering the space landscape like snowflakes in the night. In front of them lay twenty fireships and twenty smaller versions of the fireships, which their database told Toevph, were firestars. Their specs flashed on her monitor as well as B'Kailine's monitor. The firestars did not have the rhetonic cannons, but contained a lethal array of shockdel plasma cannons.

After her readout displayed the information, the front five firestars raised their deflectors and spat out several blasts from their shockdel plasma cannons. The bright yellow melenai ionic plasma balls of energy spread through space like a spider web. The balls slammed into the newly modified slitanium-chromerion field surrounding several of the starguards.

Just like Terilela back at Millmum Capitol Station, Toevph expected the field would neuter the energy ball, but that wasn't what happened. The energy bolts smashed into the fields, crushing, pawing and tearing the field, pounding so hard it toppled five starguards head over heels before exploding in a cloud of white energy. B'Kailine popped out of his chair, shocked at the sudden destruction of his starguards.

"Five starguards destroyed," Toevph yelled in surprise, awakening the fight within B'Kailine's heart.

"Target front ship…K-gun fire," he snarled.

Toevph thumbed her sensors and fired three quick K-gun bursts from starguards six through ten.

The energy deflector on the lead Tuit firestar absorbed the blasts, with a red glow at the point of impact. It bloomed symmetrically, and then vanished within two seconds.

"No effect sire!" Toevph yelled.

Tuit firestars, I–11 through I–15 activated their cannons and let loose with a flurry of shockdel cannon blasts, destroying starguards six through fifteen in the same white blinding energy bomb, which B'Kailine thought he could see out of the observation glass.

"Starguards!"

"I know, Toevph…I know," B'Kailine whispered. He sat back in his command chair, shaking his head, trying to get a sense of what was happening. "What the hell is going on?" he questioned to no one in particular.

"They've adapted to our weapons sire," she said.

"Okay...okay!" he screamed. "Plan B...Vezec maneuver...repeat, Vezec maneuver. Target the tribolemincic core...repeat, target the tribolemincic core."

The first five Tuit ships' fire arrays came to life again, spitting multiple blasts. However the shockdel blast sailed through the ghost image of where the starguards use to be. Toevph had maneuvered the remaining fifteen starguards at hyperlight speed and made them suddenly appear behind and below the firestars I–1 through I–15. She discharged both K-gun and pagenay blasts, aiming at the tribolemincic core on the bottom of the each ship. Then she maneuvered the starguards again at hyperlight speed, causing them to seem to disappear.

The K-gun opened a path in the deflector shield, allowing forty percent of the pagenay energy to penetrate and hit its target. The pagenay blast connected on the enclosed structure hanging precariously from the ship like a pair of testicles. However, an additional energy deflector encased the core like a suit of armor.

Soon the entire fleet reappeared, fired all weapons and disappeared again, playing a dangerous game of hide and seek, straining their dialairtic converters to the max. Toevph used a rhythmic approach to their headings, safely separating each starguard in the formation from each other. They would appear like Christmas lights, blinking on and off in the fabric of space, targeting the nearest Tuit ship they happened to appear next to. She concentrated their energy weapons against the Tuit tribolemincic energy core as B'Kailine instructed.

Starguard sixteen popped up fifty kilomarks and twenty on the galactic plane, behind firestar I–15, and fired her K-guns followed by her pagenay gun. The pagenay ripped through the firestar's deflectors and connected on the core chamber, dispersing fifty percent of its energy. Starguard twenty-nine followed her from another position, firing all energy weapons onto the energy chamber. Then they jumped into hyperlight, and appeared twenty-five kilomarks below the Tuit firestar, designated as ship I–13 by the ARIT, and released their weapons, weakening the firestar's deflectors and cracking the energy chamber. Then in unison, the starguards popped one hundred kilomarks behind and below Tuit ship number five, again, releasing their weapons, slicing through space like the light of the sun.

Several other starguard pairs followed their path, popping into the laws of light, releasing their fury, hitting the ships in the same exact spot, weakening the field and pushing the energy around the chamber into critical. The Tuits tried to compensate for the holes in their deflectors, but the starguards were unpredictable.

With the Tuit deflectors weakened, Toevph went to work, slowing their hyperlight transfers and pausing several minutes between hits. This lessened the strain on the converters, allowing them to cool before jacking them into MOP again. However this still violated the fifteen-minute cool down rule, keeping the converter strain in the red.

This was the mistake the Tuit weapons officers were looking for. Tuit ships I–1 through I–5 captured five starguards in rest with their targeting away, and without a second's hesitation blew them out of existence. The blinding light was like a nova, consuming all in its wake, and spitting out splinters of what was once USSTAP's newest defense armament.

"What are you doing?" B'Kailine yelled.

"I had to slow them down," Toevph pleaded. "Their converters were about to go critical," she continued, realizing her mistake. She swept her hands over the console again, placing the remaining ten starguards in stealth, making it close to impossible for a weapons array to detect, let alone target.

"So, let them go critical," B'Kailine's huffed. "At least they will take out a ship or two when they do. Leaving them out there like that does us no good," he scolded. Then he looked at her, as the thought seemed to transfer between them. "Can you tell when the starguards are about to go critical?"

"Tiah," she responded. "I'm way ahead of you!"

Her fingers swept over the console, bringing the ten starguards out of stealth and applying her rhythmic dance. Her search array told her that Tuit ships I–1 through I–20 deflectors had significantly weaken. A slight smile perched her lips as she continued pelting the ships with energy waves. Then by accident, because her hands were flying so fast over the console, she punched off Asher missiles for starguards twenty-five through thirty after they fired their energy weapons. The missiles punched through the deflectors and slammed into the converters of targets I–2, I–6, I–15, I–18 and I–19. The targets disappeared in a dirty gray mushroom cloud, sucking in the energy for a split second and then releasing it like a cosmic sneeze. "Damn!" B'Kailine screamed. "Whatever you did, do it again."

Toevph didn't have time to absorb what had happened. All she knew was that those starguards that just fired their missiles were about to go critical and give off an explosion ten times as large as the Asher missile just gave her. She pushed them within ten kilomarks of five other firestars, I–1, I–5, I–13, I–17 and I–20.

As soon as they popped into the visible spectrum of light, the blue arch of death surrounded their hulls, shooting out like bolts of lightning. The pressure of the converter's implosion, crumbled the hull. Then the ensuing explosions engulfed her entire display as it blossomed into a fiery red, blue and orange ball, shooting shredded metal, dialairtic gas, and dialairtic radiation. The waves pushed out and collapsed the hull of the nearby target ships, as it pushed and rocked them under the energy. Then like firecrackers, the firestars exploded releasing bits and pieces of the ships along with dead bodies mixed together in a stew of death and destruction.

Now Toevph had five starguards left to defeat ten firestars and twenty fireships. The odds were against her and she didn't know what to do. The fireships had sat back about one thousand marks from the battle and had drifted unscathed by any weapons. She wondered if she should bring the fight to them. After all, those ships were the planet killers…they were the ones that had to be stopped.

She huffed in disgust as she calculated new courses for her starguards to travel, but as fate would have it, the starguards' dialairtic converters registered critical. They were going to explode if she attempted to maneuver them again in hyperlight speed. So she fired all weapons, including the Asher missiles at her targets: I–3, I–4, I–7, I–8 and I–10. The energy from the K-guns, pagenay and coronet cannons blasted a hole in the deflectors as the red blotch indicated, allowing the Asher missiles to knock through undaunted and undeterred. The melody of mushroom clouds filling her monitor told her the weapons had hit their target with deadly accuracy, but she had no time to celebrate.

She had her remaining five starguards pushing critical and ready to fire up this area of space with the radiation of the gods. At least, she hoped, the radiation would affect the Tuit engines like they did USSTAP engines and that would stop their advance for a while, but she wasn't sure. It appeared from the *Y'Tamin* incident that the dialairtic radiation might not affect the Tuit engines.

Enough thinking she told herself. "I'm moving the last starguards under targets I–9, I–11, I–12, I–14, and I–16. I have to use hypersonic. If I engage the light drive engines, they will blow where they are."

B'Kailine nodded. He knew the fight was out of his hands and only destiny would know the outcome.

With the touch of an angel, Toevph pushed the last five starguards under their targets, praying the Tuits would not engage them, but her prayers went unheeded. The last five firestars activated their cannons and shot three quick bursts. The starguards, on the verge of exploding on their own, ruptured spewing dialairtic gas into open space and then exploded with the light of God.

Toevph's heart sank as she watched her last defensive line destroyed, but something was different about these explosions. Fiery red, blue and orange balls, characteristic of dialairtic radiation shot from the white cloud in a reverse pattern heading straight for the Tuit ships. Back energy from the impending dialairtic converter rupture had found particles of energy from the melenai ore's path to burn. The balls followed a path straight to the Tuit cannons, eating the invisible energy like a Pac man.

The balls hit the Tuit ships with the same fury of a converter explosion. The gun ports seared off, breaking the hull off the tip of the cone. Then a blue arch engulfed the ships, covering the cones and wrapping them in its essence. The ships were paralyzed, and so were Toevph and B'Kailine. Fate had played a cruel trick on the Tuits.

Somehow their last shots acted like a homing beacon for the dialairtic energy to go. It was like the energy had a mind of its own and would not be denied the pleasure of exploding something this day. So it reached out and tapped the Tuit ships. The static danced in and throughout the hull, sucking and draining energy from its tribolemincic energy. Then like a supernova, the ships exploded, one by one, in a series of death lights, marching in the heavens.

Toevph shrugged her shoulders as she stared out the port. This time the light was visible. It was as bright as a small sun. It shone for several seconds, before the space reclaimed her authority of darkness. When the light dissipated, nothing was left, no debris, no bodies and no evidence of mankind at all. Space was clean, not even the normal radiation that follows a dialairtic explosion existed. The tribolemincic energy had erased the dialairtic radiation.

Yet, in the distance, twenty fireships came to a halt, waiting, investigating and interpreting what just happened. B'Kailine whispered, "Go! Go away!" And just for a moment, it seemed like they heard him, but fate was unpredictable this day.

They held their position, hovering at fifteen on the galactic plane for five minutes. Then without warning, Tuit ships advanced again at hypersonic speed, circumventing the area of space where they just lost five thousand of their sisters.

B'Kailine turned to Toevph, "Do you have any more ideas, because I'm fresh out!"

Chapter 39—The Lost Osguard

"You know, you're acting like an Osguard," Lo challenged.

"Who…me," Angela teased back.

"Yeah…you," Lo snorted.

"Well general, I know I haven't been trained, but you've confirmed I am an Osguard."

Musoto's head snapped around, not trying to hide his surprise. "You're a what?"

Angela did not respond. She didn't even acknowledge his presence anymore. She stood up and walked to the big screen, peering at the board, studying it with deep reflection. She then tapped the general on the arm. "Show me what you can do."

"Tiah," he responded, taking Angela's words as an order from an Osguard. "Intercept authorized," he commanded.

***

Both Kim Salmot and Sheri Filgo acknowledged the command over the interlink. They were piloting USSTAP defenders, flying in the Earth's stratosphere. Kim was shadowing Elderidge's firefighter and Sheri was shadowing Mona's firefighter. Lo launched them as soon as they picked them up on the threat board. He guessed their targets were the presidents traveling to New York, and he knew he had to stop them at all cost, even if it meant exposing them more. He just wished there was another way.

Kim descended at hypersonic speed, heading toward Elderidge's firefighter. She had two minutes to intercept her before she reached firing range, at least what she figured would be firing range for the firefighter—another piece of information robbed from the Tuit database onboard one of the captured fireships.

She engaged her ARIT search array, trying to get a weapon's lock. Inside she was cursing Lo for waiting so long to give her authorization to engage. She wanted to engage as soon as she launched, but Lo was playing some sort of political game. She never did like politics, especially when it involved military decisions. This decision should have been simple. As soon as the Tuits showed themselves they should have engaged them. They should have blown them off the face of the Earth. While Lo played his little game, she was screaming in her mask for engagement approval.

When it finally came, she maneuvered the nose of her black defender toward the firefighter, pushing the engines to maximum speed, almost MACH ten by American standards. She also knew at that speed, her maneuvering was critical. If she had to make a turn it would eat up a lot of miles, a radius the size of Texas, just to make a forty-degree turn. If she had to make a one hundred and eighty-degree turn, because of a missed shot, it would be fatal for Air Force One.

The tone wavered in her ear as the ARIT locked on to Eldridge's firefighter. However, Eldridge must have caught the targeting array signal. Her firefighter veered right forty-five-degrees. Kim knew she was traveling too fast to get another shot. She thumbed her pagenay cannons, two blue rays of death downward. The ray from her port gun flew pass Eldridge's port side, but her starboard gun clipped it.

Eldridge tilted left and then snapped left, pulling her out of her right turn and pushing her into a flat spin. She tumbled downwards, spinning at a fast-rate of speed. Kim watched with interest for a split second, and then she thumbed her cannons once more. The blue rays shot from her gun ports on a true course to Elderidge's ship. Kim had prematurely counted it as a kill. Eldridge was a sitting duck, but at the last second, the cone straightened and shot forward, causing the rays to just miss her.

Kim pulled out of her dive, leveling the defender co-altitude with the firefighter. She had to turn right to chase the butch. Her turn was wide, eating forty miles, never losing ARIT contact with the butch. Relief entered her soul as she realized she had pushed the butch from targeting range from Air Force One. However, the ARIT calculated the butch would be in targeting range in one minute. She then calculated her time to intercept with the butch. It was one minute and fifteen seconds.

She mentally swore, for time was no longer on her side. She pushed the engines again to full hypersonic, cracking the air around her as the pressure she was creating washed over her ship. Then in a flashed thought, she pushed the nose over, descending, increasing her speed.

When she checked the clock she saw she had ten seconds left before the butch reached targeting range. She then swooped the nose up, pickled the butch and fired with two seconds left. The rays shot up toward Eldridge, causing her to jerk her firefighter left. The blasts shot pass her way wide right.

Kim knew she bought some time, but only a few seconds. She screamed skyward, maneuvering her nose left, tracking the firefighter while holding her pagenay trigger down. The blue rays followed Eldridge in her turn. Her speed caused her to eat up several miles, pushing her out of targeting range to Air Force One once more. Eldridge then jinked back right, causing Kim to redirect her nose once more. This time Kim led the butch in the turn, like a quarterback leading his receiver, and fired her pagenay cannon.

The blasts tore through the bottom of the firefighter, splitting the cone-shape ship into two pieces. The cockpit piece hurled toward the ocean, while the rear piece sailed away and then exploded, sending a bright white flash, like lightening to spark the clouds.

Kim leveled her defender, watching the cockpit piece fall earthward, wondering if she should finish the job and blow the Tuits out of the sky. In her subconscious mind, she prayed for the cockpit portion to explode as well. As the seconds ticked by, she realized it was going to stay intact. So she watched for a chute. She did not see one, as the cockpit fell through the clouds and out of view. Only the ARIT could see it now, and the display was not showing a chute either.

"Lilly Station…Defender zero—one—nine—zero—eighty-one," Kim called out. "Package saved…Splashed one butch…coordinates Delphi four—one—six—two, Calto seven—four—eight—eight…repeat… Package saved…Splashed one butch…coordinates Delphi four—one—six—two, Calto seven—four—eight—eight."

Twenty-minutes later, the cockpit slammed into the Atlantic Ocean, fifty miles off of Long Island Sound. Within four minutes of that, a USSTAP cleanup crew was on scene, disguised as the United States Coast Guard.

***

Meanwhile, one thousand and two hundred miles away over the North Atlantic and fifty-eight miles off the west coast of the island continent of Greenland, Sheri put her defender into a dive, angling to her target—Mona's firefighter. She energized her pagenay cannons and slapped on her targeting array. The ARIT used onboard scanners and sensors to narrow the targeting solution for the guns. The targeting-pipper jumped on the firefighter and the markers ticked off on the side of the monitor. She was well within range, but she wanted to get closer. Somehow getting closer made the fight more personal and it was personal for her. She didn't know if it had become personal because of the billions of lives the Tuits had terminated or because they declared war on USSTAP and her beloved Osguards, or if it was because the person in the firefighter had targeted her best friends with bombs. For whatever reason, the rage percolated in her, clouding her military instincts and delaying her training from kicking in.

Mona's early warning system rang in her helmet, detecting Sheri's approaching defender. Sheri was fifteen seconds from releasing a *'Beyond Visual Range'* (BVR) shot on the Russian president's plane. She knew her orders were to scare and not to destroy, so she triggered her cannons, releasing a shockdel blast in the plane's direction, knowing it would miss.

The blast punctured the cold air, and sliced below the Russian president's plane's left wing. The shock wave rocked the air, disturbing the airflow under the wing. The wing lost its lift and the plane rolled left, and sliced downward.

Shock rolled into Sheri's heart. She knew it was her fault. She knew she should have taken the shot as soon as she had it. Now her delay had caused a wretched situation. She thumbed the fire button and shot several rays from her pagenay guns. The rays flashed like a thunderbolt, slamming into the white cone ship with no mercy, and cut the engine pods. The mixture of energy was too volatile. The small one-manned, cone-shaped, white firefighter exploded, rocking the air and shaking Sheri's defender.

Sheri's left engine went critical as the airflow swirled around it. Then it sputtered off, spinning her left, before the right engine lost its life. Sheri slammed her head in the cockpit, dazing her, while her defender entered a deep spiral dive. She lost feeling in her fingers as the binding tightened up around her arms. Her defender spun out of control, sinking toward the ocean at hypersonic speed. One hundred percent oxygen automatically flowed through her mask, forcing itself to fill her lungs and soak her blood.

Her brain soon reactivated. The dizziness that tried to creep into her consciousness now faded. She opened her eyes to see the ocean waves spinning in her canopy window. She was passing twenty thousand feet. She applied stabilizing thrusters, stopping the spin, and then she pulled her nose up, leveling off at ten thousand feet. She fired her engines, pushing them to emergency start, enabling her to sustain her altitude.

She sighed hard, blowing out the air of frustration mixed with what was left of her fear. Beads of sweat rolled down her face, spine, and under her arms, soaking her body in her own body's lubricant. However, as soon as she started to relax, she remembered—*the Russian president's plane.*

She activated her search array, while praying. The array located the plane slicing through twenty-five thousand feet at a fast sink rate. Sheri recognized the G-forces acting on the wings were too much for the pilots to reestablish control. She had to do something, or the plane would crash into the ocean.

She zoomed her defender up, climbing to meet the plane. She didn't know what she could do, but she thought having proximity to the plane would somehow give her insight on what to do. She slipped in behind the plane, fighting the vortexes swimming off the wingtips. She pushed through the violent wind swirl and edged her defender near the fallen wingtip, matching the plane's sink rate. Now the plane was passing fifteen thousand feet and still showed no signs of recovery. Without regard for her own safety, or any real thought, she angled her defender to sail into position under the left wing.

Then she slowed her rate of descent, allowing the left wingtip to rest on her dorsal edge. Now the planes were passing thirteen thousand feet and they were quickly approaching the ocean waves. Her automatic warning system blared in her ear, warning her of the impending crash. She clicked the warning off, cutting the interruption to her concentration off as well. Her eyes stayed on her instruments. She needed to lift the wing, without snapping it off, and without disturbing the normal flow of air to create the necessary lift.

Her altimeter passed through eleven thousand feet. She knew she had to risk slowing the rate faster and push the wing level. She adjusted her controls, praying, wishing and hoping for divine intervention, luck or fate to help her save this airplane.

The wing lifted, rotating about fifteen degrees. Then in a magical moment, in a lucky twist of fate, the wing captured lift as the pilot regained control and rolled the plane level. Then the pilot pushed up the engines and the plane stopped its hellish fall from the heavens. Sheri zoomed forward and looped around to the right, keeping her eye on the fateful plane. She then fell behind the plane once more as it ascended, gaining precious altitude.

Inside the plane's cockpit, the pilot keyed his radio, "Thank you!" he whispered in Russian. His thank you went unheard, for Sheri's interlink didn't monitor VHF frequencies. But something in the air told Sheri the pilot's sentiment, for she smiled, releasing her anxiety of the situation.

She then winked at the jet and veered off to the right, speeding off at hypersonic speed, signaled by the gigantic boom that vibrated through the air. A heartbeat later, the black angel of mercy disappeared, leaving the Russian pilots in awe.

"Lilly Station…Defender zero—one—seven—eight—eighty-four… one butch burned…package safe…Defender zero—one—seven—eight—eighty-four returning to base."

***

The applause rang through the command center in Lilly Station. Sounds of cheers bellowed, releasing the fear that had grabbed everyone's heart, including Lo. The first sign of a smile decorated his face. He then turned to Angela and wiped the smile from his lips, reseating his professional military look.

"Okay Osguard," Lo called. "I've done my part, now it is up to you to do your part."

Angela smiled at Lo, nodded and then stood. She looked at Musoto, who stared back, mouth agape.

He was wondering if what he saw on the screen and what he heard on the interlink was true, or was it an elaborate trick to fool him into thinking USSTAP just saved the presidents. He wanted to believe the incidents actually happened as they played out, but his gut, or more likely his paranoia, convinced him they were playing him.

"Bring him too," she commanded.

Gloria stepped down and grabbed Musoto by his arm and twisted him around to the exit panel. This told Musoto that he had indeed worn out his welcome, and once again he was considered the enemy.

Angela moved past them. Gloria pushed Musoto to follow and the trio stepped out the exit. Two guards fell in place in front of Angela and led the way through the passageways. They traveled back down into the bowels of the station, until they reached the main gate portal room.

Angela nodded to the operator, signaling for him to proceed. Three white lights of inner space pierced the room from the portal room stage. Angela stood in front of the stage, mesmerized by the light. One of the guards cleared his throat with a slight cough, a signal urging Angela to continue.

She then grabbed Musoto by the arm, walked him up the steps to the stage and shoved him into the light. She stepped in behind him and the invisible door shut. The two guards stepped into their lights and disappeared into inner space.

Inside the presidential office suite onboard Air Force One, three white lights, exposing inner space illuminated. Peters shielded his eyes in fright. He started to scream or at least call for his secret service guards who were standing watch outside the door, but something told him to keep quiet.

Musoto's body flung out the middle light, rolling on the floor and hitting the front of the Peter's desk with a large thud. Then Angela stepped through the light, followed by the guards on either side of her. The guards held pagenays in their hands, but not in the ready. Their armed hands were pointing straight toward the floor.

"Mr. President," Angela said in a faint voice. "I am Angela Santos, the secretary you hired to help Musoto."

Peters nodded in surprise. He had read in Musoto's reports about the gate portal, but to see it work before his own eyes left him speechless. Angela recognized it, because she was still in awe over it herself. She'd only had two days to get use to the idea, and this was her second trip through inner space—third if she counted when she was kidnapped.

It was all so fast, so surreal, finding out she was a descendant of the lost line from Shirley Grace, Nausona's granddaughter. Two days of cramming produced her, an Osguard in training, as signified by her green thunderbolts. Two days in training, just for this moment, for her to talk to Peters…for her to talk Peters out of what he was about to do. Her mission was to talk Peters out of revealing USSTAP's existence to the U.N. Security Council.

She needed to explain how damaging his decision would be. She needed to describe, without giving too much detail, the universal war USSTAP was in, which was easy because she didn't have any details. She needed to describe the confusion such a revelation would cause on Earth. Everything from politics, religion and science would be spun on its ears. Without proper guidance and information administered in proper doses, the results would be catastrophic. The world's geo-political atmosphere would change and lead to the collapse of its social order, because the world leaders and wannabe leaders would vie for favors from USSTAP in a game of power, which in reality had already started with Peters. She had to convince him it was in his best interest to keep things secret for now.

However, she did understand his concern about overpopulation, diseases and famine. She also understood how barbaric and immoral it was for USSTAP to hold the key to wipe out these human plagues and not share them. She was abhorred at USSTAP's refusal to do this and she could not, no she would not defend their decision. All she could do was offer to use what little influence she had to convince the sitting Osguards, who by the way, she hadn't met yet, to implement something to relieve if not eliminate these scourges from the face of the Earth. This she would promise to Peters—she hoped he would be patient and smart enough to listen.

Her divergence from established Osguard policy was the sore point between her and Lo. Lo conceded to what she wanted to do. After all, she was an Osguard—wasn't she?

"Mr. President, let me rephrase that," she corrected with authority. "I am Osguard Angela Santos and I am here to speak to you about what you are planning to do."

Chapter 40—New Osguards

Two portal gates activated and the characteristic white light of inner space caused by the radiation of benion particles illuminated over Millmum Capitol Station. Then like a ghost, or more like an angel, Laurona's ship, the *Star Cruiser Tharen* rolled out of the light as if heaven had answered Toneilk's prayers.

A female voice echoed from the ship over the interlink, "Red Osguard One on station. Please pass coordinates of butches on interlink red–alpha–two."

A chill ran through Terilela, as she imagined Laurona had returned from the dead to protect her station from the devil's own children. She passed the coordinates of the invading Tuits' position. Then she watched the ship sail out of the light toward the enemy. Soon the light spit out other star cruisers, all reporting on station and requesting coordinates.

Rani Sailon Shimak, the granddaughter of Frank Sailon, an adopted son of Laurona, was now Red Osguard One. She commanded a fleet of twenty-three of her relatives, all descendants of Laurona Osguard Sailon's adopted children, including Stelana Rican, Red Osguard Ten and her family. Rani received the message from Toneilk and within seconds the gate portal was energized and the fleet stepped, one-by-one, into the Millmum galaxy. Twenty-four ships spat into Millmum galaxy after hovering around the gate portal of Mishlyte Capitol Station, the center of USSTAP territory and the home of Osguard thirty-six, Lena Lloyd Star.

Unfortunately, the ships the Red Osguards commanded were the old star cruisers, yanked from the bone yard and modified with slitanium-chromerion field generators and K-guns. It was the fastest and simplest way to increase the fleet for protection. Each ship contained a minimum manning of fourteen to run the offensive and defensive weapons.

***

In the Siryman Galaxy, the same picture played out. The capitol station's gate portal shot out twenty-two star cruisers, commanded by Blue Osguard one, Tonjail Naylan onboard Nausona's old ship, the *Star Cruiser Nary*. Tonjail was the grandson of Nausona's adopted son, George, and was leading the descendants of Nausona's adopted children.

Toevph pushed the coordinates of the ultra space event occurrences to the *Star Cruiser Nary*, and then watched the parade of museum aged ships fly pass the station to engage in their first battle in over half a century.

"May your god be with you," she whispered to the monitor.

"The Chaktun god is named Jus," B'Kailine informed her. "And I am sure they all have said several hundred prayers since the beginning."

"Well I hope one more doesn't hurt," Toevph said with a sparkle in her sapphire eyes.

B'Kailine looked down at her and then patted her on the shoulder, "I guess not, commander…I guess not."

***

Red Osguard One, Rani wanted to engage the butches as far away from the station as she could. Her fleet was traveling at MOP thirty, the fastest she could drive the old gravogenic engines. Terilela passed her the data from the starguards encounter with the firestars, suggesting a change in tactics might be necessary. Rani eyed the reports with suspicion. She thought the starguards defective due to the rush in production. She had supervised the modifications and inspections of the star cruisers and she staked her reputation that their chromerion-slitanium fields and weapons were as solid as a galaxy cruiser's. So she wanted to engage the butches head-on.

"Butches coming into weapons range," the defensive officer informed Rani.

Rani, the C.O. of the *Galaxy Cruiser Cherokee*, until she found out her destiny, had plenty of operational experience in running a battle, but that was with state of the art technology not with museum pieces. In its day, the star cruiser was the most feared and most competent battleship in the known galaxy.

"Slow the fleet to hypersonic, fields activated, charge all weapons," Rani announced.

As if by magic, twenty-four star cruisers entered normal light, peppering the space landscape like shining arrows in the night. In front of them lay twenty fireships. Their specs flashed on her monitor as well as the offensive and defensive officers' monitors.

She did not have to wait long before the fireships acknowledged them. The front five ships raised their deflectors and spewed out several blasts from their shockdel plasma cannons. The bright yellow melenai ionic plasma balls slammed into the newly modified slitanium-chromerion field surrounding the *Tharen* and her wingman, the *Shube*.

The energy bolts sliced through the fields with such force it popped Rani out of her chair and her fifty year old Chaktun body slammed hard onto the metal floor. Sounds around her lessened and her vision narrowed, as her mind fought for awareness. She rolled over onto her back and took a deep breath. She tried to get up, but the ship was rocked again by another barrage from the five lead ships. Her body lifted up once more and she slammed down on the floor, banging her head. Pain racked her body, shooting through her like electricity.

"Field down to twenty percent," the defensive officer called, awakening the fight within Rani.

"Target front ship…K-gun fire," she ordered.

The offensive officer sprung to his seat, buckled in and activated his leg restraints. Then he thumbed his sensors and fired three quick K-gun bursts. The energy deflector on the lead Tuit fireships absorbed the blasts. The red glow Terilela reported appeared at the places of impact.

The defensive officer, who had locked himself into place, read his scanners in dismay, "No effect sire!"

Rani shot to her knees, shaking her head, trying to get a sense of what was happening. "Terilela was right, they've adapted to our weapons. I thought the starguards might have been defective. I guess I was wrong." She shook her head, "Command the fleet to regroup on these coordinates…MOP one"

Rani plotted coordinates into her command console and passed them to her communications officer. In a split second, the fleet jumped to MOP one and regrouped in perfect formation negative fifty on the galactic plane. Then Rani targeted the Tuit ships and assigned each star cruiser a target. "Engage and target their power source, use energy weapons until forty kilomarks out, then fire Asher torpedoes, your discretion. Rani had calculated a ventral attack would minimize her forces' exposure to the shockdel cannon and eliminate any shot from their rhetonic cannons without altering their trajectory. She had already warned the other Osguards, if the targeted ships changed their axis and pointed their nose toward them, to break off the attack and go to the reset area.

The USSTAP fleet raised their noses and raced upward on the galactic plane, emerging from the darkness of the lower galaxy firing both their pagenays and K-guns in a mêlée of energy, bouncing, piercing and punching at the Tuit ships' new deflector shield. The red blotches on the deflector shields grew larger and larger as it fought to absorb and deflect the energy from the USSTAP weapons. Soon, the entire ventral area's deflector shield glowed red hot.

The Tuit ships continued on their path, heading toward Millmum Capitol Station. Then they stopped. Rani's heart jumped in her throat. She knew the Tuit ships were about to employ their rhetonic cannons onto the station. She could see the spirals on the aft part of the ship start to glow.

"Fire torpedoes, all ships…fire torpedoes," she screamed. She couldn't wait to get within the prescribed range. She knew if she delayed any longer the station would be history. The rhetonic cannons were planet killers, weapons of mass destruction, but the Tuits had started using the weapons in a conventional way, especially during battles. It wasn't farfetched to see them use it against Capitol Station.

A barrage of torpedoes, eight from each ship, one hundred and seventy six in total, sprang from the old star cruisers, like sparklers in the night, leaving a short contrail of glowing radiation in their wake. The missiles punched through the Tuit deflector shields, one-by-one, undaunted, pushing on toward their target, the tribolemincic energy core.

The lead missile from Rani's ship impacted the ship just as the beams shot from their spiral ports. However, before they connected to make the deadly energy combination, the resulting explosion cracked the hull and detonated the energy core. Smaller explosions occurred throughout the ship, cascading up and down the cone like firecrackers. Then from deep within the ship, a white fireball, as white as inner space, emerged, eating and chewing the ship into tiny splinters of metal, growing and consuming all matter in its way. All around, the other nineteen Tuit ships exploded in similar surges of fires.

"Reset…reset," Rani screamed directing her fleet to break off the attack before they were caught in the matter consuming explosive arena she had just created. The eleven upper star cruisers veered right and the lower eleven star cruisers veered left, turning in unison as easy as birds in flight, leaving behind them a spectacular display of white explosions, dust and debris, which was eerily turning the darkness of space into day.

***

In the Siryman Galaxy, millions of light years away from Millmum Capitol Station, Blue Osguard One, Tonjail Naylan, heeded the communiqué from Toevph. Before his rise to the ranks of Osguard in Training, he was Commodore Tonjail Naylan, Millmum Galaxy Station twenty-three's commander, where he learned to trust his controller with his life. So he automatically trusted the words Toevph relayed over the interlink. Additionally, his field-experience as precinct commander on the planet Renniwa, and the sire his own galaxy cruiser, the *Meslico* taught him not to be too cocky.

Sitting in the command chair brought back memories of his days on the *Meslico*. However the moments of pleasure he remembered were chased away by the moments of fear he had suppressed for the last two years. Combat was one of those memories he tried to forget. Even though he had only taken the *Meslico* into combat twice in his four-year command, those memories haunted him daily. Albeit his ship came through virtually untouched both times, the other ship was destroyed. Combining the two battles with the Mosleck pirates, he regarded himself responsible for over four hundred deaths. He gave the order that ended the lives of four hundred people, fathers, mothers, brothers and sisters to someone…somewhere. Now he was about to give the order again.

He was leading an entire fleet of his relatives and his children, Lear, Nard and Drefi into battle, so they could feel the same nausea of combat, the same sickness of being responsible for someone else's death. Life wasn't fair, but neither was war.

"Comm," Tonjail called, shaking the fear from his throat. "Have the fleet slow to MOP four, form on these coordinates. Let's surprise them from behind." He input the coordinates into his control ARIT. Then he pressed his interlink, "Blue Osguard One to Admiral B'Kailine…Ask our guest to cease and desist, or pay the consequences…all radios…all frequencies."

"Tiah!" B'Kailine responded.

Several seconds later the interlink hummed with B'Kailine's voice, translated in Tuit, "Tuit fireships, this is Admiral B'Kailine, Siryman Capitol Station Commander. You are infringing on our space. You are not authorized to be here. Please halt and respond to contact or you will be fired upon."

Tonjail listened, hoping against hope that the Tuit ship commander would come to her senses, but just as he figured, the ARIT displayed their continuing advance toward the station. He huffed so loud, it appeared to his small crew he was crying.

"Approaching coordinates," his pilot reported.

"Tiah," he responded, still sighing. "Tell all ships…all stop…all energy weapons to bear…target engines on their designated targets…on my mark." He looked toward the heavens as he stood from his seat. "Jus be with me!" Then he walked up between the pilot and navigator seat to get a full view of the screen, which was displaying digital images, because of their light speed. "Three…two…one…mark!"

The screen switched to visual as soon as they dropped out of light speed. The aft portion of several Tuit ships popped into view and filled the screen. His target was in front of him. The weapons generator hummed to life and spurted pagenay rays and K-gun blasts. Energy weapons fire bracketed the darkness all around him, like blue neon lights, lashing out and whipping across the heavens and smacking the rear deflector shields of the Tuit ships.

The red spots, Toevph recorded, appeared at the points of impact, growing larger and larger with every hit of the energy weapons. The Tuit ships, recognizing their vulnerability, began independent evasive maneuvering, breaking up the battle into individual dogfights between the mammoth ships and the smaller spear-like star cruiser.

"Pursue…engage…all weapons," Tonjail ordered over the interlink. "We need to char those deflector shields and then slide Asher torpedoes up their ass," he pushed. Then he tapped his pilot, "Stay with her." He peered over his shoulder at his weapons officer, "Keep firing, and don't let her get a bead on us. When their shields fall to fifty percent, fire torpedoes."

Both nodded their heads and the fight went local. His target veered to the left ninety degrees, and started to descend. The *Star Cruiser Nary*'s engines fired up into hypersonic speed and pushed forward, chasing the target down, spitting energy flames in chaotic randomness.

Tonjail smiled for a second, realizing his first objective was about to be achieved. He was stopping the attack on the station. Well he at least was delaying it. To stop it, he had to disable or destroy the ships. He was hoping he could get away with disabling the ships. If he could capture at least one ship, the amount of information the intelligence corps could retrieve would be invaluable.

"Shields down to sixty percent on the port aft quarter," the weapons officer reported.

"Fine! Narrow spread…concentrate on port aft quarter," Tonjail ordered.

The weapons officer narrowed his targeting parameters, but that increased his miss rate, due to the accelerated maneuvering of the targeted ship.

"Shields up to seventy percent," he reported.

"Change, spread fire range…I need to increase the hit ratio," Tonjail commanded.

"Tiah," the weapons officer acknowledge, moving his fingers across the old targeting system.

The targeted ship slid right, and decreased its rate of descent. The *Nary*'s pilot matched course and speed. Trying his best to stay in tight on the targeted ship's tail, not allowing the ship to turn and fight and giving the best aspect for targeting to his weapons officer.

"Shields at fifty percent," the weapons officer reported with glee.

Tonjail sat back in his chair. It seemed too simple to him. They had not encountered any resistance from the Tuits. Something was wrong…something wasn't right. His gut was churning.

"Disengage, break right!" he ordered.

Even though the pilot's mind wanted to question the order, he obeyed without murmuring a word. At that instant, the rhetonic cannons came to life, the port guns glowed and the red and blue energy spikes shot out backwards, stretching to converge into one spiraling color twisted beam two thousand marks off their stern, nearly hitting the *Nary* as it snapped right.

Tonjail pushed the interlink to the fleet, "Disengage…all ships disengage…break off…break off." Without hesitation, all the star cruisers broke off the attack. Some ships barely escaping the rhetonic cannons.

Thc *Tain's* port engine ruptured from the near proximity to the heat, blowing a hole into her port hull. The *Tain's* sire Ley Bioka, Blue Osguard Twenty-two, ordered the engine severed and ejected. Automatic fire suppression contained the fire at the severed spars. The *Tain* was out of the fight and now was a sitting target for any Tuit ship. The *Jetter's* engines decoupled from the near miss, leaving her adrift and also a target.

There were twenty-two star cruisers attacking twenty fireships, leaving two ships that were doubling up the firepower on single fireships. Toevph read the situation and diverted the *Michell*, sired by Blue Osguard Eighteen, Ilal Naylan and the *Jackmil*, sired by Blue Osguard Two, Haidz Rener, to lay down cover fire for the *Tain* and the *Jetter*.

The *Michell* pulled right and went MOP to cover the area of space in less than a second, straining her dialairtic converter, but it was to save her sister ship, the *Tain*. She fired a barrage of energy weapons, grabbing the fireship's attention. The fireship turned toward the *Michell* and fired several shockdel blasts. The melenai ore burned through the chromerion-slitanium field and rocked the Michell's starboard aft quarter. The hull ruptured, slicing a four-foot gash in the ship's skin. Luckily, no one was occupying the rear section of the ship. Blue Osguard Eighteen, Ilal Naylan ordered the aft section closed and for the pilot to execute attack option Blue five.

The *Jackmil* was closer to her objective. She turned right and fired her weapons, followed by two Asher torpedoes. The weapons electrified the force field at the rear of the newly targeted ships, clearing a path for the torpedoes, which crashed into the rear engines. The fireship's tail exploded, tearing the rhetonic cannons off and causing it to list forward, dead in space with energy spikes sparking throughout the hull.

Toevph saw the resulting carnage and keyed the interlink, "Blue fleet, fire Asher torpedoes after opening a weak spot in their rear shields…repeat, fire Asher torpedoes after opening a weak spot in their rear shields."

Tonjail heard the directions and signaled the fleet to re-engage, "Blue fleet…hit and run…repeat, hit and run."

Then like screaming eagles swooping down on their prey, twenty arrows of death, spitting fire and flame, pounced on the remaining nineteen Tuit ships as Toevph directed. Then when they were within one hundred marks, the ships released two to four Asher torpedoes, looping upwards after the release, screaming like a bat out of hell to put distance between them and the rhetonic cannon.

Clouds formed at the point of impact, tearing the rhetonic cannons, engine parts and large chunks of the hull off into oblivion, pushing the ships down and over, spinning them onto their point as the energy, the ship's life, faded from them.

The barrage of fire was quick, deadly and massive, leaving a graveyard of fireships listing lifelessly on their sides, bows and tails. Several sisters of the consortium were crushed to death, banged up and buried alive under falling debris throughout the new graveyard. Suddenly, space was quiet as an uneasy hush blanketed the area of death.

The Blue Fleet regrouped seventy five below the galactic plane, ready to target the tribolemincic core of the Tuit ships. Tonjail's fear faded as a light of jubilation snuck into his demeanor. He had achieved his objective. He had stopped the Tuit attack. Furthermore, he had achieved his personal objective. He did it with no loss of life for USSTAP and minimum loss of life for the Tuits. He hit his interlink, "Commander Toevph, please report."

"All ships down, weapons down, and life support failing on all ships," Toevph reported. "You did it Osguard," she further commented. "You did it!"

Tonjail nodded…being called Osguard made him feel good. It made him feel real good. "Send the call for surrender," he said, moving to his chair.

Chapter 41—Release the Lolwes

Daring, dangerous, risky, hazardous and treacherous were some of the words he heard describing his plan. Words that would make an average man cringe. However, for Michael David Genesis, the First Osguard and Chairman of the Osguard Senate, all these words did was make him more determined, more focused and more confident, for he did not hear the word that would change his mind, that would make him alter his plan, that would put doubt in his ability—he didn't hear the word; impossible.

Below him was one of twenty camps on this planet, spread throughout six landmasses, one of three hundred and seventy planets throughout the Tuit home galaxy, where the lolwes were kept like cattle, in solid-walled cells, isolated from each other. There were others in other galaxies and in the other dimensions, but Michael wanted to contain the fight inside the Tuit home galaxy.

Michael had learned about the lolwes from the Tuit database that was extracted from the captured fireships in the Siryman Galaxy. Additionally, Rina, after receiving the spirited persuasion counseling session from Rachel and Timothy Stone, confirmed the existence of the lolwes. It seemed fitting for him to use this information now for his benefit.

Michael veered his defender, the lead of Alpha Flight, First Squadron, to the right forty five-degrees. The other four defenders followed without losing an inch in formation. The other forty-five defenders from his ship combined with the fifty defenders from his cousin Osguard Two, Roger Genesis's ship from the Andromeda system, the *Galaxy Protector Llamdion*, would cover the other nineteen camps on the planet.

A simultaneous concurrent attack would be the key to his plan. It rested on strict coherence to timing, in order to achieve the proper surprise. He had studied the camp layout from obtained diagrams. The search array had confirmed the diagrams, which told him the Intel was correct.

Below him sat a square four-story, twenty-five square-acre enclosure, made of the same material as their ships. The structure had underground layers where the lolwes were housed—some five thousand as recorded by the ARIT. The upper structures housed five hundred Tuit guards, scientists and service staff. A surprisingly small number considering the number of inmates they were responsible for. Yet, since the inmates never had any type of contact with each other, and lived their entire life, from birth to death, in solitary confinement, with their sole human contact being that of their captors, it made sense that the number of Tuits watching them would be small.

Michael tried to imagine a life in stark isolation, only let out of an eight feet by five feet cell to have the Tuits medically experiment on you and then humiliate you further by extracting your sperm to be used to create more of them. However, he couldn't imagine the complete indignity of the situation. Somehow thinking of it bruised his male ego more than his sense of morality. For this he was more ashamed. Or was he more angry than ashamed?

At the moment the two feelings vied to feed his rage in the most unusual but exhilarating way. Revenge was the downfall of many military leaders, only his Sixana training kept his thoughts from being consumed by his thirst for revenge as he channeled his mixed feelings into a professional demeanor. He was on a mission, and control was the word he must fight by…not revenge.

The time was upon him. He angled his defender toward the structure and targeted his pagenay and coronet cannons toward the northeast corner. He had to take out the shockdel cannons at this corner, and then move in to level the top floors without caving in the bottom layers. The ARIT picked out the proper stress points to complete the job.

"Defender Alpha Lead…firing," he announced over the interlink, while thumbing the trigger. Blue rays from his pagenay cannon kicked out of his defender, connecting to the northeast corner tower, blowing the gun port up with a violent explosion, sending brick and mortar spewing into the blue night sky, signaling the beginning of war on Tuit soil.

The other four defenders locked-onto their targets, one on each corner and one on the middle tower. The rays lit up the sky, reminiscent of thunder with a high pitch whine, capped with the explosion of the gun turrets on the tower. The explosions were huge, loud and destructive, tearing the tower to half of its original size.

Then the Tuit warning horn sounded in the air, blaring in a wavering pitch awakening the Tuits to the fight. Inside the building, lights switched on, as the enemy awoke, not knowing what was happening, and not being able to guess in a million years what was about to happen. All their weaponry was designed to keep the inmates in; none was designed to fight intruders breaking in.

Michael looped around for his second pass, flinging his defender skyward and pulling several Gs. The ARIT adjusted the atmosphere in the cockpit, but there was always a split second delay, allowing for a pinch of pain and a hint of dizziness whenever the defender produced high-G maneuvers inside a planet's atmosphere. During that split second, Michael tightened his abdomen and squeezed the blood back to his head with a grunt.

Then his ARIT warning receiver went off. He enabled the voice feature, allowing the ARIT to articulate the warning in human voice.

"Butch…five o'clock…mark four," the ARIT spouted out.

Michael swept his head to the five o'clock position and saw faint images of ten cone-shaped ships moving toward him. This was a development he had not counted on. Nowhere in the intelligence reports or in the search array sweep mentioned anything about fighter support.

"Alpha Flight," he announced, "multiple firefighters behind us. Disengage attack on structure…engage fighters now!"

With the words still ringing in their ears, defenders two through five separated in a bomb burst halfway through their loops, turning toward their aggressors. Michael calculated their position and assigned targets to each defender. He took the first two firefighters, and selected coronet guns. He swore in disgust about the K-guns being too big to be placed on a defender, as he triggered his guns. The coronet guns shot eighteen rounds per second of invisible energy pulses at the speed of light to his targets. The firefighters could not maneuver in time, before the pulses hit them. The resulting explosions sent white sparkles throughout the sky.

Michael glanced at his ARIT situational awareness screen and saw that somehow, one of his defenders got turned around and was being chased by two firefighters. Michael turned his defender one hundred and eighty-degrees, angling his defender to engage the firefighters. The targeted defender zoomed skyward, hoping that the intelligence reports were right, and that the defender could out climb the firefighter.

The firefighters began their climb to chase the defender, giving Michael, from his distance, an unbelievably clear shot at them. He thumbed his pagenay guns and fired two double bursts. The pagenays caught the canopy of the right firefighter, sinking in and setting the oxygen rich cockpit asunder. The nose sliced to the right and down, sailing toward the ground without a living pilot commanding her. The left firefighter's nose caught the blunt of the pagenay blasts. It leveled off and limped away about four marks before succumbing to the fire and exploding in a great white ball of flames.

Behind Michael, several explosions rocked the night, catching his attention. He careened his neck toward the explosions; where he caught the last microsecond of Defender Three evaporate into thin air. The killing Tuit firefighter sailed through the smoke like it was performing a victory dance. At least Defender Three achieved a kill on one of the firefighters before he died. However, that thought wasn't comforting enough for him. Revenge now mixed with the hatred he had tried so hard to suppress, produced a deep anger that hardened his heart and took control of his thinking. He turned his defender in the direction of the killer firefighter. He glanced at his monitor, which showed five firefighters and four defenders still up.

"Defender Two, this is lead. Defender Three is down. Join up on my wing," Michael ordered.

Defender Two joined up on Michael's left side as they pushed their engines to maximum to cover the distance between them and the killer firefighter. The firefighter didn't see it coming. Both Michael and Defender Two held their pagenay and coronet gun triggers down as they pierced the light blue sky, looking like a pair of black bats flying across the green-lit moon spitting blue venom.

The energy weapons slammed into the firefighter, cracking the ship's hull, breaking its spine and sending it into a high-speed spin. After six revolutions the ship's engines burst into flames. After four more revolutions, the ship exploded, engulfing its remains in a white inferno of smoke, light and fire.

Michael took some pleasure in watching the ship suffer before it exploded, imagining the pilot panicking inside the cockpit, knowing death was imminent, but still ineffectually fighting for life. He imagined he saw the pilot honing those skills learned in training, but useless to her in this situation. For some perverse time, this thought put glee in his heart—something he would later be ashamed to admit, but for now, he gained some pleasure in the kill.

Then behind him, two more explosions rocked his attention. He glanced at his monitor and saw two firefighters left to his four defenders. Relief entered his soul as he realized the two explosions were two more firefighters being blown to hell. His monitor now showed Defender Five in the chase for the kill, with Defender Four moving in on his wing on the remaining firefighters. At the moment, all he could be was a cheerleader, wishing and wanting them to complete the intercept. His eyes widened as he fought to adjust his night vision while scanning the skyline. The explosions had played havoc on his vision and he knew he couldn't see the fight very well through the canopy. So he glanced back at his monitor, letting the entire scene play out electronically.

He pulled his defender within striking range, just in case they needed backup, but they didn't. The monitor displayed the firefighters succumbing to the onslaught of energy weapons, and disappearing from his monitor. They were dead.

"Alpha flight," Michael commanded. "Converge on the camp. Let's finished what we came here to do."

Then like avenging angels, the bat shaped defenders flew out of the night punching, cutting, burning and slamming the camp with their pagenay and coronet guns. The building rocked, swayed, and crumbled in spots, falling upon itself like a well placed demolitions display. In five minutes, the four-story, twenty-five square-acre, squared enclosure was reduced to rubble. Thirty minutes after that, Michael was back on the command bridge of the *Neraka* organizing his team for the next step of his plan.

***

He stepped through the light of inner space in full combat armor, wearing his delta belt, and with his coronet pistol at the ready. In front of him stood a man…strong, healthy with aerobic muscular tone. He wore an olive pair of pants, sandals with no shirt. His eyes were the same eerie cat-like shape with yellow pupils.

He was a lolwe, the male half of the Tuit race. The half used for breeding and horrifically raised for medical experimentation and organ donations. The lolwe stood in stark surprise, with his eyes wide and his mouth opened. Then he dropped to his knees, bowing in reverence to Michael, who he confused as a spiritual being.

Michael reached down as the invisible door slammed shut behind him, to pick the man up, and slipped the translator ARIT, nicknamed TARIT onto his forehead. The TARIT was the next generation of the mind reading MARIT that Jarod's officers used so effectively on Tuit Prime. Michael was wearing one as well.

"Please stand," Michael instructed. The man stood up, still awestruck at Michael's heavenly entrance. "I don't have much time. I hope you can understand me."

"Yes, I can understand you," the man whispered.

"Good," Michael sighed. "My name is Michael Genesis," he continued, omitting the Osguard reference, just in case the hatred for USSTAP crossed over the gender line. "What is your name?"

"Name?" the man questioned. "I have no name."

"What do they call you?"

"I am three—eight—three—eight—seven—five," he responded.

Michael was shocked. This man referred to himself as a number, stripped of the dignity of owning a name. It was appalling and unfathomable, but effective in keeping a prisoner meek and obedient to his captor. He recognized that dignity was a precursor to pride, and that both were the main ingredients to self-assertion and defiance. So the job of any good captor was to target both for elimination when breaking someone. That was who was standing in front of him—a broken man.

Michael thought for a minute. He didn't want to call this man a number, it would add to the indignity of the situation. After all, this was the first Tuit male he had contact with. The first Tuit he spoke face to face with. It was his first contact. He didn't want to insult the man, but couldn't stand the thought of calling him a number either. This was strange from someone known as the First Osguard. Then the thought hit him. He was the first man…that was it. He was the first.

"I'm not good with numbers," he said. "How about I call you Adam?" This was ironic, he thought. A man named Genesis, the name of the First Book of the Bible, also known as the First Osguard, using the name of the first man—Adam. The name fit the situation; it suited the man as well.

"Adam?" the man repeated with a smile. "Adam," he said again. "I like that. I like it. What does it mean?"

"It means First Man…I think," Michael admitted.

Adam's smile widened. Apparently, the thought of being called the First Man appealed to him. He swelled with pride as he stuck out his chest.

Michael saw it. He saw what the name did to Adam. He had just given him part of his dignity back. This was good. This is what Michael wanted.

"Listen Adam! All hell has broken loose. I need you to come with me," Michael insisted activating his PGP.

Adam looked at Michael; fear now gripping his face as the thought of stepping into the light meant Michael was the angel of death coming for him. Michael placed his hand on Adam's shoulder, reassuring him not to fear the light.

"Don't be afraid. If you come with me now, your life will be spared."

Adam saw the truth in Michael's eyes and stepped into the light with Michael. The door slid down close behind them, and the chromerion field engulfed the two. Adam became more frightened since he couldn't move. He tried to lift his finger, his hand and his arm, but his body wouldn't respond, but the immobility was just a split second. Because a door slid open in front of them, giving them mobility again. Michael stepped through the door first, motioning for Adam to follow. Adam took a deep breath and stepped through the opening. They emerged on the other side of the light, inside the main gate portal room of the *USSTAP Galaxy Protector Neraka.*

With Adam's help, the two galaxy protectors were able to liberate the entire lolwe population from the planet, but at a huge cost. They had lost twenty-five defenders, two and a half squadrons' worth between the *Neraka* and the *Llamdion.* As the reports came in from the other ships, the liberation cost grew. Firefighter protection was not part of the original equation. That oversight cost USSTAP sixty defenders and their pilots. Nonetheless, this was for the liberation of only thirty planets. Michael adjusted his plan for the next rescue operations to use three galaxy protectors per planet.

Chapter 42—Treasonous Acts

"You told me you would take care of the Osguard fleet," Miam screamed into the monitor on her desk. Her brunette hair was frizzled and her eyes were bloodshot, indicative of several nights of going without sleep.

The monitor crackled and hissed, characteristic of long distance communications through ultra-space. A faint voice, barely audible above the crackling tried to explain, "I did neutralize the fleet. I ensured USSTAP was dissolved, there shouldn't have been any resistance."

"Shouldn't have been…shouldn't have been," Miam volleyed, trying to keep her composure and what was left of her dignity. "You told Rina, she would only meet with minimum resistance."

"It was only supposed to be a minimum resistance," the voice declared, and then fell silent. Miam stared at the screen, fire glazed in her cat like eyes, imploring the speaker to continue. "I gave Rina the location of all of our dialairtic mining planets, I gave her our patrol schedules…I gave her everything she asked for. I pushed the disintegration of USSTAP through the Parliament and the sixty Galactic Congresses—no easy feat I must tell you!"

"Temporary disintegration, T'Mock…temporary disintegration," she stressed to him.

Miam heard T'Mock clear his throat.

"I didn't count on the resuscitation of the old star cruisers, or the inexplicable stroke of luck Michael had in finding a war-ready, battle tested set of lost Osguards to command the fleet or the uncanny effectiveness of the starguard defense nodes"

"Yes, the starguard defense nodes, why didn't you warn me about those?

"Like I said, they appeared to be of no consequence when I was briefed about them."

"Apparently, you're not a military man," she condemned, "so why would you have the audacity to make such a judgment? Why did you ever presume a lonely lolwe such as yourself had the intelligence to make such a call?" Miam took a deep breath, trying to rein in the anger that was bubbling to the surface, but lost the struggle. "You idiot!" she screamed. "You were supposed to tell me everything, no matter how small or how inconsequential you thought it might've been."

T'Mock huffed, bristling at the onslaught of insults spewing his way. A moment of silence hung in the air before T'Mock spoke again, "I'm sorry you lost so many ships…so many lives…but doesn't this work for you? Doesn't it paint the First Daughter into a corner?"

"How come you didn't tell us about the Osguards coming here?" Miam asked, trying to change the subject.

"This communication protocol only works one way. Someone from your end must contact me. I can't initiate contact…remember. So the question should be," he took a deep breath and blew it out hard, summoning the strength to finish his words, "why did it take you so long to contact me?" A smile flashed across his face. "Why?" he punctuated.

Miam fell quiet, remembering how she was challenging Tisha at the time in when she should've contacted T'Mock as Rina had instructed.

"Why?" T'Mock continued, knowing he had hit a sore point.

Miam closed her eyes, cursing her actions as the vision of the destruction wrought on her sisters flashed in her mind. After a few torturous moments, Miam spoke in a whisper, "Because…"

"Because what?" T'Mock pushed with more confidence.

"Because…that's all…because," she pushed back with equal confidence.

"Well, because of your *'Because,'* the Osguards may actually come out of this unscathed and more godlike than ever before. The former domains will flock back to the association like puppy dogs to their mother's nipples." His voice strengthened with each word. "Basically, Ms. Tuit, Daughter of Fire, or whatever you want to call yourself…you just messed this entire thing up for the both of us. There is no way now, you can get your revenge on the Osguards, and now there is no way that the D'Ardin Empire can reclaim its glory as the mightiest domain this side of the universe."

"All is not lost yet," Miam assured T'Mock. "You are right. This catastrophe could work in our favor. I'm one step away from becoming the Fist Daughter of Fire, and when that happens I will push the Osguards back into the pits of hell. Leaving a void in your side of the universe in which the D'Ardin Empire can swoop in and claim their rightful place in the heavens."

"How?" T'Mock questioned.

"Let me worry about that, T'Mock," she concluded, disconnecting the communications link.

***

Five days after the great attack, the fourth moon was rising over the second southern continent on D'Ardin Two, signaling the start of the nightlife and the liberation of the partygoers onto the city. The red lights freckled the greenish night, a disorienting effect for non-D'Ardins, but an intoxicating view for the native D'Ardin.

On a crowded corner in the sixth district of the city of L'Gybe a shadowy figure draped in a tan cloak stalked into the Star Bird Bar. Once inside, the figure surveyed the bar with his haunting golden eyes. The dark, dimly lit bar was crowded with several D'Ardin men in colloquial conversations culminating in a dull roar throughout the small room that was punctuated by the clanging of drink glasses. The figure stood at the door soaking in the atmosphere, and then moved across the dirt floor with fluid agility. He walked toward the booth in the back corner that was occupied by a man in a dark green shroud.

"Good evening Ambassador T'Mock," the figure greeted the man at the table.

T'Mock looked up with a curious smile, "Good evening Admiral B'Kailine."

B'Kailine removed his hood and sat down across from T'Mock, not breaking his glare from the ambassador. Several awkward seconds expired before a waitress stepped to the table. B'Kailine waived her away.

After she left and B'Kailine was certain she was out of range to overhear their conversation he straightened his back and let out a disappointing huff.

"Well?" T'Mock pushed.

"B'Kailine opened his hands in a questioning manner, "You tell me."

"Tell you what? You're the one that called for this covert meeting, not me."

"Yes I did," B'Kailine whispered in disgust.

"Look Amierwat," T'Mock rang, trying to exert his authority, "I don't know what game you are playing, but I'm a busy man."

"A little bit too busy for my taste," B'Kailine interrupted.

"What do you mean by that?"

B'Kailine reached into his pocket, retrieved a corynx crystal and threw it on the table. He smelled the fear emanating from T'Mock's aura. He saw the sweat glistened on his brow. And most of all he felt his own stomach tighten at the realization that he was correct. He had wished he was wrong, and this was some elaborate deception, but the look in T'Mock's eyes told him differently. "You know what that is," he declared.

"A corynx crystal," T'Mock croaked.

"Yes, but it isn't just any corynx crystal," B'Kailine explained. "It is a corynx crystal of ultra space communications we have been monitoring since the attack."

T'Mock swallowed hard, "Oh."

"Yes, one of the little intelligence bits we garnered from the captured Tuit ships…communication protocols and encryptions."

"That's great," T'Mock manage to crack through the tightness in his throat.

"Do you know what is on this particular crystal?"

"No, I really can't imagine," T'Mock lied.

B'Kailine shot a piercing glance at T'Mock, letting him know he didn't believe him. "Agna, don't play me for a fool," he warned. Then he adjusted his seat and leaned over to emphasize his words. "What you have done is despicable and treasonous…not only to the association but to the empire. I just don't know how deep your actions go. And I pray it doesn't go as far as the Kinsile."

"What if it does?" T'Mock challenged.

B'Kailine squinted, pushing his thoughts so hard; T'Mock didn't need to be a mind reader to understand, but B'Kailine voiced his thoughts anyway. "Whoever is behind this is a dead man…you're a dead man."

"Amierwat, we raised three sons together; you don't mean that. We have history together. I was your I'nmo. We have a life bonding charge between us…our sons."

"And because of our sons and our history, I'm giving you two universal days to make things right, or I will!" B'Kailine roared as he stood, his stone face never showing a sense of escape or compassion, "Agna, I will make good on my promise…I'nmo or not, the life bond between us be damned!" He turned and pushed his way through to the exit, leaving the shaken and scared Prime Ambassador.

***

The clamor in the Hall of Fire was excruciatingly loud. The Consortium had delayed the Vote of Confidence until today to give Tisha the opportunity to fight in-line with the eloquent speech she gave after the discovery of the Osguards in Tuit space.

Miam sat in her chair on the leadership balcony, awaiting Tisha's entrance. However, she no longer wore the aura of arrogance, or the heart of a chosen challenger. The reports of the Osguards tearing through their space unfettered and releasing the lolwes was somewhat sobering. Any other time, she would use this information to challenge Tisha, but the results spoke for themselves—Tisha had lost. And any sign of gloating would be ill perceived. Unfortunately, she had been unable to contact T'Mock for several days now, and she felt somewhat lost on what to do after the Vote of Confidence came in.

"Maug!" a voice came from the shadows.

Miam turned, startled to realize the insult flew from Tisha's lips. Then the speakers rang out in her own voice, playing the conversation she had with T'Mock several days earlier, spewing out her duplicity in the downfall of the Tuit fleet in USSTAP and Tuit space. Paleness shadowed her face, as she turned flush with every word. The conversation lasted several minutes, but the damage lingered in the air for several more deadly seconds as the entire Consortium stared at her in disbelief.

"Guards…" Tisha barked

Several white robed guards carrying firestaffs appeared on the leadership balcony, charged after Miam.

"What is this?" Miam questioned

"You are under arrest for treason," Tisha chirped. Then with a solid command voice of judgment she continued, "You and Rina have thwarted me at every turn. You were seeking to overthrow me as First Daughter and take over the Tuit Consortium. Now you will pay for your treachery."

Two guards grabbed Miam's arms and pulled her from her seat and began to drag her to the edge of the balcony.

"I tried to save the Consortium," she bounced back. "Under your guidance we would never received our revenge…the Osguards would have never felt the mighty fire of Tuit justice. You preferred to wait and bargain the Tuit justice away, so you can stay comfortable in your ivory tower. Now she faced the Consortium, "Under Tisha, the Tuit Consortium was weakening, turning into a blithering replica of a Belin Beetle, waiting for the Osguards and their so-called association to step on us, and then wipe us from their shoe. We are pests to them." Her voice softened as she preached to the consortium, "At least with Rina, we had an opportunity to step on them first.

"Enough!" Tisha commanded. "Now look at the situation. Our worst fears have come true. The association is here and they are ripping through our galaxies like firestaffs through flesh. And it is all your fault," she attacked with condemnation. With a graceful turn and a more somber voice she addressed the consortium, "Sisters, here is why we have failed…here is why the enemy is upon us…here is why we must fight for our lives instead of for our principles. Miam of Solwick!"

Miam turned toward Tisha. "You think it's just me?" she posed. "You may have control of the civilian forces, but I have control of the military," she pronounced

Tisha winced and cocked her head to the side with disbelief.

"Command Daughter!" Miam screamed.

Suddenly, five red ovals opened from ultra space, releasing five black-robed warrior sisters armed with fireclubs, a weapon similar to the firestaff, but small enough to be strapped on the forearm, and hidden underneath the robe sleeve. They raised their arms and without any word the two-barrel weapons glowed red and fired two beams, blue from the right, and red from the left, that merged into one spiraling beam. In a millisecond the beam shot from their arms and burred into the guards surrounding Miam. Their chests burst open, ripping bone and flesh, sending chunks of blood, cartilage, lungs and hearts spewing into the air in a deathly poetic three hundred and sixty-degree arc.

The howls from the consortium members added to the gruesome picture being played out on the balcony. More red ovals shot open throughout the consortium. Black-robed warrior sisters darted from some while white-robed sisters of the guardian force darted through others. Chaos erupted in the hall. Beams shot through the air, dealing out destruction and death with every hit. Blood, bone, flesh, guts and various other body parts littered the hall. Sisters of the consortium frantically disbursed, some heading toward the warrior sisters and the others running toward the sisters of the guardian force, making their choice on which side of this dispute they sided with.

Miam shook free from her captors' dead grasps and analyzed the onslaught happening below her. Her smile told the deadly thoughts running rampant in her mind. She was cleansing the consortium of the weak-hearted and feeble-minded. Her warriors surrounded her, protecting her from any stray shot that may find its way to the balcony.

In the back of the balcony, Tisha screamed. It was bone chilling and blood curdling. It was a scream of desperation bounded by hurt and seared in frustration.

Miam turned back to Tisha, relishing her victory with a diabolical laugh. She pushed her bodyguards away and marched over to her nemesis, until they were almost nose-to-nose. Miam could feel Tisha's breath against her cheek, sweet smelling lilac breath. Then with the rage of disgust she'd harbored for almost twenty years, Miam spat into Tisha's face. But as soon as the delight of pushing the wet insult from her lips manifested in her conscious, a sharp fiery burning pain slammed into her stomach. Acid and blood mixed in her throat, and with her next gurgle she released the crimson mixture from her lips.

She saw the large smile adorning Tisha's face and wondered, *what is happening?* She looked down and saw Tisha's ceremonial knife sticking out of her stomach. *I'm dead,* was the last thought that occupied her mind as she collapsed at Tisha's feet.

Tisha's smile turned into a frown as her eyes widened when she saw the five warrior sisters fire their weapons at her. No thought crossed her mind, just the feelings of fear and hopelessness. A few more seconds, the other three Daughters of Fire lay dead next to Tisha's mutilated corpse, murdered by the vengeful warrior guards.

Chaos was the new god in the hall, and she spread like a firestorm throughout the building, feeding her carnivorous appetite with mayhem and destruction. She stomped through the city, grabbing common sense by the throat and strangling the life from it, strewing dead bodies and blood in her wake. No one was safe, neither child nor woman; all fell by her mighty hand. Thousands of years of steadfast dedication to the religion honoring the spirit of the fire disappeared in one crazed moment of disillusionment. Screams pierced the day and provided the music for the night. Buildings faltered and fell under the potent devastation overwhelming the planet. Confusion reigned as black-robed and white-robed warriors fought one another to the death, killing all who challenged them, innocent or not. The Tuit society was committing suicide.

Chapter 43—Armageddon

In the distant Tuit Prime skyline, the silhouette of sixty galaxy protectors shone. Michael had sent a hail several hours ago, but it met with no response. It had been six universal months, since he entered this realm of space. Michael and the other Osguards had led the liberation of countless lolwe camps over three hundred and forty planets, and had destroyed over twenty Tuit shipyards and listening posts that lay in their path. They met no resistance, since the Tuit powerhouse, the fireship fleet, had been decimated in USSTAP territory. The USSTAP fleet moved with impunity, from planet to planet, from galaxy to galaxy, in this sparsely populated star cluster, using their newly gained knowledge of ultra-space.

He wanted to punish the Tuits. He wanted to throw their civilization back into the Stone Age, but Ortho's words would not allow him to stay on that path of destruction. He needed to talk to the Tuit Consortium. He needed to quell this war as quickly as possible. He needed to stop the senseless bloodshed of innocent people over what he perceived was a misunderstanding.

So after his hail met with no response, he had the HVP, detailing the first encounter with the Tuits, played on all visual and audible spectrum frequencies and piped to the Tuit home world. He knew Gail French, Regina Dawson and Kelly Sterling left a corynx crystal of the event. Yet he wasn't sure that the First Daughter had viewed it. So this was a way to force her to view it. Additionally, he pushed the reports of their fleets' destruction at Millmum and Siryman Capitol Stations, along with the news that their lolwes were now free men, transported to other worlds, armed and ready to defend their freedom with their lives.

"Sire!" Tirana called.

Michael looked up from his chair, signaling for her to continue.

"We are reading wide spread fires, explosions and a number of dead throughout the planet."

"What?" Michael questioned.

"It looks like a worldwide riot…more like a civil war."

"Let me see!" Michael demanded, adjusting his chair monitor.

The readings were commensurate with Tirana's assumption. The ARIT search array recorded massive explosions and fires throughout the planet. Entire cities were ablaze. Rural as well as suburban areas were destroyed. The ARIT registered millions of bodies littering the streets, under fallen buildings, in the wide-open fields, and in the forest. The ARIT read millions of others pushing through the planet with a wide variety of weapons.

"Jeez! What the hell happened down there?"

Tirana looked up to the heavens and then she shrugged her shoulders. "I believe in every society there is a period of time we all know will come, but pray doesn't. The Kulusks call it Charmlinga, the Moslecks call it Toligama, and the Pierones call it Telihick. I believe you call it Armageddon. I believe the Tuits have just achieved Armageddon!"

Michael closed his eyes in shame. He had done worse than sending the Tuits into the Stone Age. He had brought about the end of their world. A tear formed in his right eye, squeezing out of his closed eyelid and sliding down his face. He groaned, turning his face away from Tirana, so she would not see the emotions playing out on it. He wiped the tear from his cheek and choked back a cough.

"Tell the fleet," he stopped to clear his thoughts. He stood from his chair and went to his favorite perch on the railing, overlooking the control bridge. He put his hands in his pocket and shrugged his shoulders. "Tell the fleet," he continued, "…the war is over…we're going home now. Hell has come home to roost…Armageddon is here, and we don't want her catching up to us."

Chapter 44—Jarod's Letter

TO: MICHAEL D. GENESIS, OSGUARD, MILLMUM GALAXY
FROM: JAROD D. STONE, OSGUARD, SIRYMAN GALAXY
REFERENCE: AMBASSODORIAL INTRODUCTION
UNIVERSAL DATE: 12.05.48256

Michael, first let me congratulate you on the birth of your son. I know it was a great feeling to see your daughters, wife and your newborn son. I understand you named him after your first CO, Eduardo Sanchez—Edward Samuel Genesis. I believe that is a great tribute to one of the finest officers that has served the association. Centurion Sanchez's contribution and death in the first battle of this war with the Kulusks will always be remembered and honored.

I also want to take this opportunity to thank you and the other Osguards for arranging my father's accommodations and allowing him to meet me at Siryman Capitol Station when I arrived from the Centaurus Star Cluster. I didn't realize how much I missed him, and how much pain had passed between us. We are on the road to recovery. And when I say we, I mean, my brother, sister, mother and me. It will take some attempts to finally get use to my father's partner, Calvin Martin. But he seems an amenable fellow.

Now for the real purpose of this letter, Agna T'Mock, the parliament's prime ambassador from D'Ardin, has passed away. He apparently had a fishing accident during his vacation. Also, the Kinsile of D'Ardin has passed. He had an allergic reaction to a special meal containing Tealicmyn. I hear if not prepared correctly Tealicmyn can be fairly dangerous. Understandably it must not have been prepared properly.

These are only two of several deaths of high stature personnel in the D'Ardin Empire that happened during our foray into Tuit space—in my appraisal, all of them are suspicious. In the back of my mind, I wondered why the Siryman Galaxy bore so much from the Tuit attack. I dare say they may have had help. These deaths may be a coincidence, but I doubt it. I fear they are attempts to cover up any treasonous acts done by association members, especially from the D'Ardin Empire. Which may mean, we still have Tuit infiltrators amongst us? I caution vigilance from now on to all Osguards.

Luckily, the new Kinsile has appointed my former station's admiral, Amierwat B'Kailine to the post of parliamentary ambassador. B'Kailine is a man I trust to do what is right, no matter how difficult it is. Therefore, I give my full endorsement to B'Kailine as the D'Ardin Empire representative to the USSTAP Parliament. If anybody can weed out the sins of Tuit infiltrators amongst the D'Ardin Empire, B'Kailine can.

Finally, our operatives in the former Tuit reign of power report there are several domains vying for power, including domains that resided outside the Tuit sphere of influence. Many of these powers have not demonstrated friendly intentions toward the association and thus I am afraid another foe may eventually replace the Tuit Consortium. With this in mind I advise we retain the Tuit prisoners of war and continue interrogations for intelligence purposes.

In this respect, I know we will have the support of B'Kailine and I value the assistance he will render in the Parliament for the protection of the association and its members. Again, I warn we must stay vigilant in our endeavors.

Your Cousin and Brother in the Osguards
Jarod D. Stone,
Osguard 11, Siryman Galaxy

Epilogue—Return to Normal

"Osguards," Michael addressed the new Osguard Senate in the modified arena, which now housed one hundred and twenty Osguards. "It has been two universal months, and our contacts in the Tuit star cluster have assured us, the Tuit Consortium is of no consequence to us now. They are too busy fighting each other, but we must stay *vigilante.* The victor of the Tuit conflict may be a problem in the near future. So you have in front of you my proposals.

However, first I want to thank the engineering corps for responding so quickly to the changes. They worked at amazing speed to upgrade our fields, outfit our ships with K-guns, build the defense starguards and pull the old star cruisers out of the shipyard. I can honestly say, without the ingenuity and dedication of our engineering corps, we wouldn't be standing here today."

The Osguards all clapped in appreciation of the engineering corps; several yelled to bring home the sentiment.

"Second, I want to welcome the Osguards in Training to their first Osguard Senate meeting, even though this is an unscheduled meeting. The Red and Blue Osguards have already trained through our academic system, but will go back for the Osguard Top-off Training, which will last approximately twelve universal weeks. Then they will graduate to the rank of full fledge Osguard, be given a galaxy protector and train under the eye of an existing Osguard. Afterwards, they will be assigned to an upcoming galaxy as they come available. The fourteen Green Osguards, who are with us today, are the descendants of the lost line of Osguards. It appears our ancestors, Shirley Grace and Betty Nightman had moved to Victoria Texas, near the place the Tuits took them. They thought that Nausona and Laurona would start their search for them there. I can't fault them for their premise. They didn't know the mother's concentrated their efforts around New York City, where they were first contacted.

Due to a wonderful stroke of luck, we are finally reunited. The fourteen Green Osguards will enter the academy for the full three point five years of academic training as an Osguard. When they graduate, they will be given their own galaxy protectors and will train under the guidance of an existing Osguard, until a galaxy of responsibility becomes available, including those unexplored galaxies.

Furthermore, their relatives who could not serve as active Osguards, such as parents and grandparents, will be allowed all the rights and privileges thereof. New houses and townhouses will be built in Osguard Gardens to welcome our newfound relatives."

Michael then cleared his throat and switched the display on the ARIT. "Now to the business at hand—redefining USSTAP's fleet." He walked toward the middle podium, pointing to the holographic display. "Because we no longer are the sole owners of gate portal technology, we must guard against intrusion in each and every corner of our space from unknown enemies. Within one hundred million light years, there are over one hundred and sixty galaxy groups, twenty five hundred galaxies, twenty five thousand dwarf galaxies and billions upon billions of countless stars. There are only one hundred and twenty Osguards. Albeit, not every galaxy sustains life, but they have planets of natural wealth and strategic importance just as essential as the sixty galaxies in our sphere of influence now."

Michael sighed, emphasizing the sheer magnitude facing USSTAP. The hologram displayed a chart of the known universe, shading the regions not covered by USSTAP in red. Blue islands freckling the chart represented USSTAP covered regions.

"We Osguards cannot canvas all of them. We haven't even touched the Fornax Cluster or the Eridanus Cluster in our own supercluster of galaxies. We need help. Therefore, the ranks, which Ortho deactivated when we Osguards came to power, of Nolvar, Solvar and Vanguard will be reactivated, effective immediately. We are going to increase the galaxy protector fleet in each galaxy by two hundred percent, giving each galaxy eight more protectors for a total of twelve. Senate appointed Nolvars and Solvars would sire these ships. Furthermore, Vanguards will lead new USSTAP fleets as our representatives, in galaxies without Osguards. They will sire new galaxy protectors, new stations and have new galactic fleets at their disposal."

The blue islands spilled out, turning the display into a sea of blue with red freckled islands, suggesting the plan would reverse the situation in a short matter of time.

With a mixture of pride and disappointment in his voice, Michael continued, "Additionally, we will increase the galaxy cruiser fleet in each existing galaxy." The display changed, now showing black ship silhouettes. The Osguards watched as more silhouettes joined the display, signifying an increase in USSTAP ships, military, economic and scientific. When the display stopped it represented a USSTAP fleet ten times as large as the present fleet. "Defense starguards will now protect every capitol station and space station. Correspondingly, we no longer have the monopoly on gate-portal technology and must defend our interest against those who share this technology and wish to do us harm. So I propose the institution of a rapid response force to combat the possibility of more sneak attacks, similar to the ones that the Tuit Consortium perpetrated on us. This rapid response force will consist of two types of starships. The first starship will be the new star protector. The star protector will be a larger version of the star cruiser with an aft launch and landing bay that housed one squadron of defenders. The star protectors will be stationed at each capital station."

Michael stopped to collect his thoughts, wondering why USSTAP starships had to have such lame names. Deep down inside he admired the strong names of the Tuit Consortium starships: fireships, firestars and firefighters. The names exuded fire, bite and tenacity, characteristics Michael thought should represent starships with awesome destructive power. But USSTAP regulations called for non-threatening and non-offensive names, like cruiser, protector and defender. A shudder ran through him as he came to grips with the knowledge that this was the price of keeping the association united.

"The second starship," he continued, "will be the star cruiser stationed at galactic precincts. The star cruisers will come out of mothball and we will build new ones to outfit all precincts as necessary. The force's size and complement will be based on the amount of space in each precinct's territory. This rapid response force will use the gate-portal system, giving them the capability of literally stepping within one thousand light years of any spot in the galaxy. Additionally, these starships will be outfitted with Intergalactic Portal Engines that they can use to step to any fight in minutes. These ships will be on constant alert and will train to reach any part of their galaxy within ten universal minutes. The vote won the requisite approval throughout the sixty congresses and the Universal Parliament, and was unanimous amongst the Osguard Senate. In other words, we will have expansion and security build-up."

The holograph terminated and Michael gazed upon his family. "I know this is a far cry from what Laurona and Nausona began, but I feel…we feel, we can only continue in their spirit with the knowledge we are secure from outside aggression. Our laws have not changed and our charter remains the same. We will provide common defense, shared technology and fair trade practices to every domain who subscribes to USSTAP."

The secure head nods affirmed the other Osguards agreed with the new direction, causing Michael to pause in thought. He didn't want this incident with the Tuits to alter any freedoms Laurona and Nausona based the organization on. He understood his ancestors lived through American slavery under a government that professed individual rights, but did not practice them. He also understood the price of freedom was not free, and he had for far too long accepted the freedom his ancestors paid for with their sweat and blood, on Chaktun, in space as well as on Earth.

"Also, the Universal Parliament has ordered production increase of dialairtic crystals from our remaining facilities, along with issuance of bonds for private sector development of dialairtic mining facilities. Until then, the commercial industry is authorized to conduct business with the Kulusk Maxum to substitute pialairtic crystals in place of dialairtic crystals."

The one hundred and nineteen other Osguards nodded in submission to the idea. It was a bleak situation, but the reality of the circumstances forced them to accept the inferior substitute, pialairtic gas, which was highly toxic, but low on combustibility. The Kulusks had developed several decontaminating procedures that increased the safety of pialairtic gas, which meant Kulusk personnel would be used throughout the USSTAP commercial lanes to implement and oversee pialairtic crystal and pialairtic gas adoption into USSTAP mainstream—an initiative that a year ago would have been unacceptable to any Osguard.

The holographic display began again, displaying the image of Earth. Michael turned to the display and gave a faint smile. "Now the real headache," he poised. "The war has brought unsuspecting consequences with the governments of Earth—in particular the United States of America and Russia. Green Osguard One, Angela Santos, has come up with a simple compromise. It will be up to the presidents of these two nations to accept it or not. Everyone has had an opportunity to review and comment on the proposal, and no one has dissented. So we will offer them the proposal, which calls for our front business, Unlimited Associations, to open up international medical facilities in every major city, every country and every state, whose government will allow us!" Michael's voice then escalated like a Baptist Minister, preaching to his flock. He felt the energy swirl inside the room and he felt his next words would be timely if not appropriate to say at this moment. "The facilities will be free to those suffering from incurable diseases and also engage in activities to combat famine and hunger. It will be the job of these presidents to ramrod legislation, pull favors and play their political and diplomatic games to see to it that this happens. If it doesn't, the blame will lie with them, not us!" he bellowed, clinching his fist in anger.

He did not like what Peters was going to do at the U.N. Security Council, making USSTAP out to be the bad guy, blaming the Osguards of abandoning Earth. Peters didn't see the repercussion of increasing longevity on Earth, the overpopulation it would cause. Nonetheless morality needed to prevail over scientific data, models and simulations, and Michael always knew that. He just refused to face it—until now. Angela had spoken so eloquently and forcefully for USSTAP involvement, he couldn't refuse his inner voice any longer.

"Besides," he continued in a calmer tone, "this will give us a leg up during our recruiting initiative. We will be able to move openly, without restriction to recruit the brightest and bravest of the population to augment our forces...Thus giving us a prime vehicle to alleviate overcrowding and overpopulation due to our involvement with Earth. Of course, our services will still be *'covert'* and not for public knowledge. It will be difficult, if not damn near impossible. But I have faith in General Lo, and his ability to implement the plan."

***

President Frederick Walter Peters and President Sergey Repustinov disappeared behind the closed doors of his Camp David office. This was a rare event since Peters was accustomed to receiving heads of states in one of the other more ostentatious rooms. For some reason, Repustinov was accepted into the folds of Peters' inner empire, Camp David. However, this was no ordinary stately visit. Repustinov was there on special invitation by Michael.

Two white lights of inner space opened up inside the office and two black clad members of USSTAP's security corps wearing delta belts stepped through the light. Peters looked up, trying to hold his surprise, and acting like he was an old hand at seeing such an event. However, Repustinov was not attempting to hold his surprise. He was open-mouthed, gushing out his breath in an almost panic. Then the invisible doors closed behind the men, emitting the normal light.

"President Peters...President Repustinov; I am Captain Mark Owens, USSTAP Security Corps. This is my partner, Captain Vladimir Chenkov." Owens offered his hand for the presidents to shake.

"You are Russian?" Repustinov asked Chenkov."

"Da!" he said. "I was born and raised in St. Petersburg."

"So we have Russians as part of USSTAP?"

"Yes, we do. There are ten precincts in Russia alone.

"How many in the United States?" Peters asked, showing his diplomatic jealousy.

"Eight or nine," Owens answered, knowing what Peters was trying to do.

"Well, what is it...eight or nine?" Peters snorted.

"Mr. President...all your questions will be answered in due time. If you would just follow me into the light," Owens remarked activating his PGP.

"Don't worry Sergey," Peters offered. "It's alright."

Sergey looked at Peters with suspicious eyes. "Are you sure?"

Peters wasn't sure, but he had to act like it. "Yes, I'm sure."

The two men stood and walked up to the USSTAP officers, smiled and stepped into the lights. Owens and Chenkov shrugged at each other and then stepped into the light after their charges. They emerged in the Main Gate Portal Room of the *Galaxy Protector Neraka.*

"Welcome Mr. Presidents," Tirana smiled. "I am Tirana Ritchen, Centurion of Operations for the *Galaxy Protector Neraka*." The presidents exchanged pleasantries with Tirana, recognizing she was a Kulusk, someone they were afraid of over ten months ago.

Tirana escorted them to the command bridge and placed them in the seats on either side of the command chair. She took the command chair and gave the orders to proceed. The ship melted out of stealth mode and sped into hyperlight speed, taking the Oart departure. The presidents were awestruck by the magnificence of the bridges. The view port screen really caught their attention as they watched the screen blink in and out and then show the electronic display of their path. Once outside the Gentry solar system, the ship stopped and engaged its IGP engines. A white glow of inner space sprung to life in front of them and the ship swaggered into it. When they exited the light, Millmum Capitol Station in all its grandeur filled the screen.

"Mr. Presidents," Tirana opened. "Welcome to Millmum Capitol Station the capitol of the known universe. We will dock in a few minutes and then I will escort you to the Osguardian Senate."

ABOUT THE AUTHOR

Malcolm Dylan Petteway is a military analyst and a twenty-year veteran of the United States Air Force. He flew B-52's as an Electronic Warfare Officer and has 3,000 flight hours and 300 combat hours. In his distinguished career, Malcolm has used his knowledge in the art of war, military weapons and combat defenses in planning over 400 combat sorties. Besides his Meritorious Service Medal with three oak leaf clusters and numerous other awards, Malcolm is the recipient of the U.S. Air Force Air Medal and the U.S. Air Force Air Achievement Medal for his actions during Operation Enduring Freedom. Malcolm Petteway is a graduate of the U.S. Air Force Academy and California State University.

ISBN: 978-0-9843645-2-7

5 1 5 5 0

9 780984 364527

www.ingramcontent.com/pod-product-compliance
Lightning Source LLC
LaVergne TN
LVHW020659110826
845149LV00012B/2048

* 9 7 8 0 9 8 4 3 6 4 5 2 7 *